W9-BBC-699

A

MILLION

JUNES

Emily Henry

RAZORBILL

An Imprint of Penguin Random House

RAZORBILL®

An Imprint of Penguin Random House LLC
Penguin.com

RAZORBILL & colophon is a registered trademark
of Penguin Random House LLC.

First published in the United States of America by Razorbill,
an imprint of Penguin Random House LLC, 2017

LIBRARY OF CONGRESS CATALOGING-IN-PUBLICATION DATA IS AVAILABLE
Hardcover ISBN: 9780448493961
Paperback ISBN: 9780448493978

Printed in the United States of America

7 9 10 8

Design: Eric Ford

For Jack, Patrick, and Daniel,
who gave me a name worth keeping.

For Ceili, who loved well.

And for all those who find ways to go on:
Better days are coming for our little hearts.

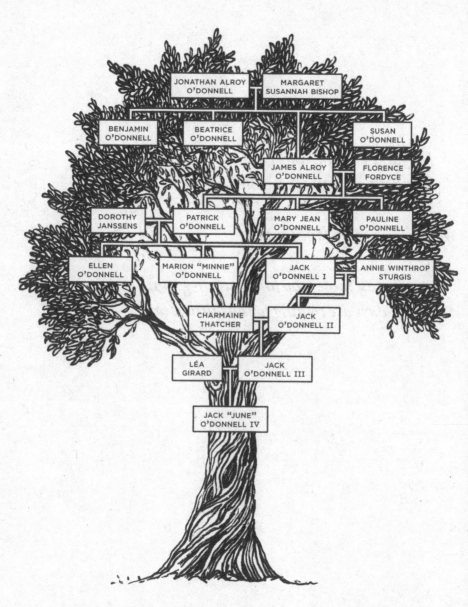

The O'DONNELL FAMILY

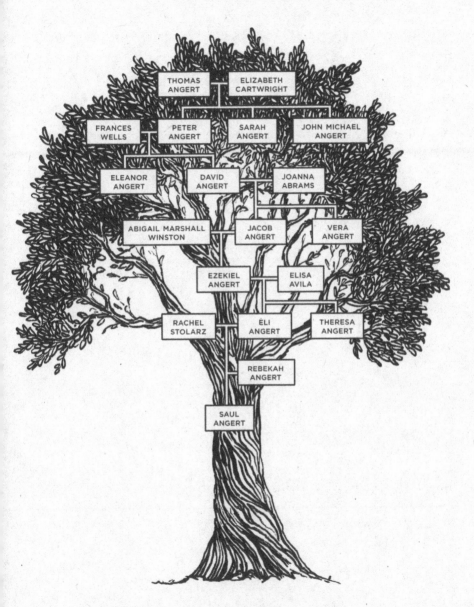

The ANGERT FAMILY

One

FROM my bedroom window, I watch the ghost flutter. She shifts and warbles in the dark yard, her pink sheen caught in moonlight. I wonder if she's looking up at the spread of stars or if she's facing the farmhouse, watching us. Maybe things like her don't have eyes. Maybe they wander, unseeing, through the world.

At the edge of the clearing, the sudden shuffle and bob of branches draw my eyes from the ghost. A couple of giggly sophomores I recognize break through the brush and hesitate, half-shadowed, as they scour the hilltop our house sits on.

They look right past the shimmering pink spirit and focus instead on the cherry tree that sprawls out in front of our porch. The tree's as old as the town itself, planted by my great-great-great-great-grandfather, Jonathan "Jack" Alroy O'Donnell, when he first settled here. He, like Dad, could talk roots into spreading anywhere, but part of the reason Jonathan stayed in Five Fingers was

1

the taste of the cherries that grew on this hill. *Like heaven on earth*, Dad used to say, *like the silent world before anything had gone wrong.*

Within months of his arrival, Jonathan had started a farm a couple of miles from here, closer to the water, where the earth mixed with sand. For two generations, the O'Donnells built a legacy of roots and branches. It's been four more since the Angerts, my family's mortal enemies, foreclosed on the farm. But the cherries from that land are still sold in grocery stores and farmers' markets, at festivals and fairs, beneath hand-painted signs and vinyl banners reading JACK'S TART.

The sophomores, Molly Malone and Quincy Northbrook, run toward the tree now, folded in half like they're trying not to block a movie-theater screen. Neither of them sees the ghost, but they both shiver as they pass through her, and Molly stops and glances back. Quincy's halfway up the tree, trying to shake down the empty branches. He hisses at Molly, and she runs to stand below him, folding her shirt up like a grocery bag as a few shriveled cherries drop.

Gravel crunches then, and headlights swing up the curve of our long driveway. In the tree, Quincy freezes like a raccoon caught robbing a trash can, but Molly's already running, halfway back to the woods with her spoils. At the breathy honk of the car horn, Quincy drops from the branches and takes off full tilt after her.

Hannah rolls the Subaru's window down and shouts, "Yeah, that's right! You'd better run, punks!" She shakes her head in mock disapproval then looks up at me, affecting surprise. "But soft!" she calls. "What light through yonder window breaks?"

"It's me," I yell back.

"Wait. June? You're positively glowing. I thought that was the east and you were the sun."

"Yeah, I'm ovulating. Common mistake."

"Well, get those incandescent ovaries down here. We've got death traps and deep-fried John Doe waiting for us."

I pull on my canvas tennis shoes, swing my leather backpack over my shoulder, and flick the lights off. But something makes me take one last look at my room from the hallway, at the wild constellations of green star stickers Dad and I tacked on my ceiling when I was six years old. I'd been sure back then they'd glow forever—that nothing Dad touched could dim.

Mom even used to say, "June, your daddy's the sun."

And he was. He could make anything grow. He warmed every room he stepped into. When he touched an animal, it would lie down and nap. He even went away in the winter, like the sun so often did, and without him the house became cold, lethargic.

It's been almost ten years since he died, and not a single star sticker still glows. But some people are too alive to fully die, their stories too big to disappear, and he was one of them. I see traces of him all over our magic house. I hear him in the creak and groan of the floorboards as the summer nights stretch them, can visualize him sitting at the foot of my bed, saying, *Other houses have support beams and foundations. Ours has bones and a heartbeat.*

I close my eyes and listen to the house hum and yawn, stretch and curl. Outside, Hannah honks, and I close the door and jog downstairs.

In the soft light of the kitchen, Mom and Toddy, my stepdad, are laughing and tickling each other like freshmen on a first date while they choose a bottle of white wine from the fridge. Shadow and Grayson are in the living room, standing on the couch, playing a gladiator video game with motion sensors.

"Han's here," I announce, and Grayson screams something like *katchaaaaaaw* over my words and kicks the air.

Mom yelps with laughter and squirms in Toddy's arms, turning her sparkly Torch Lake eyes on me. Dad always said they were the first part of her he fell for. They met far away from here, but she was a little piece of home to him, so he swept her up and brought her back with him, because he wanted all the home he could have in one place.

Mom smooths her T-shirt down over her improbably toned stomach. "Tell Hannah hi!"

Toddy wraps her waist in his arms and rests his chin on her head. "Go anywhere else after the carnival and you need to let us know, Junie," he adds. "Don't you girls get in any trouble."

"Never." I feign indignation and turn down the narrow hall for the door.

"Love you, baby," they both call.

Outside, the throng of moths surrounding the porch light disperses around me. The hens, as usual, are asleep in the grass beyond the decrepit chicken coop, no cares in the world. As I slide into Hannah's passenger seat, everything feels particularly *right* in a way I can't explain. Like the whole world's in harmony.

The house, the woods, the hens. Hannah in her floral minidress and me in my ratty summer tank top and shorts. The spirit.

I scan the yard for any hint of the wobbly pink thing. "Saw the ghost," I tell Hannah.

Hannah pops a piece of gum into her mouth then holds the pack out for me. "Which one?"

The cozy pink presence isn't the only one that has drifted across our yard since before I was born. "Feathers," I answer.

Hannah chews on her lip. "Good."

The other ghost—the shadowy one we haven't named, that plume of darkness that makes you feel nauseated and cold if you brush against it—only ever appears before something bad happens. Even when we hadn't actually seen the blackish thing, we'd know it had been there because all the animals on our land would freak. The always serene hens would flap, peck, break their wings, sometimes even kill one another. The normally merciful coywolves would mutilate rabbits and sparrows and leave their uneaten bodies on our hillside, scatterings of grisly omens. The last time it came was three years ago, the night before our porch collapsed and I broke my foot, but I haven't actually seen the dark ghost in ten years.

Not since before the worst Bad Thing.

Hannah starts to reverse down the hill and into the woods. "Ugh, your house always makes me feel the feelings. I swear, there's no place more nostalgia inducing than that leaning stack of lumber."

I nod and look out the window.

"Is she here now?" Hannah asks as she reverses slowly down the driveway. "Feathers?"

I point out toward a curve in the edge of the forest where I can barely make out a pink tendril caught in moonlight. "There," I tell Hannah. She gazes out toward that point with a dreamy, contented

5

smile, then returns to easing down the driveway. "I wish you could see her."

Hannah lifts one shoulder in a shrug. "I just like knowing she's there. You know, not everyone gets to be best friends with someone who has a guardian . . . ghost."

"Han, if she were my guardian ghost, don't you think she would've intervened when I got bangs?"

"Who says guardian ghosts don't have a sense of humor?"

When we were little, I saw the pink ghost all the time. Hannah couldn't, but she could *feel* it. Sometimes we'd chase the shimmer across the yard and run through it, as if it were the spray of the sprinkler. It felt soft and lush, like running through a million falling feathers, thus our nickname for it. Dad always called it the Sprite, and when Mom shot him dubious looks— *you shouldn't toy with the kids like that*—he'd wink and say, "You know, Léa, to enter the kingdom of heaven, you must become like a child."

Then she'd smile as she turned back to hanging laundry, or rolling dough over the floured counter, or trailing her fingers along the gauzy wind-rippled drapes, and say, "Five Fingers loves its stories."

Like most transplants to this place, Mom had a hard time accepting the strange things that happened on our land as anything other than the shared imaginings of wild, summer-dazed minds and a town-wide tendency to exaggerate.

Five Fingers *did* love its stories, but Dad's were true. Our house *is* magic, in some small way. The skinny halls and wallpapered rooms, the gnarled forest that encircled our hill—together they do all kinds of impossible things. My whole life kids have crept onto our property at night to make wishes and look for spirits, or to steal cherries from the first Jack's Tart tree with hopes of shrinking their dogs' tumors, healing their grandparents' melanoma, even clearing up their acne.

As we pull onto the wooded road beyond my driveway, something flutters in my peripheral vision: the shift of a shadow, the undulation of something inky in front of the gatehouse.

My blood chills. My stomach clenches, a knot tightens my throat, and there's a jarring halt in my heart. But when I glance in the rearview mirror, there's nothing there. No shadowy thing, no darkness.

It's gone, I tell myself. *It's been gone three years. It's not coming back.*

Hannah flicks the frayed edge of my jean cut-offs. "June?"

"Huh?"

"You okay? You look sort of . . . not."

I shake my head. "Sorry, just distracted."

It's gone.

Still, tonight's feeling of rightness has been disturbed. Something *off* buzzes in the air, like a single hornet circling my head, always out of sight.

Two

WE leave Hannah's car parked by Meijer and join the crowd rollicking across the highway toward the high school. The organ music playing on loop in the Tunnel O' Love overlaps chaotically with the *whoop* and *dingdingding* of carnival games, and sweet, fatty smells mingle with the pine in the air.

We follow the curling path to the red-and-white ticket booth at the entrance to the school's parking lot, and I try to leave behind any thoughts of the dark presence I imagined back at the house. *It's gone; it's not coming back. It was never there.*

Hannah squeezes my arm and squeals in excitement as we step into the ticket line. She may be painfully shy, but she loves crowds.

Our friendship couldn't be any more of a teen-TV-drama cliché if we tried: Hannah Kuiper is a shy yet extroverted, violin-playing salutatorian. I'm a socially comfortable yet severely introverted underachiever who, if given the option for a weekend excursion, would choose Desert Island over Theme Park. She's a waify, blue-eyed blonde, and I'm a dark-eyed, even darker-waved brunette who wore Hannah's current pant size back in the seventh grade. Mom attributes my relative brawn to the fact that I, like Dad, never stop moving.

As we near the front of the line, Han rises up on her tiptoes, searching the crowd beyond the booth. "I think I see Nate Baars," Hannah says.

"How," I say, "in this writhing mass of Vineyard Vines shorts and North Face fleeces, did you pick out one little Vineyard Tendril–North Freckle?"

"Why are people crowded around him like that?" she asks, completely ignoring me. I squint and follow her gaze to the base of the Ferris wheel. Nate's standing with a dozen kids from our school, most of whom have already graduated.

"Weird," I say. "I've never seen people line up to hear someone make a fart noise with their armpit before. Is that Stephen Niequist with him?" I gesture to the rail-thin blond boy in the grandpa cardigan, Hannah's academic rival.

She shrugs. "Weirdly enough, they're friends. *No* idea what those two have to talk about, but I see Stephen's car at Nate's house all the time."

Nate and Hannah live on the same street. We used to ride bikes with him when we were kids, before the natural current of high school took him and us in two very different directions. One direction being distinctly *toward* flatulence-based humor.

"Maybe the world's ending and Nate just found out he's allowed to choose one person to save," I suggest. Truthfully, Nate is *exactly* the kind of boy who might draw a crowd—he's all suntanned muscle and shiny, chocolaty hair—if he weren't so ridiculous. But he is, and so this visual makes no sense.

"Maybe he won the lottery," Hannah says, "and now he has fifty new best friends who want a piece of the pie."

The gaunt woman in the admission booth calls us forward, and we trade twenties for highlighter-pink wristbands. We wander partway down the aisle on the right and stop before the House of Mirrors, staring up at the pink archway over the entrance. "Hey," Hannah says gently, taking my hand. She juts her chin toward it. "Maybe this year?"

The House of Mirrors was always Dad's favorite, and it's mine too. There's something so thrilling about wandering around only to get yourself un-lost—especially when the thing you're lost in blurs the line between dream and reality, possible and impossible. Like our house and our land. Like Dad himself.

Hannah and I come to this carnival every year, but I haven't been into the House of Mirrors since Dad died.

"What do you think?" Hannah says, studying me.

I shake my head. Hannah squeezes my hand then lets go. "Maybe next year."

We stand in silence for a few more seconds, like we're at an altar or a grave and not five feet from a game where you shoot plastic clowns with mounted water guns.

"Huh," Hannah says, breaking the reverie. I glance sidelong at her. Her eyes are back on the group at the bottom of the Ferris wheel. Now that we're closer, it's apparent that Nate is not, in fact, the center of their attention. He and Stephen are standing off-center, a little bit behind the others, and as a gaggle of middle schoolers jostles past, a gap in the group shifts to reveal the person they all seem uniformly focused on. At first, I can only see his back. He's on the tallish side of average and the thinnish side too, but he somehow takes up more space than someone his size should, as if his presence bends everything around itself.

He turns a bit, and I get a partial view of his profile, but I still don't recognize him. Clean-cut dark hair, uniform five-o'clock shadow. A T-shirt whiter than I've managed to keep one in the time it takes to get from the cash register to the door. The kind of dark, slim-fit jeans you can get away with wearing to a Five Fingers wedding.

I realize then that the reason he stands out so starkly against the backdrop of our lakeside town is because he looks unnaturally *clean*. Even the tattoos covering his pale arms manage to look cleaner than plain Five Fingers skin.

Hannah takes a step past me, trying to get a better look. "Is that . . ."

A couple of people laugh, and Nate Baars smacks the stranger on the back. He turns then, so I can see his full profile, and he forces a fraction of a smile before discreetly maneuvering away. The curvature of the group shifts to accommodate his movement.

"Is that . . . a moderately attractive stranger?" I finish Hannah's thought. "The most elusive legend in all of Five Fingers?" Hannah doesn't seem to hear me. "Han? Do you know him?"

Mandy Rodriguez, who graduated two years ago, grabs the boy's arm and pulls him into a hug. Something along the lines of *good to see you* passes between them, and Hannah releases one crack of laughter before red splotches rush into her cheeks. "Not exactly."

11

The boy turns to wave as Mandy and her friends move off toward a cart selling fried-dough elephant ears. In that moment, his face becomes fully visible.

Unmistakable.

"Oh my god," Hannah gasps. "It *is*. It's him."

"Saul Angert."

The buzzing I felt back at the gatehouse swells within me now. It's not a hornet or a bit of darkness circling me. It's everywhere, everything. It's Saul Angert. Saul Angert, and the fact that he shouldn't be here.

And that I definitely shouldn't be here with him.

Three

"HOW long has it been since anyone's seen him?" Hannah asks.

"Three years," I answer automatically.

"Right," Hannah says. "Of course."

Three years ago everything changed for the Angerts, like ten years ago it changed for my family.

I was about to start high school, and for the first time since second grade, he and I were going to be in the same building. We'd spent the fourteen years prior avoiding each other, and, barring a few brushes, we'd done a good job.

I was nervous to see him on a regular basis, but a little excited too. My parents had never been the rule-setting type, so the more they drilled into my head that I *must, at all costs, stay away from the Angerts*, the more I obsessed over keeping tabs on them. I wanted to know everything about the people I wasn't allowed to know.

Saul and his twin sister, Bekah, were my personal forbidden fruit, the one thing in Five Fingers I could never touch.

"God, why do you think he's back?" Hannah says.

I shake my head. The snag in my throat returns. At this point, it's more like a double knot.

"Maybe Santa got my letter," Hannah pans, then shoots me an apologetic smile. She's had a crush on Saul for nearly as long as I've been under strict orders to avoid him.

One of my earliest memories is of Dad perching me on a stool in our summer-warm kitchen and telling me about the Angerts— what they did to the O'Donnells way back before I was born, how they still treated us. And, most importantly, what happens when we cross paths with them. I have dozens more memories like that one, snippets of panic and curiosity whenever I spotted one of them at the grocery store or in our elementary school's bus lane, fear and embarrassment when we met at the neighborhood pool and I watched Dad's face storm over.

Hissed insults in parking lots.

Ignorant backwoods dick, from Saul's father, Eli.

Elitist asshole, from Dad.

Yanked arms and hasty retreats.

Slammed doors and peeled tires.

Even years after Dad was gone, Mom dragged Shadow and Grayson away from the Cone's walk-up window, milkshake-less, when she saw Bekah Angert working the register.

So I spent much of the summer before freshman year mentally preparing myself to get regular, prolonged, and up-close looks at the supposed face of evil. But when my first day came, Saul wasn't there.

"We should go say hi," Hannah says timidly, like not even *she* believes that. She knows the sordid saga of the O'Donnell/Angert feud, but as with most things that cause her displeasure—spiders and peplum tops and that Richard Harris song about the melting cake—she tries to ignore it.

"Hannah, *no*."

When the bus dropped me off after my first day of high school, I wandered toward the Angerts' summer cabin. I watched from the woods as Saul trekked in and out of the front door, carrying taped-up cardboard boxes and milk crates full of records. He looked less solid then than he does now; he looked wilty and tired.

"I was seriously starting to resign myself to never seeing him again," Hannah forges on.

That was what I'd thought three years ago: that the packed car meant the Angerts were leaving town. But the next day a group of upperclassmen—Mandy Rodriquez among them—marched up to my locker and asked if I was the reason Saul had transferred last minute. It turned out he was going to spend his senior year at boarding school, the pretentious arts academy two hours south of town.

The news traveled fast, and by lunch everyone was speculating that Mandy was right. People paid attention to what our families did. They knew about the bad blood, and the pains we took to avoid each other, because, for all intents and purposes, Dad and Eli Angert were local celebrities: Dad for the cherries and general magic surrounding our house, Eli for a series of boring-ass man-vs.-nature

15

novels the *New York Times* had lauded, and the both of them for the roles their ancestors played in the founding of Five Fingers.

I understood why Saul's friends would think Eli had yanked Saul out to keep space between us, but it was impossible to be sure. After all, the Angerts had had their own Very Bad Thing happen a few months before, and even from a distance, I could see the family slowly falling apart. A few weeks before Saul left, Rachel, his mom, had ditched her job as the school nurse and moved to Chicago without his father, who—much to Mom and Toddy's displeasure—moved full-time into the summer cabin that bordered our property.

Weeds had quickly overrun the once magnificent garden, beer bottles and cans had piled up on the front porch for weeks, newspapers had lain at the lip of their driveway getting soggy, and when someone knocked the mailbox off the post, Saul's father hadn't bothered to fix it.

I expected things to settle down and Saul to come home, at least for the summer. But he didn't, and, after art school, he left for Vanderbilt without so much as a weekend home first. Then I resorted to tracking his movements through covert Google searches, history cleared on the off chance that Mom or Toddy ever used my computer. A year ago, Saul turned up in a "10 Under 30" feature *New York* magazine ran. Six months ago, I watched Toddy angrily stuff the local newspaper into the kitchen trash can, and when I fished it out, one of Saul's terrible junior high yearbook photos stared back at me alongside a piece alerting Five Fingers that its very own Saul Angert had sold an untitled book of essays to

Simon & Schuster. I'd been watching for it to pop up online or in bookstores but never heard another peep about it.

Three years, and in all that time, he'd never come home. And yet now here he is. Standing a few yards away near a pile of puked-up popcorn, as if he never left.

"It's a miracle," Hannah says hazily. "A back-to-school miracle."

Or a tragedy I've brought on with the sheer force of my curiosity. My mind flashes to the darkness I saw undulating across the gatehouse earlier.

The nameless thing is gone, was never there. You imagined it.

"How long do you think he's here for?" I say. "I mean, he can't be staying, right?"

"I have no *idea*, Junie." Hannah's voice strains under nerves and excitement. "That's why it's *essential* we hang out with him tonight."

A thrill of curiosity and panic shoots through my stomach. "Hello? Hannah? It's me, June, your best friend who's forbidden from interacting with him."

"I know, I know!" she cries, glancing between me and the group below the Ferris wheel. They've rearranged again so that Saul's facing our direction, and I jerk my gaze away before he can catch me looking at him. "But," Hannah begins, "this is quite possibly a once-in-a-lifetime opportunity. Don't act like you're not curious."

"You know what curiosity did to the cat."

"Convinced it to help its shy cat-friend woo her childhood crush?"

I laugh despite myself. I can't blame Hannah for trivializing my family's feud with the Angerts. Even Mom used to roll her eyes at Dad when he did things like steer us away from the shore and back to the car when we turned up for a beach day only to find the Angerts there. Backing out of the parking lot, Mom used to sigh in exasperation as Dad mumbled under his breath: *Think they're better than everyone, just 'cause they paid thousands for a piece of Ivy League paper and some froufrou shoes.* Before he died, we stayed away from the Angerts only because *Dad* did. But after, I think we all started to wonder if he'd been right: if the Angerts' hate for us really *did* somehow cause our bad luck.

It wasn't just us who said it. The whole town did—maybe just for fun, but they said it. Once, when I was in middle school, I even overheard a teacher explaining it to a substitute in the lounge: *The families hate each other so much that when tragedy strikes one, fate lashes out at the other. And when they cross paths? Well, they don't. And for good reason.*

But Hannah would never hear of it. *Bad things happen, June,* she'd say. *They just do. To everyone.*

"Pleeeeeeease." she says now, bouncing on the balls of her feet. "Let's just say hi."

"Hannah, my mom and Toddy have literally *two* rules: no swimming at Five Fingers Falls and no Angerts. You know this."

She squeezes my arm and says, "Sorry. I get it. I do. I'll just have to be happy knowing that, in another universe, the one where your family doesn't hate Saul's, we're having a lot of fun tonight. You, me, Saul, and"—she pauses, tipping her head toward the Ferris wheel—"*Nate*."

I look over, and as if on cue, Nate spots us. He waves with the unfettered ferocity of someone stranded on a desert island trying to catch the eye of a chopper flying past.

"Are you kidding, Hannah? You just dreamed up another universe and you made *Nate Baars* my unofficial date! You could've chosen anyone!"

She laughs and waves back. "He's not that bad," she says. "Besides, he's Saul's cousin. He's the whole reason I know Saul."

"*Know* is a pretty strong word for someone you've never spoken to. Aloud, I mean."

Hannah waves off my comment. "You used to think Nate was super cute."

"In the fifth grade!" I say. "He didn't have that walk yet."

"Oh please, since when aren't you into boys who walk like they just dismounted a horse after fifteen hours of riding bareback?"

"He probably has chronic hemorrhoids."

"Junior," Hannah says reproachfully, and I know she's serious because she never uses my full name. Or, at least, my full*er* name. Despite my being a girl, my full name is Jack O'Donnell IV, after my father and his father and his father's father, who apparently got *his* name because he was the spitting image of *his* father's father's father, Jonathan "Jack" Alroy O'Donnell, pioneer settler of Five Fingers and purveyor of magic cherries.

Mom used to call me Jackie, but Dad always called me Junior or June. After he died, everyone else started to too. "Oh my God!" Hannah grabs my arm again. Her face is reddening rapidly. "They're coming over here. I'm so sorry—I think I just willed that to happen. Oh my God, am I a witch?"

The tension in my throat snarling again, I glance over my shoulder. The Ferris wheel group is disbanding, but Nate and Saul are distinctly headed in our direction.

"Shoot," Hannah says, as if she weren't just begging the universe for this exact scenario to unfold. "He's actually coming over here! What do we do?"

I search for somewhere to hide. Hannah, realizing how actually terrified she is to talk to her forever-crush, also searches for somewhere to hide. I book it toward the House of Mirrors, and she chases after me. I spin back to her, my heart jarring at the realization of what I'm about to do. "Wait."

Hannah stops short, wide-eyed, and I glance toward the entrance, the spurt of adrenaline from seeing Saul spurring me on. "I want to go in alone," I say, and Hannah's face twists with worry. "You want to talk to Saul; now's your chance."

She and I lock into a staring contest. I can practically see the debate happening in her mind. "Hannah. You can do this. You can talk to him."

She shoots another glance over her shoulder and takes a deep breath. "Okay. Okay, go."

I kiss my pointer and middle fingers and hold them out to her. Hannah does the same, our two fingers meeting in the middle like a tiny high five. "When I get back, be ready to tell me which song you chose for your wedding processional."

Hannah's eye roll evolves into a grin, and I turn and step into the dark, where everything becomes me.

Four

THE room glows neon. Blues, purples, pinks cross-fade along the edges of mirrors, and so do the versions of me they reflect. The whirring of the fans dulls the screeches and giggles of the other people hustling through the maze as I take my first steps.

I come up against an unexpected pane of glass, then veer right. As I move, I allow myself to forget where I'm going, like Dad used to do—he loved to lose himself first. Then, only when he was sure we were in the epicenter of whatever maze he'd led us into, he'd make a plan and swiftly guide me out.

"When you've been as lost as I have," he once said, "you get good at finding your way home, June-bug."

I feel him in the whip of the fan-stirred wind. Like he's rustling my hair, egging me on. *By the time Jack the First was your age*, he'd tell me, *he'd flown across the Atlantic with Amelia Earhart, gone over Niagara Falls in a rubber ball, and climbed Backbone Mountain to*

*catch a falling star. By now, Jack II had saved dozens from drownin'
in an Alaskan mega tsunami, using only a sliver of glacier for a row-
boat, a broken pine for an oar, and a box of cherries for medicine. By
your age, Junior, I'd stopped a tornado with a matchbook and a glass
factory.*

I turn into a new room, all semblance of laughter and chatter fading. Blue-green arches frame the mirrors here, and swipes
of glow-paint on the floor create the illusion of ornate tiles. This, I
decide, must be the epicenter.

Channeling Dad, I become more purposeful with my turns,
but when I change directions I come up against cool glass, and
my breath catches in my chest. I laugh off my surprise the first few
times it happens, but eventually my lostness, my aloneness, starts to
unnerve me. It's been too long since I've seen anyone else.

And I keep remembering that outside these walls there's an
Angert, and Bad Things happen when an O'Donnnell crosses
paths with an Angert.

Bad Things happen, and I'm locked in a glass labyrinth with
no escape.

I stumble forward and collide with another mirror. My pulse
quickens. I try to calm myself, try to keep moving.

Another collision.

Keep moving. I turn and jolt to the left.

A pane of glass stops me. I spin right.

Keep—

I slam hard into someone as I turn the corner, barely managing
to stifle a scream.

"*Shit,*" someone—a boy—gasps. In the strand of neon green

light, I see his hand clutching his collarbone. Either my skull or my teeth just slammed into it, but apparently I'm too high on adrenaline to feel any pain.

"I'm so sorry!" I stammer, moving forward with my hands held out apologetically. "God, I'm sorry. I thought you were—"

He looks up, the light slanting across his face.

Saul Angert.

That's who I'm looking at. Who I just bit. Saul "If You See Him Dying on the Side of the Road, Keep Going" Angert.

He raises one hand and massages his clavicle with the other. "It's fine. You were right. I *was*."

"—the ghost of Jack the Ripper." The words escape like air from a tire.

"Oh," he says. "I thought you were going to say, *having a complete meltdown about being trapped in this god-forsaken nightmare*."

My heart hammers against my ribs. "No. The vibe I got was definitely Jack the Ripper."

His laugh is gravelly and warm, so at odds with his coolly rigid appearance. His dark hair is cropped close on the sides and a little longer on top, pushed back in a smooth swoop away from his forehead, and now that I'm closer I can see the minor imperfections that keep his face from being perfectly symmetrical: the slight turn of his right canine tooth and the lone dimple on his left cheek. He takes a half step back. "Well, I'm sorry I scared you."

"Oh please. I scared myself. *I'm* sorry I bit your collarbone," I reply. "If it helps, it's super unlikely I have rabies." *Despite what you might have heard.*

Although if he knew who I was, would he be standing here?

He gives me that scratchy laugh again. "Oh yeah. Right. I'm not sorry—*you* are. That's what I meant to say."

"I was just being polite," I say. "I feel no remorse."

"Wow," he says with mock disbelief. "Stone cold."

I tip my head down the mirrored aisle. "Most of me *is* made of glass, so."

"Most of you *are* made of glass."

"I feel like if you're not in uniform, you're not allowed to police someone's grammar."

When he smiles, his mostly straight white teeth glow blue along with his white T-shirt and pale arms, except for where his tattoos cut inky shadows through the light. He *is* handsome, in a way. Just not *my* way, which is usually either (1) brawny pseudo-lumberjack types whose personal hygiene regimen amounts to a lone spray bottle of Febreeze or (2) NOT SAUL ANGERT.

It would be best for me to walk away now. I know that. But I'm standing face-to-face with someone I've heard about my entire life, Googled regularly for at least three years, and never, before now, spoken to.

And I haven't burst into flames. The ceiling hasn't collapsed, the earth hasn't opened to swallow us, and he's acting pretty . . . normal.

Which, I assume, can only mean that he doesn't recognize me. Did *not* Google *me*.

I'm a little offended. And guilty. Also curious, and shaky with adrenaline. Like I'm about to jump off a diving board or crest the peak of a roller coaster.

"Well," I say, not so much *returning* to my senses as chasing them down with a hatchet. "Good luck."

Saul nods, and I turn a corner toward the outer ring of pink and blue mirrors. I watch him in the reflections in front of me as I go. He's trailing me a couple of yards back, the faint trace of a smile curving one corner of his mouth. I stop and face him. "What are you doing?" I say. "You can't follow me. That's cheating."

"Who says you're going the right way?"

"If I'm not, then why are you following me?"

"I'm not," he says. "This happens to be the right way. I'm just trying to get out of here. It's purely coincidence."

"Fine. Then you can go in front of me."

He shakes his head. "Are you kidding? I'm not going to let you cheat off of me. You bit me and didn't apologize."

"That was self-defense," I say. "At that point, there was still a *ninety-nine* percent chance you were the ghost of an English serial killer."

A slow smile spreads across his face, and for a second we're silent. Another thrill bubbles up in my chest. My midsection feels like a shaken-up champagne bottle, fizzy and light.

"Fair enough," Saul says.

I start moving again.

He gives me a few yards' head start before he follows, and again my eyes keep rebounding toward his reflection. Whenever he catches me peeking, a microscopic river of embarrassment jolts through my atoms, and the corner of his mouth twists up in a quiet way, like we're sharing an unspoken joke whose punch line is *our families hate each other, ha-ha!*

Or at least that's what the punch line is for the few moments before I take a distracted yet forceful step and slam my face into a mirror. Saul lets out one rough laugh, then jogs over to where I'm clutching my nose and groaning. He ducks his head to get a better look. "You okay?"

"Could be worse," I say, still covering my nose. "A cartoon anvil didn't fall on my head."

"Lemme see." He pulls my hand away from my face, and his dark eyes zigzag over my nose, which hurts way less than my dignity. Now we're *really* close, and I can smell his wintergreen toothpaste and his laundry detergent, and something else that's warm and a little earthy.

He brushes his fingertips over my nose. "That hurt?"

If his voice had a taste it would be like one of those artisanal chili-pepper dark chocolate bars. If it were a color it would match the eyes that are currently boring into mine.

A memory resurfaces: his name at the top of the MARRY column in the KISS/MARRY/KILL chart Hannah wrote on her closet wall in seventh grade. The image doesn't quite exterminate the butterflies in my stomach, but it *does* remind me that if Greg Schwartz turns up dead, Hannah will need a very good alibi.

"Doesn't look broken or anything," Saul says, narrowing his gaze to peer at me through the neon light.

It's probably my turn to talk, but his hand is warm on my shoulder and we're standing, like, six inches apart, and the vast majority of my brain has already rejected the memory of face-planting into a smudgy fun house mirror so that it can fully devote itself to screaming, I WONDER IF SAUL ANGERT'S MOUTH TASTES MORE LIKE COOL MINT OR SPICY CHOCOLATE.

Finally, Saul releases my shoulder, and it's then that I notice the fullness of the noise in here, the eerie music and wash of voices pulsating from everywhere. I spot the barely visible gap where one mirror flares right and another just left to hide the opening between them. I lean to the right until the two separate in my vision. "Hey, guess what," I say.

Saul stares at me for a long moment. "What?"

"I win." I slip between the panes and out into the buzzing night. As soon as I set foot on the asphalt, my eyes land on Hannah and the bowlegged boy beside her.

"June *freakin'* O'Donnell," Nate Baars calls to me.

Saul's shoulder bumps mine as he emerges behind me, and all the fizz in my chest turns to lead and sinks. He lowers his mouth beside my ear and murmurs, "O'Donnell, huh?"

But he doesn't say it like it's an accusation. He says it like a joke.

He brushes past me to meet Hannah and Nate, then looks back with a faint, mocking smile.

He said it like he was waiting to, like he knew who I was the whole time.

Five

"HOW is it I went in after you and I've been out for, like, fifteen minutes?" Nate half-shouts at me, because he half-shouts everything. "Whooped your *ass*, girl."

"So you guys met," Hannah stammers and gestures toward Saul and me as we awkwardly join them.

"No," I say at the same time Saul says, "Yes."

I think I was wrong; it was hornets in my stomach, not butterflies, and now they're migrating toward my face. Saul's gaze meets mine, and his coal-black brows pinch together, wrinkling his forehead. We both mumble some variation of *sort of*.

Nate guffaws. "You guys don't know each other?"

"We haven't *formally* met," Saul replies. He holds out his hand to me. "I'm Saul."

"Oooh, that's right," Nate says. "Your families hate each other. Dude, this is *Junior*." Then, as if worried Saul might mistake me for one of the *other* Juniors whose family the Angerts hate, Nate adds, "You know, like Jack O'Donnell IV." And then one final clarification: "She lives in the haunted house."

Dryly, Saul feigns shock. "Oh, *that* O'Donnell."

I can't tell if he's mocking Nate or me. His pupils stretch and shrink as they take me in: tiny telescopes honing in on a predator, or maybe prey. Fine—*good*. If he hates me, that will make it easier for me to hate him too. Like I'm supposed to.

He's still reaching out to me, and Hannah nervously titters, so finally I take his hand. I'm hoping for a floppy palm, preferably slick or sticky. Instead, his hand is a lot like his voice: both leaner and rougher than you'd expect from his almost sterile appearance.

Not my type, I think.

Your best friend's childhood crush.

The son of your dad's mortal enemy.

"Nice to meet you," Saul says.

A voice like late-summer corn husks.

Laugh like brewing coffee.

Hands like sun-warmed sand.

"You too."

Hannah laughs nervously again, then Nate claps his hands together and barks, "Well, that was weird." Saul barely acknowledges him, and I study my shoes and wonder how Nate managed to get him here when the two of them seem to be the sort of cousins who've never met. "Anyway, what do you kids want to do next? Ferris wheel? Scrambler? Carnival-food binge session?"

I look to Hannah for some assurance that she didn't promise our night to Nate Baars while I was in the House of Mirrors. She sways on her feet, one hand on her hip, as she scans the carnival, studying everything but Saul and me.

Dear god, she promised our night to Nate Baars.

"Actually," I start, "I'm, um . . ." *Not allowed to hang out with you.*

"Scrambler?" Hannah says abruptly, voice high and wobbly. She looks faintly green and less faintly miserable.

"Scramblaaaaah," Nate wails and then—no exaggeration—whoops and gallops toward the line. Saul strides past us with his hands in his pockets, leveling a glance over his shoulder. I grab Hannah's arm and hold her back from the group, infusing my glare with the heat of a thousand Junes.

"The moon, Junie!" she hisses. "I'll owe you the *moon* if you go along with this."

Glancing between her and where the boys are walking ahead of us, I feel my resolve crumbling under my curiosity. "Fine," I say. "The moon, a million dollars, and one solid kick to Nate's crotch."

Hannah drags me after them into the queue just as Nate's launching into an unnecessarily long story about his weekend that roughly amounts to: *I climbed a rock; I jumped into a lake.* Saul just sort of nods along, his expression lacking any sign of interest. Even the way he moves seems contained, cautious, thoughtful compared to how Nate bounds and gambols.

I try and fail to picture clean-cut Saul Angert among the mucky bike racks and beat-up kayaks attached to the cars in the Five Fingers High parking lot.

Though they're both lean and dark-eyed with weirdly elegant posture, it's equally hard to reconcile Saul as the son of Eli Angert, several of whose books I read for a Michigan literature unit last year. Mom and Toddy had offered to write me a note to get out of it ("As you know, our daughter's allergic to Angerts . . ."), but I was too embarrassed.

So I read (and appropriately loathed) Eli's books about Men Learning to Be Men: full pages describing brown liquor in crystal glasses, paragraphs devoted to the silence of the woods, diatribes about mercy-killing injured does, and more than one passage juxtaposing a masturbation scene with a sermon on the brutality of nature.

You could take the average Five Fingers boy, age him up forty years, and get an approximation of Eli Angert. But I can't understand how a boy like Saul could be born in a place like this, or what would bring him back once he escaped.

At the front of the Scrambler's line, a man with pitted cheeks and a straggly ponytail checks our admission bracelets, and a stroke of benevolent genius hits me.

"Hey, Saul," I say, pulling my backpack off my shoulders as the four of us cross the metal platform to some open cars. "Ride with Hannah? I wanna get a picture of her on the ride, and it'll be easier from another car."

He shrugs and pulls his hands out of his pockets, only to stick them right back in when he realizes he has nothing to do with them. "Sure."

Hannah shoots me a mortified look. It was a sort of mom-y thing for me to do, I know, but I wasn't the first person to make this night uncomfortable.

"I'll ride with you, Han," Nate offers.

Hannah's eyes widen, and she opens her mouth like she's about to excuse herself from the ride entirely.

"Saul already said he would," I say and grab Nate's leathery elbow to steer him into the car across from Hannah and Saul's. I rest my backpack on my thighs, and once we get the lap bar down, I rifle through my bag for my phone to maintain the pretense of taking a picture.

"Smile!" When I glance up, I find Saul's eyes already on me. A spurt of heat blooms in my chest.

Oh no. I definitely think he's hot. And worse, I want him to look at me.

Meanwhile Hannah's grimacing with anticipation of the picture I'm about to take, so I force my eyes to my screen and snap a few. Saul's not smiling in any. He's just staring intensely at the camera.

"Good?" Han calls to me.

"Good." I will my voice steady. "You guys look like you just found out bacon doesn't exist anymore, so good."

"Don't eat bacon," Saul says. "Vegetarian."

"There is no such thing as a vegetarian in Five Fingers," I say.

He lifts one shoulder in the barest of shrugs. "I know. That's why I was exiled."

Hannah laughs, a bright sound that makes Saul crack a partial smile. When his eyes flick toward me, they burn my skin, and I'm horrified and embarrassed and guiltily thrilled.

I swivel in my seat toward Nate and wait for my blush to fade, my heartbeat to slow. "Smile," I say, and Nate flips off my phone.

The metal arms of the Scrambler screech to life, the ghoulish music resumes mid-note, and we start to spin. I catch the tail end of a gravelly laugh hidden in the noise.

I feel it in my stomach as neon colors whip around us.

Because I have an insta-crush on Saul Angert. Because I am a horrible friend and a traitor to my father. Because when Angerts and O'Donnells get together, Bad Things happen.

Six

BY the time we've disembarked the Scrambler, I'm still not sure Hannah has looked Saul in the eye, and her misery has become more blatantly visible. I grab her elbow and say, "Would you run to the bathroom with me?"

"God, yes."

As soon as we duck between the port-o-potties into the shadows of the parking lot, Hannah blurts, "This reminds me of when I had that hot dentist."

"The one whose hand you accidentally licked?"

"Saul keeps *trying* to make conversation, but, like, there's a giant invisible hand in my mouth, and I'm suddenly deeply convinced I still have braces."

"Open," I say. Hannah sticks her tongue out. "Oh shit, Hannah, they're back! Your braces are back! You have haunted teeth!"

She sighs. "This is terrible. I've set off a chain reaction that culminates in my dying alone, in a doily-covered apartment, beneath a pile of coupons."

I kneel on the asphalt and dig through my backpack for Dad's old flask. Hannah glances anxiously between it and the crowd beyond the port-o-potties, then rubs the spot between her brows. "Will that make me puke?"

I wave a hand toward a sign that reads, DEEP! FRIED! CANDY! "*Everything* here will make you puke."

She sighs, swipes the flask, and takes a quick swig. "Okay, now put that away before we get arrested."

I laugh, though I'm pretty sure she's not kidding, and take a long sip myself before tucking it back in my bag.

"What was I thinking?" Hannah says. "I can't even *talk* in front of him. I couldn't when we were kids either."

"To be fair, when we were kids, he was, like, thirty-eight."

"Juuuuune," she groan-laughs. "He's twenty-one! I'll be eighteen soon—it's not a big deal."

"Whatever. Let's get back to your sugar daddy and make sure he gets you into his will before it's too late."

"I hate you."

"Love you back." I kiss my fingers and hold them out to her. Still shaking her head, she does the same. "By the way," I say as we head back toward where the boys are waiting for the bumper cars, "if you guys get married, should I call Saul Dad?"

"Jack O'Donnell IV," Hannah says, "you're so grounded."

Maybe it's the shot of whisky I took, or the meteor shower glittering across the sky; maybe it's the group of fifth graders clustered on curbs watching trails of light streak across the black with sleepy awe in their eyes, or how the night air cools and thins, but from this moment on, the carnival becomes something gentler.

The music mellows, voices simmer. The trees sway as if rocking to a lullaby. And as the four of us meander from ride to ride, Hannah loosens up and acts like herself. She talks about school and tells Saul about how she got into violin. She asks him questions about Tennessee, Vanderbilt, the summer writing residency he just finished at York St. John. She even laughs good-naturedly when Nate makes jokes or just generally does something to suggest he'd like some applause, like jumping over a trash can for literally no reason.

Each time Nate out-Nates himself, I catch myself meeting Saul's gaze, like we're sharing another private joke. It happens so many times I resolve to hang back and walk behind the others just to stop myself from eye-flirting.

I keep forcing Hannah and Saul to ride with each other "so I can get pictures," but after the Kamikaze—a pendulum ride with a metal arm that swings you in a loop—I don't have to force them anymore. It's evident this pairing is becoming permanent all on its own, which makes my head feel cloudy and my spine burn with an unprecedented and sickening breed of jealousy.

Fifteen minutes from close, we join the line for the last ride, the Ferris wheel.

"Okay, not that I don't love me some Junior," Nate says, "but I demand a ride with Hannah."

She blushes and glances sideways at Saul, who shrugs and says, "Sure."

I hate it. I hate that Hannah just asked Saul's permission to ride with Nate, and worse still I hate that I hate it. I shouldn't care.

I shouldn't *be* here. I should've left as soon as I saw him.

We reach the head of the line, and Nate and Hannah file in first. Their bench rises, and another lowers to the metal ramp. Saul holds out an arm, gesturing for me to go first. I do. Silently. Awkwardly. Miserably.

He slides in beside me and waits for me to get my backpack into my lap before pulling the scuffed bar down. We're mute as our bench lifts to lower the next for loading. Both of us look around for a while, studying anything but each other. The possibility of our car detaching and plummeting to the concrete doesn't gnaw at me like the immediate distress of being alone with him, of feeling Saul Angert's hip against mine.

"Did she blackmail you?" he says.

I finally look at him, and his face is serious. "What?"

"You clearly don't want to be here with me. So how's Hannah keeping you here?"

"Oh. She asked."

"Do you want to know how Nate got me here?"

"Guns?" I hazard.

"Yeah." Saul nods. "Guns."

I fight a smile. "Wait, really, how?"

"He likes your friend," he says coolly. "He needed a wingman. Shit, sorry—that sounds a lot creepier than the last time I said it to a seventeen-year-old girl, four years ago."

"God, this is rapidly becoming a bad teenage retelling of a Shakespearean comedy."

"How so?"

"Hannah's not into Nate," I say. "I don't think they would be a good match."

Saul shrugs lazily. "I don't know. He's a little goofy, but he's a good guy."

Neither of us says anything. Moments pass, and the silence accumulates, thick and heavy between us. To break it, I say, "Eighteen."

"What?"

"You can rest easy. You said the word *wingman* to an eighteen-year-old girl. Far less humiliating."

One corner of his mouth curls up. "Agreed. Far less humiliating."

"The bigger concern is that you used the word *wingman* and it's not 1986."

Saul's eyes narrow, but his grin widens. "Wow, you *do* hate me, don't you, Jack O'Donnell IV?"

My stomach turns inside out at the sound of my name in his voice. This isn't how he's supposed to be, and it's definitely not how *I'm* supposed to be *with* him.

Saul swears and grips the lap bar as we jolt up another notch to let more people board below. Nate's and Hannah's feet dangle over us, swaying in the lake wind, but Saul's just staring at the ground. "Not a big fan of heights?" I say.

"What gave it away? The fine sheen of cold sweat that just sprang up all over my body?"

"Actually it was your white-knuckling." I flick his hand with mine.

His fingers latch on to my hand and hold it there. "Hey, sorry about your hand," he says, tightening his grip. "Turns out I need it now, so you're going to have to find a new one."

I laugh. I warm. I burn. Guilt springs up in me. "I have something more effective than a hand in my purse, if you'll let me go," I say. When he does, I fish out the flask.

His smile now looks like how his laugh sounds: inviting, warm, uneven. I pass him the whiskey and watch his throat move as he chugs a little. He wipes his chin with the side of his hand and passes back the flask. "Thanks. Aren't you a little young to have that?"

"No, haven't you heard? They've changed the drinking age since your childhood here thirty-five years ago."

"Hilarious. So funny."

"I can tell you think so by your raucous laughter, Saul."

"I have to admit," he says, "I'm a little surprised it's true."

"What's true?"

"You O'Donnells hate us."

Heat rushes into my face. After making it this far without broaching the feud, I'd expected to finish the night without acknowledging it. "Oh, deeply," I answer, unsure whether I'm kidding or serious. Right now I don't hate Saul Angert. Nor do I want him to know I ever thought I did. "And you guys hate us too, right?"

He nods solemnly. "I'd wish you dead, but we don't need another ghost in that house."

I don't laugh. I can't. His gaze has me frozen. Like he's a Gorgon and I'm the sap who wandered into his temple. I'm worried I've lost track of the silence, that maybe we've been sitting here like this much longer than appropriate. "My house isn't haunted," I say.

"Glad to hear it," Saul answers.

"It's magic, but not haunted."

His face remains neutral. "Magic."

"I'm serious."

"Okay, Junior." He braces himself against the bar as we rise higher. "What's magic about your house?"

"You don't have to call me that," I tell him.

"What would I call you?"

"June, Jack, Jackie, whatever you want."

"I want to call you Junior."

"Fine."

"But I like Jack too."

"Whichever."

"And June's cute."

"Adorable," I agree. "Makes me sound like a tiny golden retriever puppy."

We surge upward one last time, straight to the top of the Ferris wheel, and again Saul locks my hand against the bar with his, and again I like it more than I should.

"So, June." His voice is taut as he pries his gaze from the asphalt below. "What's magic about your house?"

I shift my hand in an attempt to free it, but instead Saul slides his fingers through mine and grips them for dear life.

"Well, what have you heard?" I ask.

"The coywolves." He closes his eyes. "That if you leave shoes in the yard, the coywolves take them."

"One hundred percent. Every time."

His dark eyes open to find mine. "You're messing with me."

"I'm not. You really never left flip-flops in our yard when you were a kid? I thought everyone did that."

"Everyone did," he says. "I didn't. What else?"

"The coywolves never—or *almost* never—kill our chickens. Dad said it's always been that way, since Jonathan Alroy O'Donnell first came here."

Saul fixes me with another serious stare. "That can't be true."

"Dad called our woods a thin place, where the world and heaven overlap. He said that's what made our house magic—why that first cherry tree Jonathan planted grew overnight and the animals would lie down together."

Again all true, except, of course, when the dark ghost appeared. But that seems like a tally in the *yes, definitely haunted* column, so I don't mention it. A chill rolls through me at the thought of the writhing darkness I imagined tonight.

"And do you have proof of this, Jack?"

"We've never kept our chickens in their coop. We just let them roam the hill."

"Wild." Saul stares vaguely at our hands as the Ferris wheel begins to twirl in earnest. Cool wind ripples over us, carrying the contented noise of carnival-goers upward, and he relaxes a little. "What about the ghosts?" he says. "I remember kids used to go to your house at midnight, try to see ghosts in the yard."

"There are two of them, and anyone can feel them, but my dad said only Jacks could see them. He called them sprites. We don't really know what they are."

"And the Window Whites?"

He's talking about the little white puffballs that float in our windows and doors, like sentient, unblown dandelions. No one knows what they are or why they sometimes drift listlessly in our doorframes and other times disappear for weeks.

"They land on the glass and move around for a while, then float back into the woods," I tell Saul now. "My mom thinks they're just blossoms or pollen."

"And the rearranging hallways and rearranging woods?"

I shrug and look down at Saul's hand and mine. My stomach dips. "You think it's all just made up?"

"I think Five Fingers likes its stories."

I laugh. "You don't sound like someone who was born here." He says nothing, and I continue: "I have some hazy memories of opening a door and finding myself back in the room I thought I'd just left, and a dozen memories of walking straight out from my house through the woods toward the setting sun, only to end up back at the hill. And there's this massive tree Dad called O'Dang! We'd go looking for it all the time and only find it, like, ten percent of the time. We always knew, though, that if we stepped into the forest and the sky was misty but sunlit, we could find it."

As the words spill out, all my blood feels like it's freezing and breaking through my veins. I try not to think about the tree. I try not to think about the woods, because the next thought I have is always of the Worst Day.

All the minuscule details stored in perfect vividness by my eight-year-old brain: the dryness of the air and dirt that week, the blue petals that fell in a perfect circle from Mom's hydrangea, the weeks when she fed me only Froot Loops and macaroni, either because she was too sad to cook or because I was too sad to eat anything real.

If our house *were* haunted, there'd be more than two ghosts fluttering on our hill. If it were haunted, Dad wouldn't be gone.

"I'd like to see it." Saul's husky voice brings me back to the humming night.

"The tree?"

"The house," he says. "All of it."

I study him for a long stretch during which neither of us blinks. "You really never sneaked over? Not once?"

"Once I got as far as the woods." He shakes his head. "I remember when you did, though. When you got stung by the bees?"

I stare down at the purple stripes of a psychic's tent. "Yeah?"

That was the day I started to believe that being *close* to the Angerts was dangerous. It was also the day Hannah's crush on Saul reached legendary heights. Hannah and I were seven, so Saul must have been about ten. She and I had snaked through the woods out toward the Angerts' summer home. We found Saul and Bekah building a tree house—or, rather, *she'd* been nailing boards to a trunk, hanging on them to check their strength before climbing up to nail the next one, and Saul had been taking pictures with a clunky film camera that looked like a prop from a movie set.

Hannah and I crept close to get a look at the kids I wasn't allowed to play with—she knew them a bit through her neighbor Nate. Saul had his back to us as he crouched in the mud, snapping photographs of something we couldn't see.

I study him in the Ferris wheel's light, comparing him to the boy I saw on that day. "Your ears were bigger back then."

Saul's head tilts back, and the corners of his eyes crinkle in laughter. "Actually, I think they were the exact same size they are now, but the rest of me was considerably smaller."

His hair was longer then too, but just as neat. Bekah was the opposite, hair wild and limbs muddy and thorn-scratched. As I watched the mysterious Angert twins that day, a fallen branch cracked under my foot, and when Saul spun toward the noise, I stepped onto a collapsed log. It made a hollow sound beneath my sneaker, because it *was* hollow, or mostly hollow, give or take a hornets' nest.

The wasps swarmed at once. Hannah started screaming and ran toward the Angerts' cabin. Bekah and Saul both came toward me, like they were going to fight the things off with their hands, but even in my earth-splitting panic I knew: The wasps hadn't just attacked me for stepping on their house; they'd attacked me for getting too close to the Angerts.

Going toward the twins for help would only make things worse, not to mention the trouble I'd be in when Dad found out.

I turned and ran. Through the woods all the way back to my house, the hornets trailing me the whole way. Mom saw me hurtling toward her from where she was sitting out front, reading on a papaya-yellow blanket beneath the cherry tree. She stood and came running full speed. She swept me off the ground and over her hip, barreling for the front door. Inside, she dumped me into the tin tub downstairs and cranked the faucet to full blast. As the icy water spit from the showerhead, I watched the hornets die in the pool forming around me, the beating of their wings slowing to a fizzle and then nothing, no movement at all.

I spent the rest of the day in a Benadryl haze, covered in cala-mine lotion, and Dad had had to pick up Hannah from the Angerts' cabin, which had him more furious with *them* than me.

When he got back, I heard him and Mom talking in the hall-way outside my room. *Angert girl got hurt too*, he said, and I could tell from his voice that he thought this was only fair. *Completely covered in poison ivy. I mean, eyes swollen shut, everything.* Mom's heavy sigh disapproved of his obvious glee, but she didn't say any-thing. That was how it was. He couldn't be talked out of anything, and he could talk other people *into* anything.

"That was the first time I saw you up close," Saul says beside me. The breeze lifts my hair from my shoulders, and goose bumps wriggle up where Saul's gaze just glanced off my neck.

"No it wasn't."

He lifts his eyes to mine. "What do you mean?"

"The hornets were the second time. The first time was at the YMCA pool. I couldn't have been more than five years old. We showed up after you, and your dad made you leave. On your way out, you dislocated your shoulder. Like an hour later, I nearly drowned. That was the day my dad first told me about your family."

Saul tilts his face skyward and shakes his head as if addressing the stars directly.

"What?" I press.

"Nothing. It's just . . ." He slumps into the bench again. "What a convenient concept. That every bad thing that happens to you was caused by the person you hate."

"So you don't think bad things happen when our families cross paths?"

"June," he says. "Every single outdated, low-budget, under-repaired ride we've taken tonight not only *could have* but *should have* killed us, O'Donnell and Angert or not, and yet here we are. Together."

"I'm honestly kind of surprised the guy who's currently drawing blood from my hand with his fingernails as we dangle three stories above an asphalt parking lot would be willing to jinx us like that, but okay."

He faintly grins. "You already bit my collarbone *and* got your just reward when you plowed into a mirror that's probably never, in its forty years of life, been cleaned. Even if we *were* to be disciplined by the universe for speaking to each other, I think we've gotten enough punishment for the night."

"How did you know the mirror was the same age as you?" I ask somberly. "Were you born in the same hospital? Hey, what was the world like before the Internet?"

"How old, exactly, do you think I am?"

"I don't know—what's the last year a person could've been born and still know what a *fortnight* is?"

"It was one thing when you took *wingman* from me. I won't let you disparage *fortnight* too."

"Seriously, though," I say. "What about the thing at the YMCA? I mean, you left in an ambulance, and an hour later a pimply lifeguard was hunched over me, forcing water out of my lungs."

Saul lifts one dark eyebrow. "That shoulder's been on the fritz my entire life—all forty? Fifty years of it? Loose ligaments. Ended my baseball career before it ever began. I'd call that a blessing, not a curse. No, Jack O'Donnell IV, I don't believe your mere presence dislocated my shoulder. I believe our great-grandfathers pissed each other off and this town turned it into something big and impossible and legendary because this is Five Fingers, and everything has to be big and impossible and legendary. It's a coping mechanism for our ungodly winters."

I stare at him, trying to decide whether or not I agree. Five Fingers might be a town of tall tales, but that's because enough of us have seen enough of *it*—the stuff that's worth repeating until it becomes a tall tale—to believe in it. Dad said we lived in a magic house, and we do. He said the Angerts were dangerous to us—do I really draw the line there?

And then there's the thing too big to ask about: If *our* bad things don't turn into *their* bad things and vice versa, then what about what happened to Dad and Bekah? Ten years ago, he was totally healthy, then weeks after *she* was diagnosed, *he* was gone.

And three years ago, when she . . . on the day they lost her . . . my foot plunged through the porch and I broke a bone for the first time in my life.

We're silent for the rest of the ride, and when the car touches down, Saul disentangles his hand from mine, and we step off to meet Nate and Hannah. Talking about all this has stirred up memories I do my best to leave settled on the floor of my mind, and it's impossible to pack them away so quickly.

As the four of us make our way toward the Meijer parking lot, I feel empty, like a wrung-out sponge. I don't have the energy to care when Saul and Hannah walk ahead of us, though I *do* notice Nate's disappointment now. And I don't care that the only goodbye Han and I exchange with them is a walking wave, like, *Probably see you never!*

I don't care when I see Saul loiter against Nate's passenger door, watching us climb into Hannah's Subaru, or when he calls scratchily, "Have a good fortnight!"

Because I'm Jack O'Donnell IV, and for at least three reasons, I have no business having a crush on Saul Angert.

Seven

"WELL, I hate to say it," Hannah sighs, as we cruise into the blue-green forest that hides my house, "but a night with Saul Angert was hardly worth the moon."

I will myself not to blush, to stamp out the traitorous hope in my chest. "What about the tracker I'll have to wear on my ankle if my parents find out about it? Was it worth that?"

"He used to seem . . . *sparklier*, didn't he?"

My insides twist and snag. "Yeah, super sparkly. Like a tiara for a Barbie doll. I thought you were having fun."

"With no help from him. What a wet blanket. Almost makes you appreciate the Nates of the world."

I think my face is on fire, or maybe just crawling with fire ants.

"But still." Hannah bumps the volume up a couple hundred decibels and cranks the windows down so the heat can beat and roar against our ears. "He is *fine*, isn't he?"

"Just not Barbie-tiara fine," I shout.

The moon shines through the foliage cupped around the raw-boned road, turning everything silver and sublime. "There, June!" Hannah cries pointing up at the sky. "Your gift in all her glory. Please accept this as payment for causing your perfectly good night to be Angerted."

"Do I still get to kick Nate in the crotch?"

Hannah's laughter gets lost between the layers of sound, and I laugh too, because that's the way the lake air works: It carries the feelings you exhale into someone else's inhalations, it syncs your heartbeats, connects you to everyone else who loves it like you do.

That's what Dad used to say, anyway: *Lake people are sponges; we all absorb the same mix of life and minerals. We recognize it in each other and share it when one of us gets dried out. You're a sponge, Junior, like me. When you're dry, you have to go back to the water to survive.*

Hannah sings along, her right arm flinging out to gesticulate wildly and her wispy hair flaring around her face. She's most beautiful when she's this relentless kind of happy. Maybe that's when everyone is their most beautiful, especially to those who love them.

I thrust my right arm out the window and catch Hannah's hand with my left. We sing until our throats fray, and for a while, everything is how it should be.

By the time we rumble past the shabby gatehouse to the grassy hill my home sits on, I'm starting to feel full again. Hannah parks beside the green-trimmed garage Dad built, and the motion sensors catch the car's hood, triggering the porch lights. A flutter of moth wings stipples the ghostly glow of the bulbs, and my eyes skim the windows, the Whites bobbing in their corners.

Hannah kisses the index and middle fingers on her right hand, and I do the same. "Love you, baby girl."

"Love you more." I climb from the car and jog to the porch, listening to the crunch of gravel as Hannah reverses into the ring of woods.

I pull my keys out but freeze, a sudden prickling on my neck. When I turn back toward the yard, Hannah's headlights have vanished beyond the hill. Everything is dark and still, apart from the twin glints of eyes a few yards beyond the porch.

A lone coywolf stands with its reddish tail high and front leg bent, its narrow face caught in the edge of the porch light and its fox-like ears trained toward me.

I don't know quite what makes me do it, but I lean down, slowly, to untie my sandals, my gaze still locked with the coywolf's eyeshade.

Tapetum lucidum, Dad explained to me as a kid. *Eyeshade. A special reflective surface behind the retina that lets some animals see better at night. It gives the image another surface to bounce off of toward the brain, if the first one fails in the dark.*

The coywolf watches me step out of my salmon-colored espadrilles and lift them by their leather ties. I take a few cautious steps, set the shoes on the walkway, then retreat.

The coywolf sets her foot down and picks her way toward my shoes, haunches rolling as she moves. In one swift motion, she drops her snout, snatches the shoes, and darts into the trees.

I stare after her, a laugh building in my chest, followed by an ache. I can picture it so clearly: Dad's back and mine silhouetted by the moonlight as we sat in the yard listening to the cicadas and crickets. So many calm nights when we just *listened* to our thin place for hours. "Can you hear it, June-bug?" he would whisper. "The heartbeat of the world?"

Eventually we'd hear the door creak on its hinges and Mom's bare feet patter across the porch. "Bedtime," she'd hum, and Dad would look back at her and smile, say nothing. Then she would float down to the grass and sit on my other side, pulling my head against her chest to run her hands through my hair.

"Magic," I whisper, aching for those lost nights. I turn to go inside and find one lone Window White bobbing in the doorframe. I cup it in my hand, its softness barely palpable as I lift it toward my face. Something strange happens then: One moment it's floating along my lifeline, the next it seems to disperse into my skin, as if it were never there. I wait for it to reappear, but when it doesn't, I stifle a shiver and let myself inside.

The house is dark and silent as I creep through, nearly tripping over an amorphous pile of shoes in the foyer. Mom and Toddy aren't great at laying down the law, and while I'm not a particularly tidy person, the hands-off approach works even worse with Grayson and Shadow. They're always leaving their stuff all over the house, and I'm always tripping over it.

I steady myself on the credenza against the wall, and my stomach twists and jerks low at the sight of the vase full of blue hydrangeas resting there. I wonder where Mom got them. After Dad died, she let the bush out front wither to nothing, and when the winter snow finally thawed, she yanked it up by the roots and left it down on the curb with the trash.

The sight of it, for some reason, had started to make me sick to my stomach; sometimes when I saw it, I forgot how to breathe. For ten years Mom made sure there were never hydrangeas in the house.

I push the vase behind the only framed picture that sits there: one of Mom and me—I'm just a toddler—both of us perched in Dad's lap in the yard, wearing crowns of weeds we made together.

An ache begins behind my heart and spreads through my chest like roots.

People used to ask if it bugged me how quickly Mom and Toddy got together. I'd tell them it bugged me more when people didn't mind their own business. Those who didn't *really* know Dad would balk; those who did would laugh.

The general consensus in Five Fingers seemed to be that Mom married Toddy because she was helpless without Dad, because he didn't have life insurance and she didn't want to work or know how to fix the toilet when the tank wouldn't stop running. Because she was too pretty to be alone. All these arguments I now understand to be Midwestern ways of shrugging and saying, *She's French*.

For as long as I can remember, my friends' parents have regarded Mom with a mix of intrigue and wariness. But if they assume she doesn't know how to work hard, it's only because she makes work look easy. Earthy and romantic.

She won't wash a dish unless the lather of the soap will please her hands at that moment. She doesn't bake a pie unless she can delight in rolling the dough, in using flour-covered hands to brush the sweat off her forehead, in pressing the crust's lip with perfect dessert-fork indents. She can turn something as strenuous as toiling in the garden into an almost euphoric ritual.

But she also regularly gets massages, visits gourmet shops to buy tiny blocks of herbed cheeses that cost the same as oversized bags of shredded cheddar, and has her favorite perfume shipped to her from Europe.

In Five Fingers, shoe-stealing coywolves are less of a mystery than she is. But she always says that what she loved best about Dad was that, to him, she wasn't a mystery at all.

I sometimes think that's also what drew her to Toddy. He's stable and predictable. Kind. Plus he and Dad knew each other all their lives.

I think Mom married Todd Kemper because they understood one another and what they had lost. They fell in love while they held each other in the wake of that loss, and, together, in the bitter work of staying upright while their hearts broke, they found something sweet.

He'll never be Dad. And, *yes*, sometimes that bothers me. But with Toddy, there's no pressure to strip, bleach, or scrape Dad from the walls. He's in the floral wallpaper that lines the kitchen and the deep grooves in the mudroom's hardwood floor, where we stomped around in ice skates. With Toddy, it's okay to keep all the old pictures on the walls, to leave the albums set out in the wicker basket by the massive television he brought when he moved in. It wasn't even a question that Mom would keep wearing that first, jewel-less wedding band on her ring finger, beneath the one with the large princess-cut diamond that Toddy added.

He gave me a ring at the ceremony too. It was beautiful—peridot and two side diamonds—but I couldn't bring myself to love it like the fifty-cent spider necklace Dad got me from the quarter machine at Camponelli's Pizza.

My eyes trail away from the photograph but carefully avoid the hydrangeas as I turn up the creaky staircase. I reach the end of the hallway and ease open my door but then come up short.

My room should be dark, but it's not. Should be empty and silent, but it's not.

Wave after wave of this paralyzing shock crashes over me, but no matter how many times I blink, nothing changes.

The lamp beside the bed casts a shallow pool of golden light across the worn pink-and-blue quilt, the little dark-haired girl tucked into it, and the gap-toothed man sitting at her feet.

I'm looking at myself. I'm looking at Dad.

Eight

"DAD," I choke, but there's no sound. I try again, feel the vibrations in my throat, the movement of my tongue and lips, but still no sound.

"Tell me another one," the little girl—*me*—says from the bed.

Dad scratches the strawberry scruff on his chin. "Another one, huh, June-bug?"

"When Great-Great-Great-Great-Grampa Jonathan found our hill."

Dad nudges the younger me aside and swings his booted feet up onto the bed as he stretches out beside her. "So how's it start again, Junior?"

"Jonathan set out looking for a place to call home."

I take a shaky step forward, and neither of them looks at me.

"So he did," Dad says. He wraps an arm around the girl's skinny shoulders and kisses the crown of her head. My eyes shut for a long moment before I force myself to open them again, to keep watching. "And he looked all down the East Coast, but it was too hot and sticky, and the water was too salty, and the hills were too hilly. And when he planted cherry trees, their roots wriggled and writhed in the dirt, and their branches withered, and when the cherries came, they tasted like tears, and not the good kind."

"Was he sad?" she asks.

"Nah. Jacks don't get sad, and we get that from him."

"Was he scared?"

"Do *Jacks* get scared, June-bug?"

"Was he lonely?"

"Jacks like a lot of alone time," Dad says. "They also love an adventure, and Jonathan Alroy O'Donnell had plenty of both. He knew he'd find the right place, and that's why he never settled down anywhere else, no matter how many friends he made and adventures he had in a single place. You know, the night of Annie Oakley's debut at the Baughman and Butler Shooting Show, Jonathan bought her a soda and they spent the whole night wandering Cincinnati together. By the time the sun came up, they'd caught a band of bank robbers on the Ohio River, planted a dozen cherry trees, and gotten engaged. But Jonathan was looking for a home, and the cherries didn't take to the Ohio soil, so in the end, they parted ways, and he went south to Florida—too hot and sticky for the cherries, of course—then out west, and you know what he found?"

The pink floral drapes billow like wisps of hair as a warm breeze pushes through the open window, carrying quarter-sized specks of ethereal white: Window Whites.

I remember this moment. It's coming back to me, as it happens.

"He found sand." It's not a guess—it's the answer Dad taught me. Every part of every story was a line in a play we performed hundreds of times. I'd nearly forgotten about that.

"Sand," Dad repeats. "So much sand and sunlight. The cherries he grew there, they lacked that first-snow-of-the-year tingle a good Jack's Tart always has. But Jonathan took advantage of being in California, even if his cherries didn't. Jacks—you know Jonathan was the *first* Jack—are good at getting things un-lost. The gold rush was winding down, so on his way north to Washington, Jonathan followed the Siskiyou Trail. But one day, as he waded in the Columbia River, he dropped a cherry pit in the water and it jumped back out like a snake had bit it.

"He saw a glint there, and when he brushed aside the river muck, he found a solid brick of gold. Most people would've thought, *A brick of gold? Nothing more valuable than that*. But Jonathan wasn't most people. He knew you couldn't eat a brick of gold or bake it into your favorite pie. You couldn't bite into it and taste the whole world in its juice. So you know what he did?"

The girl sits up, her tangle of waves splaying against the headboard. "He traded it for more pits," she says.

Dad leans forward, grinning. "That's right, June-bug."

Tears prick my eyes, and the world slants in too many directions. I don't understand how this is happening. How I can see him so clearly. He's *here*, and of all the impossible things that happen on our land, something like this never has.

Dad, I say, still voiceless, and move toward him. His eyes stay locked on the sleepy eight-year-old in the ratty CHERRYFEST

T-shirt. I study the wrinkle in his forehead, the uneven tan from always riding with his left side half out the car window.

"So he went up the coast," Dad goes on. "And when he got to Washington, he liked it. Don't get me wrong—he did like it. But still, the ocean was too dark, and it rained too much, and it lacked that Special Thing, that *home* thing."

"So he came to Michigan." I mouth the words, but it's not my voice I hear. Or it's *mine*, but a slimmer, scraggly, younger version.

Dad's eyes crinkle and take on a gloss. I don't remember that—I don't remember him on the verge of tears maybe ever, so how can I see it now?

"He came across the North, and by then it was winter, and he passed through all kinds of snowstorms and blizzards and over lakes made entirely of ice."

"And was he scared then?"

"No way, Junior!" Dad replies. "He was having the time of his life. He loved the wildness of it. But he couldn't stand the landlocked-ness. Minnesota was better—tons of water there—but it wasn't a perfect fit. So he went on through Wisconsin and Illinois and over the lake into Michigan. It was spring when he finally reached the tiny town of Five Fingers, between the Five Fingers offshoot of Torch Lake and Lake Michigan. The water was a beautiful turquoise—so clear you could see your hand through it—and the rocks and cliffs were all red and gold, like a sunset. The forests were thick and thriving, full of pure sunlight and cool shadows and tiny, fluttering things. The women were strong as sequoias but lovely as the northern lights, which you could see on a clear night, a great blanket of green and purple and blue spread across the sky.

"Most dirt's just dirt, but in Five Fingers, the dirt *sang*. It *coursed*. It wanted to make life. It beat like it had a heart, and Jonathan, he knew this was home right off the bat. So he trekked through the woods until he came to a grassy hill, and he climbed it to choose where he would plant his first tree. But do you know what he found at the top of that hill?"

"A coyote."

"That's right." Dad nods. "And what else?"

"And a wolf."

"And?"

"A robin."

"Sleeping on the wolf's haunch," Dad finishes. "My great-great-great-grandfather knew right then that he'd stumbled into a thin place, a plot of land where, on a sunny day or a starlit night, you might get a glance at heaven. And he tore up a bit of earth and packed a cherry pit down nice and neat, and right there, he sat and watched the first tree grow before his eyes. By morning, the grass was covered in dew, and the boughs were heavy with plump cherries, and when he bit into the glossy skin, his eyes teared up. *Home*, he said, *it tastes like home*. And it was."

"I love that story," the little girl says.

I love that story.

"Someday I'm gonna write it down," Dad murmurs. "I'm gonna write down all my stories for you, June-bug, so you can know just where you came from." He rustles her hair and kisses her head again, and then my tears blur the scene.

You didn't *write them down*, I want to say. They're already lost, shadows flitting across my memory. *You're lost.*

And yet there he is, just out of reach. Real and impossible.

"Night, Junior." Dad stands to go. He ticks the lamp off and strides right past me, like I'm invisible, a ghost.

I chase him. "Dad," I beg. "Dad! Please."

He doesn't hear, and by the time I reach the hallway, it's dark, empty, as if he were never there.

Something tickles against my palm. I gasp and jump as the white tuft emerges from my lifeline, hovers for just a moment, then drifts toward the stairs.

I follow it, chase *him*—wherever he went.

He's dead, I think, *his trillions of cells sprinkled in Lake Michigan, and that little girl back there hasn't existed in ten years.* But still I'm running down the steps, searching for him, dodging the pile of shoes at the bottom, though it's unnecessary because, somehow, all those shoes have vanished.

I don't understand.

Why is this happening?

Why did I see him, and why is he gone again so soon?

I spin uselessly, tear through the dark kitchen. Dining room. Living room. The sunroom off the side of the house, its windows overlooking the hill and woods and stars. I find nothing. No one.

I barrel back up to my bedroom.

The lamp's off. The window's shut, the Whites gone. I'm alone.

But he *was* here.

At least I think he was.

Nine

"HAPPY Wednesday! Happy first day of senior year," Hannah sings down the hallway as she literally prances toward me. Her hair is slicked into an alarmingly neat fishtail braid that, combined with her gingham dress, makes her look like she should be running through a field of daisies, arms spread wide to catch the sun.

I swing my locker shut and kiss my fingers to greet hers. "You glorious sunburst of a person, did the birds dress you this morning?"

"Basically!"

It's been four days since I saw Dad in my bedroom, and, unable to bring myself to tell Mom what happened, I called Hannah immediately. After days of texting her feverishly during every break she took from her AP summer homework, it's a relief to finally be with her in person.

She slumps against the forest green lockers and jogs her violin case up her shoulder. "P.S. *One* of those little birdies passed along a rumor that Saul's planning on sticking around for a while."

"Oh?" My stomach clenches, and I forget what people usually do with their hands. "I thought you two weren't speaking after your messy split."

"Relax," she says. "I'm not going down *that* rabbit hole again."

Relax? Who, me? The girl leaning against her locker with her thumbs hooked into her belt loops like the hard-ass female cop in a CBS crime thriller? I am the definition of relaxed.

"Nate told me," she adds. "He thinks the four of us should 'totally chill again soon.'"

A pulse of heat drops low in my stomach. "Oof."

She laughs. "That's essentially the reaction I expected."

"I just . . . sort of think . . . Nate likes you."

Her face twists into a mask of not-quite-repulsion. "Nate?"

"Mhm."

"Nate Baars?"

"Yep."

"Nate, who walks like he's auditioning for the role of Cop Number Three?"

"The very same, Han." I rearrange my books in my arms, thinnest to thickest.

"Oof." Hannah tips her head back against the locker. "Maybe you're wrong."

"Maybe." I don't mention that Saul told me so. It'd be too hard to reference our private conversation on the Ferris wheel without broadcasting across my forehead: I HAVE A CRUSH ON

MY SWORN ENEMY SLASH THE (EX-?) BOY OF YOUR DREAMS. "Hey," I say, fumbling over a binder in my locker, "did you ever find out why Saul's back, anyway?"

Hannah scrunches up her mouth. "Nope. Just that he's here for the foreseeable future."

"I thought you would've done some expert digging by now."

"I know—a decade of Saulitis cured in one fateful night. Seeing him as the tragically beautiful stick-in-the-mud he really is freed me up to spend the last three days finishing my AP summer reading."

"Speaking of which, why haven't I seen you all day? Do they keep smart people in a separate wing now?"

Hannah's top lip curls. "Practically. If I have to sit next to Stephen Niequist in one more class, I'll freak. He's gunning for my salutatorian slot."

"Maybe you should flash him some boob, throw him off."

"Stephen Niequist is not into boob."

"Ah, see, I didn't know that, because they keep us simpletons in a separate pen."

"Oh please. You're in the simpleton pen by choice."

"Your misplaced confidence in me is charming, Han."

"And the fact that you won't even *apply* for the same schools as me is decidedly not."

"I'm not *going* to college," I remind her. I'm as incapable as I am uninterested. Instead I'm going to do what Dad and his dad and his dad's dad did: travel, see the world, rest up in Five Fingers, repeat.

"Anyway," Hannah says, "this doesn't matter in the scheme of things right now. How are you doing? Did any more of the"—she glances around furtively, then lowers her voice—"*you-know-what*s happen?"

I sink my teeth into my lip, fighting the drop in my chest. I know she's trying to help, but right now I almost regret telling her about what happened.

The weight of loss is so familiar to me by now that I've become a master at misdirecting myself: pinching my hand, biting my lip, grinding the heel of my shoe into the top of my other foot—any physical sensation to distract from the nonphysical pain.

I don't want to talk about this.

"No, no more hallucinations of my dead father," I murmur.

She squeezes my arm apologetically. She's sorry it happened in the first place. *I'm* sorry it hasn't happened again since.

"What class do you have next?" she asks, expertly steering me from the grief ledge.

"Creative writing."

"Hey, good for you, taking an elective instead of a study hall."

"I already have two study halls this semester. They wouldn't let me take any more."

Hannah laughs as the warning bell rings. "That's it, babe. Aim for the stars. I'll see you later."

"Probably not," I call after her. "Unless—wait, are you in my seventh-period *Would you like fries with that?*"

"Ha. Ha. Ha."

I straighten my books again and turn toward 204, the classroom listed on the schedule taped to my binder. Creative writing is always held in the same space: a cozy offshoot of the library's second floor with three walls and a ceiling comprising mostly windows. Originally, it was a greenhouse where some of the science classes would go for site-specific lessons, but most of the time it was basically treated as a vitamin D–rich alternative to the official teacher's lounge.

In Michigan, especially this far north, you take all the sunlight you can get, no matter the temperature outside. *If you wait for warmth to enjoy the outdoors*, Dad used to say, *the sun might die before you get there.*

It's almost funny, in a tragic way, that the fiery thing at the center of my universe did die and that I, a girl whose name is synonymous with summer, am expected to live without it.

A handful of kids are already seated in the blue Herman Miller scoop chairs lining the rectangular arrangement of tables. I take an open spot along the wall so I can look out the window at the pine trees beyond, though it will probably mean squinting into the sun most days. I recognize a few kids, most notably *the* Stephen Niequest, who plops down immediately to my left and opens a calculus textbook for some light reading until the bell rings and the final stragglers hurry in.

Everyone knows this class is pretty much a blow-off elective, taken by seniors like me who can't have a third study hall, but usually in classes like these, teachers still hand out detentions for tardiness—since, like, what else are you even getting graded on? Mrs. Strand is no exception, but, ironically, the moth-eaten woman isn't here yet.

Other kids have started to murmur about it when a girl at the head of the table formation rises from her seat and claps once.

"Hello, class." She rubs her manicured hands together, as if she's trying to start a fire. "I'm Ms. deGeest, and I'll be teaching creative writing this semester."

Everyone looks around at one another, and if I had to guess, it's because "Ms. deGeest" looks like sixteen-year-old Alicia Silverstone in *Clueless*.

"Are you kidding?" Drew Goodall calls from the back.

Ms. deGeest purses her lips and checks her student roster. "No, Andrew. Our satire unit's not for a few weeks. I'm here because Mrs. Strand retired, and I was thrilled to get the opportunity to work with all of you."

That elicits some chuckles, mostly from the group of boys surrounding Drew, who murmur variations of *Can't wait to work you either, baby*.

Her eyes blaze a trail across the corner the catcalls came from. She makes a swift gesture, like she's bisecting them with the edge of her hand. "You three. Office."

The boys exchange confounded looks. "Seriously?"

"Make sure to memorize some of your classmates' faces. You'll need to get today's assignment from someone later so that you'll be ready tomorrow." She doesn't seem mad, just calm, her tone deadpan. It has to be an act—the Tough Guy persona they teach any Dallas Cowboys cheerleader who decides to go into education.

Drew and his friends volley a few unsure looks back and forth as they pick up their books and mosey toward the door. "Close the door on your way out," Ms. deGeest says almost sweetly.

She has performed her first miracle: They obey. She faces the rest of us and claps once enthusiastically, and it's like the whole thing never happened.

"Narrative," she says. "All writing contains it. Even research papers have some semblance of story in them—conflict, resolution, specific evidence to build a thesis. A persuasive essay comes together through rhetoric, the tricks you use to *suggest* a narrative or outright portray one." She selects a marker from the shelf beneath the board and quickly scribbles, *For sale: baby shoes, never worn.* "Anyone recognize this quote?"

"Hemingway," Stephen says.

"Possibly," deGeest answers. "That's the legend, at least. Arthur C. Clarke, Ernest Hemingway, and John Robert Colombo were sitting around a table, eating lunch one day, when Hemingway bet them each a dollar that he could write a story in six words. When the money was on the table, he grabbed a napkin and wrote this line on it. Allegedly. But there had been a similar story in a 1910 edition of the *Spokane Press*. The week before there'd been an ad for a handmade baby bed and trousseau that had never been used. The *Spokane* piece homed in on the sadness of that statement, all the possibilities for why such an ad might exist.

"Today we're going to talk about story, and tonight you're going to write your own piece of flash fiction. Yours, however, will be one to five pages rather than six words."

A groan travels throughout the room. It's unanimous, an aural wave, until it reaches Stephen, who I suspect somehow already knew about the change in plans for this semester's creative writing class. His owl-like hazel eyes are fixed on the middle distance, and I can practically see the dozens of ideas skating over them.

I don't find myself disappointed about the homework either,

though unlike Stephen I have no slew of concepts barraging my beautiful near-salutatorian brain. I have exactly one idea, exactly one story I want to write down: Dad's.

That night, after dinner—and after the handful of minutes I spent staring into my room from the hallway, trying to summon my vision or hallucination or strangely vivid memory from last weekend—I sit at the kitchen table and start on my story.

Grayson and Shadow sprint circles around the downstairs, attacking each other with Nerf guns, and Mom and Toddy lie snuggled up on the couch, sipping wine and flirting in French.

French is Mom's first language, but Dad never learned it, and so I didn't either. I have all the touristy stuff down—*Où sont les toilettes? Je veux aller à la plage. Donnez-moi tout ce que vous avez*—but don't have a firm enough grasp on the language to have full conversations. Sometimes it makes me mad that Dad didn't learn, that they didn't teach me. Mostly when Grayson or Shadow is screaming, *À moi! T'as perdu!* (I win! You lose!) at the end of a wrestling match or particularly bloody round of video games.

Toddy, who's about as different from Dad as two friends could be, studied French in college and brushed up on it when he and Mom started dating. Sometimes they'll pass through the room and stop to muss the boys' hair, telling them to *rangez votre chambre* (clean your room). They'll share a quick back and forth beyond that, but it's lost on me.

It's not that I feel excluded, exactly. It's more like I thought that Mom's life with Dad and me was supposed to be the better one.

Like when we lost him, no one could possibly replace him or what he meant to us. And no one *could*, and Mom and Toddy both made sure I understood that.

But as I sit at the timeworn table beneath the pendant lamps Toddy installed, watching my half brothers, powered by sugar, surge through the house and hearing my parents laughing into each other's necks and speaking a language I don't understand, I can't help but feel like Mom's life wasn't supposed to be this good without Dad. Like things should be noticeably worse, and in a lot of ways, they're not. And it feels . . . *wrong*.

I know Dad would want Mom to be happy, for Toddy to take care of us. I've understood that since I was a kid, and their happy life hasn't made me hurt this way in a long a time. Reliving that memory four nights ago has left me feeling like I *just* lost him all over again. And *that* makes me feel like none of us should be happy right now.

All the good things in the world shouldn't make up for the best thing we had but lost.

But if I write down the things he told me, if I tell his stories and hold on to his memories, maybe it's not too late to capture some small part of Dad.

Mom glides in from the living room, carrying her and Toddy's empty wine glasses. She stops just in time for stocky Grayson to pound past her and into the hallway, followed by lanky Shadow, whose footsteps sound like snowfall by comparison—that's the way he got his nickname, actually, his impressive quietness. Poor Grayson's the only one of us without one, but then again, he got a pretty normal legal name, whereas I got a man's, and for some reason

Shadow got "Eustace." I think shortly after they filled out the birth certificate, Mom realized that "Eustace" sounds like Crayola code for "vomit," and he was such a quiet baby that he became Shadow. "Whatcha working on, June?" Mom asks, leaning over me.

"Hoooomework," I say.

"Hoooomework," Toddy calls from the couch. "Those jerks gave you homework on the first day, Junie?"

"Yeah, will you sue?"

"Course we will, honey."

"Thanks."

"I think it's good you're being challenged," Mom says, setting the glasses in the blue-tiled sink Dad installed for her while he was between jobs. "It'll prepare you for medical school."

I snort, and she shoots me a disapproving glare. "Mom. What am I going to do at medical school? Like, is this homework going to prepare me to be the long-winded janitor there?"

She exhales and dodges the boys again to come sit at the table with me. "Baby, we can send you anywhere. You can do anything."

"Anywhere?" I gasp. "Anything?"

"Dental school," Toddy chimes in.

"Dentistry's a great business." Mom squeezes my hand in hers. I wonder if she and Ms. deGeest get their nails done at the same salon. "Toddy loves it, don't you?"

"Yep." He turns off the TV, stretches his arms over his head, and shuffles through the kitchen, stopping to kiss me on the head. "Night, Junior."

"No one loves dentistry," I mumble.

"They love the paycheck." He plants a kiss on Mom's cheek and ambles toward the stairs. "They love the hours, the vacation, and the fact that the worst news you have to deliver is that someone needs a root canal. What else is there to love?"

"What about gum cancer?" I ask. He waves me off.

Mom smiles at him like he's giving his first presidential address, then shoots me another semi-worried look and squeezes my hand again. "He's right, baby. Even if you didn't love college, who knows? Maybe you'd meet someone. Dentists really do have way better hours than other kinds of physicians—and less baggage too."

"Great, Mom. I'll keep that in mind. When I'm hitchhiking through Texas, I'll think fondly of the dentist I could have married had I gone to college."

She smiles, but it's a sad one. For a moment the veil of perfect contentedness slips from her face and I see her heartbreak all over again, just the way it looked back in the days right after Dad died, when I was binging on comfort cereal and Easy Mac and she was eating nothing at all.

"I had dreams, you know," she says softly, pushing her chair back to stand. She kisses me exactly where Toddy did. "I had them, and I waited too long to chase them."

She turns and sweeps toward the hall, clearing her throat. "Boys! Bedtime!"

They groan and whine, but Toddy claps his hands three times in this faux-authoritative manner at the bottom of the stairs, and they run past Mom and pound up the steps. He's always backing Mom up like this, the opposite of how Dad's smile and quiet refusal to be reined in for the night would draw her out onto the grass to stare up at the stars. Tonight, the discrepancy grates at me.

I love Toddy, but I'm not like him. I'm not a sensible dentist in the making. I'm like Dad—*hungry*, he would say. *So hungry you want to taste the sun and lap up the lake.*

I'd never thought of Mom as *hungry*, but as I watch my family retreat down the hall, I wonder what she meant. *I had dreams.*

To me, her story has always felt like Jonathan Alroy O'Donnell's: a part of some distant tapestry of fact turned legend. She moved to the states from her tiny hometown in France when she was sixteen to study ballet at Joffrey, and at eighteen she took a job with a professional company in Miami. There, she met Dad on one of his trips, when he walked into the bar where she waitressed part-time.

Jacks, according to lore, do *not* dance. And apart from the occasional waltz or twirl in the kitchen with Toddy, Mom doesn't either. I asked her once, when I was small, why she stopped. She just looked at me, smiled, and said, *With your daddy, life is the dance.*

Thinking about it now, I wonder if her dream was simply to dance, or if it was just to have the life she thought she'd signed up for, the one that was torn down the middle ten years ago. Either way, I feel sick for having thought she wasn't sad enough about Dad. She's in love, she's married, but her heart will always be a little bit broken, and there's nothing she can do about it.

Toddy intercepts Mom again on the bottom step at the end of the hall, and his voice drops into a whisper I strain to hear: ". . . know the Angert kid's back?"

She glances my way, and I feign concentration on my laptop.

I catch only one word from her mouth as they turn and climb the stairs together: *"Trouble."*

I quell the guilt burning up my stomach and focus on the

blinking cursor on my screen. I close my eyes and let my mind drift away from Saul. I try instead to remember the story of how Jonathan Alroy O'Donnell discovered our hill, our heavenly slice of thin space. Then I let it all pour out of me, gushing like it can't escape quickly enough.

When I look up from my work, it's one A.M. All is silent, all is still, apart from the chirp of crickets and the moths dancing around the pendant lamp, grazing my hair and shoulders. At some point, the sheen of pink appeared against the wall across from me.

Feathers flutters softly. She watches me.

Ten

MS. DEGEEST cuts a slow trail around the table formation as she passes back our first assignment. She's dressed in all black and gray: black shoes, gray skirt, black blouse, gray blazer, black earrings. She's more formal than most teachers, in both dress and attitude, probably another attempt to look old enough to work here.

At lunch yesterday, the first words out of Hannah's mouth were, "Tell me everything about creative writing, and don't leave anything out." Halfway through my rundown of what we'd read and written so far, she groaned and dropped her forehead against the table. "I can't believe Stephen Niequest got to take that class and I'm in AP U.S. history that period. God, I'd better get into it next semester."

"You realize it's not AP, right?" I pointed out.

"Doesn't matter. Colleges love well-roundedness."

"You literally told me the exact opposite of that last year."

"That was last year. Last year colleges wanted niche students, people with an intense focus on one itty-bitty thing. That's why I spent all freaking year volunteering with the music branch of the Arts Council. *Now* they want well-roundedness."

"Who tells you these things?" I asked. "Is this information dispersed telepathically to all you freaks? Do the thoughts just appear in your head with a little purple signature from Dawn at the Harvard admissions office?"

"Something like that," Hannah said, then went back to smacking her head on the table.

I didn't and don't care about well-roundedness, but something about writing down Dad's story two nights ago got to me. The work felt almost sacred, like one still, perfect instant of clarity and purpose—jumping from a cliff into the turquoise water of Torch Lake or the icy blue of Lake Michigan—that stretched across the many silent hours I spent hunched over the kitchen table.

Just like the memory or hallucination or *whatever* that spurred it, I haven't been able to stop thinking about the story that spilled out of me.

Ms. deGeest pauses in front of Stephen and me, first setting our stories facedown on the table.

"Great work on your first assignments," she says. "I was truly impressed. There's a lot of potential in this room, and it was evident you put a lot of thought into these flash fiction pieces. These grades, however, won't be counted toward your final grade. This is merely a marker for you, so you have an idea of what to expect from me as a teacher and what I expect from you in order to earn an A."

She's still rambling about work ethic and progress and the

importance of honest criticism when I catch Stephen positively beaming at the red and emphatically circled B+ on the front of his story. I slide my own story off the table.

My heart plummets into my stomach at the sight of the D+ scrawled over the entire first paragraph. I fight back tears and then feel so embarrassed that I have to fight back a *second* wave and basically spend the rest of class as an emotional pendulum swinging between humiliation and anger. As soon as the bell rings, I break for the door and hurry to my locker.

I've never been this upset by a grade. It's possible I've never been upset by any grade, *period*. I've known all along that I want to travel after graduation, then come back to Five Fingers, like all Jacks do, and a plan like that limits my college options to approximately zero.

But this isn't about college apps or career paths.

I loved that story. And either I butchered it or Ms. deGeest flat out hated it. Either way, it feels like I'm failing Dad—desecrating the only part of him I have left. That I'm not worthy of that memory, or hallucination, in which he held my hand in his and I felt his skin and breath and love.

"Hi," Hannah chirps, appearing beside me in a blur of blond.

"Hi." I don't look up from riffling through my locker for my backpack.

"What's wrong?"

"Bad grade."

Her eyebrows pucker together. "I'm so sorry, June." After a second, she shakes her head. "Wait, why do you care?"

"I don't wanna talk about it."

She lifts her hands, one of which is clutching the handle of her violin case. "Fine, totally understandable."

"Thanks."

She studies me. "You know what you need?"

"Bourbon."

"Girls' Night."

"Hallelujah."

"Yes?" she confirms.

"Very yes."

"Girls' Night it is."

Except it's not. At least not for long.

It's Girls' Night when we get to Hannah's neighborhood, a series of rustic lodges surrounded by a gorgeous mix of evergreen, and eat spaghetti with Mrs. Kuiper, who, rather than returning to "Miss Sowerbutts" kept her married name even after Hannah's dad left her for his pregnant mistress. It's Girls' Night when Han and I lie on our stomachs, flipping through the newest *Rookie* yearbook and laughing over flirting tips in her mom's old magazines ("Wear your underwear as a hair band!" "Be entirely naked!").

It's even Girls' Night on the drive to the movie theater and the blissfully ignorant walk from the parking lot to the lobby.

But that's where Girls' Night ends: in the popcorn-scented lobby of the Cineplex, with Nate Baars shouting, "Laaaaaaadies!" into his cupped hands and Saul standing next to him, looking a little horrified and a little amused.

At that point, Girls' Night crashes headlong into a four-way not-a-date in which no two people are in agreement over which couple they're not part of.

I look to Hannah accusatorily. Her face is pale, eyes wide as she waves back to Nate sheepishly.

"Are you serious, Hannah?" I demand.

Her eyes dart to mine, and she mumbles like a ventriloquist, "I swear I had no idea. Nate and I were texting, and—"

"Since when do you and Nate Baars *text*?"

"I told him we were going to the movies. He said, *See you there*, but I thought he was kidding!"

"Why?" I hiss. "*Why* would you think that was a joke?"

"I don't know—he used a winky face!" she whispers, teeth still gritted. "What do we do?"

"Leave?" Even as I say it, an itch of curiosity coils under my breastbone.

"Are you kidding?" she cries. "That's so awkward! They think we're meeting them here. Intentionally. We can't *leave*."

As I glance across the lobby toward Saul, that curiosity spirals up through me like a charmed snake. It's just a movie. Saul and I won't talk; we'll sit in silence and then part ways.

"You owe me," I say under my breath, then start across the planet-spangled carpet toward the boys.

"Add it to my tab," she says.

"*Finally*," Nate says when we reach them. He seems completely unconcerned about the forty-five seconds Hannah and I spent whisper-arguing on the far side of the lobby, and he folds over each of us in a hug. His arms are particularly linger-y with Hannah, but she must be in a good mood, because she doesn't shake him off. "Glad you girls could make it."

To our own Girls' Night? Same.

"Hi, Nate," I manage, which is a downright cheery greeting compared to Saul's single nod toward us. "Saul," I say in return. "My mortal enemy, good to see you in fine health. Frankly, I thought my voodoo doll would've been more effective."

He smiles, and I anticipate then physically *feel* the cusp of his gritty laugh rise then slip back down his throat, and a tiny and hopefully nonessential piece of my heart flakes off.

Nate laugh-barks. "You're so freakin' weird, O'Donnell. Love it."

I shoot Hannah a stare like a steak knife. "What can I say? I'm not like other girls. I've literally never eaten a salad in my life."

This time The Laugh surfaces, and my face heats. I can't look at Saul, so I look at Nate, who's nodding. "Really? Wild."

Hannah gifts him with an encouraging smile and saddles me with a pleading look.

Okay, technically speaking, Nate Baars is hot. He's an olive-skinned, espresso-haired stack of muscle who surfs in summer, snowboards in winter, and rock climbs year-round. But at this point, my brain replaces the sight of him with a giant, slobbering golden retriever.

"I want to be drunk," I accidentally say aloud to myself.

"Anyway," Hannah interrupts before this not-date can get any worse. "What are we seeing?"

Saul juts his chin toward the banner hanging over us. *"The Axe Murderer on Thirteenth Street."* He could not look any smugger that this is his first contribution to our conversation. I try to imagine that he has baby-soft hands and smells like Axe Body Spray and that his favorite food is mayonnaise, because otherwise he's so, so charming to me right now I want to die.

"Great," I say, heading to the counter. "Can't wait."

"Don't have to." Nate brandishes a strand of four red tickets. "You think we gentlemen would let you girls buy your own tickets?"

Saul stares at the floor, and I know he did not pay for a single one of those tickets.

"Great," Hannah says quietly, reverting to the timidity of the first hour and a half we spent with Saul at the carnival.

We file into the theater along the back row. Somehow Nate manages to corral Hannah between him and Saul, making the final seating arrangement Nate, Hannah, Saul, me. The lights dim and previews begin.

Saul leans over and whispers, "You didn't know you were meeting us here, did you?"

In the cool dark of the theater, his voice rushes over my skin like a creek full of cattails. "Long story. It involves a misinterpreted winky face."

"Oh, naturally." He straightens up, but a second later, he leans over again. "You wouldn't have come if you'd known?"

"I . . ." . . . have no idea what to say. "Don't know."

"Because I'm an Angert?"

I stifle a laugh, not wanting to draw attention to us. "No." *At least not entirely.* Part of me feels guiltier than ever for being here after seeing, or imagining, Dad; another part wonders if *this*—disobeying him—is the way to trigger another moment like that again. I lift my backpack off the floor and sneak a swig from the flask.

"I drive you to drink," Saul whispers.

"Well, yeah, but that's not because you're an Angert."

"Is it because I chose this shitty movie?"

"You chose this?"

"I also wasn't thrilled about coming tonight." He lifts his feet up to rest on the back of the seat in front of us.

"Because I'm an O'Donnell?"

"Yes," he pans. I narrow my eyes, but he doesn't break into a smile for a full five seconds. "Because it's a little pathetic to drop out of school, move home, and start hanging out with your younger cousin's friends all the time—don't you think?"

"Sorry, I have no idea what you just said," I say. "I don't speak Baby Boomer."

"Hilarious, Junior."

"Hey."

His eyes snap to mine, and in the dark, they look almost black. "Huh?"

"I don't think it's pathetic," I whisper. "I mean, I have abnormally high self-esteem, so take this for what it's worth, but I don't think it's pathetic for you to hang out with us."

He's quiet for a second. "I never said *you*, by the way."

"What?"

"I didn't say it was pathetic to hang out with *you*."

I feel myself smiling like an idiot, but the slow burn of the whiskey takes the edge off my embarrassment. "Shh. I think the worst movie of all time is starting."

He trains his eyes on the screen. His Adam's apple shifts as he swallows. I do everything I can to make his words stop replaying in my mind. It's not enough.

I never said you, *by the way. I didn't say it was pathetic to hang out with* you.

Eleven

"WHAT'D you think?" Hannah asks Saul as we stream out of the theater. I try to hang back with Nate, but he keeps pace alongside them, so basically I'm just walking behind the group.

"It was probably in the top three worst movies I've ever seen," he answers. His eyes flash back to me, and he slows, as if to let me catch up.

I slow too, and he must notice, because he stops trying to lessen the gap between us and devotes his full attention to Hannah.

"God, it was *horrible*," she says. She sounds relieved to get that opinion off her chest. She eyes Nate accusatorially. "Why the hell did we go see that?"

Nate shrugs sheepishly. "Sorry."

"I chose it." Saul itches his collarbone, and I'm 60 percent sure he catches me zoned out on him, remembering plowing into him in the House of Mirrors. "My fault. I have famously bad taste in movies."

"I don't believe that," Hannah says. "When we were kids, you were always watching Hitchcock and Coppola and Stanley Kubrick. You were super into that stuff."

Saul's mouth opens a fraction of an inch, then closes. His ears turn pink, his chin and eyes dipping toward the floor. I'm *watching* him realize what's going on here, that the neighbor girl who barely spoke to him was silently spending her childhood gathering these details.

"Yeah, you're right. I was." Saul looks back up, all signs of embarrassment wiped clean from his face. "I was super into that stuff back then, but . . . I don't know, I'm kind of over art."

Nate laughs and slaps Saul's shoulder. "Totally, dude."

Hannah looks dumbstruck. Understandable, since the phrase *I'm kind of over art* is both striking *and* dumb. "Hey," Nate says, "we should all drive out to the falls tonight, take a night swim and rinse off the stink of that movie."

"That sounds awesome," Hannah recovers. "I'm in."

"I have to get home," Saul says, at the exact same time I say, "I can't."

Of course I've always been curious about the falls. They're a Five Fingers point of pride, famous for their preternaturally warm water. But I'm already breaking one of my parents' two rules, and in my house, going to the falls has always been treated as just as dangerous as walking through alleys alone in the dark or crossing a highway while wearing a blindfold.

"Bummer," Nate says. "Next time."

"No, you guys go on," Saul says, tipping his head toward Nate and Hannah.

"Hannah and I rode together," I point out.

"No problem," Saul says. "I can take you home. I'm staying with my dad at our old cabin. It's, like, two miles from your house. Nate can ride home with Hannah, right?"

"Hannah might not even want to go to the cliffs," I say. "Why don't you take her home and Nate can take me home?"

"In what universe does that make sense?" Nate laughs. "I didn't even bring a car. Saul drove, and Han drove you."

My mind scrambles for a way to rescue Hannah and finds nothing. I look toward her helplessly, but she's focused on Nate. "Sure," she says brightly. "I can take Nate home after the falls, and Saul can run June home. If that's okay?"

She meets my gaze, and the apples of her cheeks turn Jack's Tart pink.

Nate's face lights up. "Okay," he says. "Right on."

"Okay," Hannah repeats, face still reddening. I try to meet her eyes, to silently ask, *Is it really okay?* But she's actively avoiding my gaze and focused instead on Nate.

Oh my God. A slim but distinct new possibility blooms in my mind. Maybe Hannah really is over Saul.

Nate and I were texting, she'd said casually when we arrived. She'd been *texting* Nate Baars.

"Okay," Saul says, looking toward me for final approval. My whole body feels warm and fizzy, like my heart just started pumping ginger beer through my veins.

Or maybe I just *want* to believe Hannah's into Nate. Maybe she's being optimistic and kind because Hannah *is* optimistic and kind.

"What say you, Junior?" Nate says. "Okay or nay?"

"Okay," I murmur.

"Okay!" Nate guffaws one last time and hooks an arm around Hannah's neck. "We're off to have an adventure while you two downers go home and journal."

"Let me know you get home safe, Han?" I shout after them.

"Yeah." She nods. And then they're out the doors, and I'm sure I've made a mistake. I'm alone with Saul Angert.

"Ready?" Saul asks.

"You shouldn't have done that."

"What?"

"Forced Hannah into hanging out with Nate," I fume.

"I didn't force anyone to do anything. Seems like she wanted to go."

"How was she supposed to say no, Saul?"

"That didn't bother you when *you* were trying to force *me* to hang out with Hannah."

"What?"

"'You take Hannah, Saul,'" he imitates. "'Nate will drive me home in the car he doesn't have to the house he doesn't live by!'"

"It's not the same thing."

His body shifts as he lets out a huff of laughter. "Oh? How's that, Junior?"

"Nate likes Hannah. *You* told me that."

"You're going to make me say this, aren't you?"

"Say what?" I demand.

"I can't hang out alone with a teenage girl who's been harboring a childhood crush on me for a decade. Is she even eighteen?"

"Okay, this just got weird," I say, holding up my hands. "Do you have some kind of criminal record? I mean, should *I* be alone with you?"

He tips his head back and rubs the crease in his forehead. "It's different with you."

"That 'not like other girls' thing was a joke, Saul. I love a good salad."

"It's different because you're not into me."

"How would you know who's into you and who's not? It took you ten years to figure out Hannah was!"

"Fine, you *could* be into me," he says, meeting my eyes. "But my cousin's not trying to date you—you're not going to put me in a weird situation."

It's like the voice is coming from someone else. Like someone else has taken over my body and I'm just a ghost floating outside it. "Again, how would you know?"

"Because your best friend likes me."

"It was a childhood crush," I say, lowering my voice. "And she's over it. I believe her exact words were *tragically beautiful stick-in-the-mud*."

His smile spreads slowly until his laugh crackles out like burning charcoal. "I still couldn't take her home when she and I were the only two people who drove."

Looking at him, I feel sort of like a burgeoning lightning storm staring down at the temptation of the Eiffel Tower, promising not to touch it. "Sorry," I say.

He lifts one eyebrow. "Sorry?"

For having a crush on you.

For trying to make you take Hannah home.

For starting a fight in a space-themed movie theater.

"For biting your collarbone."

His smile is faint. "Come on, Jack. Let's get you home."

That's the best idea anyone's had all night. The lobby might be empty now, but soon a more heavily trafficked movie than *Axe Murderer* is bound to let out, and I don't need to be standing here with Saul Angert for all of Five Fingers to see.

We walk out into the hot night, and some of the tension between us dissipates as we cross the lot to a dumpy black Saturn. Things feel almost normal, friendly. "This is your car?"

"That impressed, huh?" he says. "Maybe I *should* start hanging out with high school girls."

"Not impressed, Saul. Mystified. Perhaps no one's told you: You live in northern Michigan. It's unsafe to drive a tin can up here."

He climbs in, but when I pull on the passenger door's handle, it's locked. "Sorry," he says, his voice muffled by the glass. "I can't in good faith let such precious cargo ride in my tin can. Too dangerous."

"Too dangerous for *you*, Saul," I say. "Jacks are hardy stock."

"Got it." He unlocks the door, and I get in. "Angerts: small, weakling babies. O'Donnells: muscular, demigod Michiganders."

His grin glows in the half light, and I can't help but smile too as the silence stretches out.

During the two hours we spent watching body parts and blood spurt across the screen, the sun has slunk low on the horizon. Its nose barely juts between the trees, and the moon already hangs in the rapidly deepening blue, stars poking through like pinpricks in a sheet of colored paper. As we pull away, Saul manually cranks his window down, which I take as permission to do the same.

The air is stiffer than it's been all week—summer's last cry before fall crushes it—and as we slice through the night, I feel like we're being enveloped in a fleece blanket fresh from the dryer. We're quiet for a while, the hazy sound of the suburbs fading behind us and night a deep, yawning indigo unfurling ahead.

The air pulls my hair from behind my ears and whips it around, tickles me to the point that a laugh slips out, and when I glance at Saul, he's watching me, one corner of his mouth quirked. "I like having you around, Jack," he says over the snap of wind, and I grin like the maniac I'm quickly becoming.

"Why'd you come back?" I ask.

He looks my way again, takes a deep breath, slowly exhales. "My dad's sick."

"Oh," I say. "God, I'm sorry. Is it . . . ?" I trail off, thinking of Bekah.

"Cancer?" He shakes his head. "Alzheimer's. Runs in my family, but with him, it's happening fast, or—I don't know—maybe it's been happening for years. His agent just told me. If I waited any longer, I might've lost my last chance for him to recognize me."

"I'm sorry," I say weakly. It's not enough. That's what I learned from losing Dad: There are no right words. There's nothing another human being can say that makes it better or eases the pain. *Sorry* is a white flag, an *I can't help you.*

"Yeah." Saul swallows. His fingers tighten over the steering wheel. "We were never close. My sister was his pride. But."

"Still," I say.

"Still."

"I know another *sorry*'s nothing," I say. "I'd give you something better than that if I had it."

"I'd give it back," he says. "You know what they say about Angerts and O'Donnells. Your violent blow from the universe might be right around the corner, and then I'll have nothing to give you either."

"I think mine's already come for me," I murmur toward the glass, then turn to speak to him directly. "I thought you didn't believe in that."

I also thought *I did*, but would I really have gotten in the car with him if that were true? I glance at the windshield, almost expecting a tornado or out-of-control semi to come shrieking toward us, but we're alone on the road, slinking through a peacefully swaying copse of trees.

"Old habits," Saul answers. "Or, I don't know, maybe it's being back here. It's like nothing ever changes."

"Some things do."

His mouth curls up, and his eyes flash between the road and me. "Some things do."

"You're making it hard to hate you," I tell him.

"All part of my evil plan."

"Did you hate leaving school?"

"Nah," he says. "That was the easiest part of all this."

"You know, I had a brief career as a writer."

"Oh yeah? How'd that go?"

"Quickly. Jacks are more doers than thinkers. I got a D on my first assignment and haven't touched the second."

Without a moment of pause, he says, "Do you want help?"

"Are you offering to take out a hit on my teacher?"

"Yes," he says. "And to tutor you."

"Oof. *Hi, Mom, here's my new tutor. He's the tattooed twenty-one-year-old dropout formally known as Saul, the youngest living member of Dad's least favorite family.*"

"Twenty," he says.

"What?"

"You said twenty-one. I'm twenty."

I swallow the knot of heat in my throat. "Twenty. Okay, yeah, I think she'll *totally* go for it."

Saul nods in time with the yellow lines shooting past our car. "Okay, remember how you were definitely *not* going to put me in a weird situation or turn me into a creep?"

"Fifteen minutes ago? Vaguely."

"What if we don't tell your mom who I am? How would she know I'm an Angert? I haven't been here in years, and hardly anyone knows I'm back. How would you and I have even met?"

"In a mirror maze, Saul! That's the first place she'll guess!"

He laughs: husky, warm. "Good point. Look, I'm not telling you to lie to your parents. But if you want help, I'll help you. Even if that includes lying to your parents."

"Your resolve against being put in a weird situation sure lasted long."

"I'd do anything for the written word, Jack."

"Really?" I lean over the middle console and rest my chin on my hand. "'Cause I'm kind of *over art*."

"Whoa, whoa, whoa!" He pushes my face away with his hand. "Low blow, Junior."

At the sound of my name, whole forests grow from saplings into moonlit redwoods beneath my collarbones. I can't wait for this feeling to stop, so I can be on Dad's side like I always have been.

But I also never want this feeling to stop.

"You wanna do something fun?" he asks.

I study his profile. "Such as?"

He flips on his blinker and follows the corkscrew road toward the street lined with million-dollar vacation homes overlooking turquoise water. "Break into one of the vacation homes' pools for a swim. I used to all the time in high school."

So did I, every summer including this last one. Sometimes with visiting boys I'd never see again. Or with the friends Hannah and I grew apart from since that last day of the summer before sophomore year, when we all (except Hannah) got tipsy on five-dollar champagne and swore we'd be friends forever. Or, most often, with *just* Hannah, whenever I itched so badly to do something risky that I pushed until she caved. We did it three weeks ago, on my birthday, floated beneath the moonlight in inflatable donuts, drinking Jones Soda and boxed pink wine Hannah's cousin got us.

"Don't you have somewhere to be?" I ask Saul.

"Yeah, tons of plans. I'm a busy guy."

"I just mean, you had your chance to go swimming at the falls and you passed. Or were you really so determined to land Nate that date?"

"Yeeeeah," he says. "Okay, so this is weird because I'm a grown-ass man and all—at least, kind of—but my parents always had a rule about the falls. They were freakishly strict about it. Basically convinced me I *would* die if I went. Again, old habits."

"No way." I don't realize my hand has snapped out to grab his arm until I see his eyes fixed on it. I retract it immediately.

"I know—not the parenting style you'd expect from the *New York Times* best-selling adventurer Eli Angert."

"No, I mean, my parents had—*have*—the same rule."

"Huh." Saul rubs his collarbone through his faded black T-shirt. He seems a little less put together than he did a week ago at the fair. I'm a fan. "A hint about why our families hate each other?"

"They never told you?" I say.

He laughs. "Oh, they've told me. It's because O'Donnells are arrogant, self-righteous assholes who thrive on my family's misfortune."

"Well, that's all true, but there's more to it. You don't know this?"

"June." He fixes me with a reproachful look. "Think about whatever story you're about to tell me, which no doubt makes my ancestors out to be fork-tailed demonoids, and ask yourself whether it explains why *my* family would hate *your* family back."

"It's about the cherries," I say confidently.

Saul snorts. "Isn't it always?"

"My great-great-whatever, Jonathan Alroy O'Donnell, came to Five Fingers looking for somewhere to grow cherries," I explain. "Your great-great-whatever owned the land Jonathan planted our first tree on. Ancestor Angert traded Ancestor O'Donnell the land for a basket of cherries. Jonathan wanted to build a farm nearer to the water, where the soil was sandier, so he talked Ancestor Angert into renting him *more* land. They shook on it, agreed on a fair yearly payment, swore on *the land itself*, and—what?" I interrupt myself to ask when Saul laughs.

"This is so rehearsed. You've clearly heard this story a million times."

"Anyway, as I was saying before I was brutally *Angerted*, they swore—"

"On the land itself."

"Right. Now fast-forward a couple of generations and *your* great-grandfather Jacob came to *my* great-grandfather Jack the First and demanded he pay him in full what the land was worth *then*. Like, fifty years later. Jacob told Jack he could either buy it or vacate it, but Jack had put every dime he'd made back into the farm, so he didn't have the money. Jacob kicked him off the land. He took everything Jack the First had, my family's entire legacy."

"Bullshit," Saul says immediately.

"What?"

"You want to know *my* family's version of that story?"

"The lie version?"

"Jonathan O'Donnell agreed to lease the land. There was a handshake and an oath *on the land itself*. Only, a couple of generations later, the O'Donnells hadn't paid in literally years. They'd send Jacob boxes of cherries instead of payments, and Jacob put up with it out of pity for a long time, until he stopped by the farm and realized Jack the First just kept buying more *stuff*. Equipment,

95

tools, trees, employees. It was a huge operation, and Jack wasn't paying even pennies for it. Jacob gave Jack six months to come up with a down payment to buy the land. Five months into that, Jacob's son had a major breakdown. He needed full-time care. Medical bills piled up. Jacob needed the money, but Jack told Jacob he needed at least six more months. So Jacob evicted him. And rather than let the farm be sold, you know what Jack did? He burned the trees to the ground. The people who bought that land started all over, and for years the cherries tasted like ash."

I stare at him, hard, and he glances at me sidelong as he eases onto the break in front of one of the gated mansions. He holds my gaze, like we're playing eye chicken.

"You don't believe that, do you?" I say.

"No, June. That's the point. Eli can spin a story too. This is Five Fingers—*everyone* can. That was the tail end of the Great Depression. Times were tough for everyone. It doesn't justify being terrible to each other for three generations after that. Either something else happened or our families are assholes."

The idea that something else could have happened, something Dad *didn't* tell me, eats at my stomach like acid. I shake my head. "If your family destroyed *my* family, that would—"

"Even if they did," Saul says, "did *I* destroy your family, June? Did I ever hurt you?"

The longer we hold eye contact, the higher the pressure in the car rises, until the air feels so thick we're swimming in it.

I used to think what happened to Dad was somehow the Angerts' fault, or at least that they'd celebrated my loss.

But if that were true, then what about what happened to Bekah? Was that somehow *my* fault? Did Mom and Toddy revel in her death? The day I heard, I went home sick from school. I couldn't eat, sleep, do anything but lie in bed staring at the stars on my ceiling.

"Do you?" I ask. "Think I destroyed your family?"

His smile unspools like fishing line, nearly invisible yet luminescent all the same. "Every time you make fun of me, you cut me to my core. But no, June, I don't hold you personally responsible for anything bad that's happened to me or the people I love. In fact, if you're a fair representation of what a Jack O'Donnell is, I feel a little cheated."

Heat swarms my cheeks, and I'm grateful for the cover of dark. "If only you'd saved my life that day with the wasps. Could've saved you years."

"Nah, that wouldn't have worked out in my favor. You would've liked Bekah way more than me. I was the boring twin."

His easy smile fades, sending an ache through my center. "Well. I wish I'd had the chance to like her more than you."

"Me too." He stares at the steering wheel for a second. "Anyway. Now or never, June."

I balk. "What?"

He tips his head toward the glowing aquamarine pool visible behind the mansion beside us. "Up for a swim?"

The thrill in my chest fizzles at the memory of that day at the pool years ago, when I almost drowned and Saul dislocated his shoulder. Maybe it *was* just a freak accident. Maybe Saul's right about all of it, but I still feel guilty being here with him, especially without knowing for sure how Hannah would feel about it. "I probably shouldn't."

He holds my gaze for a beat. "Yeah, I probably shouldn't either."

I stifle a wave of disappointment. What did I expect, for him to beg me to go after I already said no?

"Some other time, maybe," he says. "If you want."

"Another time," I agree.

"Wow, that was easy."

"What can I say? I'm eas—not going to finish that sentence, because I didn't think it through."

Saul laughs more loudly, more openly than usual. I can almost see the dotted line that connects the quality of the sound to Nate for a second. It makes me appreciate Nate's bark more.

I smile involuntarily, and Saul smiles too, turning his eyes back to the road and drumming his fingers on the wheel as we pull away from the curb. In the moonlight, his tattooed arms make me think of ravine-riddled glaciers: icy white and etched in shadows of blue-black. "What are all your tattoos?" I ask when he catches me examining him.

"A whole lot of bad decisions, mostly." He shakes his head. "Next time I turn eighteen, I'm listening to everyone who tells me to wait awhile."

"They look pretty cool."

"Really?" His eyebrows pinch, and he inclines his forehead toward me as he lifts his forearm in front of his eyes, revealing the inked outline of a camera held between hands. It makes it look like he's taking a picture of me. "*This* is cool?"

"Wow, that's . . . a camera. Did it mean anything to you at the time?"

He smiles, nods, glances in his rearview mirror. "Yeah. It did."

I wait for him to go on, but he doesn't. We reach the mouth of my driveway, and he clicks the headlights off, ducking his head to look up at the farmhouse.

I try to see it how a stranger might. White, rickety. Lattice overgrown with ivy. The wild garden that Mom and Toddy rarely touch sprawling before the porch. A green-shingled roof, warped and sunfaded, and the first Jack's Tart tree leaning right, its branches like a gnarled umbrella. The plywood chicken coop off to the left and some of the Girls, as Dad called them, asleep in the grass beside it. Some beams partially chewed by termites, though never enough to warrant an exterminator—even the pests cooperate in thin places.

"It's beautiful," Saul says.

"Yeah," I agree.

"Can I walk you to your door?" His dark eyes meet mine, and I shake my head. He nods once. "Good night, June."

"Good night, Saul."

Twelve

THE following Tuesday I'm sitting on the blue metal table outside the cafeteria where I've eaten lunch every reasonably warm day for four years, glaring at the red *C- Needs more plot! More conflict!* burned into my latest creative writing assignment, when Stephen Niequist walks past on his way to the parking lot.

He jerks his chin toward the paper in my hands. "Ms. deGeest?"

"The one and only."

"She's a real ballbuster. She gave me a B," Stephen says. "On the one hand, it's like, if she's going to ruin my GPA, maybe I should drop. But on the other, I'm obsessed with getting that perfect grade from her."

I couldn't reach a perfect grade with a space shuttle. "Yeah."

Stephen messes with the strap of his messenger bag. "*Anyway,* you and Hannah are, like, best friends, right?"

"Yeah." I fold the story in half. "Why?"

"Is she dating Nate Baars?"

"Noooo."

"Good."

"Good? Why, are you interested?"

Stephen snorts. "Nate's one of my oldest friends. He's liked Hannah for years."

"And so she *shouldn't* date him?"

Stephen lifts his eyebrows. "Not if she doesn't get how real it is to him."

"What do I owe you for the advice, Stephen?"

He rolls his eyes. "You asking my fee, Junior? Don't drop creative writing. I heard we're going to start doing critique groups, and I do *not* want to get stuck reading any more *scoring the winning goal* personal narratives than absolutely necessary."

"Okay, done."

He sways on his feet, then sets off for the parking lot, leaving me to wallow. I shouldn't have made such an effort on the second assignment.

But when Saul dropped me off after the movie, one of Dad's stories *had* come to me—even without the help of another hallucination—and I'd needed to write it down: the story of the time Dad found the place the coywolves take the shoes. Whenever he told it, the purse of Mom's lips said she didn't believe him, but she couldn't see Feathers either.

I knew the story was true, that once, when he was small, my father ran outside and saw the farmhouse disappear before his eyes, leaving behind a towering pile of shoes surrounded by coywolves.

It was another story he'd never get to write down and another one I'd apparently butchered.

"Ready?" Hannah's voice drifts across the sunlit courtyard from the school's side doors. "What's that?"

"Another bad grade."

"In what?"

"Creative writing, forever and always."

"Girl, you know who can help you with that?"

"I already asked Toddy to buy me a better grade. Mom vetoed."

"Okay, second idea?" Hannah says. "Saul."

"I don't think so."

"Why not?" Hannah cries, looping her arm through mine and steering me toward the Subaru. "He's a prodigy! And Nate says he's doing, like, nothing with his time. No one knows why he's back."

"Huh," I say. Hannah's barely mentioned Nate since their trip to the falls. If something's going on between them, she's being tight-lipped about it. "I still don't think using my poor academics is the best way to design a third meet-cute for you and Saul," I say, watching her for a reaction.

She rolls her eyes. "Junie, you care about doing well in this class. *Let* yourself care. Let yourself succeed."

"I'll look into a tutor," I promise.

"Not *a* tutor. The *best* tutor. Nate says Saul's stuff is amazing."

"And we're trusting Nate's opinions on literature?"

Hannah buckles her seatbelt, cranking the windows down and radio up. "He's smarter than he seems. I think he's just shy, and it translates into . . . well, you know. Anyway, we actually had a good time last weekend."

"*How* good?" I ask. *Totally-over-Saul-and-into-Nate good?*

Looking over her shoulder, Hannah shrugs and backs out of the parking space. "Good," she says simply. "Which—segue—the weekend after next, camping at the dunes?"

"With Nate and Saul?"

"Yes."

"No."

"Think about it."

"Okay. No."

"Whyyyy?" Hannah says. "The weather will be perfect—chilly and cozy, probably foggy. Your fave. My fave. Everyone's fave."

"I find hanging out with Saul and Nate stressful."

"Seriously, I'm telling you, Nate's not that bad. Give him another chance."

"If you're so over Saul," I press, "why are you pushing this, Han?"

Blushing badly, she takes a deep breath. "Please know that I am deeply, thoroughly humiliated by what I'm about to admit to you."

"Hannah, what's going on?"

"Ooooooh my God," she groans, then, "ahhhhhhhhh," as if the car is plummeting over a cliff but she's on too much anesthesia to properly scream. "I might, maybe, possibly have a small—nay, *tiny*—crush, which is probably nothing, on Nate Baars."

"Oh my god!" I yelp. "Nate Baars. I knew it."

"You did *not*," Hannah cries, ocean-blue eyes flicking from the road to me.

"I wondered!"

"It's probably *nothing*," she insists, face rapidly reddening.

"Like, a total fluke. I'm ninety percent sure it was a full moon at the falls that night."

"Right." I erupt into laughter, and Hannah smacks my arm, fighting a smile herself.

"It's probably nothing," she repeats. "But going camping might be a good way to confirm it either way. At least consider it, June."

I consider telling her then, blurting out that I'm into Saul Angert, and if any part of her is still hung up on him, I can't be around him. But admitting it aloud seems like an uncrossable line: dangerous, traitorous.

The truth is, no matter how Hannah feels, I can't be around him, because he's Saul Angert.

"Junior?" Mom calls from the door. "Someone's here for you."

I heard the bell from the sunroom, where I'm writing, a process that can be described as staring at a blank page for fifteen minutes, typing a few choice swear words, backspacing, and repeating, while Feathers undulates in the corner.

I pass through the kitchen and living room, where the boys are annihilating zombies on the TV screen. It's seven thirty on a school night, and I have no idea who could be waiting at the door for me.

Halfway down the hall, I spot the boyish man, or mannish boy, on our porch, and my stomach flips.

"Hi." Saul stretches a hand out. He's wearing a long-sleeved button-down, but I think I can spot the outline of the camera tattoo through it. "I'm Mike, the tutor. Sorry I'm late."

I look, probably suspiciously, toward Mom, whose hand's still resting on the doorknob. "You didn't tell me you were expecting anyone, Junie."

"Sorry," I manage. "Totally forgot that was tonight."

"Huh." Mom doesn't seem totally convinced. Her turquoise eyes narrow on Saul, probably trying to place his familiar dark eyes, his lean build and sharp angles.

In a rush of panic, I step aside, blocking her view, to let him past. "Come in, Mike."

He regards the swarm of moths around the porch light uneasily, then ducks inside, hands wringing his backpack straps.

"You guys can work in the sunroom," Mom offers. "Down the hall and to the right, through the dining room, Mike. Junior will be right with you."

He nods and moves off, leaving Mom to appraise me. "You hired a tutor?"

I try to keep my face from broadcasting the truth. "I mean, yes, but the school funds it," I say. I have no idea if that's a thing schools do. "For seniors. For college prep."

Mom's smile practically explodes into a fireworks display. "College, huh?"

I roll my eyes. "Maybe." I turn down the hall. "Don't get your hopes up."

"My baby's going to college," Mom sings after me. Her pride makes my heart trill. And then freeze over. Because college is for Hannahs and Sauls and Toddys, not for Jacks, and she should know that.

"So, Mike." I step into the sunroom and close the door. Saul's already set up on the floral-padded wicker chaise, pulling books from his backpack. "How long have you been named Mike?"

He grins up at me. "Since my boring parents realized they gave birth to a boring baby who definitely would never be a part of an ongoing family feud that would bar him from tutoring a friend who happens to be both younger and a girl."

"You can trust your daughters with a Mike," I agree.

"Mikes have no sex drive," Saul says. "They don't even have genitalia. They're basically L.L. Bean mannequins."

"Ooh, sorry for your loss."

"It's okay. I'm Mike now, so I don't miss having a dick."

"That's good. But, hey—why are you here? I thought we agreed it wasn't a good idea for you to tutor me."

His smile falters, and he runs a hand over his mouth, clearing his throat. "Um. I was under the impression you'd changed your mind."

"Based on . . . ?"

"The *forwarded text* in which you asked Nate to schedule tutoring with me, which I'm realizing based on your facial expression wasn't from you."

I perch on the rattan chair, pulling my knees into my chest. "I'm guessing Hannah."

"You want me to leave?"

"No," I say, heart hammering. "I want you to help me."

"You have something I can read?"

"Do you want the D+ or the C-?"

"D+," Saul says.

I stand and slide the story off the garden table, handing it to him. I take a seat beside him and tuck my legs underneath me. "Now what?"

"Shh." His eyes roam back and forth across the first page. We sit in silence for probably twenty minutes, and the whole time, I'm as bored as I am embarrassed. I can't stop tapping on the back of the lounge until Saul reaches out and presses my hand flat on the cushion without interrupting his reading.

I expect him to take his hand away, but he doesn't, and I'm acutely aware of every spasm in my hand, the way my fingers involuntarily arch up between his as if to pull his fingers down through mine. His thumb starts moving gently back and forth on the back of my hand, which makes my whole body feel like I'm standing outside in a lightning storm. His fingers skim up mine and back down between them, and I don't totally remember how to breathe.

I watch him swallow. His hand leaves to turn the page and doesn't come back when he's finished, which is the worst kind of relief. Finally, his eyes drop off the last page, and he stacks the papers. I cover my face with my hands, and he grabs my wrists to pull them back down.

"Are you ready for the bad news?" he says.

"Fine," I groan.

"First, you didn't follow the assignment." He taps one of Ms. deGeest's notes: *FLASH fiction = SHORT.* "That probably lost you a letter grade, at least."

"Because I wrote *too much*?"

He nods. "That's not the biggest problem though."

"And what would the 'biggest problem' be?"

"This isn't a story."

"Okay. Have you considered becoming an ER doctor? Your bedside manner is killer."

"I have a *great* bedside manner," he says, and I pretend not to notice the innuendo. "If I were your teacher, I'd dance around it like these comments do, but I'm not your teacher. I'm your friend, and your writing—June, it's beautiful. It sounds like you, or like how you would sound if you had all the time in the world. You, but better. It's weird and good and—honestly, I'm relieved how good it is."

"Relieved."

"Yeah. I mean, I was a teaching assistant for a freshman writing class, and it was fine, because I wasn't friends with any of the students, but when friends and relatives ask me to read their stuff, it terrifies me. I've had relationships end because I didn't like someone's writing."

"That kind of makes you sound like an asshole, Mike."

"I know," he says. "It does. I am. It's not intentional. It's just, if I'm friends with—or drawn to—a person, and then I hate the thing they make, or think it's bad or bland or unoriginal, my interest just shuts down."

"You should stop explaining. You're making this sound worse."

He laughs, rubbing at his eyebrows. "June, you have a strong voice. Strong and singular. I wish I could write like that. All I do is imitate. Your language still has its own strangeness. If you can learn the rules but keep your idiosyncrasies, you'll be unstoppable. It's great. Except there's no *story* here."

"Stop saying that," I say. "There *is* a story. A man travels the entire country and finds a thin place to build his home on."

"Yeah, exactly," Saul says. "A man travels the country, making friends, tightrope walking across the Grand Canyon, picking the winning horse at the first Kentucky Derby, saving children from drowning in the street after a molasses-plant explosion, pulling babies from burning buildings—"

"That last part doesn't happen. When does that happen?"

"He wins his way across the nation," Saul continues, "and at the end he scores the jackpot of a homestead, and . . . nothing . . . happens. No conflict, no struggle, no sadness or pain of any kind. No opposition."

"I don't *want* to write something sad," I say.

"Junior, you're too smart to think this is the truth. You *know* life's not like this. Even when it's good, it's hard and terrible and you lose things you can't ever replace."

"Fine," I snap, "I know that. Why do I have to write that? Why can't I write the parts of life that *are* perfect?"

Saul sets my story on the couch between us: a moat, a wall, a ravine. "Okay, so the best story I ever wrote—the only one I really believe in—*was* about a perfect day. My parents and Bekah and I went on a picnic at the dunes. No one talked about Bekah being sick. Mom didn't look at her and start crying, Dad didn't *refuse* to look at her, period, and she ruthlessly mocked me after a bird shit on my head. We pretended she hadn't gone off chemo, that she wasn't sick. She fell asleep in the sun, and I watched her breathe. I saw my sister smile in her sleep."

"That's your happiest memory?"

"Not my happiest," he says. "The one I'll never let go of. If Bekah had never gotten sick, that day wouldn't exist. There'd be hundreds like it, and none of them would feel like that. I never would've appreciated a moment like that."

"So you're saying it was worth it."

"God, Junior, of course not," he says, looking hurt. "I'm saying that's the way it is. I'm saying a *narrative arc* should do more than capture an ordinary day, even if the main events take place on an ordinary day. Your story captures extraordinary adventures, but they're coming out bland because Jonathan Alroy O'Donnell never fails, never hurts. He doesn't have something to lose or want something he can't have."

We fall into silence, the chirp of crickets hanging in the air between us. Saul's teeth skate over his bottom lip, and his chin drops toward his chest. "There's a lot of stuff happening, but no tension. Does that make sense?"

"Take off your shoes," I say.

"What?"

I slide off the couch and start pulling at Saul's boots. "What are you doing?" He tries to move his feet out of my reach, but it's too late. I grab his boots and walk toward the back door of the sunroom, throwing it open. A few Whites who'd been batting against the door dodge the shoes as I toss them and then reconvene against the frame.

"What are you doing?" Saul asks again, scrambling off the couch.

"I'm throwing your shoes to the coywolves."

"*What—why?*"

Because I was thinking about kissing you, because I don't want you to leave, because talking about the things you can never have makes my heart ache for the things I've already lost and I'd rather stop thinking about it. "Because you insulted my story!" I squeal as I dodge his reach. "Because you're rude and elitist for a Mike."

He laughs, reaches for me again. "June."

"Better get your shoes before it's too late."

"Did I really hurt your feelings?" he asks, leaning against the doorframe. "I didn't mean to. I just think you can dig deeper. Your brain can't be entirely rainbows and candy."

"I see glinting eyes." I nod toward the flashes of white prowling at the forest's edge. "Better hurry if you like those boots."

"What?" he says. "I can't go out there *now*."

"They won't mess with you."

"Then you go get them."

"Fine," I sigh. "Back to Mike, I see. No fun at all."

"Wait, I'll—"

Right then—right as we both step through the door into the starlit backyard—I see the floating White get caught between us. I watch it sink into my arm or his or both. And when our feet touch the grass beyond the door, the night sky vanishes, a blindfold ripped off.

The yard isn't starlit anymore. We're facing the setting sun, golden light so intense that when we turn to each other we have to squint.

The biggest difference, aside from the change from night to day, is a four-foot-high pile of shoes in the middle of the yard. As we stand there, a coywolf picks across the grass, Saul's boots dangling from its jowls. It drops the shoes at the edge of the pile and turns aside, pausing to meet our eyes before trotting off.

Saul points at the shoes and says something. I can't hear him.

"*What the hell?*" he mouths, but makes no sound. He scans the sky like he's expecting to find a UFO hovering overhead. Instead, wispy cirrus clouds hang low across the yellowing expanse, and birds blot out bits of the sunlight as they sweep overhead to perch in the treetops. The gentle cluck of our hens draws my eyes to the coop.

Dad.

He's crouched low, holding one suntanned hand out toward a yellow beak. A little girl with dark braids stands beside him—*me again*. Like the other night.

Saul is still spinning beside me, searching for a way out of *whatever this is*. I take a few steps forward, heart burning from Dad's closeness, from his sweat-dirt-cut-grass smell and the particular hunch of his shoulders, which I'd nearly forgotten.

Saul notices then that we aren't alone. He jogs past me, trying to call for Dad's attention, waving his arms over his head.

Dad doesn't see or hear him; he doesn't see or hear me either.

"C'mere," Dad murmurs to the smaller version of myself. She moves closer, careful not to startle the hen bobbing toward Dad's outstretched hands. Dad swiftly catches the bird, subduing its flapping with sure fingers. He draws it in so she—*I*—can stroke its feathers. He lifts the now calm chicken to his ear, as though listening for the tick of a clock. "Wanna hear?" he asks.

Saul taps on Dad's shoulder fruitlessly then steps back,

bewildered, searching my face for answers. His eyes bounce from me to the little girl, examining the similarities in our bone structure and coloring. As his eyes lock back onto her, his mouth quivers open.

The girl crouches and presses her ear to the hen.

I remember this. How we listened to the bird's quick, viscid heartbeats.

The two heads stay bowed together, listening and counting. Three hundred and eight heartbeats in one minute. They hear three hundred and eight pulses, like a tiny mallet hitting a glob of paint. Three hundred and eight disseminations of blood and oxygen, of life. There's sweat on Dad's neck from working out in the yard and dirt on my knees and cheek from following along, pulling wild onions up and pretending to mix potions from them, biting into their sweet white heads only to spit them out across the grass.

It's warm, so warm, and they're huddled together, and I can't hear the three hundred heartbeats, but I remember their sound and the way I looked into Dad's eyes while I listened and how he just barely smiled and I knew he loved me.

"Do you hear it?" he hums. She nods, and he releases the chicken to strut toward a sunny patch. Dad lies on his side and presses his ear to the earth. She does the same, facing him. "You listenin', Bug?"

She nods. He smiles. The heartbeat of the world. That's what I'd been sure I heard that day. It made me feel small but safe too, like I was a tiny part of an unbreakable thing.

When you lose someone, you start to feel like there's an expiration date on your crying. All your friends and neighbors and teachers expect it for a couple of weeks. They'll ask you how you are, and as you're saying *Okay*, you'll begin to shake, and they'll fold their arms around you until it passes, maybe send you to the bathroom or the office. They expect that for maybe a month, any innocuous question might trigger a process in your brain: homework > you used to do homework at the kitchen table > Dad used to lean over you, chewing on chips as the crumbs fell onto your paper > Dad > Dad's dead.

It's not like anyone *says* you should get over it. But they think—and they're mostly right—that someday you won't think about it so much. Or maybe you will. But you'll only remember things you loved and appreciate that you had them, and the hurt will have burned off like morning mist does as the sun rises higher.

They don't expect that, in the middle of the night ten years later, you might find yourself lying in bed, staring at the stars that no longer glow on your ceiling, trying to remember how it felt when Dad threw you over his shoulder and carried you, squealing with laughter, around the house. Or how he'd hold on to your wrists and spin you so fast you flew out in a circle like those carousel swings. They don't know that, the more time passes, the more you forget, and the more you forget, the more it hurts—less often, sure, but worse. You want to dig your fingernails and teeth into the ghost that's slipping through your fingers.

I couldn't have known how much it would hurt to see him again, to remember his minutiae.

I watch Dad's and the little girl's mouths turn up in matching smiles, and I'm still a tiny thing and the world still feels unbreakable, but that no longer makes me feel safe. Because Dad is gone and the world doesn't notice; its heart keeps beating like he was never here.

Dad's eyes take on a watery sheen, as if he knows he's already gone, that this is only a memory and we're lost to each other. Almost like he misses me too. He sits up and runs a hand over the little girl's head. "Bug, why don't you go inside and get ready for dinner?"

She nods, because she loves him, because she would do anything he asked, then stands, a whopping three and a half feet tall, and runs across the grass to the house.

Dad stays where he is, staring at the woods. Saul nudges my arm, pointing out toward where Dad's looking. There, I see it: a dark, warbling shape. The sprite we never named, and by default, or maybe through fear, became Nameless. The cold, angry one whose touch made you feel alone, steeped in nightmare.

Who brought with it panic and death.

Dad gazes out at it until finally it vanishes. Then he stands and goes inside.

Thirteen

AS soon as Dad steps inside, all noise cuts out, and the rippling grass and bobbing branches pause. The world freezes as I chase after him, and Saul follows me. But when we cross into the sunroom, the light vanishes; the sound of owls and crickets cuts back in. A high moon and sparkling stars replace the sunset, blues and greens encroaching on the yellows and golds, an empty stretch of grass where the shoes were.

We freeze in the doorway, taking in the transformation. I look toward the point in the woods where the dark thing hovered. I remember now: The day after Dad showed me the chicken's heartbeat, we found that same hen torn up in the yard. I'd cried, and Dad had assured me the bird was in heaven now, flying better than it ever did on earth.

By that time next week, Dad was gone, and when I saw him in his casket, I'd thought of that bird. I'd tried to find comfort imagining my dad with big brown wings that let him soar over indigo water. Instead I kept seeing the visible muscle and ligaments pulled loose from the chicken's bones. Dad was supposed to be unbreakable, an essential piece of the universe, as important to our woods as the sun itself. So was the hen. So was I. We all were, but *especially* him.

"What was that?" Saul whispers. Now that we've emerged from . . . whatever that was, his voice is back. I shake my head. "I don't know. The past? A memory?" I press the heels of my hands against my eye sockets and try to shut the door to grief before it can flood me. "No," I hear myself say.

It sounds so futile. *No*, he can't be dead. *No*, I can't keep seeing him only to have him ripped away again. "I don't want him to be gone," I half-sob for the first time since I was eight, another fruitless sentence in a time when words are powerless.

Saul draws me into him, folding his arms around me. "I'm sorry," he says. "I don't understand how that happened, but I'm sorry it did."

I tighten my eyes against a wall of tears.

"I'm sorry all I have is *sorry*."

"I'm sorry about your shoes," I murmur.

He exhales a throaty laugh. "Forget the shoes."

"I think Dad saw the ghost watching him. I think . . ." My voice breaks off.

"What?" Saul presses gently.

"I think he knew. That he was going to . . . you know. That ghost is like an omen. Bad things follow it. What if he *knew*?"

"I don't know." Saul's eyes sweep over the lawn. "Maybe . . .

maybe he's trying to tell you something. You know, like, from . . .
beyond?"

My chest constricts. When he died, I spent months watching for
Dad's ghost. I lay awake praying, begging the house, the woods, the
coywolves, whatever would listen to let him come back. I would've
taken a blob of color, an amorphous rendering of him—anything.

But in ten years, no new feathery presence arrived. No secret
messages or mysterious warmth wrapping around me like his arms.
Just the pink sheen and the black one and the tufts of floating
white, like always. I pull free from Saul. "I think it's the Window
Whites—the tufts that look like dandelions? Like, somehow when
you touch them, you . . . *see* things."

"You think . . . that could happen again?"

"It's not the first time."

"This is . . . *impossible*." He surveys the yard once more. I follow
his gaze out across the lawn, toward a flutter of pure-black shadow
receding behind a pine tree. Fear shoots through me, icy and jag-
ged. My pulse speeds and my vision tunnels until the shadowy
patch of woods is all I see. The shadow shifts as a deer picks its way
out from behind the pine.

Just a deer. Nothing else. I repeat it until the wave of dizziness
passes, until the darkness recedes to the corners of my eyes, but still
I don't totally believe myself.

That thing, Nameless, was *watching* Dad.

I swallow a knot. "Saul, you should go."

"Are you kidding?" he says. "We have to try more. I mean,
maybe the Whites *are* holding memories, but *whose* and why? That

must've been your dad's, right? And you said they all hang out in the windows and doors—maybe they're trying to get inside."

"Saul," I begin.

"And if they *are*, then why? June, maybe there's something they, or *he*, want you to see."

My heart leaps against my ribs, and I glance toward the woods again. "You have no idea what you might see if that happens again," I tell him. I think of one day in particular, *the* day . . . and yet I already know I'm going to try to make whatever just happened, *seeing him*, happen again, regardless of that risk.

"Look, Junior," Saul says, "I know what it's like to lose someone. I promise I won't pity you or try to give you something more than *sorry* just so *I* don't feel useless. In fact, I promise to be useless—but let me be useless *with* you, while you figure this out."

"It's not a good idea."

"So you're not going to try to make it happen again? You're going to pretend we didn't just slip into the past or your family's memories or some alternate reality where you're still a kid and your *dad is alive*?"

"That's not what I mean, Saul," I say. "*This* isn't a good idea. I don't think we should be hanging out, period. I think you should go."

"I wasn't trying to . . ." He opens his mouth, closes it, nods. "Okay." He turns and stuffs his books into his canvas backpack, then pulls it on and looks from his shoeless feet to me. His eyes are so dark I feel like I'm falling into them. "You should rewrite that story. It could be really good."

He slips into the kitchen, sending me one last organ-melting look before turning to go. "Night, June."

When he's out of sight, I sit on the chaise, every cell in my body simultaneously buzzing and drained. Feathers resurfaces from the wall. "What?" I demand of her.

She's silent and, I think, sad.

"Do *you* think Dad's trying to tell me something?"

She sways cryptically.

"Yeah, I don't know either." I search the windows for Whites but find none.

I pull my notebook onto my lap and start to write. This time I tell the whole truth as I know it. The story about a girl named Jack and the magic house she lived in and the man she loved more than all the water in every lake.

How one day they listened to the heartbeat of a golden hen and the slow groaning of the earth. How when she went inside, he stared out at the darkness and began to cry.

How two weeks later, he was gone forever.

Or maybe not quite.

Fourteen

IN the middle of the night I wake myself up crying, tangled in my quilt, face wet, hair stuck to my cheeks. A cool rain blows through my window, speckling my bare legs.

I was dreaming about Dad, but the details flit away like a school of tiny silver fish, darting out of reach before I can grab hold of them.

I cross the floorboards to shut my window, and I find a White skating across the frame's chipped paint. It comes toward me as I extend my hand, bouncing against my palm. I close my hand around it, willing it to show me Dad again.

It slips between my fingers. I catch it once more, and it breaks apart, squeezing between my knuckles and reconvening as a single entity outside my grasp.

"No," I whisper. "You have to work."

The White ignores my plea. Feathers shifts sadly in the corner.

The moon stares down at me, and I'm still in my unlit bedroom, aching for impossible things.

Grief is an unfillable hole in your body. It should be weightless, but it's heavy. Should be cold, but it burns. Should, over time, close up, but instead it deepens. The pain of missing Dad these last ten years pales in comparison to the pain of having seen him again only to have him ripped away once more.

I spend the next few nights doing my homework in the sunroom, constantly checking the windows for Whites. There's an itch under my skin, a restlessness, especially whenever I see the shapeless pink sprite or the coywolves slinking through the grass, watching me as if I should be doing something I'm not. I see no sign of Nameless, but every motion in the corner of my eye makes me jump. Every innocuous shadow haunts me.

Nameless was watching Dad, and then he died. The thought is a constantly deepening pit in my stomach, but somehow that's not enough to drown out thoughts about Saul: Saul's smile glowing in the dark hall of the mirror maze, Saul's gravelly laugh in a dim movie theater, Saul in my house, sitting beside me.

I sleep terribly for the next two nights, and in the middle of the third, after hours of tossing and turning, I give up on sleep entirely and head downstairs. I'm hunched over a coffee mug in the sunroom, watching the fog roll across the yard, the pinks and oranges of sunrise peeking through, when I hear Mom croak, "Junior?"

She squints at me, then reties her powder blue robe and shuffles to the coffeepot. "What are you doing up so early, baby?"

"Homework."

"Oh."

In truth I'd been writing. Not a story, just words—thoughts, snatches of conversation. About Dad, about Hannah, Shadow and Grayson, Mom and Toddy. About Saul too. Since ignoring him for the past few days hasn't eased any of the pressure in my chest, I thought maybe pouring out my thoughts about him would.

I swing the notebook shut as Mom eases into the chair across from me. "You've been taking schoolwork pretty seriously lately."

"I guess."

"You like to write?"

"Mhm."

She takes a sip, then smooths the thick locks of hair that have escaped her ponytail. In the soft gray light, she looks young, less like a mother and more like . . . a girl who couldn't sleep.

"Do you miss Grandma and Grandpa?" I ask her.

"Grandma and Grandpa Girard?"

I nod. I've only met Mom's parents a handful of times, the first at Dad's funeral. For a while, Mom thought they might move here, but they ended up staying in France, in the same town Mom grew up in, running the same bakery where she'd learned to make buttercream macarons and apricot tarts.

"Sometimes," she says. "A lot of times. It's hard being far from the people you love. In a way, you never stop feeling like a child, even after you have your own."

"Really?"

She smiles at her mug. "When I'm sick, *all* I want is my *maman*."

"What would she do?"

"She'd take care of me."

"Doesn't Toddy take care of you? Didn't Dad?"

She hesitates. "Of course. But no one's perfect, Junior. There are times when someone hurts you, or falls short of what you expect, and you remember what you *used* to have. Only in memory it looks shinier than it was. You understand?"

"Sometimes it would be easier to be someone's daughter than someone's mother?"

"Something like that."

"What about dancing? Do you miss dancing?"

She smiles, delicate, wispy. "I think life is about learning to dance even when you're sitting still. You learn to dance when you cook and clean, when you bite into cherries, and when you lie in clean sheets. It's easy to believe that if you could do it all over, you'd do everything different."

"But would you?"

"No," she hums, standing. "Most of the time, when you regret something, you haven't seen what the thing you regret can lead you to, if you let it. Some of the worst things that have happened to me have led to some of the best."

I try to see how losing Dad could have possibly brought anything good into the world—for me or anyone else. Okay, so my brothers were a pretty direct result of losing him. Two lives for one, more than fair of the universe or whatever orchestrates it, but this morning it doesn't feel like enough. Nothing could.

I force a smile. "Thanks, Mom."

"I'm proud of you, June." She sweeps a trail of kisses across my forehead and slips away to get ready for her morning.

• • •

"That's all we have time for today."

Ms. deGeest slides a stack of papers off the table and starts her twice-weekly parade around Room 204, setting stories facedown as she goes. "For Monday, I want you all to try one of the poetic forms we discussed, and do so fearlessly. The forms are meant to spread your water droplet into an ocean." She pauses in front of Stephen and me and flashes a smile. "You'll be surprised by how much smarter the form is than you. Not that you aren't already brilliant, of course."

The class laughs politely; she's got even the Problem Students whipped by now.

She sets Stephen's assignment down on the table. "Aim high. Class dismissed." The bell rings, and she places my story in front of me. "Stay for a minute after class, Ms. O'Donnell?"

Stephen shoots me what can only be described as a grimace of apology as he shovels his books into his messenger bag and mock-salutes on his way out the door. Ms. DeGeest starts wiping the whiteboard down, and I nervously flip the story over, bracing for the worst grade yet.

There's no mark on it. Maybe I'm about to be forcibly transferred from the class?

"Ms. deGeest?"

"Would you close the door, please?" she asks without turning around.

That can't be good. And why do I care? Why does it matter if I have to transfer into seventh-period gym? I've never planned on going to college. I've *always* planned to follow in Dad's footsteps.

It's not that I want the perfect grade, but I realize then that I *do* want the perfect story. I want to feel that unfettered rush of writing again, *and* I want to learn how to get everything I *feel* onto the page. To make the stories sing like they did whenever Dad told them.

And just as I'm realizing I want that, I might be losing my shot to have it.

I close the door and perch on the edge of the table. Ms. deGeest swipes her hands together, wiping nonexistent chalk off them. "I'd like you to skip the poetry assignment."

"Oh. Okay."

"You have a knack for fiction. Or, rather, narrative nonfiction. Whatever you consider your first several assignments to be, that's what I'd like you to keep working on."

"You gave me a D."

"That grade was waived, you'll recall."

"Fine, you gave me a C."

"Junior, your work is too good to grade generously. An inflated mark and words of praise are not what you need. You have raw talent. Stop worrying about the grades the people around you are getting and push yourself. *You* are the competition here. I want everything you turn in to be like your last piece."

"You want me to write twenty stories about my dad seeing a death omen?"

Her mask of cool shudders. "I'm sorry for your loss, June," she says. "But yes, I see why it might feel like that's what I'm asking. I want you to write the things you have the most to say about *and* the things you're afraid of messing up."

"That's how I felt about the first two stories, and you hated those."

"I didn't hate them," she counters. "They just lacked conflict, motivation, a clear sense of purpose—the fundamentals we've been talking about in class. The most epic character in the world isn't much without something worth fighting for."

"There weren't goals in the last one. There wasn't any of that stuff."

She laughs. "The protagonist's *goal* was to protect his daughter from seeing Death. He succeeded initially but ultimately failed. Listen, you *need* to learn the rules so your technique doesn't hold you back, so don't mishear me—but sometimes there's so much heart in your words that the rules go out the window. You had me looking at that story as a *reader*, not a teacher. Your story made me pick up my phone and meet my parents for dinner."

"Your parents live in Five Fingers?"

"Born and raised," she admits. "You know what they say: Lake girls can't stay away." For an instant, it's like I'm looking at a friend, someone who loves this place like I do, who left it for college but came back. When I think of it as a place to write, to take classes like deGeest's, college sounds at least a little less boring. The thought of a path like this flutters in my chest, a new possibility I've never considered before.

I tap my story. "I don't know if I have more of that in me. But I'll try."

"Whatever you did last time, do that again."

"Right, so take more LSD."

The corner of her mouth twitches toward a smile. "That's not the kind of joke you should make to a teacher," she says, "for future reference."

I nod, hesitating in the doorway. "So, I know you said my work is too good to grade generously but . . ." I lift the papers.

She nods. "Let's say a B."

"B?"

She must think I'm disappointed, because she adds, "*Plus*."

Mom and Toddy are going to an Arts Council event downtown—Wine & Lines, which apparently no one else thought sounded like a cocaine reference—that Toddy's office sponsored, leaving me stuck watching the boys. But Hannah's so bogged down with homework that she's devoting her Friday night to AP calculus, so there's nothing else for me to do anyway. Other than hunt for Whites, of course.

In the days since Saul and I saw Dad in the yard, the need to see him—to smell, hear, *touch* him again—has spread through me like kudzu, but still none of the Whites I've caught have done anything but float away.

It's getting chillier as fall slogs closer to winter, so to get the boys outside before it becomes too frigid, I pretend Mom and Toddy banned video games for the night.

"They did *not*," Grayson calls me out as I stuff our designated picnic quilt into his arms and shove him toward the door.

"Did too."

Shadow looks skeptical but doesn't argue. He may be older, but he's much more reticent than Grayson, who shouts, "Nuh-uh! They don't care if we play video games!"

"Remember last winter, Gray?" I say.

"Yeah."

"Okay, so then you know that soon you're going to have whole months where you do nothing but play video games. You're going to cry from how cold it is when you walk to the bus stop. You'll barely go outside. If there's a house fire, you'll feel grateful."

"What are you talking about?" he growls, scrambling out of my grip.

"Enjoy the sunshine and fresh air, and in a while, I'll take you to get pizza and three kinds of candy."

Grayson looks toward Shadow, whose bony shoulders shrug. "Okay," Grayson answers for the both of them, and I push them out the door.

At first they make a game of gathering the shriveled cherries beneath the tree and planting them in a circle around it. When they tire of that, they move on to playing aliens, zombies, soldiers, superheroes, and any other comic book subject matter they can think of while I lie on my back in the sun, eyes occasionally searching the windows. Soon the boys are circling my quilt, sighing and complaining, "We're bored. When are we gonna go get pizza?"

Eventually, this devolves into Grayson kicking my legs and Shadow rolling on top of me while I pretend to be asleep. When that doesn't work, they resort to tickling me. "Fiiiine, you little monsters," I relent, rolling Shadow off me. "Go get Dad's car keys."

Grayson whoops and Shadow punches and kicks the air as they race to the house. "Lock the doors on your way out!"

When Mom and Toddy first got married, it was a balancing act, learning how to talk to and about him. There's what I've always called him: Toddy. There's how I think of him and Mom as a unit: Mom and Toddy. The way I talk about them: my parents. The way

I talk about just him: my stepdad or my dad, for the convenience of people I don't know at all; Todd, for adults; Toddy, for people who are like family. And of course there's how I refer to him when I'm talking to Grayson and Shadow: Dad.

It doesn't feel strange to me. At least no stranger than my own absurd smorgasbord of names.

I liked how Saul couldn't settle on one. I liked feeling like maybe he thought they all applied, in different situations.

The boys come streaming across the yard. "LOCK THE DOOR!" I yell again, and Shadow dashes back to check the knob, then flashes me a thumbs up.

We pile into Toddy's truck and pull down the driveway onto the country road. I usually beeline for the scenic route through the cutesy part of downtown, but for quick errands and junk food runs with the boys, I head straight for the derelict IGA grocery store and Camponelli's Pizza next door, which sells suspiciously old but not technically expired candy.

We pull into Camponelli's and hop out of the truck, and as we pass through the front door my eyes trail back to the car parked next to us. I'm milliseconds from figuring out where I recognize the junky sedan from when I walk straight into someone.

"Sorry," I say.

"Sorry," Saul says.

Both of us freeze, rattled. "Hi," he says.

The scratch of his voice makes my stomach flip. "Hi."

"Wow, hi," he says again, adjusting the pizza box under his arm.

"Who are you?" Grayson asks.

"He's Junior's teacher," Shadow offers, which makes Saul laugh uncomfortably. "Remember?"

"Tutor," I say.

"What's a tutor?" Grayson asks.

"He helps me with school."

"That's not fair," Grayson says. "That's cheating."

"Yeah," Saul says. "Come to think of it, it's *not* fair."

"Well, tutoring isn't cheating though," Shadow explains, I guess to all of us. "They don't do your homework for you or take your quizzes or anything. They're just older kids who are good at school, and they help you go over things you learn."

Grayson must already be bored with this topic, because instead of responding, he blurts out, "Does our mom know you have tattoos?"

"I . . . ?" Saul looks to me for help.

"She doesn't like tattoos," Grayson says. "She says it makes you look like you're trying too hard."

"Are you trying too hard, *Mike*?" I say.

"Mike, trying too hard?" he says. "Mikes don't try at *all*, Jack. Mikes pretty much just get individual pan-crust pizzas and go home to play video games in their fathers' basements."

"Is the pan crust good?" Grayson asks.

"No."

"Do you like video games?"

"Yes," Saul says.

"Do you want to come over and play video games with us?"

"Mom and Dad said no video games tonight," Shadow says softly.

"Nuh-uh, that was Junior."

"No video games," I say again, helplessly.

"I'll tell Mom Mike has tattoos," Grayson says.

"Go for it."

"Does Mike get a say?" Saul says. "Because Mike would rather your mom didn't think he was trying too hard."

Grayson scrunches his face. "Why are you talking like that?"

"Can we get ham and pineapple?" Shadow asks.

"Ew, no," Grayson says. "We're getting pepperoni with extra pepperoni."

"Junior, that's not fair. I want ham and pineapple."

"No, no, no, no, no," Grayson says while Shadow begs.

"Okay, who wants to go home and play video games?" I say to make them stop.

Grayson whoops. "With Mike!"

Saul glances at me sidelong, making my stomach flip. I shouldn't have Saul over.

"We can at least get *half* ham and pineapple, right, Junior?" Shadow says.

I'm going to have Saul over. "Fine. Let's get the pizza and go."

As the boys rush the counter, Saul says, "You sure, Jack?"

"Is that what you call me when you're mad at me?"

"It's what I call you when you're smirking."

I brush past him. "I don't smirk."

Fifteen

AT ten thirty, I force the boys into bed with the help of bribery (more candy, more pizza, another god-awful eighties horror movie to watch the next time Mike comes over) and drop onto the couch across from Saul, sending my mom what I hope is a casual *When will you be home?* text.

Another hour? She replies.

In case, though, Saul asks if he can borrow a sweatshirt to hide his tattoos.

"Why do you care if my mom thinks you're trying too hard?" I tease. "Are you trying to *woo* my mom, *Mike*?"

His elusive dimple flickers into view as he says seriously, "Do you think she'd have me?" I laugh and throw a couch pillow at him, which he knocks away. "Please, June. Just let me borrow a sweatshirt. It'll make me feel better."

"So I'm June when you want something."

"I guess so, June."

"Okay. I'll grab one."

"Hey," he says, stopping me. "Can I see your room?"

"Why?"

He shrugs. "I don't know. This is your parents' house, and I want to see the part that's yours."

"It's my great-great—et cetera—grandfather's house."

"I'm less curious which pop-star poster *he* had over his bed."

I laugh. "Yeah, you can see my room."

"I don't have to," he says.

"No, yeah, it's fine."

"No, yeah?"

"Follow me or don't, Mike." I move down the hall. He does follow, and for the first few seconds after stepping into my room we're immersed in darkness together, standing close enough that I can feel his cells bumping into some of mine. I turn the lamp on, and the light breaks through some of the tension, allowing me to breathe again. I break from Saul and disappear into the closet to look for a sweatshirt big enough to fit him.

I'm not much of an oversized-hoodie girl, and while Saul's thin, he's taller than me. The only legitimate option I have is a navy crew-neck sweatshirt that belonged to Dad, which I'm hesitant to lend out. I hug it to my chest, imagining I can smell Dad on it, imagining I even *remember* his smell. I tamp down thoughts about what he'd say if he knew an Angert would be wearing it. When I come back into my room, Saul's sitting on my bed, holding a picture frame. "Your dad," he says. "I recognize him from . . . the chickens."

I hold out the sweatshirt. "This was his too, so don't forget to give it back."

"I won't." He pulls it on. "So, Nate asked me to go camping tomorrow. I think your name was mentioned."

"Are you going?"

He studies me. "I told him I couldn't."

"Oh."

"Since you and I aren't hanging out and all."

I lean against the wall. "Right."

He looks out the star-washed window then back to me. After a few still, heavy seconds, he asks, "Is it because I'm older than you?"

My body begins to buzz. My stomach pulses, and an acorn of heat catches in my throat. It feels like, all along, we've been dancing closer and closer to this, to saying aloud the last thing an O'Donnell and an Angert should say to each other. I shake my head.

Saul's dark eyes stay intent on mine. "Because of Hannah?"

"No." The possibility that she wouldn't be *thrilled* about Saul and I hanging out still lingers, but sometimes I catch her texting Nate. If things really *could* go anywhere with Saul, I'd ask her flat out. But they can't, so why torture myself?

Saul studies me for a few more seconds. "Because you don't like me?"

There, the one thing I shouldn't say: *I like you.*

"June," he says.

I laugh from pure distress. Answering truthfully would be betraying Dad. But then again, what is this? I'm *flirting* with him. I've brought him into my house—*Dad's* house—lent him Dad's sweatshirt. I'm ignoring every warning my father gave me, every rule he had for me, for a boy I've only known a few weeks. I shake my head. "Saul, I can't."

Talk about this.

Do this.

Like you.

I ignore the voice that says, *It's too late. You can't walk away from this now.*

"Do you want me to leave?" he asks finally.

"Yes," I say. "No."

"June," he says.

I let out a frustrated sigh. "Yeah. You should go."

"Okay." He stands, and I cross to my dresser to grab the B+ short story, whose grade I filled in myself. I hand it to Saul, who smiles down at it.

"Keep it," I say. It feels like I'm offering him the memory of my father and the hens itself, a tiny token, a piece of a heart I'm strictly prohibited from sharing with him.

His eyes lock with mine for a long moment, and I think he's about to kiss me. Instead, he turns toward the hall, and I follow. We're halfway through the doorway when I see the White caught between our arms.

By then it's too late: The hall is gone. My *house* is gone. We're standing in an unfamiliar bathroom, and, with one look at Saul's face, I know where we are and who the girl lying on the mint-green tile is. She looks like him, though a bit younger—around seventeen, the age she died. Her skin is sheened with sweat, her dark hair shaved to the roots and cheeks sunken.

"Please stop," the girl whispers against the floor. "Make it stop."

Saul doesn't go toward her. He stares, jaw flexed.

There's a knock on the closed door. "Bekah?" a man's voice calls. "You okay in there?"

"Make it stop." Her eyes skirt toward the porcelain tub, inside which a pile of shoes sits. A shapeless darkness writhes over it.

Nameless.

Behind us, the door creaks open, and the ghost disappears as a gray-bearded man pushes into the room.

I don't see the Eli Angert of book jackets and news stories, the one who wears a tweed coat and sits in a leather chair framed by mahogany bookshelves, looking toward a window with an expression of almost brutal indifference.

This is a secret Eli hurrying into the bathroom, a private Eli kneeling on the floor beside the girl. This Eli wears half a pajama set—the pants—and a ratty undershirt stained with coffee. He cradles the back of his daughter's head with thick, blistered fingers. "Oh, kid," he whispers, voice quavering. "Oh, kid."

"I need it to stop," she murmurs.

"I know." He gently rubs her shoulder. "Let's get you into bed."

"No," she says more firmly, "I can't keep doing it, Dad."

"You're a fighter. You'll get through this."

"I don't wanna fight." Her voice swings high. Eli scoops her into his arms and stands. "I'm tired, Daddy."

He *shh*s her, kisses her cheek despite the flecks of vomit there.

"Dad?"

"Yeah, kid?"

"You'll forgive me if I stop?"

"Stop?"

"The chemo."

Eli Angert falters. He breaks. He stops before the bathroom door and breathes. His voice cracks though he says no words. His chest heaves.

Saul stares, body rigid like he can stop himself from cracking too.

"You'll beat it, baby." Eli carries her through the door, a White glistening in his wake.

Saul catches the fluff in his hand and studies it. As it sinks into his skin, I fold my fingers over his, nodding: *I'll go with you.*

We step forward and emerge into another moment.

We're halfway up a steep white dune overlooking Torch Lake, the turquoise water rocking over the happily shrieking bodies splashing through it. On the shore, a man and woman sit in folding chairs on a polka-dotted blanket, flanking two outstretched teenagers: the girl asleep with a wide-brimmed hat draped over her eyes, the boy watching her. A pile of shoes sits yards away, ignored by the beachgoers wandering past.

Saul takes a few steps down the hillside, the hot wind rippling through Dad's sweatshirt and mussing his hair. I touch his arm. *Is this it?* I ask without sound. *The day you won't let go of?*

He nods, then squints into the sunlight. Together we watch the waves hit, the gulls dive low for Dorito crumbs and dropped grapes. I know this must hurt him, but it seems like it makes him happy too.

Saul looks my way, shielding his eyes from the sun. I do the same, and he leans forward until our hands form an awning over us. *Hi*, he mouths.

Hi.

Want to go to the water?

Yes.

The sparkling lip of the lake is riddled with millions of floating memories. We climb down to the water's edge, and when our toes *should* meet the frigid fringe of the water, we instead step onto something solid and glassy.

We're on a frozen pond now, circled in velvety snow. The beach is nowhere in sight. A gangly boy and muscular girl in matching neon snowsuits skid wildly across the icy surface, and frosty shoes tower at the edge of the lake. The kids' shouts and giggles echo as they race across the frozen pond, sliding on their snow boots. The boy slips and cries out as he falls, landing on his back with his arms and legs splayed out.

"Saul!" the girl yelps and spins, gliding toward him. She drops onto her knees beside him, and he sits up, his hat askew to reveal a considerable amount of ear. I glance sideways at *my* Saul, adult Saul. His smile is tight but wide. His eyes glisten.

"You're okay." Bekah rolls her eyes exaggeratedly and hauls him up by his coat. "Stop being a baby."

"I'm not a baby!" Saul yells.

"You're five minutes younger than me. That makes you the baby! That makes you my *servant*."

The Saul beside me shifts to accommodate a laugh, but I can see the effort it's taking to hold himself together. The miniature

Angert twins are hurling snow at each other now, and while at first they seem genuinely annoyed, Bekah shrieks with laughter when a snowball spatters her face, and Saul breaks into an open-mouthed grin.

At the top of the tree-covered ridge beyond the pond, Eli Angert appears with a bundle of firewood perched on his shoulder. His cheeks are red and eyes tight against the brilliant winter sun. "Time to come home!" he calls.

The twins skate to the bank, passing through a cluster of Whites they don't seem to see. We follow their lead, but when we step from the frozen lake onto the snowy shore, the Whites rip us away again, and we find ourselves crashing through a solid wall of water.

Soaking wet and freezing cold, we emerge into a dark space, the thundering sound of falling water echoing around us.

Saul's hand grasps for mine in the dark, checking that I'm still here with him. Wherever *here* is.

It's as if each new threshold we cross—man-made or natural—tunnels us to whatever the White contains—like when the puffs cling to a doorframe or the lake's lip, the memories they hold become rooms on the other side, places you can simply step into. That must be why just holding one the other night didn't do anything—I needed to step *into* it, like Saul and I did when we passed from the icy shore to wherever we are now.

I wipe the water from my eyes as they adjust to the meager light. We're in a cave behind a waterfall—*Five Fingers Falls?* My eyes move past the dark, glimmering falls toward the interior of the cave, and I lurch backward when I realize we're not alone.

Behind a heap of soaked shoes, a boy and girl stand coiled

together with their foreheads resting against each other's, ignoring the Whites' lazy batting.

Saul squeezes my hand to get my attention. *Who are they?* he mouths. I shake my head.

They're not much older than us, both dressed in some kind of antique undergarments: the dark-haired boy in a pair of short shorts, the girl with strawberry blond curls and full cheeks in an ivory chemise that clings to her thighs.

The boy whispers something to her we can't hear over the roaring falls. His hands skim over her arms, and he lifts her chin to his.

Saul and I trade abashed looks when the couple moves on to some pretty serious groping, and he tilts his head toward the waterfalls. I nod, and he pulls me through the thundering water.

We stumble into my bedroom, immediately dry but still so cold we're shivering. "You didn't know them?" I stutter through the chill. Saul shakes his head. I can see pain in the torque of his face, the rigidity of his shoulders. "Are you okay?" I whisper.

"Were you?" he says. "After you saw your dad the first time, I mean."

"No." I shake my head. "But I wanted it to happen again. I wanted for it to never stop."

"Me too," he says, eyes low.

"I'm sorry, Saul." I want to pull him toward me, wrap my arms around him, make him feel that he's not alone. But I don't. "I'm useless, but I'm here."

He nods, his dark eyes lifting to meet mine. The corner of his mouth twitches with an attempt at a smile. "Thanks, Jack," he says quietly.

I step back and slump onto my bed, my own disappointment spreading through me like wildfire. I close my eyes against rising tears. "After last time," I say, "I thought maybe you were right, that my dad *was* trying to tell me something. But if that last memory was a total stranger's, then, what, they're random? I might never find a memory of him again?"

Saul lets out a long breath, and the bed sinks as he sits beside me. "Hey," he says, bumping my elbow with his. "Look, if the Whites were full of random memories, what are the odds you would've found a few of your dad's? Or we would've found some of Bekah's? Those odds are impossible, June. They're miracle odds. I can't promise this is a message from your dad, but this isn't random. It means something, for both of us."

I open my eyes again and look into his. They're dark and liquid, soft and warm. "This all started the night we met," I tell him. "I thought I saw the ghost that night—the dark one—and when I got home . . . it happened for the first time here. I saw my dad.

"When I was a kid, my dad told me only O'Donnells could see the ghosts—as far as I knew, *no one* else ever had. I thought it was our own private bad omen. But in that memory . . . in the bathroom, it seemed like . . . like Bekah saw it too."

Saul swallows and nods. "Yeah," he agrees. "It did."

"What does that mean?"

He shakes his head. "I don't know. But there's a lot about our families that a story about cherry trees can't account for."

An uncanny tingle crawls down my spine, and the silence stretches out between us.

I realize then that Saul still has my hand, and my eyes flash toward the door and then the alarm clock on my desk. Though it felt like we were only gone for a handful of minutes, the numbers flash *11:22*.

"You should go," I say. "My parents will be home soon."

"June, I can't pretend this didn't happen—whether Bekah and your dad are trying to tell us something or not, we have the chance to *see* them again."

"I know." I do. I understand how everything changed when we saw Saul's sister. This bit of magic doesn't only belong to me anymore, and I can't ask Saul to forget about it, about the possibility of seeing *her* again. "I know. But my parents will be home any minute, and if you're still here when they get here, *this*—you coming over—is going to get a *lot* harder."

He studies our linked hands, then nods and lets go. "Your story—I must've dropped it."

But there's no sign of it. The pages are gone, maybe gathering dust and pollen in a pile of lost shoes. "What's your e-mail address? I'll send it to you."

"Would you believe Saul Angert is a rare enough name that I have the unique fortune of owning Saul dot Angert at Gmail dot com?"

"Stop trying to impress me," I tease.

"Send me your story, Jack." He steps through the doorway, and I feel a half-formed surge of panic before I peek into the hall and confirm he didn't vanish into some other place or time. There are no Whites in sight as Saul heads toward the stairs. His phone rings, and he answers as he descends. "Takumi. What's up?"

As I listen to the gentle grit of his voice move down the stairs,

I think about life a few weeks ago, before Nameless reappeared, before the Whites tore open the old wound in my chest, before I met Saul.

Something major shifted when he came back. It's as if all along we've been on two paths bound for collision, O'Donnell and Angert, and now it's happened. We're inextricably tangled; even the Whites know it.

A few weeks ago, Saul had a different life too. Friends I don't know, professors who shaped him, maybe non-O'Donnell enemies, all tucked away in another place.

I want to know it all.

Two hours after Saul leaves, my phone buzzes on my bedside table with a new e-mail alert, and I realize I've been waiting for it.

I tap open the e-mail, Saul's reply to the story about my dad and the chickens.

I hope you're awake, I read. *I hope you don't fall asleep before I get to tell you that you're amazing. This is amazing, and also you.*

I stare at the words, intoxicating waves of warmth coursing through me as I debate how to reply.

Even if our collision was inevitable, even though it feels *good* to like Saul Angert, every step forward I take with him moves me a little further off my old path, the one that aligned with Dad's.

The mental gymnastics—justifying some things and drawing arbitrary lines before others, straddling loyalty to Dad and my interest in Saul—are exhausting.

I try for an innocuous reply: *Who's Takumi?*

Old roommate, Saul answers. *He's been trying to get ahold of me for weeks, but I hate the phone. Turns out he's getting married and moving to Indonesia to teach English.*

WOW! Congrats, Takumi! About time, I respond.

No kidding. He and Sarah have been together for, like, four months.

Oh . . . jeez. That's . . . four months, I write.

My thoughts exactly. Whatever, it's his funeral. Whoops, meant to say wedding.

> *Well, good for him. I can't believe I haven't been proposed to yet. Honestly, I'm offended.*

This is awkward. I swear I was already going to ask this, but . . .

> *No, I will not be your date to Takumi and Sarah's wedding. I cannot support such a union.*

Damn. Maybe next time one of my friends gets married, he'll know his fiancée's middle name and you'll feel differently.

After a long pause, I type, *How are you?*

Bad in some ways, good in one.

    Meaning?

Five minutes pass before my phone vibrates with his reply. One word:

June.

I fall asleep feeling bad in most ways, happy in one.

Sixteen

TUTORING? Saul's e-mail reads.

I snuggle deeper into the blankets, morning light washing across my face.

On a Saturday morning? I respond.

Okay, then what about Not Tutoring? he asks.

You mean White-hunting?

I watch dust twirl through the sunbeams, landing on the shaggy ferns and bulbous succulents Toddy helped me hang from the ceiling.

I want to see more.

Laughter, clinking pots, and the shrieks of a hyperactive

cartoon dog drift up from the kitchen. Toddy makes breakfast every chance he gets, partly to keep the boys from overdosing on Cap'n Crunch and partly because his and Mom's definition of a hot date has always been strolling hand in hand through an organic grocery store and coming home to make creamy *cassoulet* or flaky *gâteau Basque* with Jack's Tart cherries.

They'll cook for hours, feeding each other bites of cheese and sips of Bordeaux as they go, then sit down for a three-course meal. The food is always delicious, and the process is always—like now—*very* loud.

My sweet, sugar-addicted family is downstairs having their traditional lazy Saturday morning, and here I am plotting with Saul Angert to keep chasing memories of Dad and Bekah. Guilt gnaws at my stomach, and I burrow my face into a patch of sunlight. *Today won't work*, I tell Saul. *My whole family's home.*

Then I'll be Mike.

I should say no. For Dad but also because I *know* it's only a matter of time before my parents figure out who Saul really is.

But until then, I can't deny Saul the one thing we both want more than anything else: more time with the people we've lost.

Okay.

Fifteen minutes later I'm sweatered and blue-jeaned, rooting around for bagels in the pantry.

"Eat breakfast with us," Mom says, grabbing my hand.

"I have tutoring," I say. "He'll be here any minute."

"On a Saturday?" Mom says. "Okay, well, Mike can eat too. We're making omelets."

"I'm barely hungry. Bagel-hungry, not omelet-hungry."

The doorbell rings then, right as the boys start pummeling Toddy, who has a hot pan in his hand, with their new boxing gloves. Mom has to pull them off of him, shouting things like *Faites attention!* and *Péril!* One advantage of being significantly older than your siblings is that you can usually slip away unnoticed, which I do.

I open the door to Saul's smile. The air outside is cool and dry, chilly in the shade of the porch, but I'd guess warmer out in the sun.

"Hello, Jack."

I lower my voice so my parents can't hear me, if that's even possible over Grayson's shrieking. "Mr. Angert."

He shakes his head. "God, I hate that."

"Hey." I nod toward the cherry tree, where prickly green sprouts stick up from the grass in a circle.

"What?"

"Shadow and Grayson planted those."

"Huh. And they're coming up this late?"

"They planted them *yesterday*."

"Shit," Saul says. "You're rapidly turning me into a Five Fingers Truther."

"Good." I lead him past the kitchen, grateful Grayson doesn't notice his bud "Mike" walk by. We close ourselves in the sunroom along with the morning cold and plop down on the wicker couch. For a minute, we're caught in heavy silence, just staring at each other.

"So." Saul clears his throat. "Whites." The gravel in his voice rustles through me, and I want to touch him, or maybe tap my hand on the back of the couch until he sets his over it. He bumps my knee with his. "June, look."

A White skates across the sun-warmed glass, heading straight for the back door. It hovers there, expectant, and Saul and I exchange a look.

He holds his hand out, and I take it shakily. We stand, reaching for the White. It bumps against our interlaced fingers, rolls onto our hands, and settles.

"Ready?" Saul whispers.

Desperate.

Overwhelmed.

Terrified.

"Ready."

We take a breath and step outside.

Nothing changes.

At first, I think we've stepped into a memory of a day nearly identical to today, but then Saul's voice cuts through the morning quiet: "Where are the shoes?" He looks surprised to hear himself too. "I guess that answers my question."

"What do you mean?" I ask.

"In the memories, there's always a pile of shoes," he says. "But it didn't work, so of course there aren't any shoes."

The White is pushing up from our skin again, bobbing against our hands like it can't find a way in but also doesn't want to leave.

"I don't get it. What did we do wrong?" I say helplessly.

We step back into the sunroom, searching for some clue as to why it didn't work. My mind cycles through the other times we've stepped into memories. "The *shoes*," I say. "We were barefoot the other times."

Saul releases a gruff laugh, but he's already bent down to yank his shoes off.

"We should throw them in the yard."

"How many pairs of shoes do you think I own, Jack?"

"More than the rest of the boys in my graduating class combined."

He smirks and kicks my foot. I untie my boots and, with mild regret, toss them outside. No coywolves appear, but the White is still drifting, and Saul slides his rough fingers through mine again. This time, there's no *Ready?*

We catch the ball of fluff. It melts into our hands, and we take a step together, leaving the sunroom and the present behind.

It worked, I say silently.

Saul's grip tightens as we survey our surroundings. We're just inside the woods, and everything, even the pile of shoes behind us, is blanketed in a layer of frost. The sky is bright and cloudless, and in the distance, a boy and girl, all sharp elbows and big ears and black eyebrows, are trudging our way. Saul and Bekah can't be more than nine here, but they already look so *themselves*: he neat and elegant, she mud-smudged and tough.

I glance at *my* Saul and tug his ear teasingly. He rolls his eyes and bumps my shoulder with his, sending a rush of heat down into my stomach.

We look back toward the twins. Though he's taller than her, Saul's still struggling to keep up with his sister. "We're not *allowed*," he calls at her back.

Her laugh has a shade of his grit to it, but where his is level and low, hers is loud, unapologetic. "That's why it's fun! We're like spies."

As they pass us, we turn and follow them toward the edge of the woods, where white slivers of the farmhouse are visible between trees.

The boy stops walking a few feet from the lawn. "He'll be angry."

Bekah looks at him over her shoulder. "Just keep watch, okay?"

She takes off across the lawn, beelining toward the first Jack's Tart tree. She scrambles up it, if not *gracefully* then at least *powerfully*, and picks through the branches.

It's too early in the season, I think. Patches of snow still blanket the grass, and the end of winter nips in the air.

Bekah shakes a branch, and green pellets tumble down. Her brother takes a few steps closer and wraps his arm around a tree trunk as he watches her rearrange herself in the branches. She moves fearlessly, higher and higher, picking and rustling. Minutes pass.

Behind us, birds scatter noisily. We spin toward the commotion.

Eli is coming toward us in angry strides, and little Saul's eyes rim with white as he looks between his father and the cherry tree. He runs toward Eli, as if to hold him off. "It was just a game," he pants. Eli rips him out of the way and keeps moving.

Bekah's spotted her father from up in the tree. She slides down to the grass, watching him progress toward her. She barely bats an eye when he grabs her arm and drags her toward the woods. Both Sauls lurch out of Eli's stormy path, and the boy chases him. "It's not her fault!" he cries helplessly, pulling at his father's jacket.

"Completely disrespectful," Eli growls at Bekah. "If Jack O'Donnell had seen you, you have any idea what he might've done? He'd've had grounds to *shoot* you, kid."

Bekah writhes against him, huffing angrily. He tosses her over a fallen log and spanks her once. She grits her teeth and stares hard at the mud. Eli spanks her again, and Saul starts to cry. Eli spanks her a third time, and Saul runs at him, pulling at his father's arms. They scuffle for a second before Eli throws him off.

"*Please*," Saul says.

The ruddy heat leaves Eli's face. He straightens, studying Saul for a long beat. He wipes the sweat from his upper lip and jerks his head in the direction of their cabin. His eyes sweep over both twins. "Go home," he grunts. "Both of you."

The boy remains frozen, but Bekah slumps off the log and takes his hand, pulling him away. Eli sighs, resting his fingers on his hips, and watches them move off. He looks back and shakes his head at the cherry tree in the distance.

This must be Bekah's memory, because as she moves off, the natural rustle of the woods catch in a kind of loop. Like the woods are doing what she might have expected them to do in her absence: birds trilling in the same unsettling rhythms, her father sighing again and again.

We hurry away from the nightmarish scene and catch up with the twins. They walk in silence for a long while before Bekah says, "You shouldn't let him get to you."

The boy says nothing, and Bekah adds, "It doesn't *hurt*."

His voice is small: "He doesn't do it to hurt you. He does it to embarrass you."

"I'm not embarrassed," she says, matter-of-factly. She stops walking and dips her hand in her pocket, plucking from it two cherries, mostly pink though spotted with green. "You're a bad lookout," she says. "But an okay brother."

The boy grins, revealing a missing front tooth, and gingerly takes a cherry. "On three?" Bekah says. He matches her gaze and nods. The two of them count to three, then press the still-crunchy cherries into their mouths and bite down, jaws working awkwardly against the not-quite-ripeness. "What do you think?" she says around a mouthful, her face scrunched. "It's kinda sour."

Saul closes his eyes and chews slowly. "Not sour. *Bitter*."

Bekah lets out a bark of laughter and spits her cherry out. "Gross," she says. "Still worth it though. To say we did."

"The last taste," little Saul says. A crescent of smile passes over his face. He opens his eyes, and his grin cracks all the way open. "The last taste is like honey."

"The last taste should always be sweet," Bekah says solemnly. They start moving again, the crisp leaves crumbling loudly underfoot. Without looking over at him, she says, "Saul?"

"Yeah."

"You don't need to keep me safe. I'm older than you."

"Five minutes," he says. They've reached the end of the woods. They climb the cabin's stairs and go inside, leaving the world still and noiseless, as if without them it doesn't exist.

Whites wait along the edge of the forest, and Saul and I exchange another look. He nods, and we step through.

We're back outside the sunroom, but the grass is cropped, gleaming in the sunlight. A few wisps of cloud sail across the pale sky, and a breeze snakes through the treetops, sending dried-out blots of orange frittering from the branches of yellow birches and plasticky green ironwoods.

Two elegant coywolves pick across the yard, dropping our shoes at the edge of a pyramid of boots and sandals, then trot into the woods again.

A peal of laughter draws our attention to the sunroom as a little girl bursts from it: a blur of yellow dress and nearly black curls streaked rust-red by sun. She squeals with delight as her bare feet pound the grass. Saul looks from the little girl to me, comparing us.

"Watch out for nails and rocks, June-bug," a man's voice shouts. A second form careens through the sunroom doors, barreling down the hill in the opposite direction.

My stomach jerks within me.

No.

We can't be here.

My eyes judder to the hydrangea that curls wildly up the porch, blooms spread into orbs of blue.

No.

Some petals have fallen to the grass at the bush's base. I know exactly *when* we are.

The sunlight is harsh. The dirt has a sharp, acrid scent to it, like the dehydration of summer has boiled the earth down to its essential minerals. The lawn glimmers like sea glass, thirsty, almost translucent. The birdsong rings hollow.

Any moment but this.

"I'm gonna beat you, Daddy!" the girl shrieks as she runs, throwing a look of fiery delight over her shoulder at him.

I remember how it feels to be her right now. Happiness ballooning in her chest as Dad lopes after her, clumsy and powerful like some kind of circus bear, slowing himself to give her a lead.

The part of his lips. The gap between his front teeth. The crinkle in his sweat-streaked brow.

Blue hydrangeas bobbing in the wind. Petals falling—one, two, three, one, two, three—in a half dome around the roots.

We were playing a game. Racing to see who reached O'Dang! first.

I remember how, when I saw Dad's gap-toothed grin, those blue flowers, I thought I might burst from happiness. In the moment, I had him, all the way. I didn't know it was the last moment I would. The last time I would see his living smile ignite, his chest heave with breath, his eyes squinch against the sun.

DAD. I run. I chase him. *Dad, no!*

My child self has already disappeared into the forest, and Dad's headed in the opposite direction. I try to scream for them to come back. I try to scream for her to *follow* him.

If only I had followed him, everything *would be different.*

But that wasn't how we played the game.

We ran. Two entirely separate directions. Crashed through misty, sun-washed forest. Moving, moving, moving, sometimes in straight lines, sometimes right-left-right-left. But whenever Dad wanted to play, it worked: The woods let us both find our way to the gnarled tree that, at times, simply stopped existing. It was wide as a house, bits of bark peeling away to reveal a supple whiteness underneath.

Hemlock, Dad thought. Trunk so thick you could lie on the roots like hammocks. Streamers and ribbons were strung around it. Some had been there as long as I could remember; others appeared one day as if from thin air.

Dad was gone a lot, driving semitrucks cross-country, selling fancy knives from the trunk of his car, delivering soda to vending machines or packages to doorsteps—whatever work he could find that allowed him to travel. Mom said he got restless when he was home too long. Restless when he was gone too long too.

He'd be home for a few days or weeks or months in between jobs, and in those days we'd spend sunrise to twilight together, except for the occasional morning when he was out of the house by the time I woke up and still gone when I climbed in bed.

Whenever he was home, we played this game.

Whenever he was home, we raced barefoot to O'Dang.

As I sprint down the slick hillside after him, I remember what he used to say: *Can't get into heaven with your shoes on, June-bug. If we wanna break through the veil in this thin place, we gotta go the way we came into this world: barefoot.*

For eight years, racing Dad to O'Dang! was my favorite thing. For ten, the thought of it has made me sick.

I know Saul must be chasing me, but I don't look back. My heart thunders, and my feet hit hard and fast. I scream for Dad so hard it hurts, but I make no sound. He can't hear me.

And what if he could? How could I stop what's already happened? The only reason I'm here to relive this at all is because it already happened. How can I undo this blemish on my memory? My black hole. The grief at my core, sucking everything into it.

The feeling of getting to that tree, panting and sticky and happy-so-happy. And the fear that set in when the sun started fading and the air cooled and still Dad hadn't come.

I chase him into the woods. Tree branches whip and lash at my skin. They feel solid and scraggy against my arms, though I pass through them like a ghost.

He's too fast. His gait's too long. I see slashes of red fabric—his shirt—darting through the forest ahead of me.

Wild blue hydrangea curls through the woods. Blue petals twirl in the wind, their dry tang cloying in the air. Red and blue. Red and blue. Red and blue.

"JUNE-BUG?" Dad shouts.

I follow the voice. I thrash, I claw, I fight through the brush.

I burst into a clearing, golden light pouring over yellowing grass. Dad stands there, hands resting on his hips as he breathes hard.

Hydrangea petals spiral through the air. They catch in his hair. They'll still be there. They'll still be there when I find him.

Tears flood my eyes. My throat closes. I can't breathe. I can't breathe, but I'm still mouthing the word—*Dad*—as I move toward him.

Something shifts in the trees, and I freeze, a new shock of cold coursing through my veins. A darkness writhes into the clearing.

Nameless billows toward him. The branches come alive with cheeps and squeaks as birds and squirrels erupt into panic. The trees sway and tremor as every living thing retreats from the dark ghost. Every living thing except my father.

Dad, I beg.

He stares at the black thing, tears springing to his eyes. Like he knows. He knows what's coming.

Move, Dad! Move! I'm trying to scream. I try to pull at his hand. I can feel his skin, rough and warm, but he doesn't react. Doesn't budge. He's a statue, and I'm not even a breeze.

Tears roll down his cheeks—*how does he know what's coming?*

"Please." He's panting, can't catch his breath. The darkness closes in on him: hopelessness, fear, claustrophobia, suffocation. I feel it all, and still Dad breathes hard, too hard.

"You can have me, but leave June alone."

My stomach jolts at the sound of my name. The darkness touches him then. He lets out a grunt and sinks to his knees as the thing towers over him. Dad clutches at his arm. His face twists, and eyes flutter against pain. "She's not like us. She won't be. I promise you. Just leave her alone."

Dad, I sob.

The thing folds over him. He chokes—a tight, garbled sound. The sound he made as pain surged outward from his heart. *Acute myocardial infarction*, the doctors would later tell us. I memorized the words, repeated them to myself for weeks, trying to understand how something that sounded so mundane could have beaten my father, the biggest man on earth.

"Please." He shuts his eyes tight. They zigzag under his eyelids. *"Please show her."*

I fall onto my knees and wrap my arms around him, right

through the darkness and its cold. I try to drag him away. I try to shield him. I try to make myself solid for him. Audible. *Dad. Dad. Dad.* I say it a hundred times.

My voice is still lost, but I swear he feels my arms as he slumps forward and passes through them. His eyes search for something—for me?—but I don't think they see. "Junie," he chokes. "Jack."

I'm so sure he knows I'm there, that I'm holding him, but then, in a small voice, he says, "Dad? Are you there?"

HELP! I scream as hard as I can. *HELP. HELP. HELP.*

My throat feels raw, shredded, and still the only sound is the chatter of robins and gray jays, the distant caw of ring-billed gulls. The world insists it's a beautiful day, while I sit on my knees, holding my father, blue petals falling around us.

The light, his being, his Himness, fades from of his eyes. *DAD.*

The torque of pain relaxes from his face.

I know. The second he's gone, I know. I feel the gap at the core of me, in the world, in the universe. I feel the place he should be, a tattered emptiness.

And just like that, everything freezes. The whole forest pauses.

And I know right then it's because this is where the memory ends. There's nothing left to it. The man who made it has *stopped*, ceased. Ended.

I push on his chest. I try to hold his head back and breathe into his mouth. I sob but make no sound. The birds are silent now; there is no such thing as sound here anymore. Even Nameless is frozen there, its coldness rendered neutral. There is no temperature, no feel to the air or smell or breeze.

Hands press against my shoulders and try to drag me away,

but I can't stand. I can't leave. I can barely see because I'm crying so hard, because the impossibly motionless sun is aflame, because what is there to see when your whole world dies in front of you?

Saul wraps himself around me. He lifts me. My head falls into his chest. Tears and snot dampen the long-sleeved shirt he wore to hide his tattoos from Mom back in another world.

I wanted to forget this feeling forever. The feeling of being ripped into two people: the you of before and the one you'll always be once you know what it is to lose something.

Saul carries me through the woods, jogging me up in his arms every few yards. When we get to the hill, he can't bear it any longer. He sets me on the grass and touches my teary cheeks. He mouths something and pulls my forehead against his throat, smoothing my hair. He pulls away, looks hard into my eyes, and squeezes my neck.

You're going to be okay, he silently promises. *It's over, June.*

I close my eyes against more tears, our hands twined together like old roots as we walk back to the sunroom. There's nothing else to do.

This moment is over. There's nothing left for us here.

Seventeen

I tell Saul I need to be alone. I beg him to leave. I tell him I never want to see him again. I tell him I need him to go, over and over, until he gives in. He slinks through the back door.

I sit in the sunroom until my face is placid, then tell Mom and Toddy I don't feel well and go upstairs.

They believe me—I don't look well.

I climb into bed and pray for sleep, for darkness to hide me. For time to stretch out while my eyes are closed so that when they next open, centuries will have passed and nothing will hurt like it does now.

Is this a sign? Punishment for spending time with Saul?

The words he said in the forest replay in my mind: *You can have me, but leave June alone.* Nameless wasn't just an omen. It *killed* Dad. Did it kill Bekah too?

Eventually, I fall into an agitated sleep.

"*No*," I wake myself a dozen times saying. "No, no. Please, no."

Don't let him be dead. Don't let that moment have happened. Wash it from my mind.

In the morning, I wake to a text from Hannah: *Need beach. Will die soon from calc overdose. Send help.*

I weakly push my covers away and sit up to glare at Feathers. She's been here all night, sorrowful and glistening, but her presence doesn't comfort me. It reminds me of the darkness wrapped around Dad in the woods. "It killed him," I whisper.

Feathers slumps, recedes into the wall.

My body's sore from crying. The precise moment the life left Dad's body is imprinted on my retinas in a way that feels permanent. I can't tell Mom what's happening; even if she'd believe me, I couldn't give her that burden. I need Hannah. And not the way our friendship has been lately, with gaps and secrets. I need her as my best friend. *Immediately*, I text her, then go to my dresser and sift through my drawers.

Fifteen minutes, she replies, then, *(read as: thirty)*.

I pull on a pair of jeans, a crop top, and a long crocheted sweater and grab my sun hat and purse from the hook on the wall. All the while, there's the feeling that I've forgotten something.

I remember this sensation, from when I was eight. For seconds, you forget. Like walking into a room and having no idea what you came for, your mind blanks. You know there's something you should be thinking about, because lately your only job has been to think about it.

But then—*ping*—it's back. You'll always remember.

I put on a pair of brown sandals then check for Whites before stepping into the hall. Part of me wants to look for a memory to overshadow last night's, some clue to understanding Dad's strange words. The majority hopes I never see a White again.

I tell Mom and Toddy where I'm going, give them both a kiss on the cheek, and step out onto the porch to wait. It's a balmy fifty degrees, and the sun's starting to haul itself over the trees—*ping*. Dad's dead.

The Subaru rumbles up the drive, and Hannah waves her arms dramatically from the driver's seat. "You're aliiiiive," I cry as I plop down beside her and offer my pre-kissed fingers.

Ping! Dad's not.

"I knoooow." She matches my hand's gesture, then reverses down the driveway and points the car toward Twin Gull Dunes. "How are you? I feel like I haven't seen you in forever."

"Or, like, Friday, when you gave me a ride home from school." My voice shakes, and she eyes me uncertainly.

"Not real, quality time," she says.

"No, definitely not." I clear the phlegmy rattle from my throat. "Is dropping out still on the table for you? Because I think we should consider that."

"Nah," she says. "The rumor mill suggests that creative writing class is draining Stephen Niequist's GPA, so I'm pretty much kicking his butt now. Anyway, what's going on, Junie? You look upset."

I chew on my bottom lip and shake my head. I don't know where to start: Saul, or the memories, or all the indescribable stuff in between. "Hannah."

Her eyes flicker to me. "Baby girl. What's wrong?"

Saul first. I don't understand how my heart can be moving so fast and fearfully while my stomach can feel so heavy and tight. "Can you pull over?"

"Sure." She swerves to the edge of the craggy asphalt.

I clear my throat again, bat my eyelashes dry.

"I need to tell you something because *not* telling you feels like lying."

"Okay," she says uneasily.

I blink back the sting in my eyes. "The reason I haven't wanted to go on those double dates isn't because I don't like Nate. And it's also not totally because of my family's problems with the Angerts."

Her hand flies to her chest. "Oh my god, did I do something?"

"No! No, Han." I swallow the tension bunching in my throat. "Okay, so that night at the carnival, when I met Saul, I guess . . . I was pretty into him."

Hannah laughs. "Of course you were! He's beautiful."

"Sure," I say. "But I don't just mean I noticed he was hot. You know he's not my type."

"He owns deodorant," she agrees.

"I was *really* into him, Hannah. Like into him enough that I didn't want to be around him because of my family, but also because I *knew* he was, like, your *forever crush*. And then you set up that tutoring session, and the more time I spent with him, the more I liked him. And I tried not to, because you're one of the most important people in my life, and I don't know how you feel, but I don't know how to turn this off."

Hannah drops her forehead onto the steering wheel and lets out a laugh.

"Hannah, I'm not joking."

"Nate and I made out!" she yelps, sitting up. Her entire face turns pink, making her blond hair look pearly in comparison. "Honestly, like, four separate times now. And I was going to tell you, but I was embarrassed, and I wanted to be sure how I felt."

"You made out. Four times. With Nate Baars."

"Don't say it like that!"

"Four times, like, for three minutes each?"

She gives me a reproachful look.

"Wow."

"I know."

"Wooow," I say. "So . . . not a full moon–induced fluke? You *like* Nate?"

She sighs. "I would go so far as to say I *really* like him."

I nod. "And . . . Saul?"

She snorts. "*You* were born to have chemistry with *dreamy* Saul Angert. *I* have been cursed to fall into Nate Baars's big, stupid mouth over and over again until I admit I don't even think it's that big! Or stupid!"

"You're seriously not upset with me?"

"Frankly, June, I'm annoyed you thought this would be a big deal. Am I so pathetic you thought I'd fall on my sword over you liking someone I've barely spoken to? I *had*—past tense—*had* a crush on Saul Angert like I had a crush on young James Dean, or Ryan Gosling. It's the kind of crush you share with the masses. If you called me and were like, *Hannah, young James Dean just brought a pizza to my door, do you think I should make out with him?* I would be like, *If you cut me, do I not bleed? What are you doing calling me at a time like this? Of course I want you to make out with him, and then I want you to call me and tell me everything."*

I shake my head. "Second of all, Saul was in your MARRY column."

"My *what*?"

"In your closet."

She dissolves into laughter and covers her face with her hands. "Oh my God, June! Damon Salvatore and Gilbert Blythe were on that list! What do you think of me?"

Now I crumble into laughter too. For the first time in twenty-four hours, the knot in my stomach loosens.

Hannah reaches across the center console and threads her fingers through mine. "You cannot imagine how loved and special it makes me feel that you were worried about this," she says. "I mean, it also sort of makes me feel like a choad. But mostly it makes me *miss* you, June."

I kiss my fingers, and she kisses her; we press them together, promising to get through anything, to still be best friends on the other side. "Forever," I say.

"Always," she agrees. She restarts the car but doesn't pull back onto the road right away. "Is this what had you all upset?"

Ping!

"Um." My voice wrenches upward, and I close my eyes. "Well. I also saw my Dad die?"

"What?"

"The Whites showed me," I say. I close my eyes for a long moment, until I'm steady enough to say the rest. "It wasn't a heart attack—at least not *just* a heart attack. Nameless killed him."

Emily Henry

"Oh my God. June," she says.

"It was terrible, Han." My voice shudders. "Dad was there, and then Nameless wrapped around him, and it was like suddenly he wasn't himself anymore. It was just his body, and I knew he was gone. I *felt* him leave."

"Oh, baby girl." Hannah folds me into her arms.

"They showed us some of Saul's sister's memories too," I murmur into her hair, and she sits back. "And some that belonged to strangers."

Her mouth quivers open, and her throat bobs. "Maybe the memories aren't at your house because they *happened* there but because of where your house is. On the thin place."

"Like they're coming back from . . . heaven?"

Hannah shrugs. "From somewhere. But there's no way you'd find your Dad's and Bekah's memories randomly, at least not more than once. *Something* must be bringing those memories to you specifically, right?"

When I finish telling her what I heard Dad say to Nameless, Hannah slumps in her seat, chewing on her lip. "June." She hesitates for a second. "If your dad *is* sending you these Whites, maybe . . ." She swallows hard, shaking her head. "Maybe it's a warning."

My stomach jerks within me. My vision splotches, and I dig my fingernails harder into my skin. *What if Nameless killed both Dad and Bekah? What if they're trying to warn us that Saul and I are next?* "Maybe," I whisper.

Hannah reaches across the car and pulls my hand into hers. "What do we do, June?"

168

I shake my head. I can think of only one thing, a thing I'm not sure I'm capable of doing again: going back into the Whites.

"I don't know yet," I answer.

"Well," Hannah says. "In the meantime, let's get our asses to the beach, lie in the sunlight, and smother you with love." She tries to smile. "You'll get through this, June. You shouldn't have to, but you will."

Eighteen

LIKE the first time I lost Dad, I'm surprised how quickly the white-hot pain fades into a gnawing ache. I've put ten years between me and that day, but today I feel eight again: mixed up, afraid of the world that once made me feel so loved, so safe.

The gaps of *forgetting* shorten until most of the time, a world without Dad is my new reality. Again.

All day at the beach, Hannah lets me talk things out. Tell stories about Dad that make me almost happy, slip back into crying, panic over the darkness that lurks in the woods, wander toward conversation about Saul and Nate and school.

I swear off the Whites then decide I *have* to keep investigating them a dozen times over.

Hannah's there with me as I settle into the rhythm of grief.

When I get home that night, I still haven't made a decision

about the Whites. I ignore the swarms in the windows and try to focus on my writing assignment.

I start, strike, and rewrite another one of Dad's stories, about the day he proposed to Mom. But thinking about the rich timbre of his laugh, the way he always leaned in when he told this story, the moments when he'd pause for dramatic effect—recalling each of these details makes me feel as if another nail is being driven through me, pinning me to the ground.

Like I'll never feel anything again except this invisible weight crushing my every inch.

Long after I've climbed into bed, my phone buzzes with an e-mail from Saul: *June.*

My blood turns to lava as I stare at it. I type a reply, *Saul*, but don't send it. Instead I stare until my phone light fades, then tap it back on and stare some more.

June.

Even if I'm not risking Hannah's friendship, the way I'm starting to feel about Saul *is* risking something. My whole life Dad told me to stay away from the Angerts, that *Bad Things happen when we cross paths*. It scares me how easy it's been to ignore all that since I met Saul.

But after what I saw yesterday, it's harder.

I close the message and think again of Dad's story, focus on it.

He'd been traveling a lot, and most recently he'd been in New Mexico when he saw smoke coming from a rounded summit to his north. He pulled his car over and left it on the scrubby side of the road as he wandered toward the stacks of soot, with nothing but the box of dried cherries he'd brought from home. He always took them when he traveled, partly because he could taste the sunlight on the lake in every bite and partly because, if he got a tickle in his throat or ache in his belly, he could swallow a few and wake up feeling good as new.

When he reached the bottom of the hill, everything was engulfed. The fire had raced quickly along the arms of dehydrated ponderosa pines to attack both cities at the base of the mountain. An overworked team of firefighters rushed around, trying to evacuate homes before the flames could stretch any farther, but there weren't enough of them. Dad set his box of cherries on a rock and dove in to help, ushering families to cars and buses. They worked tirelessly through the night, emptying the cities. Whenever they pulled a woman from a collapsed house, or dragged cats and dogs from flaming top floors, Dad returned to his box of cherries and gave a Jack's Tart to the injured, one bite miraculously healing their burns.

By morning they'd evacuated three hundred houses, and not a single person had died. Everyone was exhausted, ready to sleep when the bleary tangerine sun came up, but Dad had given out all his cherries and was tired in a different way, the kind that's run out of Home. So he got in his car and drove straight through the next day and night.

When he finally got there, he found Mom sitting at the kitchen table. Seeing her there made him homesick, even though he was back, like he realized right then how much time he'd lost with her and their farmhouse on the hill and had to catch up on all the *missing it* he'd forgotten to do while away.

Here's the thing about Dad, about all the Jacks: They're lake people, sponges. They have adventurous spirits but get restless when they're away from the water too long. Like Jonathan Alroy O'Donnell and his grandson Jack the First and great-grandson Jack II, Dad wanted to see the world, but he had to do it in spurts because he felt so wrong when he couldn't go stand at the edge of the lake and look out at the familiar way the sunlight bounced on its wriggling back. The cherries let him take the taste of home with him, but eventually, cherries got eaten and Jacks had to go home once again.

When Dad got back to Five Fingers and saw Mom at that table, the first thing he wanted to do was gather her in his arms and take her to the lake, so he could see his two loves side by side. It didn't matter that it was late January and the whole town was heaped in snow.

They climbed in his truck and drove to the falls, which had fully frozen over, turning the whole cave into a shimmering hall of ice. There, Dad got down on one knee and told Mom he would love her in warmth and cold, that she'd be as beautiful to him when she was old and cracking as she was when she was young and verdant; he would find something to love about her in every season of life, and he would always, always come home.

I loved the story as a kid. Dad told it to me all the time, and sometimes I asked Mom to too. She'd smile and say, "There are always at least two versions of everything, June. I've forgotten my own because I love your daddy's so much."

My daddy.

I start to cry.

Feathers wriggles at the foot of my bed, mourning or warning me or maybe simply being.

On Monday, the rest of the class turns in their poems to Ms. deGeest while I sit there empty-handed. When the bell rings and everyone files out of the room, I hang back, watching Ms. deGeest clean the board.

"I have a question," I say, and she turns around, swiping her hands together like she always does.

"All right. What's up, Junior?"

"I couldn't write it," I say. "I had an idea for a story, and I swear I tried, but I got stuck."

"You didn't turn anything in?"

"I was wondering if I could have an extension."

"I don't give extensions."

"Okay, well, will you at least read it when I *do* turn it in? I can take the zero—I don't care."

She's silent for a beat, her posture reminiscent of a hunting cat. "You shouldn't be okay with zeroes, Junior."

"Are you telling me to beg?"

"I'm telling you to do the work. I'll give you an extension this once, but here's what I'm going to do. I'm going to talk to the office and get your enrollment in this class re-designated as an independent study with me. You'll come here for both your study halls, so I know you're taking this seriously. And if you show up for the rest of the semester, I'm going to do two things: First, I'm going to write you an amazing recommendation letter that will at least partially explain your poor grades. Second, I'm going to talk to the principal about continuing your independent study into next semester. I'll use two of my planning periods each week to meet with you, and the other three you'll work silently in this room or the library. If you stop showing up, physically or mentally, I'll retract my recommendation, and I won't feel bad about it. Does that work for you?"

I stare, unsure what to say. *I'm not going to college? No letter of recommendation can make up for grades like mine? I want my study halls to be study halls?* Those are the things I would've said before this class, but that's not what comes out.

"That works."

She flashes a straight white smile. "Good. Close the door on your way out."

I'm distracted all night while I help Mom and Toddy cook dinner. While we're eating, Mom interrupts Grayson's dramatic retelling of a game they played at school to ask whether I'm feeling okay, and Toddy pushes back his chair to come feel my forehead.

"A little warm there, Junie," he says.

"I think I'll go lie down," I say.

"Do you feel sick?"

"A little." It's true. The thought of venturing back into memory nauseates me even as it pulls on me. What are the odds I'll see That Day again? Despite that risk, I need to see him. I need to understand what he knew about Nameless that Saul and I are missing.

Leave June alone. She's not like us. She won't be. I promise you. Leave her alone.

Shivers snake down my spine, and Mom reaches across the dinner table, worried, and touches my arm. "Take some ibuprofen, baby," she says. "It will help with the fever."

Upstairs, I slip my shoes off outside my bedroom, but there aren't any Whites in the doorway.

I scan the other doors at my disposal: Mom and Toddy's, Grayson and Shadow's, the bathroom—there, one lone White. I close the door to my bedroom so Mom and Toddy will think I'm sleeping if they check on me, then reach my hand out and let the White skate over me. It settles on my skin, and as it dissolves, I step into the bathroom.

The effect is immediate.

I'm downstairs in the dining room again, as though the hallways in my house got tangled and spit me out at the table. In this version of the dining room, it's late at night and the pink ghost ripples in the corner.

Dressed in pajamas and a long sweater, Mom sits at the table, her hand resting on the green corded phone she and Dad kept for posterity's sake well into my childhood. Her soft waves hang in a loose ponytail, and her eyes look puffy and wet. The wrinkles I'm used to seeing around her lips and eyes have vanished, and her cheeks are soft and round.

She stands and paces. Feathers follows her as she disappears around the corner into the sunroom. Everything stops, as it did in the forest—the crickets and cicadas falling silent, the whirring fan freezing. The drapes blowing inward from the moonlit windows pause. This memory is over.

A new White bobs against the doorframe Mom passed through.

I cup it, letting it take me through the doorway to another moment. I'm instantly back in the kitchen, seeing the exact same thing as before, only Mom's clothes are different and her hair hangs over her shoulders.

Again she stands and paces. Followed by Feathers, she turns and walks through the back door, pausing the memory. Again a single White waits for me.

I clasp it and follow.

I blink and find myself back at the entrance to the dining room.

The cycle repeats four more times, and every time I snap back into place beside the worn kitchen table, Mom looks more tired, her eyes a little pinker and puffier until finally she's sleeping with her head down against a place mat when there's a commotion down the hall.

Feathers recedes into the wall, and Mom lurches to her feet. She reaches for a knife from the block on the counter. Morning light spills through the front door as Dad comes down the hall. He stops, looks at Mom and the knife she's holding, then walks past and opens the refrigerator without a word.

"Where have you been, Jack?" she whispers.

"Went to New Mexico."

Mom sets down the knife and folds her arms around herself. "New Mexico?"

"I was thinking we could go see the ice caves this morning— what do you think, Le?"

Mom doesn't say anything at first. Dad smiles sort of sheepishly, and she says, "Okay."

"Get your coat." He grabs an apple from the fridge, swings it shut, and plants a kiss on Mom's forehead. She closes her eyes, the corners of her mouth tightening like metal twist ties. She pulls away and goes to the coat closet. I chase them through the front door, a White zipping to meet me there, to carry me away.

Across the threshold, I don't find myself in the yard. I'm in the cave again, and it's *exactly* how Dad described it: a wall of blue-green spears of ice stretching down to the snowy floor. The sun must be mostly up by now, because the whole place glitters as Dad circles it, running his hand along the icy wall. "Isn't it beautiful, Le?"

Mom stands with her hands in her coat pockets at the center of the cave. Dad glances at her. Shakily, she draws a folded piece of paper out and scrutinizes it. She holds it out to him.

Dad crosses to accept it. "What's this?"

"You know what it is, Jack."

"A plane ticket?" His voice sounds hollow. He storms away from her, then turns back. "Léa."

"You've been gone three weeks, Jack."

"I'm back."

"You didn't tell me where you were going or how long you'd be away." Her eyes cloud. "You left me there, alone, in your house, and I didn't know if you were coming back."

"I'm *back*," he repeats.

"How could you leave me there?"

"I don't know," he says. "I was confused."

"I miss my family," Mom says. "And now that your father's gone, there's no one here for me. When you're gone, I'm completely alone, and I can't keep doing that. I can't go through this again."

Dad starts to cry, hard. Harder than I would've thought possible, and Mom first looks stunned, then sad. She goes to him and draws his face up with her hands.

"I don't want to feel this way anymore," he says.

Mom's hands skim through his hair. "I know."

Dad drops forward onto his knees in the snow and buries his hands and face into Mom's stomach. "Marry me, Le."

She presses her fingers to her mouth, crying. "You know I can't."

Dad's eyes rove over her face. "I'll get help."

"Jack."

"I'll always come home," he promises. "I'll love you when I'm hot and when I'm cold. I'll love you as much as I do right now, forever, and I'll always, always come home."

"You know I can't say no," Mom cries into her hands. He stands, pulling her wrists down to cup her fingers between his.

"You can," he says. She twines her hands around his neck, nestling her face into the crook of his shoulder. "You don't have to believe me, but I'm going to get help. Whether you say yes or not. I don't want to live like this anymore. You can say no."

"Jack." Mom takes a deep breath. "I'm pregnant."

First his lips part. His eyes flick between her eyes and her mouth. A breathy laugh erupts from him. "You're pregnant?"

Mom nods, and Dad laughs again, which makes a smile stretch across Mom's teary face too. He grabs the sides of her face and kisses her. "You're pregnant."

"I'm pregnant."

And suddenly, they're happy. So happy they're laughing, so happy they're crying, but I can't breathe. Black splotches speckle my vision. Something heavy is pinned on my chest. The walls of ice are closing in.

This isn't how it happened. This isn't what I came from.

I wasn't the thing that made Mom stay. It was love, the thing that made me.

It was supposed to be love.

I stumble from the cave, collapsing against the frozen wall. I drag myself toward the shock of daylight. When I cross the threshold, I find myself back in the hallway outside my bathroom.

Laughter trickles up the stairs: Mom, Toddy, Grayson, Shadow. Happy, healthy, living.

I stagger into my bedroom, wheezing out hot tears. A shapeless dark writhes outside my window, watching me. "Why are you doing this to me?" I ask the house I once called magic. "Why are you haunting me?"

Nineteen

MS. DEGEEST looks up from the pages in her hand. She'd insisted on reading them immediately after class so we could discuss. My phone lights up with a message full of question marks from Hannah, who's waiting for me outside at our table.

Talking to deGeest, I type. *Be out ASAP but maybe wait inside just in case?* The temperature's hovering around forty degrees. We'll have snow by Halloween.

"You're going to be a phenomenal writer someday, Junior," Ms. deGeest says finally.

"Someday," I repeat.

"Don't get me wrong—it's good."

"Great. That seems worth not being able to look my mother in the eye."

"So this story is true?"

"Apparently. As of two nights ago, anyway." It had been

surprisingly easy to write, carried out of me in a rush of impotent anger I had nowhere else to exert.

She points a French-manicured finger at me. "You've nailed your problem. Sometimes, when we write about conflicts we're still in the middle of, we produce great emotion, strong feelings, but the technical aspects of the story fall to the wayside, because we don't understand the interconnectedness of all the elements of our own narrative yet."

"The interconnectedness?"

She opens the gray filing cabinet against the wall and pulls out one of those metal ball pendulums—a Newton's cradle, I think they're called. She sets it on the desk, lifts the metal ball on the right, and lets it drop, sending a shock wave through the three center balls that results in the far left ball swinging outward, then back in, where it sends the shock back again.

"I meant to use this for a lesson, but I totally forgot," she says. "Your work tends to create snapshots of powerful moments. But often it reads as a series of events. This happens, *and then* this, *and then* this, *and then* this. What we're looking for is: This happens, *therefore* this happens, *but then* this happens, *therefore* this happens.

"This scene you wrote works, but it might work better as part of a larger piece, once you're further off—when you can put things into perspective. I think you should consider working in the realm of fiction for a while. You can always come back to family history later."

"You don't know that," I say.

"Excuse me?"

"You don't *know* I can always come back. No one gets that guarantee. That's the whole point."

Ms. deGeest shakes her head. "The whole point of what?"

"That's why I have to piece this all together." I snatch the papers. "Because *usually*, when a person goes, the truth goes with him, and someday even the stories—the lies he told—are forgotten, and there's no way to recover them."

There's no way to recover *him*.

"Junior, wait!"

I'm already out the door.

"What's wrong?" Hannah asks as I brush past her.

"Everything," I choke. "It was all a lie, Hannah. He wasn't who I thought he was. I'm not who I've always thought I am."

Not the child of two adoring parents tragically ripped apart, but the child who made Mom stay when she should've left.

Not a house overlapping with heaven; an endless tunnel of bad memories.

Not a magic house, but a haunted one.

I'm a lie.

Hannah offers to take a night off from violin and studying to comfort me, but the look of trepidation on her face as she does is enough to make me decline. Instead, when she drops me off at home, I slip upstairs to "study," and spend the night staring at Feathers's lavalamp burbling.

What's one white lie when Mom and Dad lied to me my whole

life? I feel so stupid for everything I used to believe. Who thinks it's *normal* for her dad to be gone for weeks at a time with no phone calls, no texts, no postcards? How naïve do you have to be to convince yourself your mom doesn't mind that kind of instability, that she's happy with it?

Leave June alone. She's not like us. Leave her alone.

I wrap myself in blankets, but I'm still cold and shuddering. What did he mean? What does any of this mean?

"Some help you are," I whisper to Feathers, and she withdraws.

Minutes pass. Hours pass. The sun goes down and the moon glides up. The stars twinkle and the crickets sing, voices thin, starting to die off in the cold. Still I stare at my dead-starred ceiling, unable to get warm.

After what the Whites showed me in the ice cave, everything's different. If Dad's stories weren't true, that changes everything. Who he was. Who *I* am. What his rules mean.

Maybe that's what the Whites wanted me to see, what they started telling me the night Saul came back.

I shove aside thoughts of Nameless and open Saul's last e-mail: *June.* When I read it, I can hear his voice, warm and rattling and close. I see slivers of his teeth glowing in the dark, moonlight across the slight dent in his nose as he drove me down the forested lane, snatches of his hands cupped around his eyes as he looked at me through the extraordinary light of the sun on the waves in Bekah's memory of the beach that day. His dimple shadowed purple, his mouth moving silently inches from mine: *Hi.*

It's nearly two in the morning when I send my reply: *Saul.*

He answers immediately. *June, at last.*

I attach my last story and send a blank e-mail back. Twenty minutes later, my phone buzzes again. *It happened again? You saw this?*

Yeah, I answer.

Are you okay?

No.

I'm useless, but I'm here.

My pulse quickens and blood warms. I'm running out of reasons and willpower to avoid him. *Tomorrow?* I say.

What about it? You'll have to be more specific.

I wonder if we're the first people since 2001 to have a real-time conversation via e-mail.

I like how permanent it feels, he says, then a minute later: *So you're not going to clarify about "tomorrow"?*

Nah.

Yes to tomorrow, he says. *What time?*

I have to go to high school during the day, because I'm in high school. So after that.

Can you pick me up from the nursing home after?

> *No, you're the only old person I'm not afraid of. You come to me.*

June.

> *Saul.*

You're incorrigible.

> *How does it make you feel to know I just had to look that word up?*

It takes so long for him to respond that I'm almost asleep when I feel the vibration beneath my hand. *Strangely charmed/appreciative that you need a tutor.*

Twenty

AT lunch the next day, feeble sunlight lances through the cafeteria windows, striping Hannah's face, and wind thunks angrily against the glass as she asks suddenly, "Are you going to try to make it happen again? See another memory?"

"I don't know," I admit. "I'm so overwhelmed by all of this." She nods understanding, and I ask, "Do you think it's possible what I saw in the cave wasn't real? Like, maybe some kind of ancient mold has been giving me and Saul shared hallucinations."

Hannah twirls her hair. "June, this is Five Fingers. Coywolves ignore sleeping chickens to score Old Navy dollar-bin flip-flops, and I've run through a feathery ghost, and once when we were playing hide-and-seek in the woods, I swear I saw my Grandma Ortiz climbing a tree. I mean, that woman moved at a nebbish shuffle the last five years of her life and there she was, hair ten shades darker and dressed in overalls, perched in a branch twenty-five feet off the ground. When I got to the tree? Gone.

"I'm sorry, babe, but the question isn't whether this is happening. It's *why*. You need to figure out what the memories are trying to tell you."

"That my life has been a lie?"

Hannah swishes her mouth back and forth. "Your life hasn't been a lie. I mean, my parents married for love and my dad *still* cheated and moved to Colorado and waited three months to so much as e-mail me. Your dad never would've done that. He never would've left you or your mom willingly."

"He did all the time."

"No," Hannah says sharply. "He always came back." She examines her tray. "Maybe that's what he wants you to know. That's a pretty good message from the afterlife, as far as messages from the afterlife go."

"I thought maybe it was about the Angerts," I say. "Like he, or *someone*, wanted me to forget about the feud."

Hannah nods thoughtfully. "You *did* say it started the night you met Saul."

She shakes her head once, and I can guess what she's thinking. That theory doesn't explain what I saw happen with my dad and Nameless.

She's not like us. Leave her alone. Please show her.

After school Hannah puts off her psych research to come over. We wander the house barefoot for an hour and a half, searching for Whites with no results.

"Your magic house doesn't like me as much as Saul," she groans. "I've never felt so betrayed."

"It's kind of a bitch. Don't feel bad."

"Why do you keep looking at the clock?" Hannah asks.

"I don't."

"Do too. What's the—" Hannah grins. "Ah."

"Just a tutoring session. I can reschedule."

"Stop," she says. "I have a violin lesson anyway."

"Oh, is *that* what you're calling Nate? And how is 'violin'?"

Her cheeks dimple. "Ridiculous. Still pestering me about camping at the dunes with you and his cousin."

"Wow."

"Acclimated to the idea yet?" she says. "Keep trying. Anyway, he asked me to be his girlfriend."

"Seriously?"

"First he asked me to prom. Then he remembered homecoming comes first, and he asked me to that, and then he got nervous and asked me out for real."

"What'd you say?"

"We'll see about prom, yes to homecoming, and let's talk about making it official *after* homecoming."

"Hannah!" I shake her elbow. "Nate Baars!"

"He's great. He's so different than he comes off. I think he gets nervous or something. He's actually kind of shy, and super sweet, and he just, like . . . *likes* people."

"Weird."

"I know, right? Anyway, I feel like he's kind of *rare*. I just don't know if I want a boyfriend this year. Seems like an unnecessary complication."

"Maybe."

"I don't want to get so swept up that I blink and it's time to leave, and I've hardly seen you. I already feel like I've done that with schoolwork, and those are weeks of weekends I'll never get back."

"You're not going to lose me, Hannah. Not to Nate, not to school, not to anything."

Not even to a curse, I silently vow.

"Same," she promises.

Mom comes in then, the boys whipping past her straight toward the fridge. "Hey, Hannah!" she sings, giving her a squeeze around the shoulders. "Haven't seen much of you lately. What are you girls up to tonight? Do you want to come to Shadow's basketball game with us?"

Shadow looks over his shoulder at us and blushes shyly at Hannah. He's had a crush on her since he was born. "Oh, man, I'd love to," Hannah says. "But I have a paper to write, and I think June has tutoring?"

"Hey, Mom, did you know Mike has tattoos but he's not trying too hard?" Grayson calls, popping open a can of Mountain Dew he definitely does not need.

"I did not, *mon chou*." Mom closes the fridge. "And though we would never get tattoos, it's none of our business that Mike did, right?"

Grayson runs toward the TV. "I'd get them. They're cool."

Mom shoots Hannah and me an *Oh, brother!* look. "Gray, there's no time for video games. We have to be back at school in an hour. Wash your hands and get ready for dinner." Grayson whines, and Mom turns back to us. "And, Junior, please stay in the living room or sunroom while Mike's here, okay? I'm not terribly comfortable having him here while Toddy and I are out."

"*Mom*," I say.

"Junior, please."

"I *will*."

As soon as she's out of earshot Hannah looks at me and says, "Or *don't*."

Saul shows up fifteen minutes before my family leaves for Shadow's game, and Mom and Toddy are *thrilled* to hear he wants to take me to the library. I get the feeling Toddy had planned to (attempt to) veto Mom's decision to let us have an unsupervised tutoring session and is relieved he doesn't have to play bad cop after all.

Saul's wearing long sleeves again, which I'm fairly sure I catch Mom trying to x-ray for signs of tattoos, but at least the cutting fall wind justifies his clothing choice this time. I, for my part, am doing my best to act politely indifferent to my tutor, instead of like my brain is filling with shooting stars at the sight of him. As horrible as our last day was together, I can still feel the ghost of his arms around me, his hands in my hair.

"What's at the library?" I ask.

"Books, June," he says, then curbs the flirtation in his voice by adding, "I reserved some stuff on craft I think you'll find helpful."

It doesn't matter that my parents and the boys are running late: Toddy fuddles in the kitchen "looking for a snack" until Saul and I are safely out the door. It's mostly dark out, and the grass crunches

Emily Henry

with a hint of frost as we make our way to the Saturn. Around the cherry tree, the sprouts Grayson and Shadow planted last week have grown to about a foot tall, stringy but vibrant.

"Books on craft," I say.

"Some," Saul replies. "Mostly books on thin places."

"And with your rigorous schedule you couldn't get them ahead of time?"

His ears turn the tiniest bit pink, and he scratches his jaw as we pull away. "You seem a little bit freaked out every time I come over," he says. "I mean, *not* by the magic stuff."

"I have been," I admit.

"Yeah."

I want to say, *I'm not anymore.* It's not quite true. In some ways, I'm more freaked out than ever. Seeing a more complete picture of my father may have freed up my opinions on the Angerts, my feelings for Saul, but it has also fundamentally changed who I've always believed I am.

I am a Jack, my father's daughter. All my life people have told me they see Dad in me, and now that means something different than it used to. My blood feels heavy in my veins.

I want to forget who I am.

I don't want to be a Jack. I want to be just June.

"We can go back to my house after we pick up the books," I say. "My parents will literally not do a thing."

"I want them to like me," Saul replies.

They won't, no matter what, I want to tell him, so we might as well break all the rules.

We park outside the library and run through the shrieking cold and skittering leaves to the door. Past the circulation desk, we find the shelves where they keep reserved books, trailing along the *A* surnames to *Angert*. Saul pulls out five books rubber-banded together and tagged with his name, and he passes me a couple before leading the way through the warmly lit stacks.

We turn down an aisle toward the study tables, and a blond girl in a houndstooth peacoat straightens from where she was crouched beside the bottom row and turns toward us. Saul stops short.

"Saul," Ms. deGeest says. "I wondered when I'd run into you."

"Allison," Saul says. "Hi. I didn't know you'd moved back."

"Yeah, a few months ago." She grabs his arm and gives a dazzling smile before her sharp blue eyes wander to me and try to blink either me or her confusion away. "Junior. Hi."

Her expression moves from puzzled to shocked understanding in four-tenths of a second. "You guys *know* each other." She looks pointedly at Saul. "Junior's in my creative writing class at the high school. She's a super bright kid."

"Oh," Saul says. "Cool. Yeah, June's talented."

Allison deGeest half-laughs, folds her arms across her chest, and shakes her head to toss her hair over her shoulder. "Yeah, *June's* great."

"Okay, we should get back to work," I say.

"Oh, are you tutoring her?"

For a second she seems to consider this a real possibility, but then Saul says, "Not tonight. Great to run into you, Allison. Have a good night."

"We should meet up." Her eyes dip toward me. "If you have time."

"Sure," Saul says. He steers me toward the study tables again. "So that's a high school friend of mine, Allison, who is a little bit terrifying and also your teacher now."

"I've never heard my own name sound so crude."

"Yeah, well, what can I say? I'm drawn to laid-back, un-snarky girls."

"Drawn to?"

A heavy smile tugs at his mouth. "Are you asking me something, June?"

"I wasn't going to."

"You can."

"Isn't she a little old for you?"

His laugh rattles in his throat. "She was the older sister of a friend. There was a brief . . . *thing*."

"Oh god. This is so . . . you and Allison deGeest?"

"June, come on. Local legend has it you once kissed Nate behind a slide."

"First of all, remembering that will never be any source of comfort to me. Second of all, is Nate responsible for your future? Does he give you grades, and if so, on what?"

Saul's forehead inclines toward me imploringly. *"June."*

"Can we leave now? I think the back of my head is two seconds from bursting into flames."

"It's not you," he says, blushing. "I mean, she's probably worried about you. I didn't have a great reputation back then. Also she thinks of me as her peer and you as her student."

"Ugh."

He gives one scratchy laugh. "Sorry. That was weird."

"Let's just go." We're silent for the length of the ride home. Saul keeps looking over at me, and I'm reminded of the night he drove me home from the theater. Maybe the reality of running into his former *whatever*, who also happens to be my teacher, has brought him back to where he was that night: feeling a little pathetic. Anxiety wrings my insides, and an ache of disappointment, embarrassment, and jealousy radiates low in my stomach.

Saul and the closest thing I have to a mentor.

Maybe this is the universe's last-ditch effort to separate two fatally star-crossed people before their collision destroys everything around them.

The image of the darkness closing in around Dad sizzles across my mind. *Leave her alone.*

No matter what the universe has to say about it, Saul and I can't walk away until we understand the Whites' message. *Their warning.*

When we get home, we spread the books along the coffee table. Some center around Celtic mythology, others the musings of Catholic priests on places where miracles happened. A couple of collections of essays investigate buildings and natural landmarks where the veil between heaven and earth is so flimsy the authors accidentally passed through and the world transformed before their eyes.

"We can start with reading and then try some Whites, or we can do the opposite," Saul says. "Preference?"

"Reading." I'm still sick over the last two memories I saw. Still so confused and frustrated with Dad that I can't imagine facing him, though his words loop endlessly in my mind. *She's not like us. Leave her alone. Please show her.*

We can't put off the past forever. Tonight, I want to pretend we can.

Saul and I each pick a book and sit on the couch, backs propped against opposite ends, knees bent up and facing each other in the middle. I start skimming *Thin Places: Transformed by the Edge of Heaven* only to fall immediately into a Saul/Ms. deGeest spiral. I don't notice I'm drumming my fingers against the back of the couch until Saul sets his hand on them. "That's fairly distracting," he whispers.

"Saul," I whisper.

"June."

"Did I end up making you feel like a creep?"

He laughs. "Why would I feel like a creep?"

"You want me to say it?"

He looks at me. It's Serious Saul, not Flirting Saul. "Kind of."

"Because you like me, and I'm a *super bright kid*."

He glances at the book propped against his knees. "I don't."

"Oh-kay."

"I don't feel like a creep," he clarifies. After a few lapsed seconds, he says, "Anything else?" I shake my head, and he goes back to reading. I turn my hand over, and Saul's fingers trace slowly up my palm, then fall into the gaps between my fingers. He looks up again, and after a moment, his body shifts with a tired laugh. "I can leave, if you want."

Neither of us moves, though, and the silence stretches indefinitely. My stomach feels like it's slowly filling with lava, warm and thick, piling toward my throat.

"Okay," Saul says finally, standing. "Okay." I follow him toward the door, but he stops by the sunroom and faces me. "I do like you." He rubs his jaw anxiously. "I don't know if I said that part."

The heat has fully flooded my stomach, my chest, my esophagus. It's found its way through my legs. Beyond the open windows, owls hoot, the wind bats the trees, and a sudden vacuum has seemingly opened, sucking the universe and its many obstacles between Saul Angert and me from the house.

"I meant to," he says. "But in case I didn't," he nods, "I do."

I mean to say, *I like you.*

I manage only: "Oh."

Saul laughs and scratches at the back of his head. He turns to leave, and I grab his hand, tugging him into the dark sunroom, out of sight from the front door. He stares at me, so still he must be holding his breath. Or waiting for lightning to strike us. I touch his waist.

He touches my elbows. "June?"

"Saul?"

He draws me closer, a sliver of smile beginning in the corner of his mouth. "I'm worried you don't realize this isn't the way out."

"It's not?"

"The other thing is"—he takes the sides of my neck gingerly in his hands—"I'm getting sort of mixed signals here, so I want to clarify: What should I be doing right now?"

I knot my fingers into his shirt and step into him. "I like you, Saul. If you're on a roll, you can keep talking, or you can stop and kiss me."

His laugh is warm and coarse. His mouth is warm and coarse.

Twenty-One

SAUL'S laugh is still grating through him when his mouth catches mine. It travels through my cheeks and my stomach, hips, and fingers.

His hands slide around my back, catching bare skin and conjuring goose bumps as he pulls me closer in increments of millimeters. It's possible I've spent my whole life flexing every muscle in my stomach and now, relaxing for the first time, I might liquefy.

His arms tighten as he steps me back to the wall and presses his mouth, unhurried and deliberate, against my throat. His palms climb down my hips and thighs, back up to my neck like they can't sit still, and I don't want them to.

We're both a little clumsy, and I keep laughing because he feels so good. His smile widens, and our teeth bump together, but neither of us cares. The warmth of his stomach melts into my skin, but he's still too far away. His hands skim my back, press into my legs, rise up; they circle my waist beneath my shirt and settle at the bottom of my ribs, fingers gliding along the grooves between them.

He kisses me again, for the span of four sharp heartbeats, and when he pulls away, his hair is *almost* messy. He lifts my wrist and kisses the inside of it. "Are you going to disappear again?"

"What do you mean?"

"Will it be days before I hear from you?"

"It depends what grade I get on my next story."

"June."

"No, Saul. It won't be days."

He folds his arms around my waist and draws my stomach into his. "Now all we have to do is figure out how to navigate a thin place and tell your parents."

"No problem. I'll write them a note: *Dear Mom and Toddy, My tutor and I made out in the sunroom. Here is a diagram indicating which wall and pieces of furniture you should consider burning. Best wishes.*"

His laugh turns into a pseudo-groan as he slides his hands down my legs. "Maybe we should start by telling them my real name."

"God, sometimes you can be such a *Mike*."

He rolls his thumb across my bottom lip thoughtfully, then sinks into me again, his teeth skating across my lip. At the front of the house, the door whines open, keys jangle, and a jumble of voices flood inside.

Saul and I run into the living room and toss ourselves onto opposite couches, swiping books off the coffee table as my family's parading in.

"Shadow won!" Grayson shouts, storming toward us. "Hey, Mike, do you want to play video games?"

Saul looks at me, smirking, and adjusts the book over his lap. "I think I need to get home. Can I play next time?"

"I did *not* win." Shadow tromps in. "I *scored*, but my team lost."

Scored, Saul mouths at me, and I badly hide a laugh within a cough. "Well, at least you did well, right, bud?"

"Next time's fine, Mike!" Grayson shouts over his shoulder as he turns the TV on.

Mom and Toddy filter in last, slowly appraising the situation. "Back from the library already, huh?" Toddy says.

"Too loud," I say without looking up.

"I hope that's okay." Saul looks over the back of the couch into the kitchen. His ears don't even flush pink. "I thought it might be less distracting here."

"Yeah," Mom says vaguely. "So, you guys had fun?"

"Mhm," I murmur into my hand, then turn the page. "Studying's a blast."

Saul stands and lifts his backpack. "Read as much as you're able, and let me know when you want to meet up again."

"Yep," I reply. "Thanks for your help."

Somehow, that's the thing that makes his ears color.

"Thank you, Mike," Mom says.

"Get home safe," Toddy allows.

"Good night," Saul says.

Five minutes after he leaves, I close my book, pick the stack up, and announce I'm going to bed. I haven't even started my writing assignment for tomorrow, but I decide to put it off until study hall and climb into bed. Five minutes after that, I get Saul's first e-mail.

Felt a little bit more like a creep once I was trying
to escape without accidentally teaching your little
brothers about boners. I hope you're not reading this
in the midst of giving a birds-and-the-bees talk.

No, I type out, *my mom thought it would be best if you gave that lecture yourself. P.S. What's a boner? Asking for a friend.*

Are you hitting on me, June? And if so, can I have
your phone number?

Yes and yes.

I'm so happy I'm grinning into my pillow. I'm so happy the feeling can't fit in my body.

And then, out of nowhere, it happens. Something pink glistens in the corner of my room and—

Ping: My dad's dead.

Ping: He might be trying to tell me something from beyond the grave.

Ping: I never really knew him.

Ping: There's a dark, writhing, nameless thing that watches my house.

This is how grief works. It watches; it waits; it hollows you out, again and again.

My classmates pour out of the creative writing room as the bell rings, but I hang back. Stephen is packing his things with the speed of a geriatric sloth, and I offer him five bucks to pick up the pace.

"Twenty if you keep your best friend from ruining my best friend's life," he retorts.

"Han's not going to ruin Nate's life. She likes him."

"She also likes Stanford. Which do you think she'll choose, Junior?"

"Stanford? Hannah's not looking at Stanford," I say. "That's in California." She's looking at schools in the area. Maybe not the *immediate* area, but within a bearable drive: University of Michigan, University of Chicago, Northwestern.

Stephen's eyebrows flick upward. "If you say so." He pulls his books into his chest and walks out, leaving me alone with the person I least want to talk to.

"Ms. deGeest," I stammer. "Can I talk to you for a second?"

She faces me and rests her fingers on the tabletop. "If it's about your writing or this class, of course."

"It's about my *future* in this class, and whether it exists." Not that it really matters, since I didn't end up turning anything in today.

She nods. "I'm an adult, Junior."

I stifle my laugh too late. "Okay."

She winces. "I meant, I'm a *professional*. My offer stands."

"Wait, really?"

"June." She shifts uncomfortably against the edge of the table. "June, your personal life isn't my business. I just want you to hear me say this: *You're talented*. And I know you and Saul Angert have similar interests, and you're both clever and capable, and you've been through similar situations, but your life's just beginning. You have every opportunity in the world ahead of you. People from this town have a habit of sticking around, but if any part of you wants to try college, you should pursue it. And Saul—he's not here to stay. Once he gets back on track, this town won't be enough for him. Don't give yourself a reason not to reach your potential. Especially not a reason that's temporary."

I swallow a knot. "Is that all?"

"That's all," she says. "I want you to consider what you want from life."

I walk, stunned, into the library, where Hannah and Nate are making out. I pass them without a word to let them wrap things up, but Hannah calls, "See you!" to Nate and jogs after me. "How was claaaaass?"

"Good. My teacher told me not to date Saul."

"Wait, what? Is there any context for this?"

"Oh," I say. "That's the best part. They had a *thing* in high school."

"No," Hannah gasps, latching on to my arm. "Junie, that's awful. So she was, like, trying to stake a claim?"

"I don't think so. She basically told me Saul shouldn't keep me from going to college, and she also implied I'm his quarter-life-crisis booty call. Apparently this town isn't enough for people like Saul." *Like you, Hannah*, I think, tears springing into my eyes. "Once they're on track, they'll get out of here and leave the rest of us behind."

"Hey." Hannah yanks me to a halt outside the front doors. It's freezing and semi-dark, all the school's windows either aglow with light or blue and glare-streaked by the street lamps. "Maybe you are Saul's quarter-life crisis, but so what? Maybe he's yours. Or maybe you two are the luckiest people in the world and you've already found your fireworks-in-the-sky, holding-hands-until-you-die Forever Person. Guess what? There are drawbacks either way.

"Maybe you break up and it sucks, but then you heal and move on and fall in love again. Or maybe this is it, the last person you'll ever have butterflies for, your last first kiss, but you get to grow up together, start your life together sooner. And you know what else? You don't have to be afraid to walk away either way, because *you*, Jack O'Donnell IV, are amazing and my best friend, and there's no expiration date on soul-love. And if you and I want to go away to college, dammit, we're going to go away to college, and it's *not* going to stand in our way of finding love or happiness, and it's definitely not going to amount to *leaving each other behind*. We need to chase our dreams, Junie, and I don't know about you, but in my best and brightest dreams, you're *always* there."

There are tears in Hannah's eyes, and she doesn't blink them away. And then I'm crying too, because it hits me, hard. The words crack as they pass through my lips: "You're gonna move to California, aren't you?"

Hannah wraps her arms around me, and we stand there in the parking lot, crying, holding on to each other. "You're my first great love," she tells me. "I won't lose you."

"I don't know how to be without you."

"You won't be. Not really. Never."

I want to believe that, but I can't. No one is forever.

Twenty-Two

I wake to a tickling on my face as Feathers floats over me toward the window, a tangled blob of warmth and sadness. The clock glows green: *4:44.*

She ripples there, beckoning me, and I stand to look across the yard. Dimly illuminated Whites thread through the cherry tree's branches and bounce against the window frame.

Feathers seems to nod, a gentle *Go on.*

"I don't want to," I tell her.

Her warbling seems to say, *I know.*

"I have to. Don't I?"

She bobs.

I slide the pane up, and three Whites alight on the veins near my wrist. They melt like snow, and Feathers drifts toward the hall.

I follow her downstairs and out the back door, the world

changing infinitesimally when I step through. It could almost still be tonight, except for Dad.

Alongside the ache to be cradled by him, I feel a brutal, helpless frustration I can't exert anywhere. He's younger than when I saw him in the ice cave, no older than twenty-five, the patchy scruff I'm accustomed to seeing on his jaw shaved clean and his hair swept neatly back.

He sits in a lawn chair beside an older man with the same wide mouth and square jaw, his body spotted with age and sun damage. The man is staggeringly tall, but something about the slump of his shoulders makes him look insubstantial.

My grandfather Jack II. I've seen pictures but never met him. He died months before my parents got engaged.

Dad didn't talk about him much, except to say he was a Jack, that he craved adventure but always came home, was quiet but brave. He probably meant *absent*, an abandoner.

Mom's reviews of Jack II were mixed. Sometimes when Dad talked about him, she'd stab her broccoli extra hard or go from casually wiping the counter to scrubbing a spot no one else could see. But other times she'd stare out the window over the kitchen sink and say, "We all do our best. God rest his soul."

I asked her once, when Dad wasn't around, whether she liked Jack II. "He loved your father" was all she'd said. "I believe that."

Now he sits in front of me, sallow, drawing a cigar to his square, O'Donnell mouth for a puff. "Winter's coming," Dad says. Jack II exhales.

They're silent awhile. "You gonna marry that girl or just let her live in my house forever?" Jack II says gruffly.

Dad studies him. "I love Léa."

Jack II coughs, never once looks at Dad. "Then you're as stupid as I thought. A girl like that won't be happy here."

Dad watches Jack II for a long minute, then stands and goes inside. My grandfather stares at the ground. He throws the half-smoked cigar down and stamps it out, then pushes to his feet, his hulking form still hunched, and looks into the kitchen through the back window. Inside, Dad pulls Mom into a waltz, the gold light splashing across her teeth, throwing rusty streaks through her hair. He spins her, dips her low.

When he pulls her close, he sings in her ear. There's no sign on his face of the conversation he just had.

I never saw them like this, never saw them dance.

My grandfather's eyes are glassy, his fists clenched. He looks over his shoulder at the woods. A darker-than-dark blemish billows there. "You're always there, aren't you?" Jack II whispers. "You'll never let me go, I know that. But what about my boy?"

The memory ends.

Twenty-Three

"YOU know what we should do?" Hannah says, sprawled out on my bed.

"Duct tape the boys' mouths shut," I guess. Downstairs, my parents are helping Grayson host a slumber party, and a half dozen voices keep sprinkling our conversation with screams of bloody murder.

When I messaged Saul this morning about what Jack II said to Nameless, he'd been eager to pass back through the thin places—*figure this out* and *maybe take a break to redecorate the sunroom*, he wrote—but a spontaneous Friday-night tutoring session would definitely raise a red flag for my parents, so Hannah and I decided to hang out instead.

"Duct tape, absolutely," she agrees. "*And* I think you and I should go to homecoming together."

"What about Nate?"

208

"We could go as a group, but you'd be my date. We'd get each other corsages and coordinate our dresses and mostly dance together. Halfway through we could get into a screaming fight, and you could throw punch in my face or whatever."

"Let's be real, Han. If one of us is going to get face-punched, it'll be me."

"True," she allows. "Isn't it weird how Stephen and Nate are like the boy versions of us?"

"What do you mean?"

"Think about it. Stephen is, like, this shy bookworm type, and Nate is, like, a little louder, smart but uninterested in school, pretty content with Five Fingers."

"Oh my God, *I'm* Nate in this scenario?"

"Hey!" Hannah throws a pillow at me. "That's my kind-of boyfriend you're talking about! And it's not like I'm thrilled to be Stephen—my *arch*nemesis."

"Oh, whatever. You guys love competing with each other."

"Anyway, if you were planning on taking Saul to homecoming, I get it."

"Only if Ms. deGeest is chaperoning. I want this dance to be as awkward as possible," I say. "No, I'm all yours for homecoming. Anyway, I'm pretty sure last year they made it a rule that your date's not allowed to be older than nineteen."

"Oh, that's *right*," Hannah says. "There's always that *one* girl with, like, a forty-five-year-old boyfriend she met at the Fry Shack."

"Barf. About the guys, not the Fry Shack. The Fry Shack is the best restaurant of all time."

"True." Hannah's phone chirps, and she smiles enormously as she checks it. "You know, I think my favorite parts of life are the things I didn't know I wanted."

Ping! Your father was a liar. Ping! Everything you thought you were and wanted to be was based on a person who didn't exist. Ping! You're just like him.

Hours later, Grayson and the boys settle down, and the house quiets. Hannah and I climb into bed and turn off the light, whispering a list of our favorite things back and forth: corn mazes and pumpkin carving; picnics on the frozen lake; walks through the rainy woods and tulip fairs and cherry festivals and lying in the sun; getting tipsy on coconut rum and Diet Coke; houseplants and sunny kitchens; blueberry salads and goat cheese and deep-fried pickles; falling in love; kissing and sometimes more; sunsets and fog and jumping into the deep crystalline teal of the lake; laughing until our stomachs hurt, until we cry, until we can't breathe; and the water itself, always the water.

Hannah's breathing falls into a peaceful rhythm, and I'm left alone to stare at the ceiling. My phone illuminates with a text, and I tip it up to read.

Has your magic house mentioned anything about giving you a doorway to me? Saul says.

House isn't that nice. Why do you only text me at two in the morning? Am I your quarter-life crisis?

Two A.M. is when I lose all my inhibitions and say

*yes to everything I want. I also just ate a shit-ton of
Taco Bell.*

Ah, I'm in good company then.

> *It's also about twenty minutes after New York
> Times best-selling novelist Eli Angert stops watching
> the Game Show Network and goes to bed. And I
> think I'm having less of a quarter-life crisis and
> more of a "my dad keeps forgetting my mom left him
> and my sister's gone" crisis, and if you're entangled
> in that it's only because you're you and I'm me and I
> want you.*

You know what I have, besides a magic house, Saul?

> *What?* he asks.

*A magic forest that stretches from my door all the
way to yours.*

> *Are you asking me to meet you, June?*

I steer my thoughts away from the last time I walked those
woods, searching for the ever-moving tree. I focus on the beautiful moments instead, the day Dad carried me through the rain and
stretched out my hand to catch a White in the branches.

But even that day is tinted differently now. Dad wasn't who I thought he was; knowing that rewrites every memory I have of him.

I'm asking you to try, I type. *Meet me at O'Dang! Don't wear shoes.*

Immediately.

I roll out of bed, stuff my feet into slippers, and creep downstairs to the coat hooks beside the door. I pull a scarf and coat on over my pajamas and step outside.

A coywolf hunches beyond the porch, eyes flashing, a sentry guarding a tear in the veil. I shed my slippers and set them on the bottom step.

Maybe I could toss them inside and it would work the same— but if I'm asking the land to take me to Saul, maybe I shouldn't be stingy.

The coywolf slinks forward, bows to take the slippers, and dashes off in a blur of silver and red. I hurry past the cherry tree and its circle of growing saplings to the woods beyond the yard, tearing my mind from blue hydrangeas and inky ghosts.

I step through the first row of eastern pines, and sunlight splashes over everything, the sounds of night breaking open for the song of morning.

It looks *exactly* how it did whenever Dad and I went to O'Dang!

Mist floats in clumps, and jays flit between branches, calling to one another. Ahead, I spot the coywolf trotting toward a shoe pile. She drops the slippers and disappears into the brush.

"Thanks," I say as her tail disappears. I'm surprised to hear my voice until I remember this isn't a memory trapped in a White. It's the same mysterious forest we used to explore. In this impossible thin place where the sun can shine in the middle of the night, I'm as solid as the birds and squirrels who watch me but don't scatter.

There's no path to follow, no right way to get where I'm going. Soon I turn a corner around a mossy boulder, and there it is: O'Dang!

Saul's staring up at the mammoth branches and the bits of ribbon and string and flags tied all over them. Sunlight pours through the leaves and dapples the sleepily dancing Whites, revealing billions of veins and wrinkles.

"Hi," I say.

Saul turns and smiles. "I can hear you."

"I can hear you."

He's dressed in the clothes he wore the night we met, minus shoes. He looks different, his details more pronounced, now that I know his face. He makes the leaves twirling in the breeze seem sparklier, the birds bouncing between dew-laden branches happier.

"You found me," he says.

"Jacks have an excellent sense of direction." *Ping! They're used to leaving.*

"Look what *I* found." Saul's fingers run over one of the thousands of carvings in the trunk, words etched into a living, breathing thing: O'DONNELL + ANGERT.

"Aw, we have a tree together?"

"Well, we share it with a bunch of other losers, but yeah, it would seem so."

"I don't understand. Does this mean another O'Donnell and another Angert came here? *Before* our families hated one another?"

"I'm a little annoyed," he says. "We were supposed to be the first to have a forbidden relationship." His eyes trail back to me, making my heart speed. "Why do you think we can hear each other right now?"

"It's not a memory," I say. "I think it's a place where the thin place is *even thinner*. Like it sort of exists in both places, sometimes."

Saul nods thoughtfully at the hundreds of Whites crawling over the branches. "Maybe they're coming back from the other side. Maybe all the magic—the coywolves, the Whites, the ghosts—all slip through here from . . . the *other* side."

I swallow a knot. "Hannah said that too. That maybe Dad's and Bekah's memories were coming back from the afterlife because of the thin place."

Saul brushes at the trunk. "One of my library books talked about a Scottish town with an old bridge. In the last fifty years, fifty dogs have leaped off it. People think it's a thin place."

"Because dog suicide screams *pathway to heaven*?"

"Well, *some* townspeople think it's haunted, like something bad happened there and the memory was preserved, and animals pick up on it. But the optimists think maybe the dogs are chasing something to the other side, to something people can't see."

"Dogs don't wear shoes," I point out.

Saul laughs. "I guess that could explain it. Maybe they wandered into some other place when they crossed the bridge, but their bodies were still physically with the owners? I don't know—most of the thin places I've read about are cathedrals Jesuit priests take pilgrimages to, or natural landmarks where artists experienced inspiration. Believe it or not, the books don't have much about dead relatives sending messages via memory-spheres."

"It *has* to be them though, right?" I say. "Trying to warn us about the dark ghost—" Something stirs in my periphery.

My lungs catch.

We're not alone. A barefoot girl stands in the distance, watching us.

Saul follows my gaze to her. She's dressed in a butter-yellow dress, her coppery hair tangled over her shoulders and crowned by a flutter of downy Whites.

It takes me a moment to place her as the girl from the cave.

Her stare worms into my chest as she lifts her hand.

"She sees us," Saul whispers.

"It's not a memory." I lift my voice: "Hello?"

The girl turns. She begins to hum as she wanders along a stripe of sunlight. "Wait a second!" Saul calls.

Her gaze snaps back to us *"Hurry,"* she says, grabbing either side of her skirt. She takes off running into the woods.

We sprint after her, through low-hanging branches and thorny brush. "Wait!" I scream.

"June!" Saul calls from behind me.

I lose her around a bend, then catch a flash of strawberry blond cresting a ridge ahead. "Who are you?" I shout, suddenly sure the memory we saw of her was neither random nor accidental.

We're almost out of the woods now—I can see the bare expanse, the steep hill slowing the girl. I burst through the edge of the woods and come up short.

A White must have jerked me away.

I'm in a dimly lit bar packed with bodies and lazy music. It's sweltering hot, thatched fans spinning overhead and plastic ones plugged into every outlet around the narrow wooden-floored room. The breeze does nothing to prevent the sweat dripping down shoulders and foreheads and the necks of beer bottles. There's supple laughter, silky conversation.

From the bar, Dad watches the ebb and flow on the crowded dance floor. He looks younger than I've ever seen him, smooth-faced with hair that manages to be both short and messy. He absentmindedly spins his damp bottle, eyes following a woman with shoulders so tan they make her white halter top glow, and dark curls that stick with sweat to the edges of her round, lovely face.

Mom looks young and playful, gorgeously inelegant, blissfully sunlit, and little more than a teenager. The man she's dancing with whispers something in her ear that makes her throw her head back in laughter. Her reply gets lost in the music coming from the jukebox in the corner. As the song ends, they part ways, Mom shaking his hand and coming to lean across the bar beside Dad. His beer suddenly absorbs his attention.

Miami, I realize. *Where Mom used to live. Where she and Dad met. Is this when it happened?*

"You know," she says to him. "The staring would've been less unsettling if you'd spoken to me."

"That would've depended on what I said," Dad answers.

Mom turns to rest her elbow on the bar. "Would you have said something unsettling? You should know I'm friends with everyone in this bar. You would've been pulp."

Dad takes a swig, and a rivulet runs down his throat. "I wouldn't have said *anything*. That's the point."

Mom reaches out and catches the drop, eyeing it in the light. Somehow, it contains every color of the rainbow. Her eyes widen and narrow on it, as if she's seeing a miracle. She closes her forefinger against her thumb. "Why not?"

"You're too pretty," Dad offers. "You would break my heart."

"What a strange and backward view of women," Mom tsks. "There are plenty of beautiful women in here. You think they would break your heart too?"

"No."

Mom lifts an eyebrow. "Then what makes me different?"

"I see you," Dad says. "I see you, and somehow, from across the room, you convince me I know who you are. And if I'm wrong, you'll break my heart. And if I'm right, you'll break my heart too. A person shouldn't be so pretty it hurts to look at her."

Mom tips her head back and laughs again. "Jack, what are you doing back here?"

It's not the night they met. They already know each other.

Dad's gaze dips. "I was restless."

"I know you were," Mom says. "And I'd rather not get too attached to a man who has to up and leave because he misses a body of water, despite the ocean of it right outside that door—"

"Not that, Léa," he interrupts. "When I got home, I was restless for you."

She gives a derisive laugh and rubs at her sweat-dappled forehead. "I thought a dozen times about coming to find you," she says. "But I didn't. Because I know that's not how this works. You can't split your love between a woman and a lake. I don't want someone who can walk away like that, Jack."

Pain slices through my chest. *That's what you got.*

Dad takes Mom's hands in his. He kisses the backs of them one at a time. "Dance with me," he says.

"You don't dance."

"For you, I will."

She gives a closed-mouth smile, draws him onto the dance floor. A crackling Dean Martin song swells to life as Dad holds Mom close, rocks her side to side. "Did you know me when you saw me?" he asks.

She rests her mouth against his shoulder. "You know I did."

"And what did you know?"

"I knew you were full of shit."

Dad laughs, and Mom's smile spreads rapidly. This is how I want to remember her always—glowing beneath his eyes, not wilting. Not aching. Not staying because she had to, because of me.

"I was?" Dad says.

"You're a magic man who lives in a magic house and has magical adventures all around the country," Mom says. "Probably only half of what you say is true, but that's what I learned from talking to you."

"What did you know from looking at me?"

Mom glances at her sandaled feet as Dad twirls her. "Our whole lives," she says. "I saw it all, Jack. But I saw the best version of it, and that's not what we've got."

"No," he agrees. "We've got the broken one. We're all crooked and taped together. Especially me. Maybe if Jack the First hadn't done what he did, I could be better for you, Le. But I'm cursed. I'm destined to hurt you every time we collide, and we're *gonna* collide, because that's destined too."

If Jack the First hadn't done what he did? Cursed?

Mom steps clear of him. "Yeah, that's right, Jack. What you've got is a curse. It's not your fault you tore my heart up." She turns to walk away, and Dad catches her wrist but lets her go free when she tugs it. "I want what I saw when I looked at you. I don't want *this*. Get help, Jack."

She walks out the door, into the storm, and Dad stares after her. "I am," he says to himself. He sets a stack of bills on the bar and walks out into the pouring rain and heat-ridden wind.

Whites seethe in front of the door. There's no getting home now without passing through them.

Did the red-haired girl lead me here on purpose?

Stepping through the door, I'm returned to my yard. It's dusk, and a stringy teenager with a wide mouth and a gap between his teeth stands on the driveway wearing a bulky canvas pack.

Here, Dad's even younger than he was in the bar. He stands with his mother, my grandmother Charmaine, who wears her raven hair pinned back, its first gray streaks visible. In her plaid wool skirt and pearls, she looks like an aging Elizabeth Taylor, like Old Hollywood glamour hidden under rural dust and the callouses of hard work. She touches his shoulders lightly and draws him into a hug.

The front door opens, and Jack II ducks out, his hands in the pockets of his wool trousers, his button-down tucked and sandy hair cropped close. Standing on the porch behind his son and wife, my grandfather's height is more obvious than ever. The man I saw watch Mom and Dad dance in the kitchen light is hidden behind stern eyes and a flat, indifferent mouth.

"Jacky's going now," Charmaine tells him.

Jack II regards his wife and son.

"Bye, Dad," my father says.

Jack II nods curtly, sways on his feet, then goes inside. Charmaine rubs Dad's upper arm. She grabs his cheeks and pulls his head to eye level. "We love you, Jack."

"*You* do," Dad says.

"Your father's a haunted man," she answers. "But he loves you." Dad kisses the top of Charmaine's head, then takes off down the hill. As he goes, she shudders and eases herself onto the porch steps. Silently, she starts to cry. "I never asked for this," she whispers into her folded arms. "I've been a good person, haven't I?"

She sniffs hard, dabs her eyes with her skirt, and settles her face into a placid expression. Then she goes inside, and the memory freezes.

I want out, I say. *I'm tired of this.*

Whites surround the house in a circle; they block every door and window. They won't let me go, not until they've had their say.

I mount the porch stairs and accept the memories waiting at the front door.

I'm back in the woods. Ahead of me, massive Jack II has shed even more years. He walks alongside a freckly boy with a gap between his teeth, his jeans cuffed to show off red rubber boots. My grandfather's and father's chins are down, hands stuffed into pockets in an identical gesture.

The world is quiet, drenched in the last remains of a piercing sunset and the deep blue shadow in its wake. The dead fall leaves crunch under their shoes, life disintegrating into death. The air is cool, their noses dripping. Their cheeks are rosy with cold as they amble through the silence. Jack II reaches out and squeezes the back of the boy's—my father's—neck. He pats him on the back. The boy looks up at him, the last harsh spurt of sunlight glancing off his irises. His father smiles. He hangs his arm loose over his son's shoulders. The stiff leaves crunch. The sun glows. They keep walking.

Until they're so far off the memory fades.

I step back. I'm alone in my dark house. My phone vibrates, a message from Saul: *Did you see what I saw?*

That depends, I tell him. Did you see Love?

Twenty-Four

"A curse?" Hannah gasps. She brings the blush mug to her mouth and lets steam swirl up her nose. Her hair lies on her shoulders, glossy and untangled as though freshly flat-ironed rather than slept on.

"That's what Dad said," I confirm. "And my grandmother called my grandfather *a haunted man*. I think they were talking about Nameless. Mom didn't believe it, though. After she and Dad met, he went back to Michigan without telling her he was leaving, and she thought he used the curse as an excuse for hurting her."

Hannah lifts an eyebrow. "A fair assumption."

"Sure, but it *wasn't* an excuse—Saul saw a memory too, one from a couple of nights before my dad died. Bekah had *just* gotten her diagnosis, and that same day, the coywolves had killed one of our chickens. My dad found the dead bird and took it to the Angerts' cabin to show Eli. Dad said they *both* knew what the coywolves' behavior meant: that *the curse* was about to strike. According to

Saul, my dad was *really* freaked out—crying, begging. He was afraid I'd be next unless he and Eli 'made things right.'"

"What, like you were gonna catch Bekah's cancer?" Hannah gasps.

"You know what people say: When something bad happens to an Angert, the O'Donnells are next. I think Nameless does it—like somehow we're tied together, and if something happens to one of us, it attacks the other. I think Nameless is the curse."

"So what did your dad expect Eli to *do*?"

I shrug. "Saul said Eli was pissed—said even if he *could* help, he wouldn't. That if the curse was anyone's fault it was *ours*, and if something happened to *me*, it'd be fair."

"God. That's messed up." Hannah takes a careful slurp and hoists the blankets around herself again, forming a protective shell.

"I think the Whites *were* warning us about Nameless."

"Have you asked your mom about any of this?"

"She doesn't *believe* in it."

"But she knows what your dad thought."

"She's lied to me my whole life. I doubt she'll be any more forthcoming now."

"Why not? The jig is up." Hannah climbs out of bed and starts trading her pajama T-shirt and shorts for jeans, a top, and a thick sweater. "Even if the Whites are guiding you, it couldn't hurt to *ask* your mom about all this."

"I don't want more lies, Han. The memories have the truth."

"Okay, sure. You can walk into an imprint of the past, look around, smell the roses—but don't you think the truth is a little bigger than a play-by-play of events?"

"Meaning?"

"The Whites told you your dad left your mom for three weeks. They told you your mom was pregnant and considering leaving him—so *what*? Don't you care what your mom has to say? I mean, I get that it's your origin story, but it's your mom's *story* story. Doesn't she get a say in it?"

"I can't ask her, Hannah!"

"Why *not*?"

"I can barely look at her!"

Hannah falls silent. She reaches out and touches my hand. My face burns. "June."

"I trapped her," I say. "I trapped her here, and my whole life, all everyone's ever told me is how much like him I am, what a Jack I am to my core."

"She loved him," Hannah says.

My mind hearkens to Ms. deGeest's mini-speech: *I want you to consider what you want from life.* "All I used to want was to be like him. To live this big, untethered, rule-breaking life." I meet Hannah's eyes, tears flooding my own. "He wasn't having adventures, Hannah. He was running. He should've been here, trying to fix this, and instead he ran. He ran from *us*."

She pulls me into her arms, holding me tight around the neck, and kisses my head fiercely. "Know something great about your dad?"

"What?"

"He helped make you. And even if he was stupid enough to leave, he was smart enough to come back."

When you've been as lost as I have, as many times as I have, you get good at finding your way home, June-bug.

How is it possible to be so angry with someone you miss so much?

"Tell me about Dad," I say at the breakfast table.

Mom's eyes dart to Toddy, then to where the boys are watching cartoons in the living room. "What about him, baby?"

I shrug. "I don't know—why'd he travel so much?"

"For work."

"Always?"

Mom laughs. "What's going on?"

"I'm working on a story for creative writing," I lie. "There's a character who can't stay in one place for too long. He tells people it's because he's too curious, and it's true, but it's not the whole truth."

"Huh." Mom lifts an eyebrow.

"You know," Toddy says, "your dad saved my life once."

"Really?" A memory nudges the corner of my mind. Dad told me this story too. It got lost in a sea of similarly heroic and untrue tales, like Jack the First saving the kids in the Boston Molasses Explosion, or Jack II keeping Henry Ford and a couple of traveling entrepreneurs from turning Five Fingers into a live-in industrial compound by beating all three of them in an arm wrestling match—at once.

"We were fourteen," Toddy says. "We were down at the falls one day, jumping into the pool. Your dad, he wasn't allowed to be there—for good reason—but he was sitting down on the rocks, watching.

"It was my turn, and I stepped up, and for a second, I saw this piece of gold. I swear, a big gob of it, down in the water, and I took a step to get a better look, but the rocks were wet. I slipped. It wouldn't have been such a big deal, but it was getting dark. I leaned forward to catch myself, and my head hit the rock. Fell unconscious in an instant and tumbled right off the falls.

"Next thing I knew, he'd dragged me onto the shore. Started mouth-to-mouth until I woke up, coughing water. Your dad always insisted I said, *There! Knew I'd get you in the water, Jacky.*"

"Well, my dad had a bit of a lying problem, didn't he?" I say. I feel stunned, not by the story but by the glinting gold, the connection to the falls again. All these memories have to be connected, and somewhere within their web is the curse.

"No way, Jack." Toddy goes rigid. He's never called me Jack. It hurts in a way—that I'm not quite Toddy's, that I belong to the man who gave me his name. "Your dad wasn't a liar, and if anyone tells you that, you ignore them. He embellished, sure, but he never lied. He saw the truth of things." He looks at Mom and sets his hand on hers. "He looked at your mom and saw her beautiful heart even before her eyes, and I was there when he held you for the first time, and you know what he said?"

Mom's eyes sit low on the table. They lift heavily to mine.

"My life has been so small. And now it's finally big. Look at her. Look at my world." She stands from the table and turns away. "It was like he saw your whole life right then. He didn't miss a moment. He wouldn't have dared."

I think of Dad, of his own father watching him through a softly glowing window.

I think of Dad leaving home, of his mother kissing him good-bye. *Your father is a haunted man.*

I think of Dad as a boy, in a striped T-shirt and stiff Levis, looking up at his father in the forest, love in his sunlit eyes.

I wonder if, before he went, Dad remembered that moment. I wonder if he ever realized his father had been watching all along.

Twenty-Five

I'M getting ready for homecoming when Feathers's quivering reflection appears on the wall across from my window. She moves like a sheet dancing in the wind on a clothesline, carrying Whites toward my closet door.

They're here for me, as if I called them. As if they know I'm finally ready.

"Who was he?" I whisper. "Who was Dad?"

The Whites land along my arms and sink into my skin.

I step inside.

This time, it's different. I'm standing in the middle of a field, and on all sides of me, he's there. Dozens of places and times, dozens of my father living moments that have passed. Only when I focus in on one does it gain volume, the rest playing out as if muted.

In the first I latch on to, a gap-toothed little boy pounds down the porch steps and throws himself over a blue bike, pedaling down the hill after two other boys through failing sunlight. Their hoots and whoops echo through the trees as they careen away from the porch, where hulking Jack II stands watching.

In another, night hangs over the farmhouse, and the boy, my father, walks up the gravel, dirt smudged on his cheeks and blood visible at the knee of his jeans. The porch light flicks on, and Charmaine hurries out. Jack II pushes past her and takes sharp hold of Dad's string-bean arm, shaking it. "Where have you been?"

"Sorry," the boy says.

"Sorry, *what*?" Jack II parrots.

"Sorry, sir," the boy says.

"You get into it with the Angert kid?"

The boy's eyes stay low. After a beat, he says, "No, sir."

"Don't lie to me."

The boy stumbles over another apology. Jack II claps his shoulder hard, somewhere between affection and anger. His voice mellows: "Get on inside."

In some memories, Dad's small and gawky, his auburn-haired head too big for his shoulders. In some, his hands are thrust into soapy water, scrubbing dishes at the sink beside Charmaine while Jack II sits on the sofa, staring at the ticking clock on the wall. Listening to the crackle of the radio. Distractedly tapping a cigarette against a crystal ashtray.

Dad, tiny and chubby, dressed in pinstriped overalls and carried through a gauntlet of sprinklers by a singing Charmaine. Being lifted to pluck cherries from the tree with plump baby fingers.

Lying in the grass, his feet kicking in rhythm with the heartbeat of the earth, as his mother smiles down, tickling his cheek with leaves, and his father watches from across the lawn.

Dad, awkward and gap-toothed with knobby knees, carrying pellet guns through the woods. Dad escaping the house on bike, a silent Jack II watching from the upstairs window. Dad staring in at his father through a downstairs one, taking aim with an imaginary weapon, one eye closed tight, then dropping his hands and staring through the glass to his parents moving around behind it.

"You hate me," he whispers to himself.

There are older Dads too in the carousel of moments. Dad replacing shingles on the roof. Building the garage, then the sunroom, where in later memories a silver-streaked Charmaine sits with books or knitting spread across her lap.

There's Dad in rain-swept bars dense with humidity. Dad dancing and sweating with Mom, pushing her hair behind her ear and whispering to her slick cheek, "I will always love you."

There's Dad how I remember him: scruffy and strong, wrinkled from laughter and sun. He sits on a green chintz couch across from a man in gold-rimmed glasses who asks, "What was your childhood like, Jack?"

Dad thinks for a long moment, then says, "My father was a haunted man."

"Did he hurt you?" the man with the gold glasses asks.

"No," Dad says. "He hardly touched me."

"No," Dad says in another memory much like this one. "He was a good man."

"No," he says in a third. "He did his best."

"No," he whispers to himself in the next memory over. He sits in the dark on the bed, Mom asleep behind him. "He couldn't stand to look at me."

I turn to another scene. The same green couch. The same bespectacled man asks Dad, "Are *you* a haunted man, Jack?"

Dad regards him. "I'm trying to change."

"And do you believe you can?"

"I'm cursed. We all are."

"*We?*"

"Jacks," he says. "My grandfather, my father, me."

"And you have a new baby at home," the therapist confirms. "Do you think she's cursed?"

"She's different," Dad says.

"How?"

"She's how things were before."

"Before?"

"The curse."

The man sets his notepad aside and leans his forearms on his knees. "And what exactly is this curse?"

Dad's eyes flicker up. "Darkness."

"Darkness?"

"Inside of us," Dad says. "It watches us. It tempts us."

"What does it tempt you to do?"

"To end it."

The man straightens, but his face stays placid. "To end your life?"

Dad regards him. "It's not what you think."

"Then tell me what it is."

"It shows us . . ." Dad's eyebrows pinch. "It shows us the things that hurt us. Over and over again. And then it takes the thing we love most."

"I don't understand."

"It poisons us," he says. "And the people we love."

"And what do you think will happen if you end it?"

Dad's great shoulders shrug. "It will be satisfied. It will go away."

"What is this *it*, Jack?"

"It's Nameless."

"Jack, what do you think happens to Léa if you die? To your daughter?"

He drops his face into his cracked hands and starts to cry. "I don't want to leave. But the ghosts in that house—the ghosts won't leave me alone."

I don't know if I can take seeing any more. My heart feels cracked in half, but I have to keep going until I understand. Until I can *fix* this.

I turn toward a memory of a foggy morning on our hill, one of the earliest moments yet. My grandfather looks strong and limber. Dad is very small, one curl swooping down in the middle of his forehead. Together they carry tin buckets out to the hens. They stop at the coop, scattering the feed in the grass. Jack II's great form crouches as he reaches his hands out. A hen comes toward him, trusting and calm. He sweeps her up, lifts her to his ear, closing his eyes to better hear the *goop-goop-goop* of her heart.

The boy watches, and Jack II beckons his son forward, and the boy shuffles through the mud. He presses his ears to the speckled feathers, the tiny gasp that escapes his mouth making Jack II's smile grow.

"I used to think you could hear the whole world—even outer space—in the beat of a chicken's heart. That you could taste the sun itself in a cherry." Jack II sets the hen down and straightens. "It's strange how the smallest things and the biggest are so alike."

Dad gazes up at him. "Like you and me."

Jack II shakes his head, rustles his son's hair. "No. You're different. You won't turn out like me." Jack II seems to fade then, his eyes going vacant, his body becoming somehow less solid. He turns and goes inside.

I find my father young and old. In pain and ecstasy. Alone and with arms folded around Mom, holding me on his hip, whispering stories I'm too young to understand.

"When you were born, the sun cried," he whispers. "The lake danced. The dirt in Five Fingers sung, and all the coywolves stayed up past morning, hollering at the sky. The whole world rejoiced because *you* were finally in it."

In that moment, I find him.

The magic man who could talk roots into spreading.

The haunted man who ran from the people he loved.

My father, the sun, who warmed everything he touched. Who fought for us and for his place in the world.

The grass plot I'm standing on unfurls like a rug rolled out on top of the hundreds of scenes, vanishing them to make way for my own yard, my own hill encircled by magic forest.

My house is nowhere in sight. Nothing but sunlight and grass and pine needles.

Nothing with fingers or toes or eyes, apart from the three sleeping animals in the middle of the hill. A coyote curled up with a wolf, a yin and yang of red and gray fur, a robin resting on the wolf's snout. Their eyes are shut lightly as they nap beneath the cloudless sky.

In the distance, I see a flicker of color: a strawberry-haired girl watching me.

"Who are you?" My voice comes out. I'm no longer in the realm of memory but rather in the thin place.

She starts to walk away. When I try to follow, the threshold of the forest spits me back into my room from my closet.

Twenty-Six

WHEN I'm leaving that night for homecoming, I stop by the living room and stick Shadow and Grayson each with a kiss.

"Ew!" Grayson groans. "Stop!"

"You're a brat, and I love you," I tell him. "Shadow, you're not a brat, and I love you."

"You have germs," Grayson says. "Germs make people sick, and I don't want to be sick, because you can die if you're sick."

"I don't think most germs are as scary as you think," I tell him. "But I won't give you any more germs, if you don't want, even though I'm not sick."

It seems ridiculous to head out for a school dance in light of an *unbroken* curse on my lineage, but after everything I saw today, I feel fragile. I want this night with Hannah, and I don't want to let the curse steal it from me.

Nothing sounds better tonight than living my small life well.

I slip into the sunroom, where Mom's reading with her legs stretched over Toddy, who's watching a movie on his tablet.

"Hey." Mom looks up. Toddy takes out his earbuds. "You guys and Dad are and were the best parents in the universe."

They exchange a look. "You need some money for tonight, Junie?" Toddy asks. He's not joking. That's legitimately how spoiled we are: A compliment leads to an offer of cold, hard cash.

"No. I was just thinking about how lucky I am."

How I never would've described *any* of my parents as haunted. How all three of them have always looked at me, made me feel their love.

Mom closes her book. "We're lucky."

"So far you have been, yeah," I agree. "But when Grayson's old enough to go to homecoming, and he mentions how great you are, you might want to consider what he's going to buy with the cash you immediately offer him."

Mom chuckles, but Toddy's already somewhat small eyes narrow. "Oh shoot, Léa. You should've told me not all kids turn out like June before you roped me into two more."

Mom shrugs. "I was as naïve as you, and Shadow's angelic disposition certainly didn't help."

"Have fun, Junie," Toddy says.

"You staying at Hannah's?" Mom asks.

"Yep."

"Be safe, Junior."

"Love you."

I meet Hannah in the driveway, toss my bags in the back, and climb in. She offers me her kissed fingers. "Hey," she says gently.

I bypass our usual greeting and wrap her in a hug. "Thanks."

"For?"

"Being you."

"Anytime," she says. "Unless Adele has a sudden vacancy and I'm able to be *her*. Then I'm out of here."

I pull back. "You were right, Han. The memories aren't the whole story. But *hearing* about Dad from Mom and Toddy isn't the same as knowing him. And every time I step through a White, I get a chance to know him a little more. And it wrecks me to see him, and a lot of what I learn hurts, but I can't explain to you how little that matters. Because for the first time, I'm starting to really know him. To understand who he was, the good and bad. And I guess I'm just realizing that hurting someone doesn't mean you don't love them, and being mad at someone doesn't mean you stop loving them."

She studies me for a long beat, her mouth small. "It's different," she says quietly. "I know what you're saying, but it's different with your dad than mine."

"I know," I agree. "And it's not up to me whether you should forgive your dad, or if he can be trusted to come back into your life, but if you ever want to try, I just want you to know I'll be there. I'll hold your hand when you call, go with you to Colorado, whatever. Anything. Or if you want to fly out there and toilet paper his house, I'll do that too."

Hannah leans across the console to pull me into another hug. "Don't you ever leave me, June O'Donnell," she whispers into my hair.

"Never," I say fiercely.

"We have to break that curse."

"We will," I try to promise.

Despite the fact that Hannah and I are allegedly each other's dates, Nate and Stephen meet us at Hannah's in a hunter green sedan, our chariot to the dance.

"Giiirls!" Nate calls from the driver's side window, through which he's squeezed the top half of his body.

"Don't you feel like you should be throwing eggs at him?" I ask Hannah.

She gives me a reproachful purse of her lips and smooths her vintage baby blue minidress. "June, be nice."

The car stops, and Nate hops out to open the door for us, making a big show of bowing and offering his hand. "He thinks *I'm* weird," I mumble.

"Hey, Hannah. Hey, Junior," Stephen says from the passenger seat, giving us a tight smile in the imperfectly angled rearview mirror.

"Hey, Stephen," I offer. Hannah says nothing, her primal sense of academic competition taking over her body. Stephen seems simultaneously amused and annoyed.

Fifteen minutes later we park and follow the droves of students into the school to the gym. There's a vague Under the Sea theme, which mostly means we're all wearing various shades of blue, though some of the girls Hannah and I used to hang out with are in coconut bras and grass skirts, arguing fervently with Principal Michaelson, who's literally holding out a handful of Five Fingers High School Bears T-shirts and begging them to put them on.

I half-expect Hannah to ditch me and Stephen for Nate, but instead she grabs my hand and leads me down the bleacher stairs to the refreshments table on the floor of the gym.

We fill our cups with punch and shuffle to a dark recess to spike it with Dad's flask—though it seems someone's already beaten us to the *punch*, ha-ha-ha. Soon Hannah and I are on the basketball court, underneath the flare of strobe lights and tangle of blue streamers and metallic fish cutouts, dancing wildly with a crowd of kids who act like we never grew apart, screaming, "*Han! June!*" over the sound and pushing through bodies to give us sweaty hugs, cranberry juice and something sharper on their breath.

It's not our usual scene, but we're both determined to commit to the concept of homecoming like we never have before. Eventually we manage to reconnect with Stephen and Nate in the sea of bodies, and soon Hannah and her non-boyfriend are making out in the middle of the dance floor, where they're safe from the flashlights the chaperones keep shining into the crowd as they circle, hunting for contraband and breaking up the more ferociously grinding dance partners.

"Want water?" Stephen shouts.

I look back to let Hannah know where we're going, but decide not to interrupt. I take Stephen's hand to keep from getting separated on our way out. We fill new cups at the Rubbermaid jug and sit on the bottom bleacher. I chug my water, then flip my head upside down to pull my hair into a sweaty knot.

"I like your jumpsuit," Stephen says, leaning back. "Comfy yet sophisticated."

"Thanks." I touch the dark blue halter straps. "So you like my jumpsuit, but you still hate my best friend?"

Stephen rolls his eyes. "I've already told you I like Hannah."

"Then why do you seem sulky?"

He laughs. "I had a date—first time in all four years I had a date for a school dance. Then Hannah decides she doesn't want to go with Nate after all, so he talks me into canceling with Thomas so we could go stag together one last time, and somehow I didn't think that would end with the two of them cannibalizing each other on the dance floor while I hang out with someone who's—no offense—not even really my friend."

"No offense taken," I say. "It does suck. Senior year's just weird, you know?"

"How so?"

"I don't know—your defenses are down, you're more open to new people and things, and that means you might start falling in love with something or someone new, and you kinda feel like you have to devote as much time as you can to it until it's too late, but you're also trying to cram all your time with the stuff you already love and don't want to leave."

Stephen studies me for a long moment. "I wish I were more like you, like 'lake people.' There's nothing here I don't want to leave."

"Seriously?"

He shrugs. "I don't get along great with my parents. I hate winter. My sister's already at school in Ohio, and Nate's my only *close* friend. I spend most of my time studying, and we're so far away from the rest of the world that there's *still* hardly anyone out of the closet at our school. I can date, like, two people publicly and another six who won't be seen in public with me because they haven't told their friends or family yet. Aside from that, I'm not particularly into camping, kayaking, rock climbing, or getting drunk and eating fried food, so there's not a whole lot for me to do when I'm *not* drowning in schoolwork."

"I do not understand how you're best friends with Nate Baars."

Stephen shrugs and gulps more water. "Nate talks a lot, but he's also a good listener. And he cares about hearing what his friends care about. I'll miss him a lot, but not enough to stay."

"Hm." I think of what deGeest said about Saul, how eventually he'll move on from here and that I should too. Before her class, I'd never even thought about college. I'd never thought about leaving Five Fingers for more than a couple of months, and when I imagined those trips, it wasn't libraries and science labs I saw.

All those days I spent sitting at the edge of the driveway, waiting for Dad to come back, I told myself the same kind of epic stories Dad told about his time away. I gave myself shiny reasons why the man I loved more than anything in the world would leave me.

And when he was gone, I told myself I'd be like him. That I'd be cunning and fearless and wild, and I would never be far from him.

No matter how mad I am at him, I don't know how to handle wanting something different from what he had. I don't want to hurt the people I love like he hurt me and Mom, but I don't want to lose any more of him than I already have.

Maybe the thing Jacks *really* have in common, apart from the curse, is that we're all trying to correct the mistakes of our fathers.

But how did we get this way, cursed and Angert-hating?

"Look, I don't want to ditch you," Stephen says, "but I kind of want to salvage my last chance to take a real date to homecoming."

I glance around. "Is your date here? It's, like, eleven—the dance is almost over."

Stephen shakes his head. "No, but he only lives a couple of blocks from here, and rumor has it you can dance anywhere. Can you tell Nate I had to go?"

"Sure."

"Can you convince him I'm not mad at him?"

"No, because I think you are."

Stephen stands. "Think maybe you're projecting? Have a good night, Junior."

As he climbs the stairs to the school's lobby, I fish my phone out of my chiffon pocket and search for a new message that's not there. The music fades out, the lights brighten, and Hannah and Nate come staggering toward me, yelping about how badly their feet hurt. At the far end of the gym, I notice a woman in a svelte black dress, her white-blond hair slicked into a bun with one stray wave framing her face. All done-up, Ms. deGeest looks more like an adult. A super beautiful one. I fight a twinge of jealousy and embarrassment about our last conversation. Her eyes fix on me, and I look away.

"Where's Stephen?" Nate asks.

"He had to go. He's not mad at you."

"Huh." Nate nods. "Okay. Well, you know what we need?"

Hannah looks up from under the curve of his arm draped over her shoulders. "What?"

"A fourth person to camp out with. Any ideas, Junior?" He

practically winks, and Hannah grabs my phone off my lap and starts typing.

"Hey, Han," I say. "Maybe if you taught me how to type, I could send my own texts."

"This is faster!" Hannah chimes. "Let's go!"

On our way out, I glance back at Ms. deGeest. I swear she's still watching us. I shove my phone back into my pocket.

In the parking lot, Hannah's smile glows as bright as the moon, and Nate is nearly charming. In the car, he keeps grabbing Hannah's hand across the console, grinning almost madly.

We swing by Nate's house first and go through the gate to the basement door. We change into the sweats we brought, then pack Nate's tents, sleeping bags, a lantern, and a couple of flashlights in the trunk while Hannah calls her mom to tell her we got back to my house okay. Her mom believes her, because when has Hannah ever lied before? We're throwing the last few bags in the trunk when Saul pulls up and gets out of his car, looking too clean, too good.

"Hey, man," Nate calls.

Saul nods and drops his backpack into the trunk but keeps a sweatshirt folded in his arms. "Hannah, June."

"Glad you could make it," Hannah says.

"Me too," Saul answers.

Nate claps and rubs his hands together. "All right, let's get going. Nature waits for no man." He looks to Hannah. "No matter how beautiful."

She rolls her eyes. Saul glances at me, smirking, and the four of us pile into the car and head out. "So where exactly are we going?" I ask.

"Back to where it all began—where this beautiful woman fell in love with me."

"I don't think we can camp in the Fry Shack, Nate."

He eyes me earnestly in the rearview mirror. "Not the Fry Shack, Junior—the *falls*."

He doesn't notice the expression on my face or the way my body goes rigid; I guess it's hard to see on the outside that all my organs just set off simultaneous alarm bells. But Saul knows, and Hannah definitely knows, this is the one of *two* rules I've ever had to follow.

"Did you know about this?" I ask Saul. He shakes his head uneasily.

"Please don't be mad, Junie," Hannah says. "No one's going to make you get in the water if you don't want to."

"Hannah," I snap.

"*June*," Hannah pleads. "This is a town tradition we literally might never have another chance to take part in. I swear nothing's going to happen to you. We'll all be right here with you. You're going to be so glad you did it. Remember the last rule you didn't want to break? Total B.S."

This feels different. What does it mean that both Saul and I are forbidden from the falls?

His gaze is as warm and tangible as if his hands were on me. "If you want, we can drop them off," he says softly. "Then I'll take you home."

"Sure," Nate agrees from the front. Hannah crosses her arms and slumps aggressively in her seat. He reaches over and tugs her elbow.

"Fine," she sighs. "If you really don't want to go."

"What do you want to do?" I ask Saul.

The dark and silence between us are heavy and warm. Finally, the corner of his mouth twists up. "That last rule *was* total B.S."

I feel my smile mirroring his. His hand finds mine on the seat between us, his fingers rough and careful. "True," I agree.

And what about the memories I've seen there? The stories I've heard secondhand? Dad hadn't been allowed there either, but he'd gone. Everyone I know has been to the falls—camping there is *the* senior tradition. I don't want to miss out on that because of a rule Dad himself didn't follow.

I meet Hannah's eyes in the rearview mirror once more.

"I'll go."

"Yes!" Hannah gasps.

"*Yeah* you will, Junior," Nate says. "You're no wimp."

Saul's smile glows in the dark. I want to touch his teeth. Maybe climb inside his mouth.

Something Dad said floats into my mind. *It shows us the things that hurt us. Over and over again. And then it takes the thing we love most.*

Tomorrow, I think. *Tomorrow I'll keep working on the curse.*

Twenty-Seven

WE park on the side of the dirt road that runs up to a few formerly beautiful houses that now have shattered windows and lawns covered in old baby toys and broken appliances. This really might be our last chance to do what thousands of Five Fingers kids have done before us—Toddy's always saying it's only a matter of time until these houses are bulldozed to make room for condos. Then there will be some kind of gate blocking all the cars that park here in summer.

We pull our stuff from the trunk and climb the bank beyond the road, into the forest. It's two miles to the water, and following the single-track path with flashlights that catch creatures' eyes and mysterious shapes within hollowed nooks has me on edge. I'm beginning to suspect the hike will never end when finally we find ourselves on a cliff overlooking the falls and the deep pool below them.

One by one we come to stand at the ledge, turn our flashlights off, and stare into the water. There are some things that leave even Nate Baars speechless.

The surface looks dark, an oily blue, and in it millions of stars twinkle—the whole sky duplicated in one still basin, the churning strip where the falls hit seeming to suck up and pump out more constellations all the time.

No one says the word *beautiful*.

It doesn't feel right to give something so marvelous, so dizzy-ingly wild, a compliment. That'd be claiming that *we* have the right to look at this water and decide whether it's beautiful. And look-ing at the pool is the opposite of that: It's feeling very small, both incidental and fortuitous, like maybe the star-matted water would look at us and say, *I think they're pretty*, and the moon and the cave and the falls would nod: *You always did have good taste. How could you not? You're the center of the universe.*

Nate whips his shirt off, kicks his shoes to the side, and drops his pants and boxers, letting out a whoop as he flings his bare body into the water. When he crashes back up to the surface, we watch the warbling starlight to find him. "Warm," he calls. "Good."

Beside me, Hannah starts scrambling out of her clothes, hesi-tating when she gets to her underwear. Determinedly, she looks away and takes those off too. Her squeal and her bare butt arc up toward the sky then down. The water shouts when she hits it, and her laughter bounces back as she resurfaces. Saul and I smile tenta-tively at each other from a couple of yards apart.

"Hi," he says.

"Hi."

"Do you want to get in the water?"

"Yes," I admit.

"Are you going to?"

"Are you?"

"It depends on your answer."

"I shouldn't," I say. He nods to himself, then flicks the fluorescent lantern on and fumbles over some pieces of the tent. He holds up a post and scratches his head. "Clearly an outdoorsman."

"You love to mock me."

"You're an easy target." I spread out the bright blue tarp, staking down its corners.

He crouches beside me. "Hey, we okay?"

It's still hard to be close to him and think about anything but his mouth, but somehow my conversation with Ms. deGeest keeps intruding. I pull the posts out of his hand and snap them together. "Yeah?"

I finish with the tent frame, and he brings me the cover to slide over it. We work in silence, and when we finish, we set up the other tent too, Hannah's and Nate's voices and laughter rising up to us, then finally falling suspiciously quiet. "Hey, how long did you and Ms.—Allison—deGeest, like, date?"

Saul laughs. "I wouldn't call it dating. I would say we had about three *encounters*." I toss the sleeping bags inside the tents. "Why? Is that what's been bothering you?"

"No," I say. "So what did you mean when you said you're *over art*?"

My tone sounds more mocking than I mean it to. Saul stares at me for a couple of seconds before he walks away and sits at the edge of the cliff. I follow and sit beside him, leaving some space between us. Hannah and Nate are nowhere in sight, meaning they're probably in the same cave where Saul and I first saw the strawberry-haired girl and dark-haired boy.

"Saul," I begin after a moment. "I spend a lot of time thinking about you. A ridiculous amount, if you consider all the more pressing things I have to think about right now."

He smiles, murmurs quietly, "Feeling's mutual, Jack."

"And I love hanging out with you."

"Life-threatening curse notwithstanding," he says, "it's the best."

"But there's a lot you don't talk about. Like what's happening with your dad, or school—whether you plan to go back, and what happens then." My chest aches, and I focus on the starlit water below. "If I'm just a distraction from everything terrible you're going through, I get it, but—"

"June." He catches my hand and draws me toward him. I let him pull me across his lap and sink into him when he wraps his arms tight around me. He buries his face into the side of my neck, his breath drawing chills there. "Please don't think that," he whispers.

I fold my hands into his shirt, and he pulls back to look into my eyes, his own serious and intent under pitched eyebrows. He smooths the hair back from my face. I feel too teary and sensitive to say anything. I just nod.

"I want to know you, June," he says. "Not just who you are now, or who you were in a handful of memories, but all of you. And if you want to know me like that, I want that too."

"I do," I manage.

He's quiet for a long moment as he thinks. Finally he nods to himself. "Okay," he says quietly. "Did you know Bekah was a youth archery champion?"

I shake my head.

"She was tough," he says. "And brilliant. I mean, she could tell you the name of any tree in this forest. She and my dad used to take these trips. Do things Mom and I had no interest in. She went through a partial remission when she was fourteen, and they took a dogsled trip in Montana."

"Wow. Intense."

He nods. "I *always* wanted to be a writer. I was never interested in the hunting and fishing stuff like she and my dad were. Writing seemed like a good way to connect with him, I guess, so I started writing stories, and then when Bekah got sick, it was practically all I did, and then she died, and I went away to school."

He glances at me then back to the falls. "I'd be fine for a couple of weeks. Stretches where it wouldn't seem so bad. And then something would happen—or nothing would—and I'd *really* remember she was gone. And I'd plummet and write and plummet some more. I wanted to move on, to stop being sad, but I wasn't ready. So I crammed my schedule, stayed on campus to take classes over my first two summers, applied for a residency for this past one. I didn't expect to get in, and when I did, I felt terrible."

"You didn't want to go?"

"I didn't deserve to," he says. "I was—*am*—twenty years old, and all I do is imitate other writers. I mean, you know how some people are excellent at standardized testing and some people—no matter how smart—just bomb?"

"I'm aware of the second group," I say. "I refuse to believe in the first."

He forces a smile. "Yeah, well, I'm part of the first. I'm not any smarter than anyone else. I work hard and pay attention and I *copy*. I either got into the York residency because of who my dad is or because I studied until I could write like someone else. I burned out fast. A week in, I stopped writing altogether. I'd sold this book of essays—a lot of stuff about growing up in Five Fingers, about Bekah—but it turned out my editor wanted more of *an intimate look* at Eli Angert, and I couldn't do it. I couldn't make myself write a word about him. When Bekah died—I don't know. Writing was the only thing I could focus on. When I wasn't doing it, every minute was terrible, and all I could do was wait for enough time to pass that I could go back to sleep.

"When I wrote, things sort of came into focus for a while, and I could find pieces of my sister; I knew what I wanted to say, and I could pass the time saying it. When I found out about my dad's Alzheimer's, it was completely different. Even before Bekah died, things were complicated with Dad, and I think I'd always kind of written for him?" He says it like a question, like he's asking himself. "To prove I was like him. And then knowing that soon he'd be gone, it just felt like a pointless exercise."

I take Saul's hand, and his other tightens around my waist. "I didn't want to go to that residency. But I was scared to come back to Five Fingers. I didn't want to see what was happening to him. Or remember everything that happened here. And at the same time, ever since I saw those memories of Bekah, the past is all I think about. Except you."

I stare up at him until his molten eyes dip to me. "All *I* ever wanted was to be like my dad," I tell him. "I didn't *want* to forget. But now, with everything I've seen in the Whites—I don't know. Everything was different than I thought it was. *He* was different." I glance at Saul, moonlight slanting across his face. "When I'm with you, I remember there's such a thing as a present, and a future. It feels almost okay that he wasn't who I thought he was. Because now there are all these other things I never considered being or having, and I want them. And I feel like it's okay to want them."

Saul cups my face in his hands, his thumbs drawing circles on my jaw. He kisses me softly, and I thread my hands through his hair. He eases me back toward the cool earth, and I draw him with me. His rough hands slide to my waist beneath my shirt; his touch is light and potent. It wakes up my skin, drips heat into me. He kisses me again, his jaw gently grating mine, and the lines in his back tighten and soften in rhythm with our breaths.

His mouth slides down my neck, the side of his face settling over my heartbeat. "I hear you," he whispers, kissing my collarbone. "I can hear all of you, rushing around in there. A million Jacks and Juniors and Junes, a city of them."

I pull him back to me and lift myself against him. His knee slides between mine, and his stomach presses into me as he lowers himself, his warm mouth nestling into my throat. He moves down the length of me, kisses the center of my chest and stomach, my hips. My skin buzzes everywhere he touches and pulses where he doesn't.

"Go in the water with me," I say.

He grins. "Now?"

"Now. While we're not afraid." There are things I want to say and do that are scarier than the pool lit up with galaxies, and it makes me feel reckless and unstoppable. I want to be in the water, where our boundaries will lose their firmness. I want to do something I never would have done two months ago, and I want to do it with Saul Angert. "Let's go in," I whisper as his face lifts toward mine.

"Are you sure?"

I touch his nose, cheeks, jaw, cataloguing him. This is a moment I'll want to relive. "You were scared to come back. I was scared to leave. The last thing we're scared of is down in that water, and we can swim through it, and if we make it, we're done being scared."

He lets out a particularly gravelly laugh. "That's it? We go in the water and then we're fearless, June?"

"That's it. Nothing can stop us." *Not even curses.*

"Okay, Jack. Let's be fearless." He stands and pulls me up. He peels his sweatshirt and shirt off, and it's hilarious how exaggeratedly I am *not watching*.

Saul notices my sudden shyness and turns, leaving me to undress in semiprivate. "Do you want me to jump first?"

I look out over the ledge.

"Hello? We're coming down now," I shout. When I hear no answer, I say, "Let's jump together." Saul turns around slowly, and we both try to Not Look at each other too much or too long, but it turns out those things don't exist. I like having him look at me as much as I like looking at him—his luminous skin and gleaming hair and narrow smile. The real obstacle is the freezing cold air.

"You're beautiful, June O'Donnell," he says.

"Is that a surprise?"

He shakes his head once. "It shouldn't be, and it is."

"For me too." It *is* a surprise to see him and realize he's just a person, a handsome boy with all the same parts and pieces and lines I know to expect, and somehow everything is different too, because it's him. He holds out a hand, and I twist my fingers into his, step into him so close I feel the warmth of his body though only our hands are touching.

Together we step to the edge of the world and throw ourselves into the outstretched arms of the glittering sky.

We fall as one, and the world is nothing but strands of light and dark zooming past us. Air that's cold-hot-cold again, and Saul's hand, always Saul's hand. We hit the blanket of warmth—*yes*, the water is, like everyone says, *impossibly warm*—and it folds around us, dragging us down.

Even after eighteen years of stories about the warmth of the falls, I'm still so surprised, my eyes snap open beneath the surface.

That's how I find out that the stars in the water weren't just a reflection.

At first they look like jellyfish: fragile spheres of glowing purples and blues, swimming down-down-down toward the sandy floor we can't see. Many are pebble-small, others the size of snow globes. I catch one of the delicate orbs, and it turns foggy white, as if I'm holding a tiny cloud. Saul jerks his chin toward the surface, and we kick back up, the cloud-thing still in my hand.

We break through the water, gasping for breath. The air is as frigid as ever, and our teeth immediately start chattering.

I rub the water from my eyes and find that something's changed.

Night is gone. The pool is cloaked in the gray that comes when the sun has begun to lift enough to pierce the trees and bring color to the earth. Everything's a richer, darker version of itself, and fog coils around our shoulders and speckles our faces.

"It happened," Saul whispers, because when the rest of the world is this quiet, it feels like you *have* to whisper. "We're not where we were." He points to where our tents and lantern should be. There's nothing but fog rolling over a patch of blue-green brush.

"Hannah? Nate?" I hiss, treading water. He's right—they're gone. Or *we* are.

"What does it mean?" Saul murmurs. "We're not in a memory—is this a thin place too?" He slicks his hair back and swims closer to examine the orb in my fingers. Crooked in my palm, it looks different than in the water: soft, feathery.

"A Window White," I breathe. "I've only ever seen them by my house before." The White skirts off my hand and drops into the water with an almost inaudible *plop!*

"The one place we're not allowed to go," Saul says, "and yet multiple memories have brought us here. *And* there are Whites here. June, this place has something to do with us."

In the gray morning, the water appears opaque, the sparks of colorful light dulled to look like rocks catching enough sun to glitter. I think of Toddy's story, how he thought he saw gold in the water.

"I don't get it," I say. "Why aren't we allowed to come here? My dad broke the rule, and he was fine. And if the rule was made because the thin places are dangerous, wouldn't they have kept us out of the woods?"

Emily Henry

"Maybe—" Saul stops. A quiet rustling rises from the brush. Branches quiver and jump. The rustle grows. Louder, nearer.

"Hannah?" I whisper. Cold fear trickles down my spine. The water near the shore begins to bubble and froth. "Nate?"

All at once, a school of fish breaks the surface, mouths gaping, eyes wide and strange. Their silver bodies seize, churning the water. Two flop up onto the bank, bodies beating the mud as the fish choke over oxygen. Agitated cheeps and chirps swell through the trees. The hiss and slither of snakes undulate through the brush.

There's one beat of silence, and then the whole forest erupts. Squirrels and birds flee from the branches, clearing out from the ledge Saul and I jumped from. White-tailed deer bolt along the shore, eyes wild. A colony of bats shrieks into the sky, and two collide, gnashing at each other as they tumble toward the earth, wings twisted in sickly angles. A snake at the edge of the cliff jerks to a stop, its sinuous upper body lifting before it strikes toward its own tail, jaw yawning as it begins to devour itself.

Saul grabs for my arm in the water and yanks me toward him, face blanching.

Up on the ledge, half-hidden in the trees, a dark and terrible silhouette billows forward. Cold stabs my heart like a shot of adrenaline. The forest seems to close in, darken, seethe as Nameless moves closer. The fish are still writhing, suffocating. A stampede of tiny wings and paws reverberates out from the shadowy ghost.

"*Go!*" Saul pushes me toward the falls.

We swim. As fast as we can. Stroke toward the waterfall. He throws himself over the slick ledge and hauls me up through the falls to the cave.

Inside we stand, panting, staring through the rushing stream. My heart thrums louder than the water's angry roar, and Saul's choppy breaths jolt through my arm. We stay frozen for minutes, waiting.

"It must be gone," Saul says. I'm not sure he believes it.

Whites are drifting through the waterfall now, convening like tiny magnets until their combined mass is too thick to see through.

"June-bug?" The familiar voice echoes from behind me.

Everything in my body shoots up toward my throat, then plummets. I spin, searching the empty cave. I can hear my rapid breathing—we're not in a memory—but my father's disembodied voice reverberates against the stone again: *"Jack IV?"*

Shivers crawl along my skin. My eyes zigzag, finding nothing but wet rock and Whites.

"Hello?" I manage.

"June?" Saul's eyes look almost black against his drained face. "Who are you talking to?"

"Found you, June-bug!" Dad says. *"I found you."*

"Dad?" I stammer

Saul spins away from me, his shoulders suddenly rigid, then looks back. "You hear him, don't you?"

"He's here." *Somehow.*

"No, June." Saul's voice is strained and low. "It's the Whites, I think. It's a trick."

"He's *here.*" Desperation swells in me. His voice is everywhere now, rebounding endlessly against the walls. *June, June, June,* it swirls around me. "Dad, can you hear me?" I scream over the chorus.

"June, it's not them," Saul rasps. "I hear her too, but it's not them."

That's when I see it: Nameless, twitching against the cave wall. It comes forward, the Whites gliding along with it, and the voices rise in number and volume until they reach the waterfall. Saul jerks me back against the wall.

"*June*," Dad's voice says, fearful now as it's sucked through the waterfall. "*June-bug.*"

The sound cuts out as the Whites pass though the falls, and I run after them. I can't explain it, but the thought is there pulsing in my mind:

He's here. He's really in there this time.

You're going to lose him again. You can't lose him again.

Saul's shouting something I can't make out. I leap through the falls and hit the water, drop-drop-drop, billions of bubbles erupting, buffeting the glowing orbs away from me. There are *so* many, but I'm somehow convinced I'm looking right at the one that held Dad's voice—not a memory, but *Dad*, my brain repeats.

I dive after it, deeper and deeper, and I keep going even when my lungs start to stutter, and still my hands can't clasp the ball of light slipping away from me.

I'm out of breath.

Out of air.

I've gone too deep. There's no way back out. Panic sets in. My lungs spasm.

Ahead of me a waterlogged voice calls out: *June.*

The eerie blue glow stops its descent, then timidly moves back toward me. I can't explain it, but if I can get my hand around the

White, somehow the dark spots popping across my vision won't matter. The nameless thing at the bottom of the pool and the water seeping into my lungs won't matter.

Nothing matters but the voice.

My fingers graze the sphere.

I see his smile: gap-toothed, bright.

Twenty-Eight

I'M coughing. So hard it hurts.

No, throwing up.

"Oh God, Junie," I hear Hannah sob.

"She's fine," Nate says. "She's fine, Han."

"What happened? Where the *hell* did you guys go?"

The voices swim through darkness, emitting little meaning until my eyes focus on the faces hovering over me.

"Hi," Saul says softly, helping me sit up. Nate passes him a blanket, which Saul and Hannah wrap around my shoulders. I'm still naked. I'd forgotten I was in the first place. It hadn't mattered. Nothing had but the voice. There's a hollow pang in the pit of my stomach.

"Why did you let her get in the water?" Hannah demands of Saul tearfully.

"Han, come on—we were in too," Nate tries.

"You knew she didn't want to! You knew she wasn't supposed to!" Hannah's anger bows and snaps. She's crying again. "God, Junie. I should've listened to you." She folds her arms around me and cries into my wet hair.

Saul's eyes are intent on me, trying to understand what he must see on my face: fear and loss and *hope* wrapped into one.

He was down there.

"I'm okay."

He was down there.

We're on a lower ledge of rock, farther out from the falls. The water still glitters with the reflection of the stars, but the Whites are gone. The urge to throw myself back in and tear down to the bottom is powerful.

Saul catches my gaze. "We shouldn't have gone in."

What he means is: *You shouldn't do it again. Whatever you heard, it wasn't there.*

He's wrong.

I should've seen it sooner. If the Whites are slipping through cracks from the other side, there's a way for us to slip through too. All the way.

It's in that water. He's in that water.

"What happened, June?" Hannah asks.

"I dove too deep," I say. "I couldn't get back up."

She gnaws on her bottom lip. "We should get you to a hospital."

I scoot back from her, from all of them. "I'm fine."

"You're not fine," Saul says. "You nearly drowned."

"Let's at least get you home," Nate says. "Your lungs could have water in them—sleeping out in the cold is a bad idea."

I need to go back down.

Saul touches my jaw. "June?"

The spell of the water fades when I meet his eyes. I jam my mouth shut, force a nod. "Okay."

By the time we tear down the tents, hike back to the car, and start driving, heat blasting, to my house, the first rays of sun are poking through the forest lining the road. Faint pinks and yellows brush past, catching the leaning, ivy-smothered telephone poles and the flapping wings of newly awakened birds.

In my mind I still hear the spastic scream of bats, see the snake swallowing its own tail. I close my eyes until the image vanishes. *Nameless isn't here. Saul and I are safe.*

But for how long?

We slog partway up the driveway, and Nate parks to let me out. I'm banking on my parents still being asleep and more specifically on not having to tell them that I went to the falls with Saul Angert. That I saw the embodiment of Dad's curse. That, by disobeying their rule, I nearly drowned. And despite that, that I don't regret it.

Dad is there.

I strap my duffle bag, garment bag, and purse around my shoulders and shuffle up the hill. For the first time since we brought them home, I'm eager to submerse myself in the books about thin places. I need to understand how to get through. Could it be as simple as diving to the bottom?

I know we need to break the curse, but it falls to the back of my mind as other possibilities pile on top of it.

Like the possibility that I can see Dad again, not in a memory but in a place where he can look at me, talk to me, hold me.

As I approach the house, several coywolves vanish into the woods. Toddy's truck is gone; he must be having an early gym day. I unlock the door and ease it open, trying for silence and ending up with one shrill squeak of the hinges.

At the end of the hall, Mom sits at the kitchen table in her robe. She looks so eerily like those versions of herself from the past that I wonder if, even with my shoes on, I've stepped into a memory. Then she looks at me, her face tear-streaked and furious.

"Where have you been, Junior?"

"Hannah's?"

She stands and folds her arms over her chest. "And where has Hannah been? Because her mother certainly hasn't seen her."

"Mom," I groan. "We went camping. I'm sorry I didn't—"

"I had a call from your teacher." Mom holds up a hand, and her eyes flutter closed like she can't look at me while speaking these words.

"What are you talking about?"

"Ms. deGeest," Mom says. "She was concerned about where you might be headed after the dance. And with whom."

"Mom." My stomach drops, hard and fast. "Whatever she told you, I'm sure it's only loosely connected to the truth."

Mom's hands fall to her sides, and her voice drops to a whisper. "Go upstairs, Jack. I can't look at you right now."

"Mom."

"You lied to me. You had Toddy and me terrified out of our minds for half the night, calling everyone we could think of. I've never seen him so mad. You'll be lucky if he hasn't already started a war with Eli Angert."

"Toddy?" The combination of him and Eli in the same thought racks me with hot anger. "This has nothing to *do* with Toddy. This is about *Dad's* rule, and if *he* were here, he'd listen to m—"

"You father is gone, June!" Mom's scream hits me like a slap. She gathers herself in the silence. "Toddy and I are your parents, and we don't want you anywhere near that boy. He's trouble—"

"You can't honestly believe that! Saul's—"

"Enough, Junior," Mom interrupts. The tremor in her composure tells me she doesn't want to hear Saul's name. "Go upstairs, *now*."

Twenty-Nine

THE storm outside shakes leaves from the branches. Whites linger outside my window, as if waiting for the rain to let up before they drift back to wherever they go when they're not here.

The other side.

The place at the bottom of the falls.

My body's one ball of frenetic energy, legs bobbing and hands tapping. More than ever, I feel restless. Like I'm all dried out and I *need* the water.

Hours after our fight, Mom knocks on my door and lets herself in. She sits beside me on the bed, but I keep my eyes fixed on the rainy windowpane. She swings her legs up beside mine so we're facing each other. "I'm sure you're upset." After a long silence, she continues, "I don't expect you to understand, but the bad blood between our families runs back a long ways."

"Why?" I ask her. "Because Jack the First lost a farm you and I have never even been on?"

"It doesn't matter why, Junior," she insists. "It doesn't matter whether *you* think it's a good enough reason. Your father did, and Todd and I do too. I'm telling you to stay away from the Angerts."

"I'm eighteen."

"Fine," Mom says. "I'm *asking* you to stay away from them. And if you're going to live under our roof, you'll abide by that rule."

"It's as much my house as it is yours. Dad left it to both of us. He said it should always be owned by a Jack."

Mom recoils, hurt. I know it was cruel, but it's hard to care. "Do you think he would want you to own his grandfather's house when you can't follow his two rules for you?" she says.

"You can't let Dad's rules go because you feel guilty," I snap. "You *never* took them seriously. But now he's gone and you're sticking to them even though, if he were here, I'd get him to give them up."

Mom laughs, but the sound is empty. "Your father believed he could trace everything bad that ever happened to this family back to the Angerts. That wasn't something you or I could've changed. You need to let this go, Junior. I don't expect you to understand. I just wanted to say I'm sorry it has to be this way."

"You could try being honest with me sometime instead."

Mom sets a hand on my leg. "You could have too. But you didn't. And that's all I need to know about the effect this boy is having on you."

She grabs my phone and my laptop from my desk, then leaves my room. "Three days," she says from the hallway. "Then we'll talk about you getting your phone back."

"I kind of need my computer for homework."

"And you can use it. Down in the kitchen, where I can see you."

I want to scream, but I don't argue. Mom's never grounded me to the house before, let alone taken away my connection to the outside world.

There's a cruel lack of Whites, but I try doorways for a while anyway before flopping onto my bed with one of the thin-place books.

Like Saul described, the essays in the book are mostly meditations on the serenity of beautiful places. But there is one excerpt, attributed to a writer named Sheridan Llewelyn, that I find myself rereading.

The Celts called these spaces "thin places," places both visible and hidden, where the veil between this world and the next is lifted, and the light spills through. Space carved out to form the shape of God: holy ground.

The light spills through: the memories, the voices from the past.

The veil between this world and the next: the doorways that take me somewhere they shouldn't, the misty sunlit woods that sometimes open up to me, and the pool beneath the falls. I want to think it means what I so deeply believed while under the water, that there's a way to step through the veil and truly see Dad again.

Thunder rumbles the house, and the ivy outside my windows shivers, dispelling a few hidden Whites.

I set the book in the middle of the bed as a translucent pink blob appears in the corner. "Hi."

Feathers wobbles, her warmth palpable despite the chill sneaking through the old bones of the house.

"Are you trying to take me somewhere? Do you know how to get to him?"

She sails forward through my windowpane. I shove it open and let a White land on my hand. But every time I try to carry it to my closet, the wispy sphere blows back toward the window where Feathers billows. Beckoning me.

I slide the window all the way up. Beneath it there's a thin ledge, and under that, a platform of rickety lattice entwined in shaggy greens extends over the porch.

I swing one leg over the windowsill, setting the bare ball of my foot on the weathered wood. I give it more weight until it fully supports me. A White lands on my arm as I swing my other leg over.

Immediately, I'm down in the yard, lightning crackling to illuminate a pile of drenched shoes. A slim man with a cleft chin emerges from the woods, bent against the wind. Even with his dark hair and tailored clothes whipping in the storm, he looks *neat*. The angle of his cheekbones and the heat in his eyes announce him as an Angert. Something gray and mangled hangs in his hand, and he mutters to himself as he stalks to the porch and pounds the door.

A heart-shaped face framed in dark curls peeks out. My grandmother Charmaine. With a soft murmur, she sends the gap-toothed child pulling at her hip back into the house. She and the Angert man begin to argue in hushed mutters, then he tosses the mangled thing onto the porch. Charmaine bends to examine the lump: a dead rabbit.

She slips inside, and a minute later Jack II stoops his head to step out.

When Dad used to claim his father had been six foot seven, Mom would give him that *You're exaggerating* look. But the way Jack II carries himself now makes his height more pronounced than in other memories, those in which he seemed to hide within himself, eyes vacant and so quiet he was nearly invisible.

His sandy head towers over the thin man. His wide mouth presses into a thin line as his eyes dip to the fleshy thing at his feet. "What are you doing here, Zeke?"

"You know what." Zeke's voice is a raspy growl. "I found that on my doorstep. Coywolves are agitated."

Jack II nudges the rabbit with his foot.

Zeke runs a hand over his mouth hastily. "Call it off, Jack."

That vacant look passes over Jack II's face. He reminds me of a cellar door, rusted shut and covered in weeds. "Call what off?"

"The curse, dammit. This isn't our fight, Jack."

Jack II's face darkens, and he crosses his burly arms. "It's not?"

"You know as well as I do, it wasn't Abe's fault what happened. They were kids. As long as we keep this fight going, *this*"—he nudges the rabbit with his boot—"is gonna keep happening."

Jack II's stare is empty. It's the face of a black hole, and I recognize it as if looking into a mirror: the grief sucking the world into itself.

Right then, I know my grandfather lost something. I see it in the twist of his mouth, the tension in his right temple, the hollows behind his eyes.

What did the curse take from you?

Zeke twists his hands together. "He lost his mind with grief, Jack. Forty years passed, and he still couldn't sleep through the night. Not to mention how it all ended. Wasn't that enough retribution?"

"And what do you expect me to do?" Jack II demands. "You think I'm a sorcerer? I can wave my hand and bring Abe back, make his mind the way it was before? Sounds like your brother finally paid for his sins. I hope he's *still* paying, wherever his soul went."

"It wasn't his fault!" Zeke hisses. "They'd never have even gone to that wretched place if they hadn't been hiding from your father. So don't you go acting all high and mighty, Jack O'Donnell. Don't you *dare* pretend this started with Abe. Until we *both* make it right, it's not going to stop—not for you, not for me. Your father brought evil into this place, and it's not only Abe who was punished. It'll be all of us in the end. Your family and mine."

Jack II steps forward, forcing Zeke to stumble back. "Do you ever relive it?" he whispers, deadly calm.

Zeke's dark eyes widen. "I relive all sorts of things."

"But not that night," Jack II says. "No, you weren't there, Zeke. You were at home, asleep in your bed. And they don't come for you, do they? Maybe other Moments, but not that one."

"You're wrong." He shakes his head. "I see it too."

"Then you know I wouldn't help you if I could. The only curse I see on this land is you, Zeke. You and your damned family. Now get off my property before I make you." The fire fades from his eyes, leaving Jack II empty and trapped within himself.

He turns and goes inside, brushing aside the little boy waiting in the foyer and closing the door.

Zeke Angert stalks toward the woods, his gait lithe and graceful, like his grandson's. I take off after him, but the memory releases me when I cross into the woods. I'm still in the forest, but Zeke is gone, and my heavy breaths are audible. Dusky sunlight drapes over the foliage, puffs of mist visible in the stripes of gold breaking through the ancient branches.

I'm not in a memory, but I'm not just in the woods either. I'm in the overlap.

The answers were all there, cut into a million pieces that need to be placed together.

Jack the First *brought evil into this place.*

As long as we keep this fight going, this *is gonna keep happening.*

We were right: The Whites were warning us about the curse. But what's more, *all* the Jacks and Angerts that came before us knew about it too. They knew Nameless wandered the woods, disturbing the thin place. They knew the curse robbed us of the things we loved, and maybe—*maybe*—they even knew how to break it.

A fire blazes in my chest. Someone *must* be sending these moments to us.

He's down there. On the other side of the veil.

Thirty

IF Dad knew, Eli knows.

I sprint toward Saul's house. My lungs burn; my feet hammer the earth. I pass O'Dang!, eyes flashing across the names carved into the bark: O'DONNELL + ANGERT.

The mystery of our families is taking shape, but it won't be complete until Saul and I are together.

The forest thins, and the reddish cabin resolves ahead, but as soon as I hit the clearing around it, I'm ripped away again.

Why? I scream voicelessly. At the Whites. At Feathers. At Dad. At whoever's leading me. *I thought this was what you wanted!*

I'm back at the farmhouse, in the flat dark of night, electric light casting an imperfect circle on the front porch. Mom and Dad sit in patio chairs, wrapped in blankets, their hands loosely knotted. An owl hoots, moths flutter, but my parents are silent.

"Don't you think it's time to put an end to this silly fight?" Mom says quietly.

"You don't know anything about it, Le."

She shoots him a sidelong glance. "You never used to want to be like your father."

"He was a haunted man." Dad scratches at his pant leg. "Want to or not, I'm like him. It's his blood under my skin."

Mom lets out a long sigh. "You know, at some point you have to decide whether it's more important for you to be a Jack or to be happy."

She stands and goes inside, leaving him on the porch. He leans over his knees and eyes the sky. "What do you think, Issa?" he murmurs.

Issa?

"You think I should let it go? You ready to get out of here for good?"

He pushes on his legs to stand and walks inside.

A thousand Whites converge in front of the door, and I burst through them, my skin alive and hot as, all at once, memories hit me in sharp fragments, overwhelming my senses with kaleidoscopic color. I force myself to stay upright as the competing memories focus into something comprehensible.

I'm alone in a dark maze of mirrors. Some of the mirrors reflect me, as I am right now, but others show me as a toddler, as a preteen with braces, as an eight-year-old with a bloody knee. I stop in front of a mirror that shows my father.

He stares blankly out at me, doesn't react when I touch

the glass in front of him. Other mirrors show Mom and Toddy, Shadow, Grayson, Jack II and Charmaine, Jack the First and his tiny flaxen-haired wife, Annie. In some, my Grandma and Grandpa Girard stare out, and others show people I don't recognize, women with Mom's nose and shoulders, men with her chin. People who are pieces of her, like she's a piece of me.

Off to one side, I see the strawberry-blonde from the cave. She blinks slowly, then steps sideways from her mirror, disappearing in the gap between that one and the next.

I turn, searching for her, and face a whole new set of mirrors. Front and center, as if he's the immediate reflection of myself, I see Saul. Spreading out behind him, I see Sauls with missing front teeth, with sunburns and bowl cuts. I see a man in a tweed coat with a face as brutal as winter, Saul's father, Eli. Lean and elegant Zeke, and another Angert patriarch I don't recognize, with the same angular jaw and captivating eyes. I see Bekah, her crooked smile and thick eyebrows, and a curvy brunette with deep-set eyes—her and Saul's mother, Rachel.

And then I see the boy.

The dark-haired boy who held the red-haired girl in the cave.

He presses his hands to the glass, his nose flattening against it. He begins to scream. His fingernails claw at the surface of the mirror. He thrashes against it.

I hit the glass too, trying to free him. His eyes are wild and fearful. Whites are alighting all over the mirror, and he's still screaming.

I'm trying, I say.

I throw myself at the glass, and it shatters in every direction, leaving me tumbling onto the hill where my house should be.

There's no one here. Just a wolf and coyote and robin asleep in a yin and yang formation, and a springy green cherry sprout dancing in the breeze.

Now the scenes unfold around me, another carousel of moments.

I focus first on one that shows Jack II, middle-aged and hunched. He sits in a high-backed chair in a room lined with lilac wallpaper speckled by vines and plump golden fruit—the room Mom now shares with Toddy.

The man lying in the bed beside Jack II has a sickly yellow tint to his skin, and his breaths rattle in his lungs. Where Jack II is shadowy and insubstantial, this man is all intensity and sharp lines, despite the trembling of his puffy fingers against the quilt.

I recognize Jack the First from his one and a half eyebrows. According to Dad, my great-grandfather lost the other half over in France during World War I, when he threw himself between a friend and a grenade. Shrapnel had lodged itself in Jack the First's left knee, which never worked quite right after that, and in his left eyebrow, which had never fully grown back.

He'd been beloved in Five Fingers before that; afterward, he was a hero.

A clock ticks on the wall, and dust floats through spears of sunlight.

"You can leave," Jack the First coughs. "Don't need nobody watchin' me die."

Jack II rocks forward over his knees. "I'm not leaving, Pop."

The clock ticks onward; the dust drifts.

Jack the First clears his throat. "Why not?" His glassy eyes roll toward the corner as an inky darkness materializes there, twisting hatefully. "You find anything dead in the yard?"

Jack II's chin lifts. "No, Pop."

"Don't lie to me, boy," my great-grandfather spits. "You think I don't know? It's been watching me ever since that little shit finally drowned. It wants revenge, son."

Jack II winces and sits back, putting space between him and his father. His eyes have that vacant look again, as if his soul has walked off for a coffee break.

"I don't care, son," Jack the First says. "Don't give a damn how this spirit tortures me. I don't have any regrets, except that I didn't kill him myself."

Jack II's eyes lift. "You did."

"What's that?"

Jack II shakes his head.

"Speak up," his father demands. "You got something to say then talk like the fucking man I raised."

"You *did* kill him."

Jack the First tries to scoff, but his throat's too weak to let anything but a cough through. "You pity that piece of shit? After what he did to us?"

Jack II studies the floor. "You don't have any regrets? Not one?" His eyes glimmer, light reflecting against their abyssal surface.

His father regards him, mouth juddering open like a fish gasping for water and finding only air. He jams it shut. If the first Jack had any regrets, they're trapped within him for good. "Get me a drink, would you, son?"

Jack II tips his head toward a porcelain bowl resting beside the bed. "How about some cherries, Pop?"

"Scotch," his father replies. "Neat."

Jack II hesitates, as if considering pointing out that a man inches from death, skin jaundiced and hands shaking, shouldn't shoot liquor. He shakes his head and unfolds his great height from the chair, crossing toward the door.

Jack the First's eyes shut, and he groans. "I'm coming, honey," he whispers. "Not long now."

Jack II pauses in the doorway. I see something then, a kind of *caving in*, as if everything on the outside of him is collapsing inward, creating his black hole. He tries to say something. His wide mouth presses tight. He walks into the hall.

Jack the First opens his eyes as Nameless approaches him. "Do your damnedest," he growls at the ghost. "Show me anything you want. I'll be with her soon, and you'll still be trapped here."

The thing folds over him. Jack's eyes close, and a smile curves up his lips. The anger leaves his body, the tension abandoning hundreds of muscles at once, finally permitting them a moment of peace. The memory freezes as the sounds of others push forward.

I turn toward the memories circling me. A long-legged, sandy-haired child who must be Jack II barrels through the front door and scampers down the hillside. He pumps his arms, gasps for breath, bare feet pounding the wet grass. Jack the First stumbles out the front door, the bottle in his hand knocking the doorframe and his left leg swinging stiffly. "Come back, you little coward!"

Jack II keeps running, eyes blinking against sweat. "Take me away," he hisses, breath frosty as he sprints for the woods. "Take me away. Take me away."

He hits the edge of the woods and vanishes, the memory stilling.

I turn to the next and see Jack the First's wife, Annie, holding her only son atop her knees. She kisses his forehead, smooths his sweat-streaked hair. She murmurs, "He doesn't mean any of it, my love."

"He does," little Jack II says. "He hates me."

Annie presses her lips to her child's head again and stares at the wall of the bedroom where Grayson and Shadow's bunk beds now sit.

"Was it my fault?" Jack II looks at her. A smile blossoms then withers on her painted lips. She pulls a green-jeweled pin from her yellow hair and closes his hand around it.

"You are blameless, my love." Her eyes become distant. If Jack II grew up to be a collapsed heart, a black hole, his mother was a meteor hurtling through space: beautiful but burning out, screaming but kept silent by the vacuum. "Go to sleep, angel." She maneuvers her son from her arms into his narrow bed, then pulls the blankets to his chin and kisses him once. She hesitates, kisses him again more slowly.

He seems to know this means something—that tonight, she kissed him *again*. Annie hurries, crying, from the room. She glances backward one last time before she cups her hand over her mouth and escapes.

The memory stops, and I dread the one that comes next even as I turn to it.

Here Jack II sits on the same bed in the dark, his lanky legs dangling over the side as he stares at the pulsing pink patina. His fingers roll the hairpin back and forth. "She's gone," he tells Feathers. "She's gone and you're gone and all that's left is him, and he hates me." His fingers lift the pin and press it to his head where Annie kissed him goodbye.

Feathers encircles him, fluttering, warming. "You promised," he whispers. "You said we'd get out."

I want it to stop. I need it to stop, so I run. I run straight through another memory: Jack the First bending beneath the shade of the first Jack's Tart, putting his heart to Annie's stomach, hands gently clasping her waist. "I hear it," he says, voice soft and warm as sunlight through his smile. "The heartbeat of the whole world, and it's in my wife's belly."

"Little Jack," Annie says, touching the side of her husband's face.

I keep running.

What happened to destroy this?

What took the man I see now and made him into the one I watched die?

And what's it going to do to me and Saul?

Two families.

Two ghosts—one warm and sad, one cold and hungry.

Two tears in our world—one at an impossible tree and one in a starlit pool.

One curse, tying the puzzle together, and infinite memories holding the answer to what created the hungry darkness, the brutal cycle that will eventually swallow Saul or me.

I run to the end of the yard, right into the ice cave again, right through the bar where Dad stared at Mom in the middle of a monsoon, down a dune past a family napping on the sand, and into the water, and there—

I'm on the cliff overlooking the waterfall, sunlight-sprinkled mist hanging heavily over everything.

Whites *plop* against the surface, sinking under it.

"*June-bug?*" one says. "*Junie?*"

"*Dad.*"

I need him. To tell me how to make the flood of memories stop, how to rewrite a history of grief and break the curse before Saul and I lose any more of the things we love most.

I need *Dad* and all the things he never told me, and I need his arms.

I step to the ledge and study the delicate light beneath the water.

I take a deep breath and prepare to jump.

"NO!"

I spin back and see her: the girl from the cave, the woods, the hall of mirrors. "You'll drown," she hisses, her eyes wild. "You mustn't let him do this to you!"

"Let *who*?" I step toward her. "Who are you?"

"Come away from the water, Jack."

The Whites pull at my back, tell me not to walk away. The girl scans the misty forest, her pale arms hanging at her sides. "When are you going to stop this?" she screams.

"Who are you talking to?"

She faces me again. "Someone who has forgotten what it's like to have a name."

"Nameless?"

Her airy voice shakes. "The water doesn't lie. But it doesn't tell the whole truth either. If you want to break the curse, you must *both* go in. You and Saul together."

"But you said I'd drown," I stammer.

"Yes." She smiles sadly, then steps behind a thick eastern white pine. I curve around the tree's feathery branches, but she's gone. The mist has lifted, the sparkling sunlight replaced by thunderclouds and rain. I'm soaking wet, as though I've been standing out in the downpour for hours.

Standing there, in front of me, is Saul.

Thirty-One

HE rushes toward me and catches me in his arms. "I've been trying to get ahold of you all day," he says. "I thought you'd—I was scared you'd gone back to the water."

"The red-haired girl," I manage, still searching for her.

"From the cave?"

"She came to me—she said I'd drown. I don't know what they did, Saul, but our great-grandparents caused all of this—everything bad that's happened to us and our families, all of it."

His brow furrows. "June, what happened?"

My mind buzzes. I try to think back to the beginning. "Allison deGeest called my mom. My parents know I was with you. They know you're . . . you."

He nods. "Your stepdad was at my house when I got home."

"Seriously? What happened?"

He looks up the tree, rubbing his jaw. "He tried to hit me."

"Oh God."

"I almost felt like I should let him."

"Saul," I say sharply.

"I can't blame him."

"Look, I love Toddy, but he needs to drop the pee-on-everything-you-think-you-own outlook. This has nothing to do with him. I made my own decision, and besides, we have more pressing issues than he or my mom realize. Something bad happened here, and if we're going to fix it, we need to go in the water."

"June, you *just* said that girl appeared and told you you would *drown*."

I swallow a knot that scrapes like it's made of thorns. "She also said that we both had to go in to break the curse. I saw more memories, Saul. The dark ghost didn't just kill my dad; it killed Jack the First too. And your grandfather Zeke—he came to see my grandfather, like my dad went to see yours. Zeke had a dead rabbit—he *knew*, Saul. Our grandfathers knew about Nameless and the curse, and I think—Saul, if we don't fix this, I think we're next."

Saul trains his eyes on me. "How does going into the water fix it, June? What if that was Nameless trying to drown you? What if he's using your dad's and Bekah's voices to—"

"The girl *told* me, Saul."

"And who is she? How do we know she's not part of the curse? That she's not *helping* Nameless kill us?"

I massage the space between my eyebrows. I'd been sure I'd be able to convince Saul to go into the water with me. Not only because we need to break the curse, but because I *know* he must want to see Bekah again as badly as I want to see Dad, and we can *get to them.*

"We can't rush this, June," he says. "If we're going back there, we have to know for sure. We have to let the memories take us to the beginning."

"I don't care about the memories. I want to go through the veil, to where the memories come from, and *see him again.*"

He takes the back of my head in his hand and draws me into his rain-soaked chest. "The past is what it is, June. Can't the present be enough for you? Your mom and Todd and your brothers and Hannah. Me."

I close my eyes and breathe him in. *He's safe,* I tell myself. *We're safe. Focus on that.* "I don't understand how it can be enough for *you.*" I open my eyes again and watch the rain slide down his face. "How did you close up *your* black hole? How can *you* move on?"

The corner of his mouth inches up, and he cups my face. "Because I have to. The sun keeps rising, and the seasons keep changing, and there are still people here I don't want to lose."

Focus on that. There are still people here I don't want to lose.

"We need to find out about Abe Angert," I say.

"Abe?"

"You grandfather Zeke told Jack II he thought the curse was Jack the First's fault. But Jack II said it was Abe's—is that your great-grandfather?"

Saul shakes his head. "Abe was Zeke's brother, my great-uncle—I don't know much about him."

"We need to talk to someone who does."

Saul grimaces as he anticipates where I'm heading.

"Saul, every O' Donnell and Angert who came before us knew about the curse. We need to talk to your father."

He folds my fingers into his. "I never know what to expect when I get home. He may not remember the curse, or Abe. He may not even remember me." He looks poised to go on, but instead he rests his mouth against my forehead.

"I'll be there with you," I tell him. "If Eli doesn't remember you, I'll still be there."

His eyes move back and forth across my face, reading me. He nods and turns, leading the way through the woods.

Thirty-Two

THUNDER crackles, shivering the foundation of the Angert cabin.

It's never had quite the mythos of our farmhouse, but people *do* talk about it, guess what kinds of oddities hang on the walls or sit on dusty bookshelves. Because for all intents and purposes, this log cabin *was* the beginning of Five Fingers.

Before Jonathan Alroy O'Donnell arrived, the Angerts had already built their cabin and opened the sawmill that put Five Fingers on the map. For a long time, they'd owned most of Main Street, but they'd been selling it off for generations now. When Eli hit it big with his first novel, he sold the rest—everything except the Cape Cod–style house they bought on the water and that rickety cabin in the woods.

When Rachel and Eli split up, they sold the Cape Cod too. The original Angert cabin is all they have now, just like the farmhouse and the lone Jack's Tart tree are all *we* have.

Saul steps inside and runs a hand through his hair, shaking out the rain. I follow him past a staggeringly disorganized office piled with books and maps and old cassette tapes into a conjoined kitchen and living space, whose rear wall of windows reveals long swaths of storm gray and lush forest.

"Wait here." Saul turns to a brown leather couch draped in a set of red bedsheets, a dull plaid blanket, and some pillows. "I'll check the bedroom."

As he treads down the hall, I realize how tiny the house is. It's the kind of place you might rent for a long weekend with one or two friends, and judging by the bedding on the sofa, there's no spare bedroom for Saul. I imagine him and Bekah camped out on the couches, telling ghost stories and watching the windows for the glint of coywolf eyes.

There's sadness in this house—a fireplace overflowing with soot, counters littered with orange pill bottles, and the kind of quiet that feels less like peace and more like absence—but the warmth isn't gone entirely. A crayon drawing is still stuck to the fridge door, four stick people swimming under the lake, and notches in the back door record changes in Saul's and Bekah's heights. As miserable as they were when Bekah was suffering, I bet there still was softness and love in these walls. Moments, at least seconds, to feel bone-breaking crushes of happiness at being here together.

Beneath the coffee table, my feet bump a hidden cardboard box, eliciting a metallic rattle. I drag it forward and move aside the crumpled newspaper to find a stack of picture frames. I slide one out and stare into the black-and-white image: the gleaming eyes of a toothy girl whose dark freckles sprinkle her cheeks like constellations. Pollen and leaves cling to the sweat streaks in her messy bangs.

She can't be much older than fifteen, but she's got the crow's-feet and fine wrinkles of someone mid-laugh.

It's absolutely beautiful.

I set it down and keep riffling. Many are portraits; some were taken at wide angles; all are of kids: siblings, parents with their children. They're uniformly tender, saturated in the many shades of gray and black, eyes shining and endless, freckles and wrinkles holy.

They all have the same candidness of real living moments captured.

My chest twinges when I reach the last photograph. A girl lies in a hospital bed, tubes in her nose, dark hair a mess on the pillow. She's lifting herself up and pointing across the room, an open-mouthed smile ablaze across her face. Her unruly eyebrows are lifted in surprise.

You can't see what she's pointing at, but it doesn't matter. She is the sun. She is what matters, not whatever brought her that over-flowing happiness.

Her eyes and hair are dark, her skin fair and jaw sharply angled. She looks like her brother, only three years younger, permanently seventeen.

"He's sleeping." Saul's voice is low as he returns to the living room. I set the frame down. The sound and the sight of him, here in this place, breaks my heart. Not the way that losing Dad did, a constant, ever-deepening spiral into all the things I hadn't realized I'd lost right away. No, this is a sharp break, a flood crashing through a dam, because Saul has—and his father and mother and Bekah have—hurt more than any person should.

He sits beside me, taking the photograph in his hands. A crease burrows between his eyebrows. I touch the camera inked onto his skin. "Is this what the tattoo was about?"

His eyes barely reach mine before turning back to the photograph.

"They're beautiful," I say. "They're alive."

He raises an eyebrow. "Yeah. Can't do anything that's not ironic, I guess."

"What do you mean?"

His fingers splay on the glass, touching Bekah's teeth. "All these people, they're all dead."

"*What?*"

"I mean, not *all*. But someone from every picture. So if there's only one person, then, you know. I started this . . . um, not technically a business, because it was free . . . but this thing in college where I'd take pictures for families who had kids or partners with terminal illnesses."

I look at the open-mouthed girl again, expecting to see the haze of death, some kind of emptiness printed over her. She's obviously ill—medical equipment visible all around her—but she's still full of life, this indescribable *twinkle* I can't imagine ever being stamped out.

Dad had that too. Maybe some people die gradually, move away from their bodies over time, but others—people who shine—go in an instant. You can see their souls in their eyes until the last possible second, feel the gap in the world the second they're lost.

"They're incredible, Saul."

He sets the frame down. "You know, back when I used to pray, all I ever asked was to be able to tell stories. So I could be like my father." He juts his chin toward the box. "Telling stories never came naturally to me, but I was good at capturing moments. When I was a kid we had my photos hanging all over this place. When I left, I'd mail prints home for him—didn't tell him about the whole *sick kids* thing, just sent them along. I never expected that when I got home they'd all be in a box. Even the ones that used to be hanging. I guess that's the thing about moments. They always pass."

I thread my fingers through his. "You know what my least favorite thing is?"

"What's that, Jack?"

"When people find out you've lost someone and they get uncomfortable and embarrassed and pitying and weird."

"It's the worst."

"But not because I hate being pitied. I *do*, but it's more than that. When people pity you, it's like they honestly don't realize the exact same thing's coming for them. And then *I* feel embarrassed and uncomfortable and have to pity *them*, because, like, do you not realize it's always someone's turn? You haven't noticed *everyone* gets a few blows that seem so big you can't survive them? And then here is this person looking at you and dramatically murmuring, *I'm sorry for your loss*. And you have to look at them and hope your eyes aren't saying, *Don't be too sorry. You're next.* You have to spend all this energy making your face say, *Yes, it's horrible, and extremely* rare. *I can't believe I was the person who lost my father. You certainly won't lose anyone. You'll die first, out of everyone you love, on the eve of your hundredth birthday."*

"June." Saul says it so gingerly my eyes well with tears. He pulls me against his side and rests his chin on my head.

We both know that pain comes for us all.

It's almost a relief. Because if all of us are going to someday lose the people we love most, or be lost by them, then what is there to do but live? But that doesn't seem like a good enough answer. The answers to the hard questions *never* seem good enough.

"I'm sorry," I say. "I don't want to cry about someone who wasn't mine to lose. I feel like I'm co-opting your grief."

His hands stop tracing idle circles on my back. "I think once you've felt grief, it's hard not to catch someone else's. Especially when the person grieving is someone you love."

The word, *love*, swells painfully in my chest. "Or maybe when you've felt grief, it's hard not to love someone else who has too."

Saul eases my shoulders back to look me in the eye. "No," he says. No declarations or arguments or speeches. Just *no*, and it's all I want, all there's room for in this tiny house of ghosts.

"I'm so sure we can get to them," I tell him. "Like they're right there, on the other side, trying to help us."

"I know it feels like that. But our parents told us to stay away from the water for a reason, June. Nameless was *there*."

"I don't think I *can* stay away."

His fingers graze my spine and stop against my neck, where he knots them through my hair. "I know you think my dad can tell us what *really* happened between our families. But, June, some days he doesn't know what shoelaces are. Sometimes he doesn't remember how to ask. If he can't help us, promise me you won't go back to the falls until we're *sure* that's what we need to do."

My chest cinches. *I can't wait that long.* "He'll remember."

"Just in case." Saul goes to the mahogany liquor cabinet on the wall and pulls a notepad and pen from the bottom drawer.

"Still hiding your diary?"

"You know what I like about you?" he says.

"My bite."

"Precisely. Being mocked by you mere moments after holding you in my arms restores my faith in humanity." He sets the notepad on the ottoman. "If you *must* know, my dad uses this to take notes on different scotches. I figured we could write down—" He drops off.

"What?"

"Um." He stares down.

I pull the notebook from his hands and look at the shaky handwriting there: *Your son is Saul. Your daughter is Bekah. Bekah is dead.* I flip through the pages and find more notes: *This is your house. You live here alone.*

The name *Rachel* alone on one page; on the next, *Rachel is gone.*

Eggs go in the refrigerator.

Your laundry room is in the cellar.

Your agent's name is Miriam.

Saul pulls the notebook out of my hand, avoiding my gaze as he flips to an empty page.

"Saul."

He shakes his head. "I can't, June," he says, voice phlegmy. "I can't talk about it."

"Okay."

He scribbles names in opposite corners along the page's bottom end. He writes Bekah's beside his and Shadow's and Grayson's beside mine. "Saul, what are you—"

"Making a family tree." He starts four generations back, drawing a thin line marrying *Jacob Angert* to *Abigail Marshall Winston*. "This is when both our families say the feud started, and even if they're lying about the farm being the cause of it, Zeke blamed the curse on Jack the First, so it's a safe bet we only need to look this far back."

Beneath Jacob and Abigail, Saul lists their sons, *Ezekiel "Zeke" Angert* and *Abraham "Abe" Angert*. He connects Zeke to his wife, *Elisa Avila*, and beneath them he places their son, *Eli*. Finally, Saul links his father to *Rachel Stolarz*, then connects them to *Saul* and *Bekah* below. He slides the notebook my way. "Your turn, Jack."

As I start filling out my half, I realize how little I know about anyone but the Jacks. Like the Angerts, the O'Donnells are an antiquatedly patriarchal line. I scribble *Jack I* and *Annie* at the top, and below that I write *Jack II* and his wife, *Charmaine*, who produce a line to *Jack III*. I connect Dad to Mom, *Léa Girard*.

As I scan it, I catalogue all the evidence of the curse: Jack the First seeing Nameless on his deathbed; Jack II splitting his time between watching the dark ghost in the woods and the son he could barely look at through the window; Jack III clutching his chest in a forest clearing as the ghost throttled him and stole my whole world. "That's all I've got."

Saul analyzes the web of names, rubbing the wrinkle between his eyebrows. I'm distracted by his hands. Despite our current situation, his arm grazing mine still makes me feel a little like my organs might liquefy.

For a few seconds, the curse becomes less urgent to me than Saul's rain-dampened skin. Or the scratch of his fingers against his jaw's shadow. His eyes slope down my legs then return to the words on the page, and my stomach swelters. He glances my way again, and a slow smile quirks the corner of his mouth. "Why are you grinning?"

"I'm not."

"Yeah, June, you are. We're looking at our cursed family trees, and you're grinning."

I shrug, and he jogs my knee in his hand. I set my hand over his, and his smile widens until he lets out a heavy breath and refocuses on the notebook, leaving me to burn up by myself. I'm about to suggest we take a brief and steamy recess from the History of Grief when a low voice rattles behind us.

"What is she doing here?" Eli asks from the doorway, his mouth twisted downward. He feebly grips the doorjamb, shaking his gray head. "Can you see her, son?" he chokes out as he takes one stumbling step back, half-supported by the wall. All the heat in me turns icy then, because I see it so clearly in his face: Eli Angert is afraid of me. "Can you see the ghost?"

Saul rises and approaches his father. "Dad, this is my friend Junior. She's not a ghost. You're confused."

Eli stumbles, shaking his head frantically, eyes flashing between us in a frenzied corkscrew. "I didn't do anything," he cries at me, voice crackling. "Don't take my baby!" he screams. "Don't take my Bekah!"

I shake my head, speechless. I'm trembling as badly as he is. His eyes are clear, homed in on me. He doesn't look confused; he looks like he sees something dark and brutal.

"Dad," Saul tries again, inching nearer to him.

Eli scrambles for the door. "Leave us alone, Maolissa. You can't have her—leave us alone!"

He bolts into the thunderstorm, and Saul takes off after him, leaving me to chase them both.

When I reach the forest, sunlit mist replaces the rain.

Ahead, Saul's gaining on his father. Eli stops shambling from tree to tree and slumps against a trunk, his fingers digging into the bark. Saul gets an arm around him, but Eli's hysterical now, waving his arms against Saul's grip.

When he sees me, his knees sink onto a broken tree limb. His fingers curl into Saul's leg. "There," he cries, "you see her too. The dead O'Donnell girl. Issa."

Saul registers shock, and I look down at myself, half-expecting to see my clothes covered in blood or some visible evil circling me. But Eli and Saul are staring past me.

I turn and balk.

Within Feathers's rose-tinted aura, crisscrossed by Whites, stands a girl.

Not blood-smattered or grisly, but timid and barefoot. Impossibly still, like a tear in the world pulling everything toward her. Her strawberry waves hang on her shoulders, and her white shift clings to her, damp.

The dead O'Donnell girl, Issa? Issa, who Dad spoke to the night Mom asked him to end the feud?

Is Feathers *Issa O'Donnell*?

She beckons me from the edge of the woods, noiseless in her prompting. I look over my shoulder at Saul, who's still bodily supporting Eli. If Feathers is a dead O'Donnell, then we're on the cusp of understanding what happened to destroy our families.

On the cusp of breaking the curse.

Of diving through the water and seeing him again.

Saul gives one curt shake of his head. "June, no. I don't think—"

I step past the tree line, through the feathery softness. I've hardly caught the first desperate note of Saul's shout when a tremendous warmth sinks into me and I'm tugged into a new world.

Thirty-Three

I'M standing beside O'Dang!

Feathers—Issa—is gone.

I circle the sprawling roots, disrupting sleeping Whites that rise and twirl as I pass. Each time I curve around the trunk, I cross a new threshold and find different people there, eyes that don't see me, ears that don't hear me.

Children tightrope walk along roots. Preteens play chicken on low branches, slapping one another's hands and screeching with laughter when one finally topples off. Couples kiss in dirt pressed with pine needles, against the trunk, in crooks between branches. Dozens of people. Hundreds of bare feet.

They carve names and hearts, symbols and dates into the flaky bark. Flags are strung up, torn down. Mardi Gras beads tossed over limbs, bird feeders hung from the most inviting branches.

I walk past Dad and me.

I'm in the floral shorts that were my favorite at the time and the too-big yellow dinosaur shirt I often slept in. Dad won it for me in a milk-can toss. I'd wanted the stuffed tiger, but he'd talked me into the shirt: *You can only have the toy in the house*, he reasoned. *You can wear that shirt for years, anywhere you go, June-bug.*

That was Dad, all about mobility, being able to walk away when he wanted and come back when he needed. I wriggle my toes into the mud and watch them together until eventually they turn away.

A new White hovers at my sternum.

I observe its fragility, the way light bends and refracts through it nonsensically. I clasp it and keep circling the trunk.

I've come to her moment.

The red-haired girl, Issa, stands, facing the tree, beside the dark-haired boy she kissed in the cave. She holds a pocketknife to the bark, and he grips a nail between two knuckles, both etching lines into the tree.

"I'm writing yours." Her voice shimmers. I don't know how else to describe it. It's not purely a matter of sound; it's the way he reacts to it, his eyes squinting and mouth curling, ears pink. It's the way her words hit him and reverberate through his grin, the fullness that sparks and palpitates between them.

"I'll write yours," he says, and his voice shimmers into her too.

I feel Feathers—*Issa's ghost*—hovering behind me, watching.

A whistle cuts through the air. They both stop carving. "He's calling you," the boy says.

She folds the pocketknife and presses it into his palm. He slides his hand around her neck and kisses her slowly. "Tomorrow," she says.

"Tomorrow," he promises.

"I love you, Abe."

Abe.

"Always," Abe says. He leans against the tree and watches her retreat. Over his shoulder, their unfinished carvings are visible: O'D ANG.

Here—where wolves and coyotes lie together and robins sleep on the haunches of wild dogs, where cherries taste like sunlight and chickens run free—here, it was possible for an O'Donnell and an Angert to fall in love. So what happened to it all?

Why hadn't I heard Issa's name before?

Why does no one talk about her, though her ghost still wanders our house?

Issa's ghost leads me to the forest's edge, where another bobbing White waits for me. I cradle it, breathing deeply, and step through.

The blazing light of a setting sun skirts across the waves I'm facing. Peals of laughter rise amid the crash of water on sand. Down the shore, made into shadow by the intense last light of day, a man with pants rolled to the knee chases a little girl with long red curls in and out of the water. She squeals as she dodges him, her curls bouncing across her back.

Behind them, a petite woman with pinned-up hair walks barefoot across the wet sand, hand outstretched to a chubby toddler. The wind ruffles his Peter Pan collar and poufy shorts, dances through her yellow curls and blue dress.

The light slices around the four of them, shaping their silhouettes. Hunched like an amateur wrestler and swinging his stiff left leg, the man shuffles after the delightedly shrieking girl. "Oh no you don't!" he growls, bending to splash her. She shrieks and splashes him back, and he sweeps her into his arms, pretending to gobble her belly as she flails with laughter.

"Don't eat me, Papa!"

He swings her onto his hip and jogs her there, her hair glinting down her back like a blaze of fire. "I won't eat you, Issa," he says. "What kind of a man would eat his own heart?"

She grins, her face partially hidden under deep blue shadow. Beneath his one and a half eyebrows, the first Jack's eyes sparkle in the light. He cradles her head and kisses her above her temple.

Annie lifts a fussy Jack II into her arms and steps into the water beside her husband. They watch the half dome of sun melt into the waves; they squint against the wind. For a moment, my family—the first Jack, Annie, Issa, and Jack II—are happy.

I take a step into the water behind them, wanting to become a part of this memory. Instead I find myself back on the hill.

A pinkness, the aura of a red-haired girl, dances on the porch, and my chest aches with the memory of the one ghost who's *not* inside that house.

For the people who are left, I go inside.

Thirty-Four

"STRAIGHT to school and straight home," Mom says sharply, pressing my phone into my hand. "*Only* for emergency calls."

"You're seriously going to make me stay home on Halloween?" I say.

"Oh, you're not staying home," she says. "You're coming to Shadow's basketball game."

"Mom, come on."

"We've been over this."

We "went over it" for two hours last night when I walked in, rain-soaked, through the front door, which, thanks to the Whites, Mom and Toddy hadn't seen me walk out of in the first place.

"I have half a mind to keep your phone even during the day," she says, "and if I see you've been sending texts or using data, I *will* keep it tomorrow."

Hannah leans on the horn outside.

"I'm going to *fail* creative writing without his help. I'm not going to get a letter of recommendation."

A fifth honk from Hannah's car.

"I'll call your teacher and get a referral for a tutoring service," Mom says. It's both a genuine offer and a threat. Another *end of story, final answer, no Saul Angert for you while you live with me.*

Is this really as simple as a fight over the land, over money? Why would Mom care about that?

Since I got back last night, Feathers has been hovering against my Whiteless wall. "At least tell me Saul and Eli are okay," I begged of her, but no matter how much I hissed and threw paper wads at her, she took me nowhere, gave me no new answers, and I spent the night willing Saul to be safe, praying nothing happened to him or Eli.

Hannah honks again, and I throw Mom one last glance. "I can't make you tell me what happened between our families," I say, "but I'm going to find out either way."

Her mouth tightens. "For your sake, I hope you don't."

"But we *always* spend Halloween together." Hannah stabs her pasta salad with her fork and waves it toward the fake spider webs strewn over the cafeteria doors. "I'll beg. Parents love me."

"One of the benefits of being a real-life Disney princess, Han, which, after our attempted campout, you're officially not. You're a brazen hussy like me now. How's it feel?"

"You know, it felt pretty good," she says, "until Léa called my mom."

"I can't believe *you* didn't get grounded. I think my mom

would care less if I'd talked you into stealing a car than she does that *you* talked *me* into spending half a night at the falls with an Angert."

Hannah sets her fork down and studies me.

I'd told her this morning about what happened in the woods last night—who Feathers was, that Issa and Abe were in love, that Saul and I would have to go in the water to break the curse, and what I heard at the falls last weekend—and the crease of worry between her brows hasn't let up since.

I look down at the pathetic tacos on my tray, a mess of low-grade beef and wilting iceberg lettuce. There's some serious cognitive dissonance going on with the summery food they're serving us and the actual snowflakes falling outside.

"How did it feel?" Hannah asks quietly. "Hearing his voice."

Like nothing else mattered. Like he was really there.

I stand and swipe the rest of my food into the trash can. "It hurt so much I thought I would die."

On my way to study hall, I stop by the office to pick up a drop/add slip on my way to the library, where I slide into the last computer in the row along the rear wall. I can see a sliver of Ms. deGeest through the open door to her classroom.

A storm of anger and shame rages in my stomach.

I'm furious with her for telling my parents about Saul, but I'm also furious with myself for spending the last four years obsessed with following in Dad's footsteps. Now any other future I might want hinges *entirely* on my ability to write myself out of the hole of a straight-C student.

And I can't do it. Can't face deGeest. Can't write. Can't figure out who I want to be or where I want to go. All I can think about right now is breaking this curse before it hurts someone else.

I start an e-mail to Saul, telling him about the tree with O'D ANG carved into it and the moment on the beach with Jack the First, Annie, Jack II, and Issa—*she was his daughter, I think*. I write about Feathers guiding me through it all and my fight with Mom. I ask if Eli's okay, whether he said anything after I disappeared after Feathers, then I hit SEND and wait.

I open a word document—*one last try*—but I have no story, just broken pieces of one.

I lay my spinning head on the desk. The computer pings, and I sit upright to find an e-mail waiting for me.

Jack, I'm so happy you're okay. A few seconds later another comes in: *Sorry, I wanted to say that before I finished reading the e-mail. Back now.* New York Times *best-selling author Eli Angert is fine, but I couldn't get anything out of him. Pretty much right after you ran off, he forgot he'd ever seen you. Have I mentioned how happy I am you're okay? It's almost enough to make knowing I can't see you all right. Just kidding, I'm more selfish than that.*

Meet me tonight, I type.

He doesn't respond for four minutes, each of which takes approximately one hour to pass. When his message comes in, it reads: *Juuuune.*

Sauuuuuuul, I reply.

I didn't think I'd ever get to kiss you.

*I'll give you six dollars and kiss you again if you
meet me tonight.*

Your family's really upset, June.

I stare at the words, chest burning, hands aching, eyes stinging.
The next message that comes in reads: *Promise me you'll stay away
from the water, June.*
    Being apart sucks, I say.
    It does, he says. *Promise me, June.*

*I can't wait any longer. I can't spend every night
waiting for something terrible to happen to my
family, or to you. We have to end this tonight.*

Another six minutes pass. *Where and when?*

Thirty-Five

"JUNIOR, could you stay after class?"

It's infuriating that Ms. deGeest can even look at me, embarrassing that *I* can't look at *her*.

After the rest of the class files out, I count thirty seconds of pin-drop silence before Ms. deGeest crosses her arms and leans against the table. Her lipstick is miraculously crisp for this late in the day. Every detail of her seems curated, like her four years' advantage over me gave her the time to determine the precise message she wanted her hair, makeup, wardrobe, and posture to communicate.

"You didn't turn in an assignment," she says.

"I haven't written anything."

"Any particular reason?"

"My life took a particularly weird turn this week."

Her eyes flicker sideways, betraying an instant of discomfort before she pulls her Grown-Up Teacher mask on. "I understand why you're upset."

Now I do meet her eyes. "You're *from* here," I say. "You must know about the bad blood between my family and Saul's. You might've stepped into my business out of some misguided desire to protect me, but you have no idea what—"

"I'm sorry." She straightens the papers on her desk. When she looks up her cheeks are pink. "Okay? I'm new at this, and I crossed a line. I messed up, and you don't need to forgive me, and you certainly don't have to like me, but this thing you do? Writing? It's not a hobby, not a phase. *You* are a *storyteller*. You have a chance to shape your world. You have talent and opportunities and something to say, and you're choosing to blow it because you think this town defines you. I've watched your effort in this class dwindle—you haven't turned in *anything* since I ran into you that night—and if I overstepped, it was only because I thought you were getting involved in a situation that wasn't good for you, and if I were your mother, I'd want—"

I can't contain a jab of laughter. "My mother? To be my mother, you'd have to have gotten pregnant when you were four years old."

She lifts her hands. "The point is, don't let my mistake be an excuse to give up on this class, and don't let Saul be an excuse to stay here. Believe me, June, I know what it's like, how hard it is to leave, to let yourself be different. And I know Saul. What the world stands to lose if he walks away from writing. Look, your grammar's a mess, your vocabulary's slim, and you could line the Great Wall with your adverbs, but you *have* something to offer. That's a *gift*.

And if you master the tools that go along with it, well . . . the world will be better for it. It's okay to be angry with me—and it's okay to take breaks from writing, and fine, college isn't for everyone. But if you take this seriously, you need to fight for your future. Do *something*."

"I *am* doing something," I say, frustration mounting. "I'm just not *writing* because sometimes *writing* isn't worth anything. Sometimes your actual *life* takes over and you don't have time to stare at a computer for four hours."

"I understand." Her voice dims to a hum. "I do. But you shouldn't feel guilty about taking time to nurture a part of yourself that matters. And aside from that, you *need* to turn in your homework. I can't possibly communicate how ridiculous it would be for you to fail this class because you didn't take an hour to pull together *something* to turn in."

I take the slip of paper from my pocket and set it in front of her. She lifts it between two polished fingernails. "This is a drop slip."

"Yeah."

"We're weeks from the end of the semester."

"A month."

"It's too late for this."

"The office gave it to me," I counter. "They'll do anything to get a few more seniors though graduation."

"And you think you won't graduate without dropping my class?"

I nod.

"Because you plan to fail?"

"Are you going to sign it?"

She tears it in half and places the halves in front of me. "It's too late."

"Okay." It doesn't change anything. I'm not going to do the work, because writing down the past is meaningless. I hate so much of my family's past, who I am because of it. I want to undo it, not preserve it as record. All that matters is undoing it.

"I can't do the work for you," she says. "You can't save anyone, no matter how hard you try. I want good things for you, but that doesn't matter if you don't want them for yourself."

Her stare has at *least* as much steel in it as I imagine mine does. "I don't need saving. I just don't have anything to write."

"I'm not asking you to make something perfect. I'm asking you to put the work in."

"I'm not like you, okay? I'm stuck here. This town *is* me."

"Fine." But I can tell it's not fine. She's upset and disappointed, and right now it's easy to see she's not much older than me. While she may have *learned* you can't save anyone, she hasn't stopped trying or feeling bad when she can't.

A strange feeling tangles in my chest.

I want her to be right about me.

"I'll try," I say over my shoulder.

It feels like a lie. I guess I'm still nothing if not a Jack.

Thirty-Six

"I can't believe her." Hannah takes another slurp of her Diet Coke. We're sitting in the bleachers of the Five Fingers Elementary gymnasium, watching Shadow's basketball game. "Doesn't she realize she's your *teacher*, not your mother?"

"Shh." I tip my head toward Grayson, the only buffer between us and Mom and Toddy. Thankfully, Mom made an exception to the No Fun, No Friends rule and let me bring Hannah along. When Toddy found out, he was huffy. They'd almost certainly made a pact not to cave on my punishment, and Mom's already broken it. Out on the basketball court, tennis shoes squeal over the floor and high-pitched shouts echo as the boys call for one another to pass the ball to them. It seems like *everyone* on the court is saying, *Here! Here!* I half-expect Grayson to join in from the way he's bouncing on his butt.

Hannah drops her voice into a whisper. "I'm serious, Junie. You could probably get her fired for that. It's freaking *creepy* how she keeps getting into your business."

I feel a barb of defensiveness, like when someone else joins in when you're complaining about your siblings. "Yeah, well, it's not like she's the only problem. There are billions of things keeping us apart."

Hannah's lips turn down in an exaggerated frown. "It's a *week* without a phone, not a prison sentence. I'm sure he's at home moping and pining, like *you've* been doing all day. It's a bump in the road, Junie."

"A cursed bump."

Hannah shakes her head, bangs swinging over her blue eyes. "You're not going to try and do it alone, though, right? Issa *told* you not to go without him."

"No. We're going to try to meet up tonight."

Her gaze flashes toward my mom, and she whispers, "Maybe you should slip Léa some Ambien."

"Frankly, I think she could muscle through on sheer willpower."

"I want candyyyy!" Grayson announces then, kicking the shoulder blade of the woman sitting in front of us. She turns around with a glare, and Mom flashes an apologetic smile.

Toddy leans forward. "The game's almost over, Gray."

"I'm soooo hungry," he groans. "And I'm about to pee my pants!"

The buzzer sounds then, signaling a Five Fingers loss. As we make our way out to the snowy lot, Grayson skips along dramatically clutching his crotch and squealing in faux misery and true delight at the way the people crane their necks to watch him.

When we get home, everyone else slips inside, but Mom catches me on the porch. "Could you give us a minute?" she asks Hannah.

When the door is shut behind her, I say, "What, don't want an audience while you attach a house-arrest tracker to my ankle?"

Mom gestures toward one of the garden chairs, and I plop down as she eases herself into the other. It's freezing out, and our teeth are fighting a chatter. "You know I hate this, June. I would much rather trust you."

"Then do."

She sets her hand on top of mine. "I didn't want to tell you this, but Todd thinks you should know." After a long beat of silence, she gives her head one firm shake. "Abraham Angert was a murderer."

I stare at her, uncomprehending. "What?"

"He killed your grandfather's sister, your great-aunt. Issa. It happened when Jack II was very young, but it affected him profoundly. Your father grew up hearing about it—older people in town were still talking about it. Jack II was a sad, sad man. Losing his sister destroyed his family."

My mind grasps at the words, but they don't make any sense. Abe *couldn't* have killed the girl he loved. And even if he did, that wouldn't be an excuse for banning me from Saul.

"She was only seventeen," Mom continues. "Abe *said* he had no recollection of doing it, and by the time of the trial, his counsel had persuaded him to plead insanity."

"What do you mean he *said* he had no recollection?"

"Issa's father, Jack the First, never believed it. So her brother, Jack II, didn't quite believe it either, and your father *really* didn't believe it. They thought the Angerts were . . . dangerous."

My scoff isn't enough to show how completely ludicrous that sounds. "Dangerous. And that's what *you* think?"

"I don't know, Jack." Her face twists at the sound of my name. She frees her hand and sinks into her chair. The snowfall has picked up. The lawn is almost entirely coated with white, Shadow and Grayson's cherry sprouts bowing under the weight, and the treetops glint silver. "I think there was more to it than any of them ever let on. And I loved your daddy, but he was *not* the most forthcoming person—he wanted the world to be rosy and bright for us all the time, even at the expense of the truth."

"I know."

Mom narrows her eyes as if trying to see through my skin. Finally, she gives up, and they soften. "I don't know why he thought what he did, but he was afraid of them, June. And there wasn't much else he was scared of.

"I can't protect you forever." Her voice quivers as she stands, a cloud of ice crystals hovering in the air from her breath. "I'm going to while I can." She looks back, resting her hand on the weather-rusted doorknob. "I can't lose you too."

I know what we're risking if we go to the water. But I also know what we're risking if we don't.

"You won't, Mom," I whisper.

Thirty-Seven

INSIDE, Hannah's already got her homework arranged on the kitchen table. The boys are on the couch, watching old episodes of *Adventure Time*, flat out shrieking with laughter, and Toddy's setting up Happy Lamps, his yearly effort to sprinkle the house with imitation sunlight as we slog toward winter, which likely won't let up until April or May.

He emerges from the basement carrying the clock he bought me last year, the kind with a light that clicks on an hour before your wake-up time, intensifying gradually until it theoretically wakes you up with the misconception you're going to see the sun that day.

Against my wishes, my coldness toward him thaws.

Mom comes and sets my phone down beside me, tapping the tabletop with her manicured fingernails. "I still don't want you communicating with him," she says.

Toddy halts his dig through the hall closet, standing still in a hopelessly obvious attempt to listen in. I nod, and that's that. Toddy huffs and heads upstairs. Mom follows him, and I stare at my phone, debating whether it's safe to text Saul.

Han looks up from the calculus problem she's been scowling at and whispers, "You can use my phone to text him if you want."

I glance toward the stairs and shake my head. "We're meeting tonight anyway." I dig my folders out of my backpack, and Hannah shrugs and returns to her work. I last two minutes before I cave and start a message to Saul. I rephrase it eleven times but still find no delicate way to tell him what Mom told me. I settle on: *My mom said Abe killed Issa.*

I let out the breath I'm holding and pick up the photocopied notes I harangued Stephen for, my last attempt not to fail Ms. deGeest.

The top page is a sort of timeline printed in uneven shades of gray, covered in streaks of highlighter and Stephen's chicken-scratch notes. "STORY ARC," it says at the top.

My phone buzzes. I check the stairs again for Mom or Toddy before opening Saul's reply.

Eli won't tell me anything about Abe. He shuts down whenever I ask. I don't know what happened, but I can't imagine the guy we saw making out with Issa in the cave hurting her. There's more to this.

Agreed, I respond. *Mom finally left me alone. I'll see if I can track down some Whites before tonight.*

My phone buzzes almost immediately. *Please don't do that. What if they take you to the water again?*

I sigh. I keep making promises I can't keep. That I'll stay away from Saul, that I won't go to the water without him, that I'll do my creative writing homework despite the utter chaos inside my brain. *What will you give me if I wait?*

Apple fritters by the dozen. I'm at Egrets with NYT-blah-blah-blah Eli Angert right now.

Egrets, the storefront downtown that sells pastries and cider from Egret Orchard, is a Five Fingers autumn staple. It's only open a few months a year, during which everyone eschews their usual cafés in favor of apple everything. *See you at two then.*

I turn again to the STORY ARC timeline and try to focus.

The main horizontal path curves across the page like a speed bump, vertical lines labeled "TURNING POINT" dividing it into sections.

Stephen's labeled the first section of the timeline: "ORDINARY WORLD."

Before I met Saul, my mind fills in the blank.

"TURNING POINT 1: NEW OPPORTUNITY."

"NEW SITUATION."

"TURNING POINT 2: INTRODUCTION OF MAIN GOAL."

"PROGRESS TOWARD GOALS/TESTS, ALLIES, ENEMIES."

Feathers/Issa—ally? Nameless—enemy? Ms. deGeest—mentor? Enemy? Ally?

"TURNING POINT 3: POINT OF NO RETURN." It's the halfway point on the line, with two more big turning points marked afterward.

Point of no return: *the cliffs over the swimming hole.*

I can feel Saul's knuckles grate against mine. I remember the fall breeze rustling over our naked skin, drawing goose bumps on our arms and legs. His eyes on me, his breath, half the stars strewn across the sky and half warbling in the oily water.

There is no returning from what I heard in the cave or what I found in the water. And there's no returning to how things were before I knew Saul Angert.

I drag my laptop to me and start to type. I begin by describing the way Saul fumbled over the tent and how it made my insides turn into bumblebees. I write about the way he kissed me, breathed against me. How the water drew us into it with the false promise that anything that happened within it would be sacred, unknowable, secret, and safe. I write it all.

I could be embarrassed at the thought of Ms. deGeest reading this, but I'm not sure she ever will. I'm writing this for myself.

So I can remember.

So if someday the curse squeezes my heart so hard the blood stops pumping, I can disappear from this world knowing that night won't be lost. The truth won't be lost.

I, Jack O'Donnell IV, love an Angert.

"More coffee?" Han swipes our mugs up and carries them into

the kitchen. I look up, feeling like I've just emerged from the warm water beneath the falls.

The boys have changed into pajamas and moved on from cartoons to a boxing video game.

Shadow keeps saying, "Gray! You don't have to move side to side! Your character does that automatically!"

Grayson keeps kicking and half-elbowing Shadow as he waves the wireless controllers around in a frenzy.

Hannah glides back with our refilled mugs. "So I chose my AP psych paper topic: the fallacy of memory. Thought the research could help with your little . . ."

"Curse?" I finish.

"I was going to say *problem.*" She drops into her seat. "Anyway, it turns out memories are rarely totally accurate, and the more we're asked about them, and the *way* we're asked about them . . . well, it changes them."

"Example?"

"Um, this guy showed a video of a car accident to two groups of people. To one group, he asked questions about what happened when the cars were *smashed into.* He asked the other what happened when the cars were *hit.* A week later, the *smashed* group remembered seeing shattered glass in the video. Which there wasn't."

"Huh." I think about all the memories I've seen so far, the way that, though I'm not *really* there, I can still *feel* them.

"You know how sometimes you remember something specific from your childhood, and your parents can confirm it happened, but when you picture it, it's less like a memory and more like you're watching it happen to someone else, like a video?

Memory is mostly about making connections. We have snippets of real information, bits of imagination and emotions, and we combine them to tell ourselves stories. That could explain *how* you experience the memories. Sure. They could belong to your dad, but maybe you don't see them through his eyes because *he* didn't really either. His brain created a full to-scale replica of the moments you're visiting."

"Weird."

"If you think *that's* weird, you should hear about this rat experiment these scientists did."

"'Rat experiment' is basically my middle name."

"They found out they could pass phobias down through generations of rats."

"Everything about that grosses me out."

Hannah laughs, but her eyes widen at the prospect of talking science. "It's called genetic memory. It's present in animals at birth, leftover information gathered by previous generations. Like, rats learn to be afraid of cats, and cats learn to be afraid of dogs. Not every new rat or cat has to have firsthand experience with the enemy to learn that fear, you know? Some are born with it.

"Maybe that's how O'Donnells are with the falls and with Angerts. Maybe it's genetic memory."

"That's not the same thing," I point out. "I was freaked out by the falls *because* my parents were *constantly* telling me to stay away from them."

"True," Hannah says. "Bad example. Anyway, what are *you* working on? Seems like you're over your writer's block?"

"In this exact moment, yes."

"Well, you know what they say: Rome was built in one exact moment."

"What's writer's block?" Grayson hollers over his shoulder.

Hannah whispers, "How can one tiny organism make that much noise while simultaneously catching every word we say?"

"He's got to be some kind of reincarnated god," I answer, then shout, "It's when you can't write."

"I get that," Grayson says.

"Oh? What are you writing?"

"Homework stuff." He sends one of his controllers flying into the wall.

"Hey, bud, use the wrist straps with those things, okay?"

He chases it and picks it up, but it's too late: Shadow's character has knocked Grayson's out. "Is Mike going to come over and help you with your homework?" Grayson asks.

Shadow glances back at us. "Yeah, tell Mike to come over. Grayson's too easy to beat."

"Mike?" Hannah asks.

I'm distracted by a lone White sifting down the hall toward the stairs.

"June?"

"Mike does Junior's homework," Grayson answers Hannah.

"He's her *tutor*," Shadow corrects him.

The White twirls up the banister. I know I told Saul I wouldn't, but it's here for me—sent to me, like I'm now sure all the memories have been.

My heart begins to race. "Be right back," I tell Hannah and jog upstairs. The White clings to my closet door.

Why can't I let this go?

Because *he's* sending them.

The White dances like a dandelion in a summer breeze. I reach a shaking hand out and hungrily accept its warmth into my skin.

I can't resist. I step through the doorway.

I'm still inside my closet, but I'm facing out into my bedroom now. Shouts are coming from downstairs: screams—a man and woman—and the shatter of porcelain.

A teenage Issa hurries into the room, pulling little Jack II in after her. She closes the door, shutting out some of the noise, but Jack II is still crying. She shoots him a forced yet fierce smile, then hurries to the bed and starts ripping the blankets off it.

Jack rubs his eyes and takes a tentative step. "What are you doing?"

She flings the smile over her shoulder, golden-red curls falling into her face. "I'm building a safe house."

"A safe house?"

"Take the pillows and follow me, Jack." She carries the bundle of bedding into the closet, passing right through me. She begins tying the corners of the sheets to the shelves along the wall, stringing up a fort.

Jack II's chin snaps over his shoulder at the sound of another shout. "Jackie," Issa says, taking his shoulders.

He stares at her with saucerlike eyes. "What's a safe house?" he whispers.

She studies him, the expression on her heart-shaped face as serious as that on his round one. "A safe house is a doorway to a magical place."

"Like the thin place."

"Yes, like the thin place. When we go inside, we won't be here anymore. We'll be somewhere no one can find us. A secret place for you and me alone. How's that sound?"

Jack nods solemnly, and Issa squeezes his shoulder, then ducks into the blanket fort. He follows, a look of wonder spreading as he inspects the light spilling through the blankets. "We'll be safe," he says.

"We will."

"Why is he so angry?" Jack asks.

A sadness flickers over Issa's face. "I think because he is afraid."

"Afraid of what?"

"Of losing what he loves."

Jack's mouth forms a perfect circle of concern. "The cherries?"

Issa folds her legs underneath herself and pats the pillow beside her. Little Jack curls up there, letting his sister smooth his hair. "He's very lonely, Jack," she says. "He's watching the world as he's always known it change into a place he doesn't fit. He resents those who know how to change with it and those who pity him. I think he even resents those who love him." She squeezes his shoulders. "You and I won't ever be alone like that. Someday you'll be grown up, and when you are, we'll escape together."

"Where will we go?" Jack asks.

"Anywhere you want. With anyone we want."

"I don't want him to hate me," Jack whispers.

She discreetly brushes tears from her eyes and kisses the crown of his head. "Have I ever told you about the night you were born?"

He shakes his head, and her lips press into a smile. "Papa was in Maryland. Everyone wanted Jack's Tart, and people had money to spend back then, so he'd gone to sell seeds to a farmer down there. He hadn't wanted to go, but you weren't due for another two weeks, and Mama told him there was a better chance of every fish in Lake Michigan turning silver than your being born in the next two days.

"But you had other ideas, and sure enough, when Papa reached the hotel that night, there was a message waiting for him: You were on your way. He was so happy, he picked the clerk up and spun him around, gave him all the cherry seeds he'd brought to sell. Then he hopped right back in the car without so much as a glass of milk for dinner and headed for home. But as he drove, he saw, out of the corner of his eye, a star falling over Backbone Mountain.

"And then another, and another, until the sky was alight with a meteor shower. Papa knew then you had arrived. He started crying so hard he couldn't see—from happiness that you were here and sadness because he'd missed your grand arrival. He couldn't return home with nothing to give his new son, so he pulled over and climbed to the top of Backbone, and at its peak, with his bare hands, he caught a falling star."

I've heard this story, though in my father's version, Jack the First had chased the star on horseback and caught it on a dare from Jacob Angert. I wonder, then, if I'm witnessing the story's first telling. If it was less an exaggeration and more an outright fabrication that Issa created to soothe Jack II in this moment. Something that affected him profoundly enough that he'd pass it along to his own son, who would pass it to me, all its details chopped up and rearranged.

"And though the star badly burned," Issa continues, "he ran to his car and drove all the way home through the night with it, ignoring the heat on his palm. When he reached Five Fingers, he threw the star into the lake, and just like that, every fish turned bright, shimmering gold. Papa caught one with his hand and carried it to the hospital, where he found me and you and Mama waiting for him. *Hi, Jack*, he said to you, *I'm your father, and this is how much I love you. Enough to climb a mountain. Enough to catch a star. Enough to carry it home as it burns. Someday you'll know what it's like. Someday you'll love something so much it turns every brown fish gold."*

Jack's lungs have fallen into a steady rhythm, his eyes pressing shut.

"I love you, Jack," Issa whispers. "Even if he's forgotten how to, I won't. I love you, and I'll never let you go."

When he finally drifts into sleep, the memory freezes.

You promised, I remember Jack II crying on the bed to the pink ghost. *You promised we'd get out.*

He knew Feathers was his sister. She was supposed to take him away, somewhere safe. She *was* his somewhere safe. I know what that's like to watch that disintegrate. To lose the one thing you never thought you could.

But how? How did he lose her?

Did Abe really kill her?

Dread creeps through me, mingling with the ache of grief.

I slip back into the bedroom—mine, in the present. The sound of Shadow's and Grayson's laughter, of Hannah's playful teasing drift up to me. I'm home.

I set my alarm for two A.M. and get in bed. I must drift off, because

I jerk awake sometime later, choking, convinced my lungs are filled with the water from the falls.

The cold burn in my chest fizzles, but there's no way I'm getting back to sleep, so I creep downstairs. Mom's sitting up at the table, tearfully scribbling in a notebook. Fresh worry needles me. I want to go to her—comfort her—but I can't jeopardize my impending escape.

I sneak back upstairs to wait. My nerves spark when a text from Saul comes in. I'm suddenly afraid he'll call off our plans, feel too guilty or worried to meet me in the woods. I tap it open.

Hey. An ambiguous bait-message. An implied *We need to talk.*

I figure if I don't respond, he won't be able to cancel. There's no way Saul Angert will leave me to wander the woods alone.

Another message comes in. *That was my impression of a loser who doesn't know how to say what he's thinking.*

Convincing, I can't resist replying.

It's all about commitment. If I'd texted you any sooner, with more than one word, it might not have been so convincing.

Great, I say, then add, *Are you trying to cancel?*

No.

Then why are you texting me an hour before we're supposed to meet?

Why do you think?

So it's my job to answer the question for you.

I don't want to wait an hour, he says.

That eager to dive into memories, huh?

Sure. That's it.

*Flirting with me on the very brink of discovering what
caused a century-old family curse.*

I'm shameless. Shameful? Both?

I think you mean "hot."

Get over here, Jack.

I'm trying, I tell him.

Not hard enough, apparently.

Is that a euphemism?

Hitting on me on the very brink of breaking a
century-old family curse, huh, June?

I go into my closet for a coat and a pair of boots, then sit on my bed and pull them on. A faint illumination comes from the window. The Whites are back, silently grazing one another as they shift within the pane.

This time when I sneak downstairs, Mom's on the couch snoring peacefully, a pilled carmine throw tossed over her. Guilt coils around my stomach.

You're doing this for her too, I tell myself. *For everyone you love.*

The windows are frosted and dark, but I can make out a doe picking its way through the snowy lawn, two fawns ambling after, stopping to sniff and munch. At one point they freeze and stare at me, their ocher eyes blinking at me through the glass.

I remember a morning like this one. Dad nudged me awake and led me downstairs to show me how, through one window, you could see coywolves hiding in the trees and, through the other, a deer lying in the snow as though it were a bed of hay.

"Is it true that in another forest, the coyotes or the wolves would kill her?" I whispered.

Dad nodded solemnly and twisted the knob on the back door, nodding permission for me to step outside. Our toes purpled in the below-zero temperature, and our breath was visible as we watched the creatures. "Anywhere else the deer would run too," Dad whispered. "But this is sacred ground."

"Marta Griggs didn't believe me," I told him. "Even though her family believes there used to be a magic garden and a snake slithered into it and spread evil. She says that's why people kill one another and why they get sick too."

Dad's face tensed. "You know, June-bug, evil's something you

327

can decide to do every day, and it gets easier every time. But the more good you bring into the world, maybe the more the rest of the world would look like this. Like paradise."

I ease the back door open, and the wind cuts through me. I close it before the bite can wake Mom, and I step onto the porch, heart trilling in my chest because we're so close to figuring everything out *and* because I'm going to see Saul again. Finally.

As I set off across the yard, a snowshoe hare darts past me, followed by two more, their feet pricking holes in the crunchy snow. I watch the point where they vanish into the dark folds of the trees, amazed by how much ground something so small can cover in so little time. I pick up my pace, jumping in surprise as a deer gallops jerkily past, dashing into the forest exactly where they did, its white tail fading into the night.

An outburst of flapping wings erupts behind me, and the feeling of free fall hits me all at once, the sensation of my stomach flying into my mouth, the ground dropping out from under me.

I know before the stampede of living things hits—the porcupines and opossums, starlings and house sparrows, weasels and woodchucks all scuttling furiously past me, all shrilling and wild-eyed. Before I've turned to face the chicken coop, I know what I'll find.

The blackness thrashes in front of it, stretched out in every direction, twice its usual size, and everything caught within its grasp screams and seizes. Instead of huddling around the heater in the coop, the chickens flap through the grass, pecking and flailing; field mice move drunkenly among them, falling onto their backs and twisting in agony.

A hen—neck twisted, blood and feathers spread—lies strewn across the shining white.

"Saul." My teeth chatter, lips shiver. I turn and run, whipping my phone from my coat. I dial as fast as I can, counting the seconds as the line rings. Once.

Twice.

Three times.

Six.

Seven.

"Hi, you've reached Saul. Sorry I can't take your call. Leave—"

"No," I say aloud. I call again.

One ring. Two. Three. Five. Seven. *"Hi, you've reached—"*

I turn back to the writhing darkness, to the nameless thing following me, hating me. "You can't have him."

It vanishes.

I take off running.

Thirty-Eight

IT'S not too late, I tell myself.

I'll get to Eli's cabin soon, and Saul will be fine, I tell myself. *I'll be fine.*

I keep running, my heart raging against my rib cage.

A twig snaps within the forest—the footfall of a coywolf, or gravity taking its toll on a dead branch, probably. But I *feel* something watching me.

Another snap. A rustle. I spin.

A dark shape dives into the shadows.

I lunge after it, throw myself through the brush, feet pounding the snow, calves burning, lungs heaving, heart *aching* because *where is Saul and why isn't he answering his phone?*

A half dozen coywolves scatter from the brush as I pick up my pace. I run until everything is a blue-green blur. The trees thin ahead, moonlight breaking through.

I stumble into the clearing around the cabin. A rabbit lies dead in front of the steps, and the front door hangs open, the wind pounding it against the side of the house. Dead leaves skitter across the floor, the crispy noise like a lifeless version of Saul's laugh.

I bound up onto the porch and move into the dark hallway. "Saul?"

The house is a mess: an antique console table flipped on its side, a ceramic vase shattered, its dried-out contents spilling across the wood grain. A green lamp knocked over on a fifties walnut table, its age-yellowed shade askew and the lightbulb flickering from the loosened connection.

"Saul?" My voice crackles as if interrupted by static.

Soft whimpers rise from behind the couch. I pick up a broken slab of ceramic from the ground as I advance. "Hello?"

I sidle around the edge of the coffee table until I can see the gap between the couch and the loveseat. On the floor, a man in rumpled pajamas rocks against the wall, tears still rolling down his wrinkled cheeks.

"Eli." I hurry to his side.

His vacant eyes drift to me, blinking against the stuttering lamplight. The wintry bite I'm used to finding in his face is nowhere to be seen, but neither is the man who cradled his daughter on a bathroom floor.

"Who are you?" He sounds young, lost.

"I'm Ja—Junior," I decide on. "Saul's friend."

"Saul." Eli looks at his hands. They're clutching a triangular slice of ceramic, like mine, but his are smeared with blood. His arms are sliced in purposeless sweeps of dark red. I bite down on the words—*Oh God*—rising in my chest.

I pry the makeshift weapon from his fingers. "Eli. Where's Saul? What happened?"

"Saul." Something passes over his eyes, as if his mind just slid into place behind his pupils. A gurgle gets trapped in his throat. "Saul's my son." He covers his trembling mouth with one hand. *"Bekah's gone."*

"Eli."

His eyes snap toward mine, teeth chattering. "She came."

Shivers spring up over my legs as the wind's howl whips through the open front door. "Bekah?"

"No. Maolissa." The open door claps against the side of the house. Eli's eyes pinch shut, and he releases a half-formed grunt, the tears starting to fall anew as he slumps toward the wall.

"Eli, *what happened*?"

"Maolissa came. She tried to take him from me. I told him not to go," Eli gasps between tears. "He wasn't going to. But then *he* came."

I touch his shoulders. "Who, Eli?"

His eyes rove around the room, his face contorting. "Abe."

That familiar chill passes through me. "Abe is . . . the other ghost. Abe is Nameless?"

Eli sniffs. "I told Saul he wouldn't hurt us. Abe only hurts *them*." *Them.*

"I tried to tell him, but he ran, and Abe left too. It was just me and her then." Eli sinks into himself, wrapping his arms around his own shoulders. "She showed me," he sobs. "I don't want to remember. I don't want to see it. Please don't make me see my baby like that. I didn't do anything. *It wasn't my fault. It wasn't . . ."*

He curls up on the floor. I touch his shoulder, but he hardly seems to notice. "Eli, who are *they?*" I say, needing confirmation. "Who does Abe hurt?"

All at once, his crying stops. His dark eyes relax. He blinks up at me. "You must be one of Bekah's friends. She's out back."

I swallow the lump pressing into the top of my throat, brace myself against the hollow weight crushing my chest. He's lost. He can't answer, but I don't need him to.

"They're good kids," Eli whispers. "Good."

I hold back tears and take his hand. "They love you."

Eli's eyebrows sink. His face is open, childlike. "Who, now?"

I straighten, lifting the lamp upright as I do. I leave him huddled on the floor, like the chickens clustered in the coop, like the coywolves gathered in the woods. Like everything on this land we share that seems to know:

Death is coming.

Thirty-Nine

"SAUL." The wind swallows my voice as I emerge from the ram-shackle cabin.

Saul would've gone to my house when he saw Nameless—*Abe*—like I went to his. And what would he find?

A dead chicken and me missing. He'd think the worst, like I had about him.

I check my phone—no missed calls—and dial again. No luck.

Issa quivers in front of a furry pine, the moonlight stripping her bubbly reflection of color.

"Help me," I beg her.

The pain in my chest is deep and violent, lodged in the endless vacuum of grief inside me. As badly as I want to see Dad, I don't want to die. I don't want to lose Mom or Toddy or the boys or Hannah or Saul. I need him to live. I need *both* of us to live.

Shadows splotch Issa's non-body: Whites from the woods drift through her.

"No more memories. Take me to *Saul*!" I shout through the wailing wind. "Before it's too late."

Issa sways. I remove my boots and cross the stiff snow barefoot. When I step through Whites, I appear on top of the waterfall, current gushing around my ankles like angry salmon.

Two bare, moonlit bodies stand ahead of me at the edge of the waterfall. Even though Saul and I jumped from the cliffs to the right, I can't help but think for a second that it's *us* I see.

"Ready?" Abe Angert asks the red-haired girl beside him. A smile parts her full lips, dimpling her cheeks. She looks as if her happiness is on the verge of spilling into laughter. As happy as she was that day on the beach with her family.

Abe studies her, momentarily forgetting the breeze, the water, their nakedness. He reaches out, and she does too. They look at their entwined fingers with breathless wonder, as if watching the earth's foundations being laid.

As if they can see the bones shaping their hands, the tendons stretched there, the joints attached and ligaments tied, the veins threaded through and muscle wrapped. As if they can see the pulse of her heart racing from her chest down to her palm, thrumming against his lifeline until his heartbeat and hers are in sync.

Until the two of them are in sync.

Abe and Issa: one thing, one intangible thing that cycles between two bodies.

"I love you," he tells her quietly.

Her eyes flutter shut as she smiles. "You aren't allowed to love me."

"No," he says. "It's you who isn't allowed to love *me*. I have no such rule. What did your father call me—a snake in the grass?"

Her smile fades. "It's not you, Abe." She opens her teary eyes. "He hasn't always been so angry. The world doesn't have money for cherries anymore. He gives them away by the dozens just to keep them from rotting on the ground, and I think . . . I think he needs someone to blame, because otherwise it's just him. *Him* who failed us, who lets us be hungry. He can't look at us. He's angry all the time. He tries to find other work, but there's none here. And your father, he's been so generous, but . . . my father resents feeling indebted. I see it in his face, Abe: He believes he's losing the world, and that makes him angry with anyone who's managing to hold on. But once he *knows* you . . ."

"Issa." Abe touches her cheek, running his thumb up to the corner of her lashes. "Your father sees his land as the Garden of Eden and me as the snake trying to tempt you away."

"Then he's as foolish as the devil was," Issa says. "This may be as close to Eden as any place, but no man, not even Jack O'Donnell, can be God."

Abe's smile is so similar to Saul's that my heart speeds. "Yes," Abe replies, fighting to appear solemn, "God is much too lovely to be a man. She's far more likely to look like you."

Issa erupts with laughter. "You are shameless."

"Is that what you love most about me?"

"It is," she says. "Though it may also be one reason I'm forbidden from loving you. Or do you so easily forget the other girls you've carried on with all through town?"

A flush starts at his ears. He tucks his nose against the side of Issa's face. "Yes," he whispers. "Easily, immediately, wholly."

"That doesn't flatter me, Abe."

"Then what does?" He steps back. "How I dream of you, Is? The sketchbooks devoted to your neck and shoulders and hands? How when I bite into a cherry, it's not the sun I taste but you? How, for me, the whole world isn't made up of lakes and trees but of your millions of shades?"

"Obsession," she says. "Infatuation. And when you follow the only work left in the state to another city, what then?"

"How long have I loved you, Issa?"

She arches one eyebrow. "Always, to hear you tell it."

"Always," he says. "Before you would even look my way."

"I looked your way," she teases. "It was only that you hadn't yet grown into your ears, so looking did little."

"Maolissa O'Donnell," he says, "I have loved you since you were six years old and I found you at the disappearing tree. I loved you when you, at twelve, turned up your nose and said, 'Abe, I'm going to travel the world, probably marry a prince, so you need to understand the nature of this friendship.'"

Issa keens with laughter, and Abe winds his arms around her waist. "Tell me, Issa. Is that still your plan?"

Her smile falls, leaving tenderness and vulnerability exposed. "Sometimes," she whispers, "I think you are the snake."

"*Issa.*"

"Don't draw me away from them only to leave me," she says. "You say these things—you make me feel as though, if you stop loving me, I'll die."

"You won't," he murmurs. He shakes his head once. "I won't."

"Promise me."

He takes her hands in his. He kisses one, then the other. "I promise you. I promise the stars. I promise the lake and falls, coy-wolves and robins. I promise earth and heaven: I will love you long after the last human has taken his last breath. When the stars burn out and the oceans freeze over and the whole world is ash and dust and ice, our names will still be carved into the tree of life, side by side, and I'll still be loving you."

Issa's voice trembles. "Maybe in the water we'll be reborn. When we come up, you will be only you, and I will be only me. On the other side, nothing will keep us apart."

"Nothing *will* keep us apart," he answers solemnly.

Her smile is the kind that hides something. I think of the memory of that day on the beach, when Jack the First chased her through breaking waves and her laughter spilled out like gemstones. Her love for her father is as essential to her being as her love for Abe, or either's love for her. I think of the coyote and the wolf then, and instead of marveling at Dad's description of them lying together, it's the robin that awes me.

The delicate thing with soft feathers and hollow bones that lies between two wild and unpredictable beasts, untouched by both. Fearless, trusting.

Issa looks at Abe one last time. "Ready," she whispers.

They take a running leap off the ledge, and squeals fling out of them as they drop to the water. I rush forward and watch Abe Angert and Issa O'Donnell hit the pool below. They splash; they plunge; they sink, bubbles jostling to the surface in their wake. Everything falls silent for three breaths, and then Abe tops the water, gasping, his smile vivid. He treads water, turning in slow circles.

"Issa?" The walls around the pool catch his voice and mute it. "Is!"

No answer. He glances right-left-right, dives down again. He's gone for a long moment, too long. He resurfaces alone.

"ISSA?" The water sloshes as he twists. "IS? ISSA!"

He dives under, emerges again, hoarsely shouting her name. The cliffs absorb his voice. The water mocks him with its quiet. Still no red-gold hair or slim shoulders. No gemstone voice responding to his call.

I stumble from the ledge. Stagger, trip. Stomach bile rises in my throat, and vertigo rocks me off balance.

My head cracks against something hard, stars popping in my vision, a wall of hot whites and reds.

The colors fade; the shadows hanging over me resolve into foliage. I'm back in the forest. *I just saw someone die.*

I saw someone die.

I saw—

Saul. I'd forgotten about Saul. About the dead hen and the ghosts.

I lurch to my feet and run for my house, calling out for him in case he's still in the woods. My bare feet are numb as they trample the snow, and I try to shake the Whites from my hair and clothes. There's no time for this.

But when I reach my yard, lush grass catches my feet where there should be frost.

A warm breeze wriggles through my coat. A pile of shoes sits to the right of the porch, and the moon hangs high.

At the bottom of the hill, I see movement: a hunched blur.

"HELP!" Abe's now familiar voice is cracking, muffled by distance. "HELP!"

Lights flick on in the windows.

"HELP!" Abe screams again. He struggles to keep his legs under him, to keep hold of the limp thing in his arms.

The front door flings open. Jack the First careens out, bad leg buckling with each step. Abe lets himself fall now, now that there's someone to witness what's happened. The porch light barely spills across the girl's face.

"What happened?" Jack the First rasps. "What happened?"

He's a record stuck on a note, skipping, scarred. He touches the sides of Issa's face. He drags her out of Abe's arms and across his own lap, keening with horrible bearlike sounds. "What did you do?" he screams, voice threadbare, at Abe.

A long-legged little boy with sandy hair breaks from the front door and runs across the shadowy yard. Annie chases Jack II, her nightgown fluttering, and catches his shoulders. A strangled noise dies in her throat as she sees, then understands. She shakes her head and sinks, pulling Jack II to her. His round face is scrunched. He shakes his mother off and runs for the woods, runs right past me, runs like he can never stop. Like if he looks back, he'll die, and if he keeps moving, it won't hurt so bad.

"What did you do?" Jack the First shrieks again.

"The falls," Abe musters. He shakes his head. "I thought that if she could have the cherries—"

"The cherries?" Jack rasps, returning to himself.

"—if she had a healing cherry," Abe chokes.

Jack's on his feet, standing over the crumpled boy. He bears down on him, and Abe makes little more than a grunt when Jack kicks him in the ribs. He doesn't scream when Jack hauls him up by the neck or hits him across the face. He collapses onto his stomach, tries to scramble away, but Jack drags him back and stomps on his shoulder.

Abe goes limp though not unconscious. There's blood under his nose, and in this light it looks more like syrup or chocolate. It blooms across a cheek, an elbow, a gaping mouth on a pale boy.

A scream tears through me, making no sound. Stars dance behind my eyes, and the ground sways. I crumple and grip the grass between my fingers, wanting to stop this thing that's already happened.

Feathers flickers at the far edge of the woods, weeping as only a thing without eyes can. Kneeling without knees.

Abe doesn't see her. Does he see anything anymore? He stares at the sky, unblinking, mouth twisted as Jack hits him, sickly thud after sickly thud. Crunch after snap. Snap after thwack. There's blood, so much blood, and I can't tell where it comes from—Jack's split-open knuckles or Abe's cheek.

Whether it's Jack's thumb that's broken or Abe's eye socket.

Jack splattered in Abe's blood or Abe splattered in Jack's.

Jack's heart torn in two or Abe's drowned in the water.

A snake rustles in the grass beside me, slithering toward the woods. I wish I could close my eyes and shut out the sounds of flesh hitting flesh, lungs heaving.

The wolf at the coyote's throat.

The robin dead in the water.

Eventually Jack's throws come slower, his breathing heavier. He slumps sideways off Abe, onto the ground.

Annie sways in the breeze, her hair lifted off her neck.

Abe just stares, as though his mind has become untethered from his body.

There's blood in the grass, none of it hers, and she's still dancing, weeping at the edge of the woods.

Jack the First crawls to Issa, presses his forehead into her shoulder. He knots his fingers into the grass beside her.

The snake is gone. It's over. This place is broken, and now I understand.

Forty

I enter the house and am ejected into the present, a new sense of terror cleaving to me.

It's not just me and Saul at risk tonight.

Issa's hovering form follows me upstairs to the boys' room. I listen for their breathing, search the dark corners and shadows for the ghost we've always called Nameless.

When I'm sure Shadow and Grayson are safe, I stand outside the master bedroom and listen to Toddy's snores, then slip back downstairs, where Mom turns over on the couch, sighing in her sleep.

They're safe. It does little to ease the spastic clip of my heart. *What about Saul?*

I leave the house, feet still bare and approaching frostbite, I'm sure, but I need to be able to follow wherever Issa leads.

Wherever Saul is.

Issa takes me back into the woods. They're misty and sunlit, as though night were nothing but a dream, and in this golden haze she becomes solid: pale with strawberry hair and dimpled cheeks. She smiles sadly—the way she smiled when Abe said nothing would keep them apart—and leads me, calling for Saul as I go, through the forest.

We pass the billions of fluttering Whites, the mass of vines and branches circling O'Dang! like women holding hands around a maypole, and Issa keeps moving.

"Where is he?" I ask.

She says nothing.

Ahead, the trees thin. My heart thunders. I know where Issa's taking me—I can already hear it.

We crest the cliff overlooking the falls. Beneath the glassy surface, delicate spheres float like lazy jellyfish, membranes in otherworldly shades of blue, purple, and white.

Warmth wafts off the water, carrying a whispered word: "*June.*"

I try to shut out the sound of my father's voice. I dig my feet into the earth to keep myself from leaping in pursuit of him. "Where's Saul?" I demand of Issa, who has shifted into a fluctuating pink aura again.

She wavers at the lip of the cliff, as if peering into the water, and every pump of my heart carries ice through my veins.

"*June-bug.*"

"*Junie.*"

"Junior."

Dad's voice becomes insistent, harder to block out.

"You said I would drown if I went in alone," I snap. "Why did you bring me here?"

Issa billows, all her movement pointing to the water. The ice in my veins stops, reverses, plunges into my heart. "Did Saul go in the water?"

She dips. It's as close to a nod as I can imagine a thing like her doing. I eye the sleek surface, and the voices escalate into a feverish pitch: *"June, June, June."*

The Whites sound sinister now: hungry. Less like Dad and more like Nameless. *Abe.*

I step to the edge, sending rocks scrabbling down the cliff side.

"If Saul went down before we got here . . ." He would've been under for a full minute by now—and that's only if he went *right* before we got here. "Why would he *do* that? He knows how dangerous it is."

My mind spins, trying to piece the night together. I think back to the dead hen in my yard and the rabbit outside Eli's cabin. Issa had gone there, Abe too, and Eli had told Saul what the memories had revealed in pieces to me: that Nameless hurts O'Donnells.

He would've come to check on me, only to find a hen dead in the snow and me already gone. Whether because he assumed I'd gone there or because he knew we were out of time—

Saul went in the water.

"June. June. June. JUNE. JUNIOR." The voices mix with the hiss of creatures scuttling through the branches, slinking along the

forest floor. The voices begin to *shout* over the burbling of the water as fish rise, flailing.

An inky shadow rolls across the falls.

He's here. Maybe he planned all of this exactly as it's happening. Maybe he knew sending Saul in would send me in after.

Maybe Abe's here to drown me.

But it doesn't matter. The voices are so loud they feel as if they're coming from within my head, and the forest buzzes in anguish at the cold ghost's presence. From this close, I feel the shapeless thing's turmoil worm into me, stoke me into a frenzy.

"Saul," I say, grounding myself.

Stay focused. For Saul.

I jump.

The warm water seems to reach up to snatch me, drag me down. Hundreds of waterlogged Whites scream and moan in my father's voice. I don't fight the pull.

I dive.

Deeper, deeper, deeper, until I have to kick hard to keep moving through the barrage of Whites. I ignore the push on my lungs, the water slipping up my nostrils, the panic saying *up-up-up*.

Closer to the bottom, the Whites are packed more densely. Their light dazzles so brightly I can see nothing else. I kick harder.

Closer. So close I can touch the wall of white. I can taste it.

I push myself into it. It envelops me, light everywhere. Nothing but light.

It recedes from the center of my vision, radiating toward the outsides.

I'm immersed in a memory, the whole scene washed out by the brilliant luminescence hanging over everything. I'm downstairs in my house.

Dad sits in a high-backed chair at the console table in the dining room. He's hunched, his oversized hand gripping a pen, scribbling on a sheet of loose-leaf paper.

In the kitchen, Mom is boiling noodles. I can smell marinara, tangy and sweet and loaded with garlic. Steam spirals up from the pot, finely sheening her cheek with humidity. She sweeps her forearm up to her hairline to catch the sweat accumulating there.

"Junior?" she says. The burning whiteness seems to drape over her voice, distilling it into the pure sound of her. "Come help Mama."

The eight-year-old girl drawing at the dining room table stands but hesitates there, between her parents—her mother at the stove a few yards to her left, her father at the desk on her right. She ignores her mother and goes to her father.

I remember.

She tries to climb on his back. He wriggles her off, leaving her to squeal and giggle and try harder. "Not now, June-Bug," he says.

"Jackie, please," Mom says. "Get the silverware, baby."

She keeps climbing on him. He stops what he's doing and pulls her off. Holding her by the elbows, he leans back to study her, smiling softly. After a few seconds of silence, he kisses the wiggling girl's forehead. "You go help Mom, Bug."

She huffs and turns away. Dad folds the letter he'd been working on.

I remember. This happened the night we found the dead hen.

He writes something on the outside of the note, then walks toward the door. "Be right back," he tells me and Mom.

I strain my eyes to see the word on the folded letter: *Junior*.

White light bursts across my vision, and I feel the water all around me again. I kick one last time, but somehow I've been turned around. I'm kicking *up* not down, and that one kick sends me over the surface.

Forty-One

THE white is hot against my eyes. I blink it back, treading water. Slowly, color filters into the edges of my vision.

The forest is gone. So is the waterfall.

I'm in an ocean, or maybe a Great Lake, some vast gray body beneath a mist-filled sky. In the distance, I spy a white shore. A girl with red-gold hair sits at the edge of the tide. *Issa.*

"Hello?" I call, checking whether I'm in a memory. My voice is audible but barely; a blanket of hot wind roars over it.

The water is as dense with Whites as the pool under the falls. Billions of them filling up this massive space. They all seem to be swimming away from the shore where Issa sits, across the softly rollicking waves where I emerged. In several places throughout the watery expanse, the Whites stop swimming *out* and dive *down*, forming little cyclones of fluff.

To gaps in the veil, I think, *like the woods and the falls.*

I stroke through them, grazing dozens at a time, and even though I'm not crossing thresholds, their contents flash bright across my mind.

A red sled whipping down a hill, the sweet tastelessness of a snowflake on my tongue, the crackle of a gas fireplace, and piles of snow melting on boot toes in a tray inside a green door.

A hammer in my hand, yellow floral curtains, the earthy smell of sweat, and a buttery laugh.

Popsicles staining mouths Tang-orange, slivers in my feet, fights with a mother who isn't mine, a glass shattering in the sink, drawing blood from the skin between my thumb and forefinger.

Downy fur soft against my face.

The memories course through me, and it's everything I can do to keep treading water. Sometimes, though, the memories feel so real I forget and start to slip beneath.

A tug of the tide pulls me back to reality, and I kick to the surface and keep swimming.

Until my arms ache. My legs ache. My shoulders burn and lungs feel like someone's taken sandpaper to every inch of them, and still I'm far from the shore.

Issa sits, watching serenely.

"SAUL?" The wind swallows my voice. I don't know whether I'm calling out for him or asking Issa if he's here. I can't let myself think about what could've happened to him.

I swim until it's all I can do to keep my nose above water. And then I can't even do that.

I kick my legs, windmill my arms, but I'm no longer above the surface, and every muscle in my body throbs with exhaustion. I open my eyes and watch armies of Whites swim past.

I see full cities beneath me—sunken homes and skyscrapers, bicycles and cobblestone and awnings, Whites cloistering around the waterlogged windows. Overlapping places, maybe, or maybe places that haven't existed for a long time.

My lungs stutter until they're on fire. *It won't end here, Abe,* I think with all my might and keep swimming. *I'm fixing it.*

I ignore the voice that says it's already over. I repeat in my mind: *Saul will be okay, you will be okay, everything will be okay,* even as my muscles stop responding to my commands and my lungs twitch and cold dread tangles around me.

Now other memories crash over me—not from the Whites but from my own mind: Mom's hands in my hair, Toddy's chin resting on her head, Grayson and Shadow wrestling me in the yard, Hannah pulling me close in the school parking lot as snow falls on our hair, Saul looking into my eyes and saying, "I can hear all of you, rushing around in there. A million Jacks and Juniors and Junes, a city of them," bees awake beneath my skin, buzzing eagerly toward him.

I DON'T WANT TO DIE.

I think it like a scream, like a battle cry. Even if it means seeing Dad, I don't want to die. There, I admit it and fight a losing fight against the water, thrash, scream with my body as I can't with my mouth, and *fight.*

I WANT TO LIVE. I WANT TO LIVE. I WANT TO LIVE.

My toes graze something solid.

Sand. The valley beneath me starts sloping upward to meet the shore in the distance. I kick, and soon my feet hit ground. My knees hit ground. I'm crawling up the shore.

And then there's air.

Shocking, hot, abundantly dry.

My face is above water. I collapse onto my stomach, greedily gulping oxygen. I'm shaking, unable to stand. I curl into the fetal position, too tired to acknowledge the girl sitting behind me, and dig my hands into the sand.

It's not sand at all. It's cool on my hands but doesn't melt. Warm on the soles of my feet but doesn't burn. I let a fistful sift through my fingers. It floats to the earth like trillions of Whites crushed to bits. The ground is made of crumbled memories.

Every spare inch of me has been dusted chalky white, as if I've rolled in a vat of flour. I wipe at it, but it doesn't even smear.

Craning my neck, I look at the sky. Out over the water it's a gray-blue, but past Issa, the sandy shore extends into a desert plain, and billowing mist forms a high wall in the distance, blocking the horizon from sight. The Whites are coming from the haze, carried by the wind. I'm closer than ever to wherever they come from.

In a way this place is familiar. I imagine this is what you see when you open your eyes after a plane crash or car accident, in that moment *before* you register the truth of wreckage, blood, and rocks. This is a place you see as you're falling asleep, and you think it must've come from your brain, but you have no clue where you got the idea.

I've crossed through the veil.

Hot wind batters me, loud but strangely calming. I struggle out of my coat and stand, forming a visor with my hands to shield my eyes from the light and the whip of my hair.

"He's not dead."

Issa's voice startles me. She's standing now, water lapping at her feet. She dusts the white stuff off her skin; it doesn't cling to her as it does to me.

"Saul?"

She tips her head toward the wall of mist. "Walk with me."

My muscles groan in protest, but I fall into step beside her, her copper curls lashing her creamy face and pink lips like streaks of sunlight. "What is this place?"

Her shoulders barely hitch in a shrug. "It doesn't need a name, does it?"

"Everywhere else has one."

"Then call it the place that isn't everywhere else. Or perhaps the *other* place."

"Is it an afterlife?"

Issa laughs, a sound not dissimilar to the wind in its crisp, vital quality. She sets her hand against a twisted tree that grows out of the sand, casting slight shade. "It's just a place," she says. "Like any other. This world is outside your world. If your world is the womb, this is the person it belongs to. It carries you everywhere, but you don't see it until you're born."

"You mean *until you die.*" My voice shakes. "I drowned, didn't I?"

"You don't have to die to get here," Issa says. "Most do, but your world has cracks in its walls. Sometimes things get in, sometimes they get out. It takes a great amount of luck or coincidence for a person to squeeze through."

"And which brought *me* here?" I say.

"I did. And *you* did."

I shake my head. "I don't understand."

"I hoped you would choose to come here as you did," she says. "Alive rather than dead."

"I didn't make a choice. I came to find Saul."

"Yes." Her lips lift a blaze of smile. She keeps walking, guiding me through the Whites and wind. The gray overhead never changes. I see no sun or moon or stars, only the white underfoot, the shifting mass of water molecules ahead, and the Whites blowing past us. Sometimes I hear seagulls, distant and blithe.

"Can we go back?" I ask her. "Home, I mean."

"Perhaps." She doesn't go on.

"What about the curse—is it broken now?"

"Our house sits in a special place," Issa says. "Things were meant to be better there. Quiet, peaceful, *good*. Grief tore through it. You understand that, don't you?"

"I saw what happened at the falls, what your father did when Abe brought you to him."

She squints into the wind. "Grief isn't a curse, June. Pain affects us all, even those of us who live a little closer to paradise than the rest. But my father's grief turned into poison. It ate through his heart and changed our family: his son, his son's son, you. And Abe's shame destroyed him. Shame, many say, was the first curse."

"Abe isn't cursed," I argue. "He *is* the curse. He killed my father *and* your father. He even killed Bekah."

"What you saw between Abe and my father," she says, "was one haunted man trying to find solace in revenge against another. What you saw happen to your father was the nameless thing that used to be Abe lashing out when he saw what was happening to Bekah. He never hurt her. When you saw him linger near her, when she was ill, you witnessed a haunted ghost remembering what it is to weep."

"You're saying he was *justified*?"

"He *has* been our family's curse—exerting his pain, exacting his idea of justice—but this didn't start with him. And he's not the only one to blame, just as our family isn't the only one cursed. What my father did to Abe broke something in him, June. Abe lived with it until the day he ended his life. His curse—*Saul's* curse—is different from ours but every bit as real. Shame steals from them. It eats at their vast, vivid minds until they become small and shadowy, trapped alone in a dark, wordless place."

"What about Bekah? The cancer?"

"That wasn't the curse. That was life, all its brightness and its dark. But the way the Angerts forget—that, I think, is a little of both: life *and* the curse. Life has made them want to forget, conditioned their bodies for it. The curse takes every tendril of memory, pulse of life, every touch and whisper and golden moment from them while Abe watches and, in his pain, strikes out. The only way to end this is to release the past. To be the one who lets go first, with no guarantee the other will follow."

"Then why did you bring me here?" I demand. "Why did you show me all that? If we need to let the past go, then why haven't *you* moved on?"

She smiles wordlessly.

It seems like we've been walking for hours. There are no signifiers for time or distance, and my body never gets more tired than it already was—absolutely wrecked with fatigue. My mind feels empty as when morning draws you from a dreamless sleep, but my throat feels swollen and dry.

It's hard to hold on to the truth here, even harder to remember the outside world. I try to picture my father, my mother, but their faces are blurry. I picture Saul's eyes. I hold on to them as we walk.

"Saul?" I manage to ask her.

She smiles and walks onward. I have to believe she's taking me to him.

I keep moving, moving, moving. At some point I must have fallen without noticing. I'm on my stomach, dragging myself forward. Issa walks evenly alongside me.

Coywolves pass us, their keen eyes watching me, belly-down and crawling. Ahead, blurs of color in the roaring wall of mist become squiggly silhouettes. Wind sprays water against my face, and I open my mouth to swallow it, but it's not enough. Even without the sun, my skin feels raw and scorched.

My mind slithers toward the moisture, its tongue lolling, praying for a drink, but my limbs won't listen, and the mist remains out of reach.

At its edge, small white tufts whiz like snowflakes.

I focus on Issa's ankles and keep moving.

My skin begins to burn, as if the dust on it is poison. I scratch at it, tear into it with my fingernails trying to get it off me, more desperate with every passing second of white-hot pain.

"June," Issa says.

"My skin," I rasp, "it hurts." I slash and scrape at my arms and legs, tears pouring down my face, but still the coat of Whites won't smudge. "It won't come off." The pain hits me in waves, sending grotesque images through my mind: a pool of blood overflowing my cupped hands, spreading up my arms, covering my body.

I scream and rub at my arms, seeing nothing but red now where white was. Red all over, blood covering me, and I know—somehow I know—it's Abe's.

I'm bathed in it. The memories of that night on the hill flap against me like a thousand angry bats.

"I didn't do it," I gasp as I try to writhe away, but I can't escape the memory. It's everywhere; the blood is everywhere.

Issa crouches and gingerly frees my hands from my hair. "What's happening?" I sob.

"You were supposed to have cherries that tasted like sunlight, a house full of love, and a peaceful forest," she says. "But instead, this is what was passed down to you, and I'm sorry for that, June, but you can't get it off yourself."

I see it all: I've inherited the man who swept his daughter from the water, laughing, and who held her empty body, weeping in dew-slicked grass.

The little boy who watched it happen, the man he became, who learned to turn invisible, who saw ghosts and feared love because he knew what it was to lose.

My legacy is the little boy who grew up haunted, who thought his father couldn't see him. Who left me and my mother whenever the house became too crowded with ghosts of his childhood. The man who abandoned me again and again and didn't know how to stay, no matter how badly he wanted to.

My birthright was Issa's death, Abe's assault, Jack the First's refusal to forgive.

Two ghosts: vengeance and grace.

The blood on my hands may not be real, but I was born with it all the same.

My inheritance is grief and sunlight, and the ability to choose which to hold on to.

"How?" I sob, the pain of my own skin becoming unbearable. "How do I make it stop?"

"I'm taking you to the one who can," Issa says.

Forty-Two

ISSA helps me to my feet. The burning still sears through me, but her arm is strong under mine as she guides me onward.

We're closer to the mist now, and the blurs of color take on the shapes of people. Peals of laughter, snippets of conversation, slip through the wind.

"When you come here, you're meant to wash time off. To let your past settle." Issa kicks one foot through the not-sand under-foot. "Your Moments are meant to rest. But our two families live in a place riddled with cracks, and instead of crumbling when I washed, my Moments were drawn back through the holes by some-one who hungered for them. I was free to move on, but I stayed. For Abe.

"When he arrived, he wasn't ready to let go. He didn't wash himself, so the pull on his Moments drew him back through the veil too. For four generations, our families' inability to let go

359

has brought Moments back. The hate between our families has anchored Abe, has allowed us to stay."

"They weren't being sent to us," I whisper. "Saul and I were bringing them?"

"In a way, the memories *belong* to you—they're pieces of what made you—so when you longed for the things you'd lost, the Moments came, as they had for your father and for his. All of you were born already holding on to the pain of the past and hating Angerts, because my father had."

Genetic memory. Memory passed through DNA. I shake my head. "But I never hated the Angerts. Not really."

"Not all coyotes dislike wolves," Issa says. "In another life, perhaps your lack of hate might have been enough to let our family's darkest memories rest. But you and Saul were each looking for the person you'd lost. And there were fragments of those people—shared DNA—in the Moments that came to you, and within Abe and me."

"I thought . . . I *hoped* my dad was sending them."

Issa's cerulean eyes flick across my face. "Whenever I could, when cracks and thin places in your world and this one aligned, I came through. I didn't bring the Moments, but I guided you to those I thought you needed. Abe—the thing that used to be Abe—he guided your father and grandfather to the Moments that hurt most."

"It *all* hurt, Issa." Tears squeeze from my eyes from the effort of holding in the screams of pain. I focus on the meager relief the mist brings my sizzling skin. "The happy memories hurt just as bad, maybe worse."

She studies me. "I know. But that kind of pain teaches you something different, June."

Finally, we're within the mist, each drop cooling the burning of my skin and clearing my mind. It snags on something Issa said. "You said Abe guided my dad and grandfather to the Moments that hurt most. What about me?"

"Abe's watched you grow up, June." Her lips pull into a straight line, the wind lashing strands of hair across her face. "Of the three Jacks I've tried to guide, you're the first who was ready to listen. It was harder, I think, for Abe to hate you. Otherwise he would've come for you when Eli lost Bekah. You were too innocent then, even to the thing he'd become. But tonight, I could see it in him. He was going to hurt you."

How could he take the thing I loved most but hesitate to hurt *me*? Didn't he know he'd already torn out my heart? That he'd hurt me worse than any physical pain could? A coywolf trots past, and I clear my throat of its teary thickness. "And whose side are the coywolves on?"

Issa almost laughs. "Did you know there's a fungus that drives everything it infests to spread itself? The fungus infects hosts with a desire to destroy. Evolution—nature—did that."

I shake my head. "I don't understand."

"The coywolves are the antithesis of nature. They have no capacity for revenge, no instinct to kill. They're driven by *wholeness*, the impulse to heal. They try to draw everything here, to be washed clean. They steal your shoes so you can leave your world—you must be barefoot and wide-eyed, just as you entered it.

"The coywolves weren't trying to show you memories; they

were trying to bring you here. Thresholds are more than randomly chosen divisions between rooms. They're places where change—transformation—happens, and whenever you slipped through one, barefoot, to a thinner piece of the veil, you saw the memories as we're able to in this place."

"And O'Dang!? That's here too?"

"There's only one of that tree," she confirms. "Where you live, you might wander through a thousand different cracks to find it. The same with the water you came through—it overlaps with the pool beneath the falls and a hundred others. Our families' darkest Moments are drawn to that water, *because I died there*."

We've reached another shore. Fog hangs thick in the air above us, but ahead, the water is a healthy teal, waves topped by half domes of refracted light, and the clear sky gleams cornflower blue.

All around us, people emerge from the mist. Some, like me, are led by dustless people, but most are alone, covered to varying degrees in White-dust.

"We're meant to be washed clean, June," Issa says. "To let our burdens fall away and moments come apart like dandelions. It happened long ago, to the wolves and coyotes and birds who stumbled through, before any human tread on that grassy hill—and it's still happening."

She nods toward an old woman shuffling into the glittering froth of the tide. "Most people, when they come here, are finally free, but what they don't realize is that they could've been all along if they'd just let go."

Issa faces the wall of mist, where a shape emerges, its details filling out as a stooped man in a tartan hat limps forward, damp eyes rising and falling to take in the sight. He begins to cry as his gaze locks onto something behind us: the woman bathing in the water. Her layer of white has started to rinse off, and when she sees him, a laugh breaks free from her throat. She runs for him, falling in the water, and he catches her, gripping her tightly.

"When I first arrived, I waited here for the boy I loved," Issa says. "And when he came, I saw him, shrouded in mist but so very, clearly, excellently him."

She squints across the light-dappled water, and I can recall the feel of her sadness, the feathery warmth.

"He waded toward me, but he didn't let time wash off. The stars hadn't yet burned out. The planet wasn't cold. And I was waiting. Even then, he couldn't let go. He turned away—slipped back through, though he no longer had a body to wear there." She swipes a gold-streaked curl from her eyes. "I know what you must think, but he isn't lost, Jack. There's still hope. For you and Saul *and* for him."

I search the freckles on her nose, the glints in her eyes. "How can you say that? He's tortured us for decades, Issa."

"You must be tired from carrying all that Past around," she replies. "It must be exhausting to live for four Jacks."

"I'd rather do that than let go and lose him."

"Letting go is not forgetting. It's opening your eyes to the good that grew from the bad, the life that blooms from decay."

"My dad was supposed to be here," I whisper." He was supposed to always be here. I *needed* him, and Abe took him from me."

Issa lets a Moment alight on her hand. She sets it in mine and curls my fingers around it. I see a pure, bright memory: sun in my eyes, dirt underneath my fingernails, teeth sinking into a cherry, spraying tart juice on my chin.

She scoops another few and drops them over my fist. They hit my closed fingers, then bounce away. "June, Moments are like cherries. They're meant to be relished, shared—not hoarded. You can clutch one terrible Moment or experience all the rest. Your life is slipping past in brilliant little bits, and I know it feels as though you're holding on to *him*, as though opening your hand is letting him slip away."

Now she opens my hand, and the Moment in it floats to the ground. "But when Moments pass and crumble, they become seeds. They grow into new trees. And I promise you, he'll be in every new leaf. He will *never* be far from you.

"But if you *don't* let go of all that Abe did, you'll be haunted like the rest of them. You will miss the chance to live the life you want because you've accepted the one that's been passed down to you."

I swallow the knot in my throat. "Is he gone, Issa?"

Her mouth quivers. "When your father came here, he came in through the front door, no regrets. He shed his skin and stepped through a free man. He bathed in the water, and he wasn't sad about the way things were anymore. He was ready to move on."

I'm trying to parse out her meaning when an abrupt smile splits her face and she illuminates with happiness, bright and salient. I follow her gaze over my shoulder.

A lean boy with dark hair approaches through the mist, his angles sharpening into focus as the fog between us thins. "Saul."

My heart flares with relief so concentrated it overwhelms me with tears. He can't see me yet, but I know it's him. With every bone and muscle and ligament, I *know* him.

I look back to Issa, but she's turned away, wading into the water, her dress floating out around her. She turns toward me again, shielding her eyes against the light. "It's a miracle," she calls, grinning.

"What is?"

"That with your hand shut so tightly, he managed to slip in. That with his hands gripped like they were, he saw the shimmering possibility of a future when he met you."

Her smile widens, but tears still prick her eyes. "Wash yourselves, June," she calls. "Your curse will be broken. Abe won't be able to follow you back. If that's not enough to free him, there's nothing else I can do. It's his decision now. I'm moving on."

I run down the beach toward her. "And if I don't? Go back? If I want to stay and find *him*?"

Issa looks out across the water, where a series of islands has become visible, some drifting toward the shore and others away. "You swim," she says.

"What's there?"

Issa laughs, and while it should be eerie, it's shiny and gorgeous. "I don't know yet. Either way, don't delay your decision—there are people waiting for you, Jack O'Donnell."

I watch her shrink, feeling the wind at my back and an unbearable cleaving in my heart. Feathers, the sprite, my sweet pink ghost, is gone.

"June?"

And then I turn. I see him. And for a moment, the happiness, the light, the *deeply good* outweighs all the bad.

Everything in me swells, threatens to pop like an overblown balloon.

Saul's face is sunburned and muddy. Hair sandblasted, skin bleached by Whites. Through the crashing waves and seagulls, he says my name.

I run to him, and he crushes me to his chest. His lips are cracked and bloody as he kisses me, but I don't care. I don't care that I'm covered in blood. I forget the scalding of my skin.

I take his mist-speckled face between my hands, and he knots his fingers into my hair and laughs, gravelly, warm, *him*.

"You're alive," he says, and I nod, and laugh, and cry. His hands stroke through my hair. "Jack O'Donnell IV, we're alive."

I cling to him, damp wind cycling around us. Safe, steady, whole.

"I went to the falls," he says in a rush. "I saw Nameless and Feathers. There was a dead rabbit, and I thought the worst, June. I went to your house, but you were *gone*. I didn't know what else to do."

"Issa," I say. "Issa and Abe. That's who the ghosts are. She brought me here."

He presses his face into my neck, and a cracking sound climbs his throat. "I thought you were already gone. I told myself if I jumped, I could find you." He pulls me into him, blocking me from the wind.

"I'm here." I spread my fingers over his heart, feeling its beat. "I'm not gone." I repeat it again, a promise.

Saul straightens, and his eyes register the blood on me. "June, what happened?" He tries to wipe it off, but it doesn't smear.

"It's a stain," I tell him. "Look." I point to the bruises on his arms. I gently lift his shirt and find more blue-black welts rising from his ribs. "Did you see what happened to Abe on the hill?"

Understanding crosses Saul's face as his fingers skim the bruises. "You think these are from what Jack did to him? Takes *chip on your shoulder* to a whole new level."

"Chip in your bloodstream," I say. "Blood in my DNA."

"Are we dead, June?"

"We won't feel this close to dying when we're dead."

Saul laughs. "True. I've never been so thirsty."

We start to walk, and the pain needling my skin hits anew with each step we take out of the mist. The sparkling water and blue sky come into view. Up and down the shore, blemishes of color become visible, all moving, like us, toward the water.

"Where are we?" Saul asks.

"The world outside ours?" I say helplessly.

One of the islands has drifted closer, a small one smack-dab in the water, on which a white farmhouse basks in the light, ivy sprawling through its lattice, flowers and a cherry tree leaning in its yard. Another island floats in tandem with it, vacant apart from a massive tree with gnarled roots.

"Your house," Saul says. "And O'Dang!"

I nod. "You think that's the way home?"

"Is that the way back?" Saul shouts to a barefoot woman in an olive dress. She and several other newcomers are wading into the water, splashing their wind-beaten faces. She looks up, droplets sliding off her face, then follows Saul's gaze to the farmhouse.

"Not for me," she shouts back. "The others said the islands come when it's your turn."

"Turn?" Saul asks.

She shrugs and lowers herself into the water. As she does, something strange and lovely happens. White puffs wash off her—off everyone who's wading in. Like snakeskin being shed, snow from a window, dust bunnies blown free from a book cover.

"This is where they come from," Saul says.

The woman's grinning as she slurps from her cupped hands.

"Is the water drinkable?" I call.

She laughs and slicks her wet hair back. "It's water!"

We push our faces into the crash of the tide and gulp.

We lie in it, roll through it. The snow-sand starts to wash from our hair and clothes, settling to the bottom without a fight. The Whites shed from me, but the blood doesn't rinse off no matter how I scrub.

Saul takes my hands in his and runs his fingers through the blood, drawing wet streaks through it. He scoops water in one hand and pours it over my forearm, and the blood runs off in minuscule red rivers, though the water doesn't seem to muddy. Pour by pour, the blood disappears, rinsing off beneath his cupped hands until it's gone.

Saul kisses my clean fingers, one by one.

I touch the bruises on his cheek, those on his arms. I massage the water into them, watching the dark purple fade from beneath his tattoos until the bruises become nothing. I pull his shirt over his head and wash his sides, his ribs.

I rinse his shoulders, his spine. I watch the welts vanish, and when they're gone, I kiss his forehead, his cheeks, his mouth.

We fall under the water and sink and twist, are buoyed back up, water and Moments sliding off us like avalanches. Our Whites drift off. They crumble, one by one, and sink.

We lie back on the White-sand, smiling and breathing deep. I can't explain the feeling in my body. At first, we're both laughing breathlessly, and when the giddiness settles, I feel heavy, so calm I could melt into the beach, become a part of it like all our Moments. Saul's fingers twist through mine, and he looks over to me, a million droplets glistening on him like marbles.

"I knew who you were in the mirror maze," he says. Somehow, here, we're *below* the wall of wind, *above* the crash of water, in a quiet slice of space. "I knew who you were, and I was so happy you didn't seem to recognize me. I wanted to stay there as long as I could, to spend as much time as possible before you found out."

I try to remember why. I remember what happened but not why it mattered so much, why I believed anything was keeping me and Saul apart. I think of what Issa said to Abe on top of the waterfall: that he would leave and forget her. "What if I want to travel?" I ask Saul.

"Then you'll travel, Jack."

"What if I want to go to college?"

"You'll live in a dorm and join the literary magazine," he says. "Go to readings and sneak out with your friends the night before

National Poetry Day to cover the campus with poems; drink Jell-O shots and shave your head in a frat-house bathroom and quit shaving your armpits and live in a new city and learn how to make sushi and whatever else you want. I can wait."

I close my eyes and grin at the sun—or the *not-the-sun*. "What if our curse makes all the stars burn out and we're left in the dark?"

Saul touches my bottom lip, and I open my eyes. The crescents of refracted light in the water droplets on his face make him glitter like the ocean. "We aren't cursed anymore, June."

"How do you know?"

"Because I'm happy," he whispers. "I saw all there was to see, all the worst parts, and I'm still furiously happy."

He's right—our blood and bruises are gone, like Issa said—but what about Abe? What happens to him now? I curl myself against Saul, pressing my face into his wet shirt. "Maybe everyone's cursed."

"Not us," he murmurs in my hair.

"What makes us so special, Saul?"

"We're in love."

"Are we?" I whisper.

He gingerly takes the sides of my face in his hands. "June O'Donnell, I like that you know you can't fix the thing that hurts in me. And that you understand it gets better but you never stop missing people. I like that you *know* no human being will ever make it okay that you lost another one. And that you're smart and funny and willing to go on horrible double non-dates for your friend and that you want to write things that are happy, and of course I like your butt and eyes and teeth and hair and the way your fingernails are always badly painted and that when you laugh, you have no chin.

"And I don't know what exactly makes it love, but when I saw you in the House of Mirrors, it was like I already knew exactly who you were. And I should've been wrong—that would've made more sense—but I wasn't, and I love you. I'll always love you. And someday maybe we'll have a bad breakup or grow apart and—curse or not—all the stars will burn out and the planet will have another ice age, but I'll go on loving you because I see you, June O'Donnell, and I can't unsee you."

He lowers his mouth to mine, and we kiss how we drank the water. Our teeth collide like they did that night in the sunroom, from too much smiling.

When we pull apart, his eyes flick down my face and out toward the twin islands docking near the shore: O'Dang! and my house.

All along I'd been so sure Dad was trying to tell me something, and even now that Saul and I are here together, legs outstretched in sparkling waves and invisible sun blanketing us, I still feel a deep ache. "One will take us home," I murmur.

"And the other?"

I meet Saul's dark eyes. "To *them*."

"Is that for you?" the woman in the olive dress calls, tipping her head toward the farmhouse on the island. "You might want to wade out there while you can, if it is. Looks like it's starting to drift back out." She returns to wringing her hair out, knotting it into a braid.

She's right. The island is floating away, a new one visible on the horizon.

Saul and I stand. "Which do we take?" he asks.

"I don't know yet."

We wade into the water, and when we're in to our waists, we let our fingers fall apart. The sun on our backs and arms, we climb onto the floating island and look up at my house. "Saul?"

"June?"

Maybe for some people, falling in love is an explosion, fireworks against a black sky and tremors rumbling through the earth. One blazing moment. For me, it's been happening for months, as quietly as a seed sprouting. Love sneaked through me, spreading roots around my heart, until, in the blink of an eye, the green of it broke the dirt: hidden one moment, there the next.

"I like your hair and arms and laugh. And the pictures you take and that you came home even though you were scared and that you apologize and expect apologies. I like that you don't get embarrassed often but when you do, your ears turn pink, and I like your jaw and stomach and how you think about the worst things that have happened in a way that doesn't *justify* them but finds the tiny specks of good circling them, and I love you. I love you, Saul Angert."

His smile is slow and faint. "I know, Jack."

"Cocky," I tease.

"Confident."

Forty-Three

WE fold our fingers together and step toward my porch. It's nearly silent, apart from the gulls overhead. Butterflies spiral around the ivy-wrapped lattice, and birds chirp in the bushes.

Something crawls on the nape of my neck. I turn, and across the water, I see a shape moving out of the haze toward the shore where we bathed.

"June?" Saul touches my elbow, then follows my gaze.

Abe's blue-gray button-up ripples in the wind. The worn fabric of his pants lashes his legs, and his dark hair ruffles.

I expect to feel hate, anger, fear—but I only feel sadness. His dark eyes, the sharp angles of his face—they're so familiar, shadows of a person I love. How did the boy on the waterfall, the one who'd loved Issa since they were six, turn into the darkness that haunted us? Was it in that moment he found her? When the light left his eyes as Jack the First attacked him?

Or did it happen over years of missing her, being hated by the family *she* loved? In the end, he's nothing but a mess of color: the white of memory dust, the red of the blood on his hands, the purple of the bruises the world inflicted on him.

"Our curse is broken," I say. "He can't follow us back. Whether he moves on is his decision."

We watch him and he watches us for an extended moment.

He steps into the water, his pants clinging and rocking with the tide. I try to see the darkness in him or feel the cold that rushed into me whenever he was near, but here he's nothing but a human being. A mass of guts and cells and all the Moments that hurt him.

Behind him, a little girl emerges from the mist. A woman down the beach lets out a yelp, and the girl turns toward her, a smile breaking across her face. They run for each other, the girl's yellow braid bouncing behind her. Their bare feet slap the not-sand, making a sound like the heartbeat of the earth.

The woman's knees hit the ground as the girl collides with her, their arms wrapping tightly around each other, faces burying themselves in curves and muscle and fabric.

That.

That was the moment I had wanted. A reunion.

Saul's hand tightens, silent acquiescence: *me too.*

Still watching us, Abe lowers himself to his knees. Whites spit out from him like soap bubbles beneath a showerhead. He plucks one off, brings it to the surface, and meets my eyes again.

He shakes his head, opens his mouth, then closes it again. Silently he releases the White.

It doesn't sink. It's pulled along by the breeze straight toward me. The dead bit of memory, the outermost layer of moments, pulled away to leave behind only the supple truth.

Abe stands, his liquid eyes shifting away from us to search the horizon. He doesn't find what he's looking for there, and the light draws a vein down the silvery slope of his cheek.

His mouth forms words: *"I'm sorry, Issa."*

He doesn't wash any more of his time away. He turns toward the mist and returns the way he came.

"What does this mean?" Saul whispers. "I thought the curse was broken."

"For us, it is," I answer.

"But if he's not moving on, he'll keep torturing us."

I shake my head. "He can't come back."

"Then why stay here?"

I stare into the mist and its white noise. "I don't think he was ready to face her."

Because he blamed himself for her death. Because of the way he tore through her family and broke all his promises. Issa said shame was the first curse, and when you've held on to shame that long, it must be nearly impossible to let go. *Nearly.*

Maybe not now, but someday he'll let the girl who loved him look at him again. And when he does, she'll be waiting.

Saul nods at the White floating toward me. "What do you think is in that?"

I wrap my arms around his neck and bury my face in his chest. I can't look at it, or the house, or O'Dang! "I don't know."

He lowers his forehead to mine. "What do you want to do, June?"

"I want to know Dad's okay. I want a promise that I'll see him again. I want that love back, Saul."

Saul tips my face up. "The kind of love your dad had for you, that's not the kind of thing that can die. Look at Issa. This whole thing—she had us play out their lives so we could understand this fight and stop it. After everything Abe did, she brought us here for *him. That* kind of love—the kind that doesn't stipulate or caveat—doesn't die. That's what you had with your father. That's what I had with Bekah. That's what we have, June, and they're *here, right now.*"

"You want to stay?" A sharp pain passes through me. I never would have believed I'd feel this way, but since I dove into that water, *I'm* different. *I WANT TO LIVE* burns like an ember in my chest.

For Saul, for Mom and Toddy, Shadow, Grayson, Hannah. And for myself.

Saul shakes his head. "June, the past three years have felt like one never-ending night. And then, a few months ago, I was running through a hall of mirrors, and I collided with you, and I remembered it was just an optical illusion. Your teeth hit me in the shoulder, and I saw morning in you. And if the world can surprise me with something as bright as June O'Donnell's teeth in my shoulder once, it can do it again."

His thumb runs over my jaw, and his eyes tighten at the corners. "I love my sister, and until I die, I'll never stop missing her. But I want to be good to the people I haven't lost yet. I want to live, with you."

He brushes tears from my eyes.

"Those are some transcendent bicuspids I've got," I whisper.

He grins. "If you'd hit me with your molars, I would've seen the face of God right then."

"I bet we could catch a boat to that attraction from here."

"For sale: face of God; price: future."

"For sale: baby shoes; misread eBay description; thought they were adult shoes."

Saul's laugh is all husk and warmth. He pulls me sideways so he can kiss the top of my head. "Even if you can't see morning in me, I hope you can see it somewhere."

My heart fills with homesickness—for all three of my parents. I look up at the house in front of us. I can imagine Mom sitting at the table, wearing her two wedding bands, staring down at the smooth wooden surface she's washed clean a million times.

"June." Saul tips his head toward Abe's fluttering White as it finally reaches us. "Do you want to see it?"

I flatten my palm, and the White dances over it. Though it touches my skin, it doesn't reveal its secrets. I think of that day in the woods. *Please*, Dad said as the darkness folded over him. *Please show her*.

I tighten my fingers around the pulsing Moment, but the memory doesn't play out for me. This island must be more a part of our own world than this one, where merely brushing the White is enough to send its contents dancing through you. I need a threshold.

I look up at the only door within reach: the door to my own house.

"I think he left it for me," I say. "My dad."

Saul studies me.

377

"Thank you for not stating the obvious."

He laughs. "What, in this impossible place, could possibly be obvious, June?"

"That I'm holding a message from my dad in my hands, and the only apparent way to see it is to go through that door, probably back to Five Fingers. Away from him."

"I thought 'the obvious' was that you already had dozens of messages from him: about how much he loved you and what he wanted for you. The obvious is that whether you had that White or not, your dad would want you to go back to your life and live it well."

"I want to say goodbye first."

"It's not goodbye." Saul threads his hand through mine. We circle the far side of the island and stand with our toes in the water. There are islands coming closer, others moving out, and there, at the edge of sight, the thin line of the horizon: dark greens and browns, the hazy half image of mountains spearing the sky. Saul sweeps my hair behind my shoulders, and the wind carries it out behind me. I lock my fingers into his, and we stare.

"Are you there?" I whisper.

There's silence, but it's Dad's. Bekah's. The specific silence that can come only from their mouths. I know. I have to believe.

"I love you," I say.

"I love you," Saul says, and I know he's not talking to me, just like I wasn't talking to him.

I cup my hands around my mouth and scream, as loud as I can, as big and long as I can so it will be a promise with gravity and truth. "SEE YOU."

Saul laughs beside me and lifts his T-shirt to wipe his eyes. He cups his hands around his mouth and screams: "SEE YOU."

We stand for one more beat of silence, and then we turn back toward the house.

We climb the steps to the porch, and I stop Saul by the arm. "I think . . . I think I need to see this alone."

"You're sure? This is what you want?"

I nod, and Saul pulls me into one last hug, then kisses my forehead. "See you on the other side, Jack."

I gather all of myself, and it's not that much. All the Jacks that clung to me, all the ghosts, are gone, and I'm just me.

Light.

Breezy.

Free.

Jack IV.

I go through the door.

Instead of stepping into my house, I find myself in the side yard, behind a dark, writhing shape. Abe's ghost is watching through the window as my father sits at the console table in the kitchen, scribbling a note. Every so often, Dad stops and looks up through the pane of glass, straight at Abe.

I watch the eight-year-old version of me climbing on Dad and see him frown and disentangle her from him. "I'll be right back," his muffled voice comes. He disappears down the hall.

I follow Abe's fluctuating form to the front of the house, where Dad is bounding down the porch steps into the night. He's holding a note, labeled JUNIOR, clipped to a leather-bound book. I follow him into the woods.

Suddenly, the night blinks away, replaced by golden light and soft fog. I trudge through the strange quiet, listening to my father's breaths, counting the beats of his heart, all the way to O'Dang!

When we reach it, Dad climbs, one arm over the other, to the first level of branches, to a hollow made by an animal. He pulls the book and note from his jacket and glances toward Abe—*at me*—then at the book. He tucks it in the hole.

He left something for me. He left a note for me, something I've never seen before.

I go toward the tree as if to climb it, but he's already climbing down.

I chase his long strides back to the yard, to the sudden night and porch-light glow, the overgrown ivy and shaggy grass, the cicada chirp and twinkle of stars and glint of coywolf eyeshade.

Dad stops beneath the Jack's Tart tree, eyes lifted to the moon. He looks over his shoulder at Abe—*at me*—and gives a closed-mouth grin, full tears rolling down his cheeks.

Dad, I say, though of course I have no voice. He faces the house again.

This is the last time I'll see him, at least for a long time. I'm shaking like a leaf despite the warmth as I cut a circle to stand in front of him.

His eyes flash up to my bedroom window, then drop again. They look right at me, or through me. "June-Bug," his voice squeezes out as a throaty whisper.

Dad. My heart races so fast I vibrate with it.

He holds his arms out to his sides, like he's hugging the house, the night, the world. His eyes neither shift nor focus. They stare, wide open, lashes thick with tears. I reach out and touch his hand, feel its warmth and solidness. "Look," he whispers.

I follow his eyes to the stars. Once, when we lay gazing up at the night, he told me the stars we saw were only the tiniest fraction of the stars that burned above us.

I'm looking.

His eyes move vaguely back and forth. "I don't know if you'll find this, Bug." His voice is small. "I hope that if you find *any* of them, if you figure out how the Whites work, this is the one you find. I think I'm running out of time." His breath catches in his chest, and he wipes his eyes with the heel of his hand. "I wanted to be a better man than my father, but I made so many mistakes. Someday you'll know that. I hope you know the good parts too. I hope you know I loved you."

He waves his free arm up in a slow arc across the sky. "You look for me there, baby," he says. "I'll look up. We'll see the same stars."

I remember something else he told me about stars: that their light traveled so far we might see some shining that had already burned out. They might reach us after their lives had ended. The light was real and warm, though it came from something that, elsewhere, no longer existed.

What if there are no stars in that other place, Dad? I ask, starting to cry.

He opens his arms again—this time as if to hug me, and I walk into them. I feel his heartbeat against my chest, warm and real though it comes from someone who, here, no longer exists. *I love you so much*, I say.

"I love you so much," he says.

Don't ever let go of me.

"I'll never let go of you, June," he says. "The first time I held you, I saw it all. I didn't miss any of it. I hope you find this. I hope you know. Go live, baby. The world's waiting."

Dad.

Abe's torn-free memory shivers, breaks. Darkness spills in through it like water through holes in a ship. The woods break. The coywolves come apart like dandelions. The stars wink out. Dad's heart keeps beating. Dad's arms stay warm. "See you, June-bug," he says.

See you.

Forty-Four

I crash through. There isn't a doorway to go by. Instead the memory crumbles around me. I don't have the presence of mind to hold my arms up over my head.

I simply sob. I feel my tired legs collapsing and then solid arms around me. "You're okay," he says again and again.

"He loved me," I cry.

"He loves you."

"I miss him."

Saul holds me. We lean together on the front porch, and it's not the front porch of the *other* place. It's the true front porch. Of the here, the now. The one with a frosty cherry tree ringed with sweet saplings.

The hill Jonathan Alroy O'Donnell came to. The hill Jack the First stood on. The hill Jack II rode his bike across and where Jack III showed me the stars. Our home. A thin place.

Where life goes on and the stars keep shining and the person who loved me most has moved on but his heart has somehow stayed behind.

"We're home."

Saul nods.

I touch the doorknob. It's unlocked. I start to shake again, but this time with happiness, relief. Because of what I've come home to.

All the things of the present I'd forgotten to treasure: a mother with dreams and long, elegant fingers that dance in all they do, a stepfather who fixes broken toilets and cleans teeth and protects me like his own, brothers with boundless energy and chalkboard-fingernail voices and sometimes sweetness just for me.

And Saul, a boy who loved me when history said he couldn't.

"I'm home," I cry. "Mom! Toddy! Shadow! Grayson!"

The stair lights flick on.

"I'm home."

"*Baby*," Mom's voice says.

I am so happy, so relieved. For the first time, I feel big.

We've been gone three days, they tell us.

They thought the worst.

The police were looking, Hannah was panicking, Eli was found wandering in the street, his home torn up.

Tonight, they agree to ask no questions. ("But we *will* talk about this tomorrow.")

Tomorrow, the answers will matter again, but they'll still be impossible things.

Hannah gets here in twenty minutes, and we're crying on the

floor in the living room. Grayson and Shadow are shy, unsure how to be around the sister they thought had left them and broke their parents' hearts.

Only I will ever know how seriously I considered doing just that. How could I willingly do that to them?

The answer, deep down, is that I couldn't have. There's too much in this world, under the slowly dying stars, that I love.

For Saul, I know what hurts worst is Eli.

"We'll see him tomorrow," Mom promises. She's the one who got him into the assisted living facility after Saul disappeared, when the police found him in the median of the highway, disgruntled and murmuring with bloody hands.

"It should've been me," Saul says.

"You're here now," Mom says. "There's still time."

"Maybe," Saul says. "Or maybe he won't know me."

Mom hesitates. "He talks about you. He has your pictures on the walls."

And in this way, I know we *did* break a curse when we washed each other clean. Because my mother, an O'Donnell, or the former wife of one, at least, visited *New York Times* best-selling author Eli Angert these past three days. An O'Donnell paid his bills and made sure he had books to read and pictures on the wall. An O'Donnell took an Angert a box of dried cherries, and an Angert accepted them.

He had taken them between his teeth, and tears had flooded his eyes. *They taste like home*, he'd said.

"The ghosts are gone now," I tell Mom quietly.

She smiles knowingly. Or maybe skeptically. It's hard to

say—it's the same smile she gave when Dad told stories from his trips or talked about the magic tree in the forest.

"I know Dad wasn't perfect," I say. "I know . . . he used to leave."

Mom laughs. "Of course he wasn't perfect. But he was ours. And we were his."

"Was that enough?"

Her eyes sweep over my face. "When it came down to it, yes. That was enough."

For the first time since this started, I'm sure my father wasn't a liar. A liar would've changed his memories. A liar would've projected that shiny version of his proposal to Mom, the version he always told, not kept the truth close to his heart, guarded in a little sphere of white. "It was enough."

We eat even though we're not hungry yet.

"So you don't get sick," Toddy says gently, tousling my hair. "It's good to keep a little something in your stomach."

He wanted to take us to the hospital but settled for scheduling doctors' appointments in the morning. We eat everything they put in front of us: two bowls of bland tomato soup, one half-frozen piece of turtle cheesecake, a peanut butter sandwich apiece, slabs of reheated macaroni casserole. I let them wrap blankets around me. I let Mom comb through the tangles in my hair. Every gesture is an *I love you*, and I collect them, my way to say, *It is so good to be loved by you*. I drink every cup of water they bring, and when Mom surreptitiously pours each of us a tiny taste of whiskey, I let its warmth settle in my stomach, thinking fondly of the worst movie of all time.

"How's Nate?" I ask Hannah, and she laughs in surprise.

"He's going to be good. He's going to be really good when he gets my message that you're both okay."

"I'm sorry," I say again.

She wraps an arm around me and clears her throat. "I knew you'd never leave me, Junie."

I kiss my forefinger and middle. She kisses hers. "Never. Not in the important ways." But the sting is still there in my chest, and I pull away, fighting tears. "I think I need to step outside for a second."

Everyone tenses, Mom and Toddy especially, but they nod and let me go. This time, I won't pass into a memory. Our families' Moments are gone, but there's still something unnerving about passing through this doorway, knowing how it conspired with memory and magic to show me so much. I sit down on the porch and breathe in the pine. I can almost see the outline of Dad standing in the yard. I look up at the stars, and I see him there too.

I feel his stories burbling up in my chest, and I know that tomorrow I'll begin to write them down for Ms. deGeest, and this time I'll tell the truth.

The door clicks open, and Saul lowers himself to sit beside me. After a minute I say, "The night we met, I didn't see you coming either."

He smiles. "I would try to make out with you right now, but I don't know if in the last three days your mom and Todd had a chance to teach Shadow and Grayson about the birds and the bees, and I'm too tired to explain it."

I laugh despite myself. It's easier than I would've guessed. "Tomorrow then."

"Tomorrow," he agrees.

"And the next day. And the day after that. In every room and every Five Fingers establishment."

"A Makeout Tour," he says. "Maybe we can do a signing."

"And what about after that?"

His dark eyes are serious despite the trace of smile in the corner of his mouth. "I don't know, Jack. College? Grad school? Indonesia with Takumi and Sarah? The world is your oyster."

"And you?"

"I'll be here with Eli," he says. "For now, at least. And after now, I'll still be close, if you still want me."

"Nowhere the stars can't reach you?"

"If I have anything to say about it, I'll be well within celestial-light range."

"Good," I say.

"Good."

We sit for hours, the door opening every once in a while as, one by one, the others join us on the porch until we're a row of seven. From one end, Toddy passes a box of dried Jack's Tart. I cradle one between my teeth.

"Look." Mom points across the yard toward the first streak of yellow. "Morning's coming."

I bite down and taste it all, the heartbeat of the world.

Forty-Five

The Complete History of Jack O'donnell

I find it in the woods, in the crook in O'Dang!, right where he left it.

June,

> *If you find this, it means you see them too: the ghosts, the memories, all of it. It means they tortured you like they tortured me, with pieces of our story.*
>
> *Baby, I'm sorry, for everything. I'm sorry I gave him fodder to hurt you. I'm sorry I messed up enough that when you saw the truth, it was always going to hurt. I never wanted you to stop looking at me like I was the sun, but now you know how things really happened. At least, as well as a series of moments can tell it.*
>
> *I always meant to write the truth down, June, and here it is. This book has all you need to know about me. The things that mattered. The important things.*
>
> *I love you, June, always. Always.*

I lean into the crook of the branch and tuck the note into my pocket. I take a deep breath and push a cherry between my teeth, sunlight and warmth and dirt rushing over my tongue, a million glimmers of Jack, both sweet and bitter. I open the book, THE COMPLETE HISTORY OF JACK O'DONNELL III.

This is all you need to know about me. Not every moment, not the things I saw or the places I went. You need to know where my heart was.

That the most important thing I ever did with my life was love you, and my favorite sound was your snorting laugh. I don't have time to tell you any more bullshit stories, and I wouldn't tell you even if I did.

Here, so close to the end, all that means so little.

When I was a kid, I dreamed about exploring pyramids and riding on elephants' backs. I wanted to sail across the world and climb Mount Everest and look down over everything. I thought that was the life I'd lead and that the moments of mine that were closest to that would be the ones that made me.

The truth is, I stopped dreaming about those things, June, the day you were born.

Here is what I'll take with me from this world: a thousand moments spent watching you sleep, tracing the freckles over your mom's eyebrow as she Windexed a mirror, rubbing her wrists when the cold made them sore, combing your hair when it got tangled, a deep hurt in my belly from the way it hurt you.

I am very small, and I don't find myself wishing I were any bigger.

All I want, with my one tiny moment, is to love you.

If you remember anything about me, remember the truest thing: I will love you after all the stars have burned out, after the sun has died and ice has covered the earth, after the last human has taken her last breath.

I'm happy, so happy to be a tiny fleck of a thing alongside you. We may just be moments, June, but to love a handful of people very well, that's a good life.

I was just a blip, a spark, the blink of God's eyes. Because of you, it was more than enough. It was everything.

I was just a moment, and you gave me a million Junes.

I was just a moment, and you made me forever.

Thanks

FIRST, I need to thank my incredible parents (and grandparents) and promise my mother (and grandmother) she *will* get a book dedication, just as soon as I write the right book. I am so lucky to have spent my life with two loving parents in my corner, and I wouldn't trade you for anything or anyone.

Thanks to my brothers and sisters, for always coming through for me and for each other. If I ever move to a deserted island, I hope you'll come too. (This includes you, Megan and Noosha.)

Thank you to Brittany Cavallaro, Parker "Charker" Peevyhouse, Anna Breslaw, Jeff Zentner, Janet McNally, Katie Kennedy, Lindsay Eagar, and anyone else I am traitorously forgetting who offered early (and late) reads on this book. I am so, so lucky to have friends with brains and hearts as brilliant and beautiful as yours.

Thanks also to Kerry Kletter, Jack Sjogren, Hallie Bateman, Matthew Baker, Shannon Parker, Roshani Chokshi, Kathryn Purdie, Erin Summerill, Julie Eshbaugh, Margot Harrison, Ashley Blake, Dahlia Adler, Katherine Locke, Sara Taylor Woods, Tristina Wright, Meg Leder, Adriana Mather, Riley Redgate, Jeff Giles, Tehlor Kinney, Cam Montgomery, Eric Smith, ALL the Sweet 16s, and everyone else who makes my writing and reading world so much brighter on a daily basis.

To my Hope College family, you are the best. Always.

To all my book blogger, bookstagram, and bookseller friends:

You've made this whole process so much less daunting and more fun. Thank you, thank you, thank you.

To my agent, Lana: You have been my rock this past year. Thanks for all that you do to keep me going and to make everything I write 300 percent better.

To my editors, Liz and Marissa: Liz, I am floored by your generosity and kindness. I, and this book, owe you so much. Neither would be the same without all your hard work and passion. Marissa, thank you for stepping up and kicking you-know-what in the eleventh hour. You are a master slicer and dicer (of words), and your support has meant so much to me.

Anthony Elder and Corina Lupp: I don't think *anyone* deserves a cover as a beautiful as the one you've given me, but I'll gladly accept it.

Kim Ryan and Jennifer Dee, thank you for being such wonderful advocates for *A Million Junes*. You are empresses. Thanks you, Kate Frentzel, for fixing my many randomly capitalized phrases and so much more.

To Ben Schrank, and everyone else at Razorbill and Penguin Young Readers Group, thank you for all that you've done for me and for this book. I'm so grateful to have landed among you.

Thanks also to Hermione Granger, without whom probably none of us would be alive.

And finally, thank you to Joey: Every moment that I'm loved by you is an incomprehensible gift. You've already given me a million Junes.